Also by Stephen Box

the Way – to achieve success

PREJUDICE IN LOVE

The Odd
Patients

A Convenient Liaison

Stephen Box

A Convenient Liaison

Stephen Box

Twitter: @theStephenBox
www.thestephenbox.com
www.amazon.com/author/stephenbox

Published 31ˢᵗ May 2023

ISBN: 978-1-7396765-0-6 (sc)
ISBN: 978-1-7396765-9-9 (hc)
ISBN: 978-1-7396765-1-3 (e)

About this book

This book is intended as a social fable discussing two completely different aspects of society – the haves, and the have nots. Clara, having been forced to leave school at 14-years of age to care for her terminally ill mother and younger brother, never finished her schooling, and has nothing and no-one to help her. She scrapes a living at the abusive end of the social spectrum. James has everything he needs, has never needed to care for anyone always having people around him to care for him. He knows Clara from school days, naïvely thinking himself her white knight but to his own ends with scant regard for her dreams. His parents, both successful upper-middle class executives want for nothing in a materialistic world. His mother, a PhD biochemist and Director of a major pharmaceutical company, concentrates on her career as a female craving success. His father is a successful corporate banker but not vying to get to the top. He is the seemingly more lay-back member of the family, but the strength and calm when needed as a single event in the life of Clara brings reality crashing down upon them causing them all to engage in a journey that will transform their lives.

I met 'Clara' on a train to Cardiff where, having fought hard to get her voice heard with no formal qualifications, she was finally to be interviewed at a college to study fashion. I was so moved with the despair she had suffered during those 3-years as the carer of her mother with no State support regarding her education and ambitions during or after her mother finally succumbed to her illness. She had sacrificed formative years to care for her mother, and then forgotten; left to fend for herself at the bottom of the social ladder. The reflections expressed in this book of those 3-years are her story. I would hope that this book makes the plight of these children carers more visible as there are many of them.

About the Author

His life has been filled by one adventure after another having started as a Nuclear Physicist at the Atomic Energy Research Establishment, Harwell, UK. During the 'brain drain' of the mid-1970's he transitioned into the world of international banking using his skills with computers and mathematics and where he ultimately participated in developing the Global financial village post deregulation of capital movement and the breakdown of communism with special emphasis of engaging with developing economies to better the lives of their people. When Stephen's career as a noted International Banker was truncated by health issues, his adventurous spirit turned to writing to fill the downtime, both recording his adventures and using novels to comment on observation of social issues in today's world.

A Convenient Liaison

Chapter 1

The rising sun streaming through threadbare curtains told him it was time to leave her bed and go home. She was still sleeping. *'What a lovely lady'* he thought. She had suffered in her short life but a joy to be with for the two nights each week she provides sexual favour exclusively to him to supplement her meagre income as a waitress and bartender. But last night after their passionate sex, they had talked into the night about her hopes and dreams. He is hatching a plan and needs to know if she can play a vital role in his foreseeable future.

He needed the toilet and then dressed. She awoke. 'Morning. Are you leaving already?'

Reaching over to kiss her, 'We had a late night. You need some sleep before your shift. I'll let myself out. Thanks for a great night. Same time on Thursday?'

'Sure, but a cuddle now would be nice.'

'I'm needed in London today, so I must get going. But Friday morning I'll be happy to oblige.'

As he finished dressing, he could not help but despair at the shabby bedsit this unfortunate lady had to call home. *'Why has life been so unkind to her'*, he thought as he put £30 on her small table. He noticed some sketches. *'They look like fashion sketches.* Are these yours?'

'Yes. I have dreams one day to be a fashion designer if I can ever get the money together to go to school.'

'They're good. When I see you Thursday, I'd like to look at your work.'

'This could be the missing link in my plan', he thought. He needed to mould this new data into a credible scenario that would fulfil his needs without taking advantage of her. His trip to London would hopefully enable him to start to put this plan into action.

'Bye, Clara' as he let himself out.

As the door latch clicked shut, she curled up in bed. *'Too early to face another dreary day at work.'*

Driving the short distance home to leafy suburbs, he reflected on the misfortune that had beset Clara since the age of fourteen. He had known her at school as a lively, outgoing girl full of fun. She had also babysat him on occasion. Then her mother was diagnosed with a nasty variant of MS disease. Her school days were over as she became a full-time carer for her mum and younger brother. No father to help. He fled as soon as her mother became ill and not heard from since. Nor was there any other family to help as her mother had moved to St. Albans, far away from her family, with her husband who had moved here for work. Her mother finally died three years ago, leaving the lovely 22-year-old Clara with nothing but a severely curtailed education. Her brother had since joined the Navy and rarely visited with her, quickly forgetting the love and care she afforded him during his teenage years ensuring he finished school. She eked out a living at a restaurant bar on meagre earnings, which she supplemented with a few carefully selected clients, but only James spent the night with her. Theirs was a special friendship.

What a contrast to his cosy life. He is just two months short of his nineteenth birthday with a maturity belying his age, and from an extremely comfortable middle-class family. He has a lovely home where both parents have lucrative careers. His mother, Dr Janice Caldwell, senior biochemist, and executive director of a major pharmaceutical company, was prepared to forsake any further siblings in favour of her career, very much leaving him to look out for himself, but with love and affection available when needed. He is currently enjoying a gap year between school and university with a secure place at Cambridge university to read computer sciences, or that's what he has led everyone to believe. Since the age of fifteen he developed a keen interest in computer graphics, putting his above average skill in mathematics to the test. He generated a graphics engine that could rapidly transform still frames into lifelike animations with near-perfect mobility. A young but prosperous computer gaming company wanted to purchase this engine from him and hire him. He had other plans so, with the help of a reputable London law firm and internationally renowned accountants and auditors, agreed to licence the use of this engine. The income to date is staggering; something he kept to himself as he had more significant engines to develop, seeing a bright future for himself. But he also knew his parents would be extremely disappointed with his change of heart regarding university. Three years at university did not fit with his plans.

His liaison with Clara satisfied his natural sexual urges without the need for a conventional female relationship. He now felt so good with her he wanted her to be part of the next two to three years whilst he developed his business. He wanted an unusual liaison of convenience with her, but it could be good for them both. Time for a chat with his mother.

When he arrived home, both parents had already left for work. As he entered, he encountered Samantha, their housekeeper, known affectionately as Sam, busying herself with her chores. 'Morning James. Ready for breakfast?'

'Just need to take a shower and get changed. Say twenty minutes?'

Sam was now used to his Monday and Thursday nights with Clara. It amused her neither parent knew anything about his activities. His mother would surely be deeply concerned her ambitious son would have a relationship with such an unfortunate and older girl known to sell sexual favour. And the thought her son is a client would appal her. It always tickled her she knew James better than his parents and looked forward to the day of realisation by his parents that James had his own plans for his future.

This family amused Sam. They had it all, but they could be three separate individuals. If his parents knew the extent of the computer technology in his bedroom, they would have to ask how he could afford so much. But they never went near his room and were too self-absorbed in their own lives to question why he spent so much time there. She also wondered if they knew anything about the three days each week he spent in London with his 'friends'. He must generate real income from somewhere, but did they know, or even consider it?

Chapter 2

He was gazing out over the 4th floor balcony of a new apartment block in the trendy part of Wapping in East London. The vista over the river Thames was now a trendy area south of the river. *'This is ideal for my plan'* he thought, *'let's see what deal I can do.'*

He had completed his homework on this new development. This is the last apartment for sale. At an asking price of £485,000 for a 3-bed, all ensuite, apartment with a large open plan area living area with a well-planned kitchen and panoramic views over the Thames the price was full but not excessive. The large quarterly service fees of some £4,500 probably inhibited a fuller price. But this service charge included a swimming pool and gym, and 24-hour porterage. The purchase price also included a secure underground parking space. Even at his tender years he knew there was a deal to be done as maintaining a sales office for just one apartment must be expensive. The agent had already offered to cover his Stamp Duty tax, but as a first-time buyer he knew the Government incentive would likely make this tax nominal. There was room for negotiation, especially as he is a cash buyer.

The show apartment was furnished, which would save him the time to furnish until he was better established in London. Speed of occupation was his primary criteria. He needed to be close to his two new collaborators for the next part of his business development plan.

He invited the agent to sit at the dining table with him. 'Angela, I like the apartment as is. I'm interested to purchase fully furnished so you avoid the expense of clearing out and making good. I'm a cash buyer and can move as fast as you can. I already have a law firm who take care of my business interests, and I have primed them to quickly move to close, and certainly within one week if the paperwork is in order. And whereas you have already offered to cover my Stamp Duty tax, they inform me this is nominal as a first-time buyer. Therefore, what price to agree a purchase in the next five minutes?'

He impressed her. *'He's still a teenager but has done his homework. Better get some direction.'* 'Why don't you tell me what you have in mind, and I'll make a call.'

4

He thought for a moment about how low he could pitch a credible bid. 'My thoughts are £450,000 with completion as fast as you can deliver the paperwork.'

She paused a moment to consider his offer. 'That's probably too low, especially fully furnished, but let me make a call.' She clicked a speed dial on her phone as she walked to the balcony for some privacy. Her conversation lasted a few minutes before she returned.

'I've spoken to the owner. He informs me the furnishings in this apartment are worth over £15,000 but is amenable to an offer to leave the apartment as is. His counteroffer for a 7-day close is £465,000 and you pay your own Stamp Duty.'

He needed a moment to compose himself. He would have paid £475,000 fully furnished. 'Okay Angela, I'll go with that. We have a deal.' He shook her hand as the traditional acceptance to treat.

He handed her a business card. 'This is the lawyer who will manage the purchase. He can confirm he has funds on deposit and is ready to expedite the sale. I'll phone him now to confirm the deal. He clicked his phone to call his lawyer. 'Good morning, Simon. I've agreed a purchase at £465,000 fully furnished to close within seven days, and I pay my Stamp Duty.' He listened to Simon and then addressed Angela 'He wants to know if you're separating out the cost of furnishing.'

'Good point. I'll need to ask the owner and then call Simon.'

Simon was good to go. He had over £1 million of royalty funds on deposit for James so knew he could deliver for his young, but very capable client.

'I want to take some photos to see what furnishings I have, and what I will need to add. Once you have confirmation from Simon, I would like access tomorrow to see what I need to get fully installed as quickly as possible. I would also like the information needed to activate fibre broadband and TV. I want to move in, fully operational, as quickly as possible.'

'No problem. And thank you for your business. I think I need to follow your career with interest. For one so young, you're clearly focused on your future. Could I have your autograph to remind me of this day?'

He smiled in amusement. 'What would you like me to sign?'

He was full of joy as he purchased sandwiches and made his way to Camden to the apartment of his two new collaborators, Javid and Hashem. Their apartment was full of computer technology and reflected the chaotic living style of two young computer geeks. But they are very capable, and busy generating the algorithms he needs for his next generation graphics engine. They were now his junior partners on an earn-in basis and would soon move to new offices in Camden as soon as lease negotiations are complete.

He stays close to them during his days in London whilst not meeting with potential clients to ensure they stay focussed on his requirements. However, the thought of driving in or out of London on a Monday or Friday did not appeal. His computers at home are directly linked to Javid and Hashem so they can work together, even when at home.

Chapter 3

It was Thursday evening after dinner. He found her in her study reading some research paper. 'Mom, can we have a chat? I need your input on something.'

She put down the research paper on her desk, removed her glasses and put them on top of the paper before turning towards him. 'Shoot. What can I do for you?'

'Mom, I want your consent to have a woman stay with me overnight.'

'You have a girlfriend? Please tell all. Your father and I were getting a little concerned with your general lack of interest in the fairer sex.'

'This may sound a little weird to you, but I don't want a steady relationship at this time in my life. But I can assure you I'm a red-blooded heterosexual with all the inherent needs. I want all the benefits of female companionship with none of the baggage. Does this make sense to you?'

'Sounds like you want a mistress.'

'Interesting way to put it. And I've found a solution, but this is your home, so I want your consent.'

'What is your solution that requires my approval? You're 18 years of age. If you want to have a woman stay with you overnight, it's your concern so long as she causes no problems here.'

'Thanks mom. Let me explain. But hear me out before you pass judgement.'

'I'm listening.'

'Currently I seek my sexual pleasure elsewhere with a woman who knows there is nothing other than sex between us. We meet twice each week when I'm not in London. I spend the night in her shabby bedsit. I pay her because she only engages in sex to help make ends meet. She doesn't like it but needs must. She's drawn a short straw in life through no fault of her own, and I'm happy to help her help me. At present I'm not the only client, but the only person who she will allow to stay overnight. We've been friends for years. I want to change this situation for her. I want her to myself, and I'm prepared to pay her enough to make this happen. But I don't want to spend so much time in her bedsit. I want her to come here to stay with me on a regular basis, not least to provide some respite from her miserable life. I want to be right up front with you about this as I have no intention to deceive you or dad.'

'Who is this woman?'

'Clara Thompson.'

'My God. Which pit did you swim in to find her?'

'Mom, that's not fair or remotely charitable. You know what happened to a bright, fun loving 14-year-old when her mother became ill. Does she deserve to continue to be abused after the love and care she afforded her mother and brother? She's a lovely lady, and I value her as a friend and companion. She is forced to play slave for peanuts because she didn't finish school. She grits her teeth to provide sexual favour to supplement those peanuts just to survive. How can she ever recover with any chance to achieve her potential if no one reaches out to her? I want to help her, and she plays a vital role in my desires without commitment. A little respect and charity will go a long way.'

7

'I apologise. You have obviously thought this through. I can't say I'm fully in favour of what you're proposing, but I can also understand your desire not to get tangled in a relationship before you start university. I also find your desire to help her interesting. Helps me not to think of her as your hooker. Would she be participating here other than satisfying your needs overnight?'

'No.'

'Can you be certain she is fully protected against pregnancy?'

'She has a coil.'

'Would she have her own access to this house?'

'No. She would come with me, and I will see her out.'

'And she would agree not to sell favour anywhere else?'

'That would be a conditional part of this relationship.'

'Can you afford the cost of her commitment to you?'

'Most certainly.'

'In respect we're having this conversation I will agree in principle to this liaison on condition both of you have a full sexual health check with Dr Bryant before you bring her to this house, and after she has agreed to not sell favour to anyone else. I'll talk to your father, although I don't anticipate any problem other than her reputation. You have obviously considered this aspect so on your head be it. Does this satisfy your request?'

'Thanks mom. This means a lot to me. All I need to do now is to convince her of the merits of my plan.'

'If you're the only one who stays with her overnight, and she grits her teeth with all other clients, I think the outcome is most certainly in your favour. I just hope you don't regret your choice.'

'Mom, she will be my lovely mistress, not my hooker. We're friends and have been for some years. I value her friendship.'

'You better go see if she'll agree to your offer.'

Chapter 4

It was Thursday evening. He collected her from the restaurant as usual at 11pm. When they arrived at her bedsit, she took a quick shower to remove the grime of serving food and drink all evening before engaging in their sexual pleasure. She had taught him over some weeks how to touch and tantalise her body. Their lovemaking became more passionate as they learnt how to please each other. He was the only client with whom she did not insist on a condom, knowing she was his only partner.

They lay together, spent and content. He knew what he needed and knew he was with the person to satisfy his needs. 'Can I discuss an idea I have as I think it should be good for both of us?'

She turned to him. 'After all that passion, my ears are the only part of me not singing. What do you have in mind?'

'I want to change this. I want to change our relationship. I want to make things better for both of us.'

A little apprehensively 'What do you have in mind?'

'You don't enjoy selling sexual favour, and I don't like you being forced to engage with clients you don't like. We both have our needs, and we most certainly gel as lovers. As you know, I'm not ready for a typical relationship with the corresponding baggage involved. But I need gratification, and you fulfil this need in spades. Can I ask you how much you make in a typical week from sexual favour?'

'Between £200 and £300. Why?'

'What would you say if I was to offer you £300 per week to be my exclusive mistress? You would spend your nights with me at my house and the payment is a retainer, not based on activity. I know you don't provide favour during your period but under this retainer arrangement I will pay you every week. Even if I'm in London, you'll be paid. I want you to myself. Wrapped in your arms, I feel at peace with the world. Would you consider such an arrangement with me?'

'Wow. What an offer. You do know I only take your money because I need it. I love our nights together. In better circumstance I would not consider selling sexual favour to you. You could have it with the pleasure you give me. And you want this to happen at your house. What will your folks think? Can't imagine they want me there with my nefarious reputation. Far too low.'

'I've already cleared that hurdle with my mother.'

'What! You've already discussed this with your mother. Bet that was an interesting conversation. What did she say?'

'So long as you agree to be my exclusive partner in sex, and we both undertake a sexual health check with Dr Bryant, we have her blessing.'

'Can you afford to pay me so much every week? I don't see you go to work.'

'I do work in London, and I can happily afford to pay you. Will you be my lovely, sexy mistress?'

'I'm overwhelmed. You really care for me. I'll happily be your mistress for as long as you need me. When do I start?'

'Is now okay? Do you have any appointments which you need to fulfil?'

'I'll be happy never to fulfil any appointment again. Fear not, I'm your happy mistress from this moment on.' She clinched the deal with a longing kiss.

'Be clear, Clara, we cannot become lovers in the traditional sense. This arrangement is to negate the need for a conventional relationship. I have a business to build, and I have no time for such baggage. You must understand this. If you find Mr Right for yourself, our arrangement will terminate. If you ever have sex with anyone else, our arrangement will most certainly end. And I'll never cheat on you either. You provide all I need.'

She had a very content smile on her face. 'How many nights per week will we share your bed?

'I don't have any fixed ideas, as we must agree this between us. I spend Tuesday and Wednesday nights in London. I'm open to any other nights, subject to you needing time for your commitments.'

'If I have Tuesday and Wednesday nights free, you can have all the other nights in the week you want me there.'

'Done. I'll warn you some nights I work into the night so we would have our fun, and then I would work while you sleep.'

'What is your work?'

'Easier to demonstrate than explain, but what goes on in my bedroom is absolutely secret so you must agree never to speak about what you see.'

'Sounds very covert. Can't wait to see. Will I be with you tomorrow evening?'

'You tell me when to pick you up and I'll be there.'

'Can I leave some underwear and clothes with you so I can change in the morning?'

'Of course. And my shower is big enough for us to shower together to add a little additional spice.'

'Thank you. What a lovely guy you are. It'll be fun being your mistress; correction, your lovely exclusive mistress. I love sex with you, and I solve my financial needs. Let's celebrate with some passion.'

When he opened his eyes, it was light, and he could see her smiling at him. 'Good morning, James. Did you sleep well?'

'Very well, my lovely mistress, thank you. Are you in need of the cuddle I promised you on Tuesday morning?'

She snuggled in 'Yes, please.'

'I would like to see your design sketches before I leave. Let me see if we have a secret star designer in our midst.'

'I'll get them now. But it was just something I developed to occupy my time when my mum was sleeping. Please don't judge them against professionals. I'd like to go to design school to learn this craft to see if I have the creative talents.'

They sat in bed as he scanned her drawings. 'You have a good hand for sketching. Not really understanding fashion, I can't comment on your designs, but you've given me an idea for another computer engine. I'll think it through and then be prepared for me to interrogate you to gain trade related information.'

'What do you mean?'

'Information such as what are the difference in body sizes between say size 10 and size 12. You're a size 10. What changes to your body dimensions would require you to up size to size 12?'

'I don't know but will find out. Never thought about it before in such detail. What would you do with this information?'

'Most fashion is designed and made for slim models, probably size 8 or size 10. When such a model struts the catwalk, a woman who is size 14 cannot relate to how this dress will look on her. What about if I could build an engine that would allow this woman to input her size and the engine emulates the dress on her size 14 body? Now she can see how it will look on her. Add mobility to the computer model and information about the weight of the dress material and how it reacts to movement, and we could have a digital catwalk where our digital size 14 model moves to show how this dress looks whilst moving.'

'Fantastic. And you can build this model?'

'With enough information about sizes and material, I can't see why not. I'll give it some thought.'

He put the drawings back on her table. 'What times are your shifts today?'

'Lunch shift starts at 11:30 until 2pm, and my evening shift starts at 5:30 until 11pm. Why?'

He picked up his mobile phone. 'It's now 8:45. Let me call Dr Bryant to see if he can fit us in today. He's our private GP, so we may be lucky.' He dialled the surgery. 'Good morning. This is James Caldwell. I have a new girlfriend and my mother has insisted we both have a sex examination. Is this possible today?' He waited. 'Yes, 2:30 today? Great. We'll be there. Thank you.'

'We can have our first night at my place this evening. My mom only said we had to be examined. Nothing about waiting for the results. You up for your first taste of my bedroom this evening?'

She smiled at him 'Can't wait. Can you take a bag home with you with things I'll need?'

'No problem.' Without thinking, 'How much wardrobe space will you need?'

'Don't have much, so very little.'

'Sorry, what a crass idiot I am. I'll make amends with a shopping trip for you tomorrow.'

'You don't have to do that. We live in different worlds, so don't worry about an innocent mistake.'

'Can I please take you shopping tomorrow as part of our new arrangement? Surely I can adorn my lovely mistress as part of my pleasure with her.'

'If you put it that way, I'll happily shop with you, but not in this town. But what about a nice cuddle before we each must start our day?'

Their trip to Dr Bryant was tedious and intrusive, but the general opinion, subject to the results of blood tests and swab analysis results which would be back on Monday, was they were both clear of any sexual infections or diseases. He had satisfied his mother's conditions, so now it was time to prepare for his first night in his own bed with his lovely Clara. After dropping Clara back at her bedsit, he went home to consult with Sam as he would have to make some adjustments to his bachelor style living and add appropriate towels and toiletries to accommodate his mistress.

Chapter 5

It was 11pm. She was clearly happy to see him. They were quickly home, and into his bedroom. When he opened the door for her, she could see a nice queen size bed to her left, but as the door opened further, all she could see was two tables full of computers and other technology with four large flat screens on stands behind the desks. It was an overpowering sight for her. 'I thought this was a bedroom. Looks more like something from a space centre. You weren't kidding it would be a shock. What do you do with all this stuff?'

'Another day. Could I interest you in a shower before we enjoy ourselves?'

'That would be very welcome. Can we have our first shower together? You can show me how everything works here.'

'Let's go. Bathroom is through here.'

Their shower was long and lingering, spending more time wrapped in each other's arms with the water relentlessly splashing against their bodies. He had already cleansed her body with the love and affection he felt towards her. For her, this shower was something to be savoured.

The shower in her bedsit was a grubby cubicle she could just squeeze into, and water, if she's lucky, would be warm – not hot, otherwise tepid. The shower she now enjoyed was easily large enough for two people and had a variety of shower heads and body sprays engulfing her in lovely warm water. This was heaven to her, and she was in his arms having enjoyed his cleansing her body.

He whispered in her ear, 'Are we done? Can I dry you and encourage you into my bed?'

She looked at him with an ear-to-ear smile 'This is so lovely. I've never experienced such luxury and care before. Lead me and I'll follow.'

He switched off the shower, gently removed the excess water from both bodies and led her out before taking a large towel and lovingly towelled her until she was dry. She did the same for him. He then lifted her into his arms and carried her to his bed. They were soon consumed in the love they so enjoyed together.

When she awoke, he was looking at her. She reached for the side of his face. 'Hello. How long have you been watching me?'

'No idea. Such a lovely sight in my bed. I think a long cuddle this morning.'

Chapter 6

They were two weeks into their arrangement. James had returned from London on Thursday evening content his new apartment was ready to occupy and planned to move the following weekend leaving just one week to appraise his parents of his new plans, pack what he wanted to take with him, and move. More importantly, it was now time to see if Clara is prepared to move with him. This was his biggest concern and most important task. He liked how their relationship had developed in two short weeks and knew would be ideal for his immediate needs in London. But would she be prepared to up and leave with him? She had many friends locally and was very popular. He decided to spring his proposal this evening.

He was waiting for her at 11pm. Even after a long day, she arrived at his car with a big smile on her face, happy to see him back after his trip to London. They kissed before he set the car in motion and headed for their love nest.

She had her shower to cleanse herself for their catchup after two nights apart. Although he maintained they were not real lovers, an observer would not detect any difference. When together, they were lost in each other with an all-consuming passion.

They came up for breath, needing a drink. One benefit of them being in his room was his choice of alcoholic beverages. He was not a drinker by any stretch of the imagination, but sometimes after a long spell on his computers a drink would help him relax before trying to sleep.

As they sat together in bed enjoying their drinks, he launched his proposal.

'We are two weeks into our arrangement. Any thought how it's working out?'

'James, why do you need to ask what I think? Can't your clever, intuitive mind capture how I feel about us being together?'

'Please don't shoot me for caring how you think or feel. You're my friend as well as my mistress. You're most certainly not at my beck and call, so you are afforded a voice to air anything that needs to change or would like to change for the better.'

'Other than maybe trying some more adventurous sex, I'm totally satisfied with our arrangement. Sleeping here with you changes my entire landscape. What a difference to my crummy bedsit.'

'I have another proposal that will dramatically transform the landscape for both of us.'

She looked at him quizzically. 'I sense something the size of an atomic bomb is about to drop in my lap. What do you have in mind for us now?'

'I want us to go live in London.'

He stunned her. 'That's a big bomb. Tell me more.'

'*Excellent*' he thought, '*She's open to the idea.* My business interests in London now require me to be there, full time. I want you to come with me.'

'What about university?'

'That hasn't been on the cards for nearly two years. But I wasn't ready to tell my folks until I was sure I could make it without a university degree.'

'And where would we live?'

'I've bought an apartment on the river. It's now fully furnished and ready to occupy.'

'Wooo, backup a little. If I'm your friend and you want me to up and move with you to London, a little more explanation would be in order.'

'Clara, my lovely lady, I've been operating a double life now for nearly two years. All the technology here allowed me to develop a special computer graphics engine currently used in the development of computer games; but has far more uses. It's currently licenced to one of the major computer games companies in London who have achieved so much success with it my royalties' amount to six figures every quarter. I now have two partners and about to open offices in London to attract some of the brightest minds to develop other ideas I have. I've bought a lovely apartment in a trendy part of London, and I now need to move there. But not a word to anyone. I need to manage this bombshell with my folks.'

'I always knew you're different, but you've just blown my mind. How do you see me fitting in?'

'Let me tell you how I see it with the proviso it's all up for discussion. You're my very personal partner, not my employee. I want you to come live with me as my mistress. During the day you will also be my housekeeper, but I want you to go to design school to realise your dreams. I'll pay you £500 per week plus all your living costs, although you will be subject to tax and National Insurance. According to my calculations you will still have over £400 pocket money per week. You'll enjoy company benefits such as private medical insurance. I'll also pay all your tuition fees. And if you agree to come, I'll take you shopping for a new wardrobe as a welcome gift. When I need a partner for functions, theatre, or any other event, my lovely mistress will fulfil this role. Any special clothes for such events will be an eligible expense for which you will have a credit card. How am I doing?'

Tears were running down her cheeks 'Why are you doing this for me? There will be hundreds of women seeking your attention far more intelligent and educated than me.'

He gently wiped her tears. 'I forgot about another task. You are there to protect me from such people. I neither seek nor want their attention. You must be my guardian and ensure such women cannot woo or trick me.'

She tried to laugh under her tears 'And what weapons are at my disposal?'

'Anything you like against the women, and what we already share as my motive to stay focussed.'

She took his drink and placed both on the bedside cabinet. 'Hold me, please. I'm feeling very vulnerable. No-one has ever shown me such kindness and I'm not sure how to respond.'

'Take your time, lady. This is a big decision for you. I need to know should you agree to come with me, you'll have no regrets. I can wait for an answer. I can even take you to London on Saturday if you are available and show you it's all real.'

'James, I know you, so I know it's real. But why me?'

'Because you are a very important part of my plan, and indeed my life. These past two weeks have shown me we work well together. I trust you, and what we share makes my life complete.'

'How long do you think you will need my protection?'

'Very minimum two years, maybe as much as five years, but certainly for as long as it takes for you to finish school and establish yourself. Of course, should you wish to move on, you are at liberty to do so.'

'When would we move to London?'

'Next weekend.'

'So, I have a week to unravel my life here and ride off into the sunset with you? Not possible; but will be done.'

'Do I hear an acceptance to my proposal?'

'My prince charming rides up to my dreary life and wants to carry me off into a new world for me and help me realise my dreams. What is there to think about? Of course, I'll come with you. And I'll take Saturday off so you can take me to show me our new world.' They kissed tenderly.

He got out of bed and opened his drinks fridge, pulling out a bottle of champagne. They celebrated their new life together.

'When will you tell your folks?'

'When do you need to give notice?'

'Tomorrow. I'm supposed to give two weeks, but they've never shown me any kindness so to hell with them. They'll certainly bitch about me taking off Saturday, but I'll figure that out.'

'Can you avoid telling anyone why you are quitting or where you're moving. You can contact anyone you want to stay in touch with once we've moved. Let's keep this move below the radar. It's no-one's business except us and my folks. They will need time to adjust so I don't want anyone in the town confronting them until they have time to understand my decision.'

'No problem. Very thoughtful.'

'I'll tell them tomorrow before I pick you up in the evening; probably during dinner.'

'Will you tell them about my involvement in your plan?'

'Of course. I want them to visit with us the following weekend to give them comfort all is well with their son. You're part of my new life, so they must accept this. It will be much easier for them to accept you in London than here. No historic baggage in London.'

'How long have you been planning all of this?'

'The decision to move to London was made some six weeks ago. Obviously, I needed somewhere to live. I closed on the apartment a week ago, but then needed various services connected before I could move my computers. A woman's eye would be useful on Saturday to ensure we have everything we need to move in. I really need you to look after us both in the apartment. Although it's furnished, we can change things as we feel the need. The existing furnishings are okay and get us installed.'

'And when did you decide about my involvement?'

'Can't we skip something so close?'

'Please. I'd like to know why you chose me.'

'Our original Monday and Thursday nights meant so much to me I could not imagine losing them. But I needed to know if we could live together and thus my first plan two weeks ago. Since then, I can't imagine not taking you with me. What we have is far more than sex. You bring a needed calm to my otherwise hyper life. When you really see me working, you'll understand more. I need you to be there for me when the stresses of creativity start to crescendo. Just take me in your arms and take me to the place we enjoy together.'

'Thank you. I'll be there for you, never fear.'

She thought for a moment. 'I think there is one important aspect of this plan you may have overlooked. In the interest of ensuring we both enter this liaison with our eyes wide open, I want to air my thoughts. The arrangement you propose looks fine on paper, but paper cannot reflect human nature or emotion. Our current situation would be considered casual as we don't live together. What you are now proposing is the equivalent of marriage without certain elements of baggage, but a full-on relationship where we live, eat, and sleep together 24/7. As with all such relationships, there will be times when we disagree. What I need to know is if we argue it is as lovers, not as hired help. I'm not about to engage in a situation where I don't have equal rights within our relationship. Is this okay with you?'

'I hadn't thought about us arguing over anything, but I see this may be naïve. How do you think we should deal with such situations?'

There could be times when one of us offends the other. The offended party should quietly but immediately express their offence, hoping the other will quickly realise their error and correct it. If such offence is borne out of frustration it may persist in which case an argument may develop until some realisation takes hold. Another possibility is annoyance with one another. Better to air it and resolve the source of annoyance. Another source will be a difference of opinion. I want a pact with you we never go to sleep at night with an open argument. When we curl up together in bed, we remember why we want to be together and realise no argument is worth losing what we share, even if we only agree to differ, but respect that right. Can we declare such a pact?

'Wow. Whole new world. You're clearly more worldly than me in such things, but yes, I accept your pact and if you find me inconsiderate at any time, you must tell me and correct me. We're friends. We should be big enough to disagree and accept differences.'

'Thank you. One more thing, and this is very important to me. Whatever your argument at no time can you use the paid mistress to put me down. I want it clear between us you can pay me to housekeep and to bury the baggage such as children, family commitments and demands on your time. But you must never suggest you pay me as your lover. What happens between the sheets I give freely in my love for you. James, I love you dearly, and that's what I bring to our bed. I'm not heartless enough to accept this liaison without love. And I think you share that love. Never degrade the love we share, it's what holds everything together. I'll never breach our trust to capture you in marriage. Should you ever think of a lifelong commitment, then you must make it clear to me. Do we understand each other?'

'You're some tough lady. I get it. And I do feel the love we share. As friends and lovers, we're equal in all respects, and fully committed to each other. I will never again refer to you as my mistress. You are my partner and lover.' He paused. 'Out of interest, what would you do if I inadvertently made such an intolerable error?'

'I'd knock your head clean off your shoulders. I'm a street fighter so you would most certainly feel pain.'

'Hmm. Much to learn from you about relationships. I've never been in a relationship where I had to be thoughtful and considerate. If I give you consent to straighten me out when necessary, will you help me to understand without using physical violence?'

'I truly hope our love for each other will resolve any problems we encounter.'

'On that optimistic note, I think we should get some sleep. Too much excitement for one day. Much to do now the game is on.'

'Can you pinch me in the morning just so I know this is all real? And can I be affectionate with you? Can I call you sweet nothings such as *darling* when we're alone together?'

'Happy to give you a pinch and then kiss it better. You can be as affectionate as you like, but don't hurt yourself. I never want to hurt you. You already know, for the foreseeable future, I have no intentions towards you or any other woman besides the lovely relationship we already share. I have much to do and must be free to follow my dream.'

She snuggled in as he killed the lights. It was so nice to be in his arms. She was looking forward to her new adventure. What did she have to lose?

Chapter 7

It was Friday evening, a little after 7pm. James, his mom and dad were enjoying a relaxing dinner to end their active week. Both mother and father expressed their respective news about their week at work.

'Folks, I have some news I want to share with you. I've decided it's time to move to London and seriously pursue my business career. My initial product I licence to a computer gaming company has generated over £1 million in royalties, and I have more products under development.'

Silence. His parents looked at each other, then at him. His father spoke first. 'Son, you're telling us you have a business in London that has generated over £1 million in royalties to date and this is the first time you think you should mention it?'

'I needed to prove myself. Your expectations are, quite reasonably, I should go to university. Ordinarily I would agree with you as it's a great opportunity. I have quietly worked on a computer graphic engine for three years. It came together about eighteen months ago. I then tried to find an application for it. I found a computer games company who needed the power of my engine to make more realistic games. They initially tried to buy it from me with the offer of a job to further develop it. But I know this engine has far more applications than games, so I licenced it to them. Their success on the back of my engine generated those royalties, and they keep coming in six-figure amounts each quarter. This proves I have both the technical and commercial skills to make these models my career. I now have two partners in London helping me to generate a more advanced version, and I have interest from other sectors for my original engine.'

'Son, that's incredible. I'm so proud of you. What's your next step?'

'I've bought an apartment in London, and about to sign a lease on offices. I need to attract special talent to work on my new creations, which will certainly appeal to the movie animation industry. I realised some weeks ago I now need to take my business seriously so need to forego university and commit myself to my work. I'll move to London next weekend and invite you both to come see what I have created the following weekend.'

His mother felt the need to speak. 'You've been involved in this for three years? Why don't we know anything about it?'

'When I started this model, it was just an idea. I didn't know if I had the mathematical skills to develop the complex algorithms required to achieve my goal. I needed to prove to myself I had the capability. Many highs and lows along the way. It was only when I demonstrated it to the gaming company I knew what I had. But could I convert this model into enough money to justify skipping university and building a business? Being able to buy my apartment for cash convinced me I can be successful. This was just three weeks ago, so now I'm ready to divulge my success to you both.'

His father looked at him. 'My eighteen-year-old son is a successful millionaire business owner. This we must celebrate. Let me find some champagne.'

Whilst he was away from the table, his mother spoke. 'What about Clara? You've agreed a relationship with her, which I have to say has been good for you. Now you want to desert her? Where's all your good intention towards her now?'

'The relationship over the past two weeks was a test to see how we interacted on a regular basis. As you see it works well, so I'm taking her with me. I'm a target for every gold-digger and honey-trap female in London. Clara will protect me from such people, and I can send her to design school, which is her dream.'

'Well, you seem to have it all worked out. Does she know about your move?'

'I asked her last night. She agreed to my proposal for two to five years, depending on where things go. At least she can finish design school.'

Father returned with a bottle and three glasses and proceeded to pour.

'Son, I feel very proud today. You built this business on your own. What a star.' He raised his glass. 'To you, my son, may your business prosper, and your dreams come true. Cheers.'

Mother broke the silence. 'He's taking Clara with him as his mistress.'

'Wise move at your age. Too many charlatan women in London looking to profit from your success. I think we should properly meet her if she is part of your continuing story.'

'Mom, Clara is no longer my mistress; she's my partner. How about breakfast tomorrow as she is coming with me to London to help me finish setting up my apartment?'

'Great. Say 9am. We'll welcome her into your adventure.'

'Thanks, dad. Your acceptance of her means a lot to me.'

'Your mother explained your argument to me regarding your interest in Clara. You're right in that her misfortune is not her fault, and her subsequent lifestyle was forced upon her. The warmth you have shown her is an example to us all. We must judge as we would be judged. You have shown incredible maturity for your years, so who are we to judge your relationship with her. We look forward to meeting her.'

'By the way, son, if it's not too intrusive, where is your apartment and how much did it cost?'

'It's in the trendy part of Wapping, right on the river. Fourth floor, so magnificent views across the Thames and South London. It has a large open plan living area with a balcony, and three-bedroom suites and secure basement parking. After some negotiation I got it for £465,000 fully furnished. It was the show apartment.'

'Goodness. My eighteen-year-old son has bought an apartment in London for nearly half a million in cash. Congratulations. Can't wait to see it.'

He left the table pleased with his success. He knew his mother is not happy with his rejection of university. After all, she was a PhD and very attuned to academia. His father, on the other hand, had graduated from university but did not see university as a better alternative to the bragging factor his son was a millionaire entrepreneur at the age of eighteen. But the most important achievement was his father's acknowledgement of Clara. Again, he knew his mother would prefer to keep her involvement hidden, but his father clearly understood her role and was fully supportive. He knew her acceptance by his parents would enhance Clara's commitment to her role. His plans were looking good. He couldn't wait to update Clara on his success.

As per usual, he was waiting for her at 11pm. She got into the car but was clearly upset. 'What happened tonight? You look stressed.'

'First, I asked for a day off tomorrow to see my sick aunt. Went down like a lead brick. Then, perhaps unwisely, I told him I was quitting next Friday. All hell let loose. Threats, intimidation, you name it. Finally, he recognises my value to his business but in the wrong way. Life will be hell next week, and whether I get paid is anyone's guess.'

He took her hand. 'Enough of this crap. You've suffered more abuse than anyone I know. You're my partner in all respects, including payroll. You don't have to serve tables or bars ever again. You deserve better, and better you shall have. If this arsehole has a problem, he can deal with me.'

'You want me just to walk away?'

'Absolutely. If people don't appreciate your contribution, then forget them. They're scum. We'll go to London tomorrow as planned, but I think we should stay overnight in my apartment. You'll have Monday to unravel your affairs here. I'll take you with me on Tuesday. On

Friday we both pack and start our new future. How does that sound?'

'Perfect. Thank you.'

'Let's get out of here. It's the last time we need to do this so wave goodbye.'

When they were safely ensconced in his bedroom, he poured them both a drink. 'How did it go with your folks tonight?'

'Better than your story. But have your shower, or would you prefer to shower together, and I'll tell all.'

'Together would be lovely.'

'Go get started.'

After their shower, they were quite happy to stay naked and finish their drinks before climbing into bed. 'So, what happened with your folks?'

'They invite you for breakfast tomorrow to welcome you into our family. My mom was not so happy, but my dad was over the moon with my success. He can't wait to visit with us in London.'

'I have nothing to wear for breakfast. I hoped we could go to my place to change before going to London.'

'We could go now, or first thing tomorrow. Breakfast is 9 o'clock. We're both early risers so we'll have time.'

'It's too late tonight. Let's sleep and go in the morning. If we're staying in London tomorrow night, I'll need an overnight bag.'

With that they curled up together and slept. No sex tonight.

Chapter 8

They were both awake a little after 6am. They showered and dressed. She had a supply of underwear in his room so no crisis there. By 6:30 they were on their way to her bedsit. She quickly assembled what she needed, not bothering to change, and they returned to his room. It was close to 8am.

James, having considered what he should take with him, posed a question. 'We have an hour before breakfast. Any ideas?'

'Let's get naked and start the day as we mean to go on.'

He needed no more encouragement to this idea.

Having showered and dressed again, they duly presented themselves for breakfast at 9am. Both parents welcomed Clara to the table, and Sam was beside herself to see how this would play out.

For the past two weeks Sam had prepared breakfast for both James and Clara as she didn't leave until it was time for her lunch shift. She liked Clara and knew she was far more worldly and streetwise than James. But she could also see the love they shared. Clara would always help her clear breakfast and help with the dishes; and they would naturally chat. Sam knew Clara would be the lead in their relationship; but would love and care for James. His parents had no right to judge her without seeing into the heart of this lovely lady.

His father had sensed the attitude of his wife so used his best calm and charm to welcome Clara and engage her with her thoughts on their new adventure. This put Clara at ease. James registered he should thank his father for his kindness.

Finally, his mother softened, realising they outnumbered her. 'Clara, my dear, you know our son is precious to us. You have shown us over the past two weeks you have a special role in his happiness. Please take good care of him and don't allow his success to go to his head. You have my full support to keep him focussed on his goals and if you need our support, please do not hesitate to ask. We entrust you with the care of James and will be there to support in any way we can.'

'Thank you, Mrs Caldwell, for your kind words. I promise you I'll care for him and protect him. I'm not afraid of him so I'll keep him in check if need be.' They all laughed. 'I hope I can provide the love and support he needs to fulfil his dreams, but I'm reassured you're there for support if need be.'

'Thank you so much, my dear, but please call me Janice. You're family now.'

'And please call me Geoffrey' his father having forgotten this important badge of acceptance.

'*Job done*' he thought. '*Time to get out of here and away to London.*' 'Okay folks, we must away. Busy weekend ahead to get everything ready to move.' With that, they left the table to collect their bags and depart for London.

Being a Saturday, the drive was faster than during the week. He stopped at a Mercedes showroom. She was confused as there were no fuel pumps. 'Get your bags and come with me.'

They entered the showroom. A suited man approached them. 'Good morning, Mr Caldwell. Everything is ready. We taxed your car, you are insured for seven days, and you have the promised half a tank of fuel. If you have the documents for your old car, we can complete your transaction.'

Keys and documents were exchanged, and they were led outside to the car park where a new Mercedes Estate car responded to a key depression on the key fob. James turned to her. 'This is my new car. I can't transport my computer suite in my old Golf, let alone your luggage and mine. Get in. We're close to my apartment.' He thanked the sales agent, and they were on their way.

She sat there taking in the aroma of new leather. 'Any other surprises today? New apartment, new car. You must be doing very well in business.'

'I couldn't have the car I wanted. The insurance would be prohibitive at my age, but this will do for now. Good workhorse for the stuff we need to move around. You need to be able to drive it as well.'

'I don't have a driver's license.'

'Something that needs to change ASAP. Driving lessons for you once we're settled. There will be times I need you to take me somewhere; or collect me. For example, it's quicker to drive from here to Gatwick Airport than use the train.'

He parked in his allotted space in the basement and took their bags to his apartment. He let her enter the hallway into the living space before him. She let out a gasp as she surveyed both the room and the panoramic vista. 'Wow, James, this is fantastic.'

'Come, look at the rest of the apartment.' The first stop was the master bedroom suite which she loved; especially the spacious bathroom. Then they went to the guest suite, which again was very nice. Then to the third suite which he explained would be converted into a computer suite so he could work at home if need be.

She put her arms around his neck and held him close. 'Thank you so much for including me in your life. This place is lovely, and I'll make it a truly lovely home for us.'

He held her tight. 'It will only be a home with you in it.' They kissed passionately.

He wanted to engage her in the tasks in hand. 'Can you have a nosey around to see what's missing so we can go shopping. I want us to move in next weekend with a view to sit down and get on with our life. Let's try to fix any deficiencies this weekend. I want to check the various fibre feeds I ordered.'

'I'm on it. Anything particular you want me to check?'

'Anything and everything. You probably have a better eye for these things than me. Make a list including any food items we need this weekend.'

She was away starting in the kitchen checking every cupboard and drawer for contents against what she thought they would need. The agent had left notepaper and a pen, so she quickly recorded what she thought they would need. Then she moved to the bathrooms.

This gave him time to check both his fibre broadband and the TV/radio/DAB feeds he had ordered. The high-speed fibre broadband was essential, and he had his laptop ready to check the quality and speed of the service. All was good. It was safe for him to install his computers here, knowing he could work effectively. The desks, chairs, and screen mounts were due for delivery on Wednesday with a full-size laser body scan unit the following week.

They reconvened some thirty minutes later. She had a list. Now they needed to know where to shop. Her list content was too extensive to risk the local high street, so he scanned the internet on his phone for the nearest shopping centre. Nothing local, so they would have to drive north-east for about ten minutes to Westfield Stratford City mall. It took over two hours to find everything they needed consuming all the rear storage capacity and the backseat of the car. It took two trips to the car park to unload their purchases.

Clara busied herself deciding where to store the groceries and household goods. He busied himself setting up an account on Amazon for her. She couldn't drive, so until she could goods would need to be delivered to her.

By the time she unpacked everything, bed made up, and bathroom organised, she was exhausted. He saw this, so they agreed to try one of the local trendy restaurants for dinner. It felt strange to her to be the customer rather than the server. Whole new world.

Chapter 9

They slept late and then indulged in playful sex before taking a shower together. It was after 9am before they emerged for breakfast.

'What's on the agenda today?'

'After breakfast we go to Brent Cross Shopping Centre for the shopping extravaganza I promised you. You need a new wardrobe for your new life, so let's go get it before I bury myself in work. It's on our way back to St Albans so we'll continue home afterwards.'

'Wow. You really spoil me. I'm so excited about moving here on Tuesday. Can't wait to get settled.'

When they walked into Brent Cross, he could see she was reticent about what to buy, not really knowing how much he could afford to spend. He sensed her anxiety. 'Clara, pretend you do not have any clothes or shoes. You have one shot at selecting a new wardrobe because I'm no shopper. Run rampant until we can carry no more. As for fear of cost, you will not begin to dent my credit card so go, have fun. You have two, maybe three hours from now.'

She had fun. He had to guide her a little as she forgot things like coats and underwear, but after more than two hours she certainly had enough to start her new life. She had never owned so many clothes in her life.

They made their way back to the car. 'If you've forgotten anything, I've set up an Amazon account for you.

We'll get you an iPad on Tuesday so you can shop when you like.'

They were quickly back in St Albans. His father was very interested in his son's new car, further endorsing the success of his son. They decided to have a family dinner together, and Clara was quick to de-tag her new wardrobe and select clothes she wanted to wear.

Over dinner she related what she had seen of the new world of James in London and even fielded questions. She impressed James with the amount she had absorbed during their visit. They would soon be settled into their new life.

Both parents were keen to see the computer technology in his bedroom before it was dismantled and shipped to London. It amazed them he had amassed so much without their knowledge.

Chapter 10

There was no urgency to get up, although Clara was keen to put her old life behind her. Their first stop was to be her bedsit.

As they climbed the stairs and approached her room, it became clear the lock had been forced, and the door was ajar. As she pushed the door open, she could see her room had been trashed. She walked in, followed by James. 'Welcome to my world. This is retribution by the restaurant owner' as she burst into tears.

James held her. 'Salvage what you want and let's put this behind us. You can call the landlord. Let him know what has happened and you cannot stay here any longer. Your abuse by such people is over. Let's go start our new life together in London. I'll call the police to let them know about this outrage, but don't expect them to respond today.'

She put what was worth salvaging into a bag. She called the landlord to tell him about the break-in and her fear of staying any longer. They left back to his home, where he knew he must lift her out of this depressing situation.

He needed to move her on and concentrate on their future. 'Clara, unless you have anything more to settle here, why not accelerate our program and move to London tomorrow? We can spend the rest of today packing and be on our way tomorrow morning. If you can pack for us, I can dismantle my computer suite. We can load the car before breakfast and be on our way around 9:30.'

'I've finished with this place. I wanted to say goodbye to some people, but I'm not in the mood. We'll be back here to see your folks, so let's go. Find me some cases and show me what you want to pack.'

'Do you need a little fun before we pack?'

She smiled at him 'Let's pack. Then a nice shower, a lot of fun, another shower, and a nice dinner with your folks. Let's get this show on the road.'

'What about lunch?'

'We'll find space somewhere in our schedule.'

'Better go tell Sam about dinner. I'll bring cases back as they're stored in the loft.'

It took some two hours to complete their packing, interrupted only by a quick break for the sandwiches Sam prepared for lunch. They were now wrapped in each other's arms in the shower, having enjoyed their first shower and had their fun on the bathroom floor. He could see the events of the morning had passed. She was ready to move on.

There was still a couple of hours before dinner. She was thinking ahead 'Why don't we go to the local supermarket and get the food we need for the coming days? Will save us time in London.'

'Good idea. Let's go.'

As they prepared for dinner, they were both satisfied they were now ready to start their new life. They looked like a couple ready for a new adventure, and they both felt the togetherness which would confront any obstacle they may encounter. She made a special effort with her new wardrobe. They left hand-in-hand for the dining room.

As they approached the living room, they could hear his parents talking. James allowed Clara through the door ahead of him. His father was quick to his feet 'Clara, my dear. How lovely you look. Can I get you an apéritif?'

'Good evening, Geoffrey. Thank you, but I'll wait for dinner.'

She moved towards Janice, who stood to greet her. 'Hello my dear. Geoffrey's right. You look lovely tonight.'

'It's our last day here, so I made the effort.'

Geoffrey looked at his son 'Change of plan?'

'Yes, dad. Clara has finished her exit from her life in St Albans, so there's no reason to return on Thursday. We're all packed and ready to leave in the morning.'

Sam declared dinner was now ready. They moved to the dining room.

During dinner, James related what happened this morning at the bedsit. His parents were appalled at such behaviour. Geoffrey interjected, 'How have you left it with your landlord?'

'I've told him about the break-in, and we informed the police. My guess is he'll keep my deposit towards the repairs.'

'How much was the deposit?'

'£500.'

'My dear. Your landlord is a client of my bank. With your permission, I'll collect your deposit from him for you. He has insurance to cover the cost of repairs. I'll bring it to you when we visit.'

'That's very kind of you. Are you sure it's no trouble for you?'

'He looks to us for much financial support but can be somewhat derelict in his duty to his tenants. It will be a pleasure to see his face as he hands me this money.'

Janice sat there thinking, *'He's really taken a shine to this young lady. Why such an interest?'*

After dinner, they adjourned to the living room for coffee and drinks.

Chapter 11

They were up bright and early. No time for early morning cuddles or long showers. The car needed loading before breakfast so they could be on their way. Both parents wished them well before departing for their respective jobs.

After helping Sam to clear breakfast, they said their goodbyes to her. They were soon driving off into the sunrise of a new life together.

It was mid-morning before they drove down to the car park. They decided to unload the car, have an early lunch, and then unpack. None of the computer equipment could be assembled, as the room would not be restructured for another twenty-four hours. Unpacking clothes revealed the lack of hangars which had them both in fits of laughter. Such a simple item, but completely lost without them. It would require a shopping trip.

As they had no TV or radio, they decided their late afternoon running into evening would comprise a little fun, a long shower to purge them of any debris from St Albans and the move, an early dinner out at a local restaurant, and then an earlyish night.

Chapter 12

The first call from the concierge on Wednesday morning was a little after 8:30am to say his brother was here to collect the bed and dressing table from the bedroom destined to be his computer suite. James had sought the advice of the concierge to dispose of this furniture. During this conversation, the concierge told James his brother would really appreciate it and could collect it. James saw an opportunity to court favour with this important interface with the outside world so offered the furniture for free so long as they collected it before his computer suite furniture arrives – expected this morning.

The next call was mid-morning to announce the furniture delivery. The delivery driver moaned about the lack of parking around this building, having been told they must quickly unload the furniture and move their van before assembly and installation. James went to speak with the concierge who was most apologetic but explained visitor parking is restricted, but there was a public car park about 100 yards away. However, on this occasion, as a favour, he would allow them to park downstairs in the car park in the bay used by the trash bin collection, but only until lunchtime. He further advised James that although not common knowledge, some residents had not taken their option of parking spaces in the basement car park. The building owner did not want to carry these spaces now the apartment sales had completed, thus looking for a third-party buyer to purchase them and rent them. If he were quick, he could secure a second space at a good price which he could use for visitors or commercial vans so long as they could clear the height barrier which was high enough for emergency vehicles. On his way back up to his apartment he thought *'Can't have my folks aggravated by such problems. 'Need to talk to the property agent to secure another parking space.'*

After supervising the installation of his computer suite furniture, and rewarding the two deliverymen on their way out, he called Angela. A second parking space would cost him £20,000 plus £120 per quarter year in maintenance and service charges. He had no bargaining chips on this occasion and called Simon to appraise him of this additional transaction. Completion was not an issue on this occasion as they would allocate him the space and could use it as soon as they exchanged contracts, which would only take a few days.

At lunchtime Hashem arrived with a new iPhone, iPad Pro, ear pods, and Apple Pencil for Clara. She had prepared a light lunch after which Hashem spent the afternoon educating her how to use her iPhone including transferring her contact data from her old phone, and how to use the sketch function on the iPad so she could use it to produce her design sketches. She could use a Wi-Fi connection to one of the printers in the computer suite to print anything she needed in hardcopy.

James spent the afternoon configuring his computer suite, ensuring it worked as expected; and connected with Javid to test the internet speeds.

By 5pm all are satisfied the day has been productive. Clara had much to learn to become proficient on her new technology, but she had satisfied Hashem she was no slouch once mastering the basics. She only needed the exposure and the opportunity to grasp what she needed to know.

They adjourned to a local hostelry for much needed refreshment. It was a hot day. Although the apartment had air conditioning, Clara had the balcony doors open all day to capture the breeze from the river, resulting in the afternoon sun driving up the apartment temperature.

Hashem, knowing the story of Clara's misfortune, took her under his wing. He, as most geeks, had little time for mere mortals, but he hooked into her desire to learn, and he saw her as a delight to work with. His view was James had chosen well, as she would become a worthy member of the team.

Chapter 13

The following day Clara received her first letters since moving to London. Both were credit cards in her name – the first she had ever owned. One was on the private account of James, and the other on the account of EMULATE Corp. A new purse would be required to accommodate such cards.

Mid-morning saw the arrival of their new TV, AV, and sound systems for the living area, their bedroom, and the guest suite. They were quickly set up and tested. James had accounts with various music and video streaming services, so content was quickly available. They also had access to the building satellite system for live TV channels. Although neither were particularly TV viewers, the apartment now felt complete. Clara would have certainly missed music and radio when James was away at his office. James also set up an Amazon account on her iPad and demonstrated how to use it.

Having now mastered her iPhone, it was time to alert her friends in and around St Albans of her new life, and her new telephone number. Some, whom she knew would be working, received a text message, and others a call as she felt the need to share the joy of her new life with good friends. This took most of the afternoon. James was ensconced in his new computer suite online with the Hashem and Javid, so she had time on her hands to catch up. After all, this was no fairy tale; it was real. Her knight had saved her from her miserable life, and she was now in his castle enjoying a new life.

Chapter 14

The sky is cloudless and blue, allowing the sun to warm everything in the path of its rays. James, having assumed his usual position of not visiting the office on a Friday, decided it was time to explore the area. They walked the streets around where they lived to establish what is available to them. No large department stores but many small shops, cafes, and restaurants occupying new build and renovated old buildings reflecting the proud global trading past of this former dockland area. A detailed look at the various menus on display enabled them to select which they would like to visit to select a restaurant to call their regular. They booked an Italian restaurant to visit this evening to begin the selection process.

Clara used her iPhone to photograph both the restaurants and their menu so she could catalogue each.

They found a driving school within a ten-minute walk from the apartment, so booked a block of lessons for Clara to begin as soon as she had her provisional driving licence.

They also found two parks that were well nurtured, providing a tranquil setting when in need of escaping the hustles and bustles of city life.

After a quick lunch James adjourned to his computer suite and did not re-emerge until well into the evening when dinner became late supper.

Saturday morning was a late rise. No pressure today to do anything. Long cuddles and shower being the preferred way to start the day.

He went with her shopping to ensure she knows how to use her new credit cards and they worked for her.

Once she had settled, he left her to her chores and into his computer suite. She was quickly learning that geeks do not regard weekends as anything other than another day to practice their art.

After a late, but playful rise on Sunday, she persuaded him to explore the swimming pool and gym, which was fun, but he was back to his computer suite after a lite lunch. She had to amuse herself with TV and radio as they had both overlooked the need for reading material, and she had yet to master digital books and magazines.

Chapter 15

Clara's allotted project for the week was to research and visit various art colleges in London, specialising in fashion clothing design. He expected her to determine courses and entry requirements, returning with as much literature as possible from each including application forms. They would study this data on Thursday evening to decide which colleges could be persuaded to allow her entry without qualifications. James did not consider misfortune should stand in the way of enterprise and certainly never considered the need to comply with convention. He was prepared to apply whatever "greasing" was necessary to give her the best opportunity to realise her dream.

He stayed in the apartment on Wednesday for the delivery of the body scanner pod to complete his computer suite. That evening Clara became his first full body scan.

Come Thursday evening, she had amassed much data. The result of her visits revealed one college which stood out as her preferred choice. She made known her favourite to James being Central Saint Martins in Granary Square, near Kings Cross. Famous names such as Stella McCartney, John Galliano, Paul Smith, and Alexander McQueen had studied there, and which filled her with trepidation how she would qualify for entry to such an esteemed college. James read the literature thoroughly. He could see this college had progressive credentials; and located close to his offices in Camden. He had a plan. He would visit with the principal to discuss a joint venture co-operation using his proposed specific computer engine for the fashion industry. Clara would have to convince the college of her merits to be a student there, but such a fully funded joint venture should remove the obstacles of her lack of qualifications under the circumstances she faced in those formative years. He encouraged her to be positive, working together to secure a place for her in October. She would need to develop designs both on paper and her iPad to show her skills. He would try to secure an interview for her.

A sewing machine would be needed and mastered so she could show her ability to make her designs. She already had sewing skills out of necessity to prolong the use of her clothes, or even refashion existing clothes into new designs, which is something she enjoyed in her previous life. She had one of the famous cast iron Singer sewing machines from a Boot Fair for just £10 which, despite its age, did still perform. But she had left this in St Albans as part of her history. Another research project was needed to select the most versatile machine for her purposes. She started this project with much enthusiasm until realising there were so many options selecting became a labyrinth of twists and turns regarding optimal function ranging in price from casual to professional user. She felt a professional machine would give her the scope and quality of stitching likely to be required for college, but she would need to convince him of the merits of such an expensive, in her mind, machine, and she would need a suitable cutting table to go with it.

'Nowhere to put a cutting table of any size, so the dining table will have to do.'

Chapter 16

Friday soon arrived. It was clear to James from the start of the day Clara was overtly nervous about the visit from his folks this evening. He spent all day with her, observing as she prepared the apartment for their first visitors. He took her shopping for the food they would need and purchased champagne and a case of good burgundy – a passion he shared with his father.

They expected his folks around 8pm. A little after 5pm, he could see everything was perfect. 'Clara, let's take a break and calm you down. I've never seen you so nervous. Why don't we have a drink and then have a nice shower together so you can chill? We can prepare a cold table after 7 o'clock so everything is still fresh when they arrive.'

'Are you sure everything's okay? I've never done this before. I so want to make a good impression.'

He held her in his arms. 'Everything is great. Now I need you to relax so they see the lady I know.'

The concierge phoned to say their guests had arrived and directed to the parking space he had purchased for such visitors. James went down to the car park to guide them through the labyrinth of corridors and basement levels to arrive at the elevator. Not being a public building, the only formal guidance notices were how to get out in the event of a fire or flooding.

He reached the apartment with his parents, who were greeted by Clara. The exchange of greeting between Clara and Janice was polite, but Janice still showed her reservations. Geoffrey instantly observed this lack of warmth by his wife, and the general nervousness displayed by Clara. He reached for her, hugged her, and kissed her on both cheeks before stepping back but holding her hand. 'Clara, my dear, how lovely to see you. And how lovely you look. Would you like to show us around your new castle, and I want to hear all about the past two weeks.'

She knew he was compensating for Janice, but she really appreciated his calming influence. He brought a much-needed smile to her face. 'Why don't I show you both to your room. We have champagne on ice so maybe a little refreshment to lubricate your tour.'

'That sounds wonderful, my dear. Lead the way.'

Clara showed them to their guestroom so they could dispense with their luggage and freshen.

They all toasted their arrival to their new home but were keen to have a guided tour of the apartment and balcony before daylight faded.

Suitably impressed they sat down for a cold supper washed down with a fine burgundy wine. Much discussion about how they were settling in. Geoffrey was very keen to know how Clara was settling into her new life. He had good news for her. He had recovered her £500 deposit on her bedsit, expressing the joy from the look on the landlord's face as he handed him the money in cash, no cheque. James had appraised him she had not been paid for her last week at the restaurant, nor did she have a P45 which presented difficulties setting her up as an employee. Geoffrey explained he visited with the owner to insist on her money and P45, again refusing to accept a cheque as he knew she did not have a bank account.

He handed her an envelope with the total cash and her P45. She could not help but get up and give him a kiss on the cheek. 'Thank you so much for helping me. I'm so grateful.'

'No problem, my dear. It was a pleasure to see their faces. Both take advantage of people in difficulties. What I'm prepared to do for you, if you don't need that money, is to set up a bank account for you in our retail division so you can be issued a debit card to make withdrawals when you need cash, and to allow James to pay your salary directly to your bank account. You probably don't have a credit history, so would find it difficult to get a normal bank account. I can vouch for you to overcome this difficulty and build an excellent credit history for you. The account will be in St. Albans so I can oversee it for you to ensure you have no difficulties. But you can use it in any branch or cash machine. Is this something I can do for you?'

She just looked at him with such love for his concern for her. 'Of course, I would love to have my own bank account. Are you sure this is no problem for you?'

'No problem at all. You need to become a fully-fledged member of mainstream society. Before we leave on Sunday, you must give me your details and a sample of your signature, and I'll do the rest. You may receive some forms in the post to complete the process, but I will open your account on Monday, and you should receive the account details and your debit card by Wednesday.'

'That's really great. Thank you.'

They closed the evening on the balcony observing the ever-present life on the river as boats carried anything from noisy party people to police launches, the swell from which created the illusion of nearby lights dancing on the water. There was a tranquillity which eased any tensions.

When they were finally alone in their room, James couldn't help but comment on how much his father had taken her to his heart. 'My dad sees in you what I see.'

'What about your mum?'

'She's too insular. At present she sees me ignoring her chosen route for me through university, and you are part of that disappointment. Give her time. She'll come around as I'm sure dad will slowly adjust her mindset away from her vision of my future to the reality of where we are. Academics tend to see things in a linear progression. Life isn't like that.'

'Your dad's really nice to me. All the trouble he took to get my money and P45. I'm so grateful to have him in my corner.'

'My dad has a big heart, but also very strong. He comes across as unassuming, but don't cross him. As you've witnessed, he's not afraid to confront when necessary. He'll more than compensate for my mom's attitude until she comes around to accept things as they are, and you as a key part of my life. I also think he genuinely likes you.'

Chapter 17

When James awoke, she had been fretting for some time about what she needed to do to make the day successful. The disquieting attitude of his mother did not help her insecurity. He had only seen this insecurity in her these past two days. Before she was always comfortable and confident in what she did, but this life is all new to her. '*She will need a comforting hand this weekend. A long shower together will get the day started.*'

Saturday morning started with a casual breakfast followed by James showing his folks the facilities available within the building whilst Clara made good in the kitchen.

All four of them went on a discovery tour of Wapping, moving East along the river walkways past Shadwell Basin on to The King Edward VII Memorial Park. From there they walked along The Hwy and then along Garnet Street towards Wapping Woods through which they walked to Discovery Walk onto Wapping Lane, where they headed for Wapping Rose Garden to the West of the apartment block. From there they explored Wapping High Street on their way back towards the apartment, stopping for lunch at their nearest hostelry. The conversion of this former dockland area into a thriving modern community impressed Geoffrey.

James wasn't ready to show the new offices as it was still in fit out, so spent the afternoon demonstrated his computer suite to his father. Hashem and Javid were as usual online, allowing James to demonstrate their remote working interface. His father was fascinated by the full-body scanning pod and the wireframe images of Clara, and which could be mobilised for game purposes.

Clara and Janice opted for a swim and then gym. Their conversation was akin to a post-appointment interview to see how she was settling into her new situation and finding out how she deployed her time. Clara felt no warmth during this interrogation and noted her desire to show she was still fit. She could only hope James was right about his father bringing her around over time because this current frostiness was unsettling. She really didn't need any more coldness in her life.

They spent the evening at the theatre to see Les Misérables and then on to dinner at Fredericks in Camden Passage amongst recognisable celebrities from the popular music world. James likes both the restaurant and the local buzz, thinking he should have located here. He made a note to himself to investigate the possibilities.

After a late breakfast on Sunday, his folks departed for home, much to the relief of Clara. Whilst she enjoyed time with Geoffrey, the attitude of Janice reminded her of the bitter life she had left behind in St Albans.

Chapter 18

James made it clear he would spend his time during the following two weeks between overseeing the fit-out of the new offices, spending time with Hashem and Javid organising the computer and office equipment they needed, and his computer suite. Meals would need to fit in with this plan.

By Monday evening she had finished her research on sewing machines. A multi-purpose machine facilitating every stitch type she knew cost around a daunting £500.

'Will he agree to such a lot of money?' She put her ideas on the table for him to peruse. They ranged from a basic model around £350 to an all-singing model at £525. He casually scanned her potential choices.

'Get the most versatile version you can. Will save having to buy, and more importantly, find space for another machine as you progress with your studies.'

'But £525 is a lot of money.'

'Clara, it's nothing compared with the cost of my body scanner, and you're likely to get far more value out of your machine. Just buy it and get your show on the road. You need to be familiar with this machine before you start college. And put it on the business credit card.'

She picked up her iPad, loaded the Amazon website and ordered the expensive machine plus several accessories and cotton packs. It would arrive tomorrow.

The following morning her first surprise was the arrival of her Provisional Driving Licence. She was quick to confirm her first lesson on Thursday afternoon.

By the time she had finished her chores, the building intercom buzzed to announce the delivery of her new sewing machine. The porter decided it was too heavy for her so had it delivered to the apartment and, using her intoxicating smile, it was lodged onto the dining room table where she was quick to unpack it as though Christmas morning. New experience buying expensive items for herself and having them delivered to her. Once all the packaging was strewn on the floor, she sat and looked in amazement at her new toy.

After her blissful delight returned to reality, she realised she had no materials to try out her machine. She remembered seeing several Asian shops selling material around Whitechapel. She was quickly on her way.

This area of London was very much dominated by the Asian community, and shops reflected what you are likely to encounter in local areas of India, Pakistan, Bangladesh and the East Asia peninsula – stacked high and deep in clothing and material in a seemingly chaotic jumble. The only display of anything might be in a shop window, but don't expect rails of clothing to browse. Westerners could find these shops daunting, but not Clara. This had been her world in St Albans and nearby Luton, where she would seek exotic but cheap materials to make her clothes. She knew how to play the barter game with them, remembering to ask for quantities in yards, not metres.

She browsed the glorious array of fabrics like a child in a cookie shop. A bemused shopkeeper approached her. 'Can I help you, madam?'

Wearing her infectious smile, she looked at him and as animated as she could be, 'I've just been given my own sewing machine. I need some lovely material to try it out.'

Totally bewildered by her display, 'Can you show me what you would like?'

Reaching into her pocket, she produced money, 'I have £40. How many different fabrics can I get in 5-yard lengths?'

'Show me what you like. I will tell you when to stop.'

After selecting five different rolls, he asked her if she lived locally investigating if she was likely to become a regular customer. 'Yes, I live in Wapping. You're my nearest store', again knowing the reason for his question.

'Then you can choose one more roll.'

She selected, and he cut. When he had cut all six lengths and knowing they probably make the clothes piled high in the same building, 'Do you have any offcuts I can use for practice? Don't want to waste such beautiful material until I know what I'm doing.'

He, knowing she had her limit of £40, looked at her thinking. 'Are you making many clothes?'

'Yes. I start college in fashion design in October so will make many clothes over the next 3-years.'

'Wait a moment. Let me see what we have.'

He returned with a fistful of offcuts in a range of materials. 'Will this be OK for you?'

'Wonderful. Thank you so much,' handing him her £40. 'You've been so kind and helpful. I'll be back for more soon.'

'Enjoy. If you have excellent designs with our fabric, you tell people where you get them, and if you create something special, you come see me to see if we want to make for our customers and we share profit.'

'Sounds good to me. I'll pop in regularly to see what new fabrics you have to give me inspiration.'

James arrives home to see the dining table covered in material and machine. Dinner was on their laps on the sofa, but he found her excitement with her new machine so infectious he could not find it within him to complain.

He adjourned to his computer suite. Looking at the available space. Shouting back through the door, 'How big is a cutting table?'

This question shook her out of her next sewing task. '6-feet by 4-feet, why?'

Get one and put it in the corner in here. And some storage for your fabrics, hopefully under the cutting table.'

'Won't me in there interrupt you?'

'Once the offices are fully operational, I'll spend most of my time there. And if I work through the night, you'll likely be sleeping so no problem.'

She was quickly back to Amazon finding what she needed and ordering, including the recommended table and chair for her machine, and storage units for materials this time without consulting him. These items were scheduled for delivery over 2 – 3 days.

James arranged to meet with the Principal at Central Saint Martins. Having told her story, presented examples of her work, committing to her funding and success, and outlined the design project in collaboration with the college to be fully funded by EMULATE, the principal, contemplating the idea of being associated with such a significant advance in fashion, agreed Clara would receive an entry interview and would be tested in her first probation year. If successful, she would no longer be on probation. He explained entry to the college is not based on the educational requirements by a university, more vocational requiring a demonstration of flair and creativity. Many overseas students had no formal qualifications but had considerable experience for their ages working in sweatshops in less privileged parts of the World. They scheduled an interview for Clara the following week.

Clara decided not to attempt to impress with any of her modern designs at her interview, just her design skills on her iPad. For practical capability she would do what she already knew, create new clothes from old ones demonstrating her creativity in converting clothes of different materials, blending these materials with knowledge of their varying characteristics to create a new garment showing her creativity. Her new machine would allow her to perfect the stitching requirements. She made a pair of classy shorts with a fashionable top. The interview was successful. She was on the first step of her dream to be a designer. She would start at college for fresher's week at the beginning of October.

She was grateful for this new focus in her life, as with her driving lessons, as he now spent most of his nominal time at home in his computer suite. No more arriving home from the restaurant, nice shower together, and sex before sleep. Nor in the morning. This side of her expectation from her new deal had slowly but surely gone. And no local friends made for an otherwise lonely existence.

Chapter 19

The new office had been functional for a week. Over the weekend James let it be known he needed her to come to the office during the day to field the incessant calls they were receiving from people touting for business in office supplies, coffee machines, photocopiers, printers, et al.

Upon arriving at the office on Monday morning James pointed to the reception desk, which was located immediately inside the entrance, was some 3m long with a curved end. Sitting on the receptionist side of the desk stood a rather expensive looking white desktop computer and keyboard with a 32inch white curved monitor. There was also a modern digital multi-line telephone system.

'This is your desk. I'll get Javid to fire it all up for you, and then I'll explain what we need from you.' At that he advanced along the long open space to offices at the far end. As she looked toward where he disappeared into an office, she saw a large open space with a cluster of eight desks position back-to-back set in the middle, but by no means consuming the available space. At the end of the room, on the opposite side to the offices, she saw banks of electronic racks with masses of cables engulfing them like tentacles.

Javid came walking towards her. 'Hi Clara. Lovely to see you. Let us get you set up. I'll show you how to use the telephone system. You'll see, for now, I've put three message books on the desk for you, one for each of us. What I've done is to put a list of people for each of us who we are happy to take calls. Anyone else you will need to extract who they are and what they want. We can then decide if we wish to call them back. We are being inundated by photocopier and drinks vending salespeople, recruitment agencies, stationery suppliers, and a whole gamut of others we don't want to engage with, but don't want to offend in case we need them in the future. You will need to field these people as they take up too much of our time. I don't know what else James has in mind, but this is the task we most need you to fulfil until you recruit a full-time receptionist for us.'

She spent the entire day, including over lunchtime, fielding calls from all and sundry, all pressing to speak with a director, but not letting any through. Looking at the three geeks at the other end of the office, *'Do these guys eat?'*

She did field one call, Sonya, a recruitment agent, she engaged with to understand how to recruit a capable receptionist. They laughed their way through Clara's description of the three geeks running the business, and their desire to recruit more like them. They agreed a conventional receptionist would not be suitable, but Sonya would scan their books as she remembered a capable woman, but who is a goth – even in the workplace. To Clara, she sounded perfect for these guys.

Chapter 20

It was her third day in the office. In her waitress days she was accustomed, on busy days, to remembering ad hoc orders from up to six tables and know which table ordered, and the need to add these extras to the correct bill. But never did she feel as frazzled as she sat at her desk looking blankly at the list of tasks confronting her.

James was out of the office at a meeting, albeit he was no help in any event. Hashem saw her blank expression. Making her tea, he grabbed a chair, delivered her tea, and sat with her.

'We've really dumped on you, haven't we? Putting a functional office together is so alien to us. Why don't you tell me what tasks are alien to you? We can spend the afternoon trying to find solutions.'

'Hashem, all of it is alien to me. I've never worked in an office. This computer appears to be connected to your telephone system, but I have no idea how it works. If I'm sitting here, the telephone rings and I have the option to answer. If I'm not here, it seems to know and takes over answering a call and taking messages. How does it do this? And what do I know about what signs, plaques, and stationery you want. And I have no idea how to use this computer.'

She was almost in tears as she eased her frustration. 'I want to help you be successful in your business, but I don't understand any of what you expect of me.'

'Not true, Clara. Your skill in handling our telephone calls is remarkable. We were becoming so frustrated with the constant interruption from people we don't know. The jungle drums around here spread far and wide to everyone who wants our business, telling us what we need before we even know we need it. I hear how you handle these calls. Extremely polite, but firm. It's great.'

She tried to chuckle under her desperation, 'much experience with clients at the restaurant who could get very nasty and rude if we couldn't accommodate them for their chosen reservation time. My job was to soak up the abuse and try to give them an alternate booking. Wouldn't like to think how many times I wanted to slam the phone down on them. Even worse, face-to-face with someone trying to order something no longer available. You are the butt of their frustration but must maintain a friendly smile whilst guiding them to an alternative.'

'There you are. None of us have your interpersonal skills or patience. I understand how James defines your role, but please don't think I share his view, and I think I can speak for Javid as well. You are a fundamental part of our team, and we must all work together to ensure you have the knowledge and skills to deliver your part.'

She put her hand on his. 'Thank you. You don't know what this means to me.'

'Why don't we start with the telephone. I saw this system and couldn't help myself buying it even though it's probably far too sophisticated for us until we're much larger.' He pointed to a small hole in the middle of the bottom frame of the display. 'This detects if you're sitting here. If not, and a call comes in, the system will either divert to a predesignated extension, or take a message. When it detects your return, it will advise you of any calls so you can listen to the messages.'

'Is it actually filming me?'

Hashem laughed. 'Don't worry. It's a body heat detector. Works a bit like a motion detector. It only knows someone is sitting here, not who.'

'I find the technology is this place scary. I thought James' computer suite looks like a space centre, but the setup here is beyond me.'

'Clara, there're only dumb adding machines that allow us to express ourselves. If they become overpowering, all you need to do is unplug them. Let's look at the software on your computer. The main application is a word processor.'

'But Hashem, I can't type. I've never had any need to learn.'

'This is a skill we must teach you, and you must learn. You'll need it for college, so you need to get some practice. Come to think of it, you would be better with a laptop at college. I have a good one I no longer use. I'll clear all my stuff off it and load what you'll need for your college work. I'll give it to you tomorrow. I'll load the same word processor as is on this system so you can practice on both. I'll hook it up to the internet, to the printer in your computer suite at home for small print runs, and to the main printer here for anything over, say 20 pages. But if you send anything to the printer here, let me know so I rescue it and make sure James brings it home for you.'

'Hashem, you're so kind to me. Thank you so much.'

'No problem. I'll find an online typing course so you can learn when you want to rather than go to some course. What else is on your list?'

'Company signs and posters. I don't have a clue what you need.'

'I'll design what we need. You track down suitable print companies locally and get quotes.'

'Great. I can do that.'

They spent the next hour finding solutions to all the issues on her list. She emerged feeling much better. She had much to learn, but with Hashem and Javid prepared to help her, she no longer felt alone in these tasks. Importantly, she felt in control of the telephone system for the first time. She also worked out if there are times when telephone calls overwhelm her, she could put something in front of the detector on her screen and all calls would go to voicemail. *'So much for smart technology'*, she thought.

Sonya called back to say she had found her goth receptionist. She was available for an interview. But who will interview her?

'Sonya, I have no idea about the skills of a receptionist, nor about interviewing. And I can't see the geeks remotely interested in the process. They just want a solution. I need help.'

'Why don't I come to your offices to meet you and look at the proposed setup. I'll ask the lady, Helen is her name,' they laughed at such a name being associated with a goth, 'to come one hour later and we can interview her together. Then why don't we go to lunch and get to know each other as you sound a fun lady?'

'Sounds great. Set it up. And thanks for your help.'

'Clara, I think you and I are going to have fun, so no problem. I'll try for Friday.'

Chapter 21

Sonya arrived punctually at 10am on Friday. She was a pretty lady, probably a little older than Clara, with long brunette hair, looking very professional in her trouser suit. Clara had not really considered how she should dress for the office because the geeks are always dressed casually. James would dress in what would be considered smart casual if he had to attend meetings, but dress down appeared to be the norm in this industry sector.

Sonya was impressed with the rolling screen now in reception. It was a video advert for the latest game using their engine, and there was no doubt who produced the engine. Javid had topped and tailed this 2-minute rolling video with graphics, leaving no doubt this was an EMULATE product.

They laughed their way around the office as Clara pointed to the Geek Unit and the proposed Starship Enterprise desk cluster. Sonya thought this a perfect environment for Helen, who she had rekindled a relationship with yesterday. They enjoyed a coffee whilst waiting for Helen to arrive.

Helen appeared. Well presented. Clearly goth, but not overtly so. No goth makeup, only symbolic goth clothes. They already knew she was 30-years-old and her CV showed a variety of appropriate experience, mainly in the media sector. They sat in the visitor waiting area.

Clara broke the ice by asking Helen to describe herself, what she could deliver to the job, and any issues that may be a concern on either side.

'My name is Helen. My friends call me Hell, and this is my preferred name. As you can see, I follow the goth cult, although not the deep morbid variety. My goth calling is more to do with the music I enjoy than anything barbarian. This has caused me problems getting a job, but I try to be considerate of my role, and am looking for a more progressive employer who looks at my performance rather than my dress code. I was an executive P.A. but this did not work out with my dress code. I will not wear goth makeup in the office, nor will I disrespect the nature of my duties. I have a degree in English Literature and French from Oxford. What more do you want to know?'

Clara could feel her pain. 'Well, Hell, my ambition is to be a fashion designer and I think you look great. You look very comfortable in your clothes, and it radiates through.'

Helen looked visibly shocked. 'Thank you so much. You don't know how good that makes me feel.'

'It's a pleasure. Been there. Before I show you around, let me tell you about EMULATE as this is no regular company. This company to date comprises 3 geeks and a dog's body, that's me. The owner and primary geek is my partner, James, who developed the computer graphics engine you see on the video here. He has forsaken university to develop ever more powerful engines, having made his first £1million by his 18th birthday. The other 2 geeks are the lovely Hashem and Javid, both Ph.D.'s in their early 20s and are now partners with James. Unless they speak with me directly, everything they discuss between themselves is gobbledegook's to me. All they want to do is their geek work. What they need is someone to interface between them and the normal world. How am I doing?'

Helen was smiling. 'Sounds great. Can I meet these guys? I can do all the interfacing they need, and I don't need a job description. Sounds like they're going places and I'm up for it.'

Sonya brought some formality to the conversation. 'Don't you think with your background the job of receptionist is below your expectations?'

'From Clara's description I see this role as more full-on P.A. where dealing with interlopers from the outside world is just one important task. Sounds like they need someone to deal with all day-to-day tasks to give them the freedom to do their work. This would make me a significant contributor to their success. This job would require all my skills, especially in media, so totally meet my expectations. What a buzz to work with such incredible minds.'

Clara had a thought. 'There is one consideration I want to air in case this affects your decision. James is looking for a minimum 3-year commitment. On a woman-to-woman basis, you are now 30. What are your ambitions regarding a family life, especially children?'

'That question is a little off the normal scale of allowable questions. But I can see you're not remotely malicious about it, so I'm happy to answer. I have a boyfriend, but with no serious ambitions yet. Yes, I would need to consider children in the next 5 to 6 years, but not on my priority list. Hand on heart today, I don't see a 3-year commitment as an issue.'

'Great. Why don't we go meet the geeks?'

They introduced Helen to all three. Hashem and Javid stood to greet her; James stayed seated. None of them displayed any interest in her dress code. She was also given some idea of the intended expansion, shown the Geek Unit and Starship Enterprise zone. She was all smiles.

When back in the visitor's area, Sonya restored formality. 'Well Helen, what do you think?'

'When can I start?'

'Don't you want to know the package? What were you on before?'

'As an exec P.A. my salary was £27,000 but was below market for the job. The only perks I can remember was life assurance. What's on offer here?'

'I'll check current exec P.A. salaries and discuss with Clara. In addition, you get life assurance, London weighted medical insurance, pension scheme and 20 days paid holiday per annum.'

'Wow. Can't complain at that. What are the hours?'

Clara answered. 'With the geeks, hours are anytime. But Hashem and Javid get here around 8:30am and normal leaving is 5:30pm. As you're dealing with the conventional World, I think these are the hours you're most needed.'

'Good. No problem. If we can agree salary I can't wait to get started.'

With that they said their goodbyes, after which Sonya and Clara went to lunch.

Over lunch they really bonded. Clara described her background but not her deal with James, only, having reconnected with him, she moved with him to pursue her dream as a fashion designer. Sonya committed any support she could give, not least her agency could provide any administrative support roles needed and she would be her contact there.

'What do you think of Helen, or Hell as she wants to be called?'

'I like her. If you tell me she has the skills, she certainly has the character. That she won't concede her goth values to suit a conventional job shows she can hold her own with the geeks. So long as she stays true to her word about doing whatever is required, I'd like to give her a shot. When can you give me the salary information?'

'I already know. It's my job to know. But telling her at the interview might have closed the deal before you have time to think about it. Salary range of an exec P.A. in a small to medium company is in the range £32,000 to £40,000. As you have attractive perks, my suggestion would be to start her at £32,000 with the option to increase if she works out.'

'Do we have a probation period to consider?'

'Yes, normally 5 or 6 months.'

'I have no idea how to write an employment contract. Can you help me?'

'Of course. I know what you are offering in perks, so we only need to agree salary and probation.'

'My thoughts are we offer her £32,000 to start. If she proves herself through probation, we increase to £35,000 after six months, and then if she really does well, we'll guarantee a minimum £5,000 bonus. How does this sound?'

'Very generous, she'll jump at it. Are you sure you want to go this far?'

'We want to reward performance, and she will earn it. Can you imagine another 8 geeks in that office? She'll need to mother them because I'll be at college.'

'Okay. Let me draft up an offer letter and Contract of Employment and let you have them on Monday.'

Chapter 22

As weeks passed, routine became de rigour. Clara recruited Helen, the goth who quickly adapted to this unusual setup. Clara assumed a more administrative role trying to maintain order in a chaotic environment. Two positions in the Geek Unit had been recruited, filling two of the eight positions in the Starship Enterprise desk cluster. Both were graduates with PhD's before they were 25 years old. When Clara overheard discussion with these recruits, Hashem, and Javid, they could be on a different planet speaking an alien tongue. And when they had finished using a whiteboard, it looked like some futuristic hieroglyphics.

It took her three months to complete her driving test, which she passed first time. This added chauffer duties to her list of tasks, initially to and from the office, to give her experience on the roads of London. But college is looming, so expected to reduce such tasks.

Another very noticeable change was the continued absence of James from the office. Hashem and Javid were concerned with the behaviour of James regarding one Juliet Cranford, a young executive at ComPlay Limited, a potential client for their computer engine. They noticed James was spending much time with her where all such meetings were for lunch or dinner. They also knew part of Clara's role was to offset the need for alternative female companionship, and she was more than a little interested in this situation.

As Hashem and Javid had developed a serious liking for Clara, and they wanted to prevent a problem that could impact the business, they suggested to Clara she join them for dinner this evening. Little did Clara know they were going to the same restaurant James had booked for his dinner with Juliet. They arrived before James and found a reasonably secluded table in a corner from which they could observe the restaurant. James arrived some 20 minutes later with Juliet. He was too pre-occupied with her to even scan the restaurant, although he would have to scan carefully to notice his three collaborators.

Having ordered their meal, James and Juliet huddled closer with Juliet constantly touching the back of his hand. This was clearly not a business discussion.

The three observers allowed this closeness to develop for a further half hour just to be sure they were not reading too much into what they observed. Finally, Clara declared it was time to go to the toilet for which she would need to pass the table of James and Juliet. She was now clear Juliet had more than a computer engine in her sights.

As she approached James, she tried to feign surprised. 'James, darling, what a surprise to see you here. That's fortunate as we can now go home together after dinner.'

He looked at her startled, quickly removing his hand from the grasp of Juliet. 'What are you doing here?'

'Hashem and Javid realised I would be alone this evening and invited me to dinner. We're over there', as she pointed to her table. 'I need the toilet, but we can link up when you have finished your business' looking at Juliet.

James was in a quandary what to do. Guilt flowed through his veins, making him feel uncomfortably warm. He tried to compose himself. 'Clara, this is Juliet Cranford from ComPlay. They are interested in our computer graphics engine.' He looked at Juliet. 'This is Clara, my partner.'

Clara's look towards Juliet as she extended her hand made it clear she knew Juliet was interested in more than a computer engine. The look on Juliet's face as she shook hands with Clara told all, but she had the message. No more cosy lunches and dinners trying to catch this man.

Juliet did not wait for dessert as she made her excuses and left. James settled the bill and went to join Clara, suspecting this was no coincidence. 'I'm ready to leave if you've finished.'

'Good idea. It's been a long day. Time to go home.'

They said their goodbyes and made their way back to Wapping. He said nothing throughout the journey. She knew this would be a test of their agreement and wondered how he would react once in the sanctuary of the apartment.

He poured himself a drink. 'Please tell me this evening was not a coincidence.'

'Just fulfilling the role you asked of me.'

'Did Hashem and Javid put you up to this?'

'James, please don't tell me you're not aware dear Juliet was reeling you in hook, line, and sinker. Please tell me you're not that naïve.'

'The deal with ComPlay is potentially large, so a little flirting to secure the deal can't be considered anything other than helpful.'

'She's more than a match for you. She knows exactly what she wants out of the deal and was weaving her charms on you for some time before I intervened, but not make a scene so you can salvage your deal without selling your soul to her. That's part of my job description. Remember? No more lunches and dinner with her. Meetings only at ComPlay offices or ours. Are we clear?'

He was fuming. He wanted to tear a strip off her but knew she had caught him with his trousers down. She was mandated by him to intervene in such circumstances, so what to do.

She could see his anger. 'James, whatever you want to say, say it. Another part of our deal is we do not go to bed with any anger in our hearts.'

He looked at her, not sure what to do. 'I feel embarrassed and chastised. I do feel angry with you, but I also know if I do vent, you'll probably knock my head off, which will hurt. You've fulfilled the role I asked of you, so I must accept your intervention. So, thank you. I'm sorry I strayed and will try to be more careful in the future. Will that do?'

She hugged her little boy. 'Let's go to bed and put this behind us in the way we know best.'

Chapter 23

She no longer attended the office for more than one day each week, or should it be better phrased after the incident with Juliet he wanted to isolate her from his day-to-day dealing, and with Hashem and Javid. He did not like the idea she could collude with them against him. It was his business. Keeping a tight control on activities within the business was still his prerogative, and he intended to exercise it.

This gave her time to master her new sewing machine, which occupied the long hours he was absent from the apartment. It was easy for her to become absorbed in trying new ideas interspersed with frequent trips to fabric and pattern shops, maintain a good relationship with her now friend and ally in Whitechapel. He was always happy to see her, especially when she took with her whatever latest creation she had made. Keeping her supplied with a variety of fabrics from plain chiffons to exotic silks, he even gave her tips on how to work with such fabrics. She loved the challenge of working with such fine fabrics, never before being able to afford them.

However, there was not much else in her life besides her drive to teach herself typing, which she mastered quite quickly. Her fabric man and the building concierge were fast becoming her only face-to-face contacts outside of the office. Not even weekends changed her lonely existence. Now she could drive shopping was a lone chore added to the lack of ideas what to buy never knowing if he would want food, or already eaten with Hashem and Javid.

Thank goodness the start of college was imminent. Time to prepare and hopefully meet new friends.

Chapter 24

It was fresher's week at college. Very much a week of finding her way around the College, understanding her schedule of study, and some fun events. Books and other study materials to buy ready to start work the following week.

The first few weeks were stressful. Her class were mainly straight from school, so much younger. Although academically not demanding for someone straight from school, her lack of school education since the age of fourteen left her hopelessly struggling to understand the required process. The year comprises a mix of academic study and practical application. The academic study in this first year involves reading, comprehension, and reconstituting the study matter in the form of an essay within a maximum word count demonstrating, or not, comprehension of the study material. Whereas she can readily hold her own on the practical side, the discipline of studying, comprehending, and regurgitating academic study is alien to her.

Her allocated tutor, M. Francois Benign, of French origin, slight in stature, in his 40s tending to the effeminate, presented her with two challenges, his strong French accent which he wore as a badge of honour, and his bad breath. He did quietly acknowledge to her he was aware of her unfortunate background and would spend as much time as he could to help her to overcome any difficulties she might have settling into academia, but with a patronising and arrogant air. Without giving a thought to her background or, indeed, the other members of the classes he taught, where there is a French expression for something in the fashion world, he would most certainly use it assuming his young charges are familiar with such expressions, even if not in general use in the UK. She needed to change this situation, even if it meant a change of tutor. But how?

By the third week she felt so frustrated, and an essay to deliver. She tried to discuss this with James during a rare moment they spent together, but not really interested. She phoned Hell and explained her plight. 'Come to the office after school and let's talk about it.'

Having finished at college at 4pm, she went straight to the office sitting with Hell to explain her problem.

'Sounds like my first French teacher. Thinks French is the only language of merit on the planet. I can do two things for you. The first is I teach you how to structure essays. This we will do each day after college until you have grasped the process. The second is to come visit with Francois during your next private tutorial to see if he can better understand your situation and be a little more helpful. When is your next tutorial?'

'Friday. Midday.'

'Good. So, we have a couple of evenings to get your essay writing up to speed. Let's get started.'

Hell went to sit with James, closing his office door behind him. She knew James was no match for her, thus felt confident in confronting him about Clara.

'James. You have a distressed Clara through no fault of her own. She has an arrogant French tutor who speaks to her, half in French, and his English has a thick French accent. I've been to meet this man. He has no empathy with her situation. Could I ask you to speak with the Principal at the College to see if we can find a solution? Clara doesn't need this stress. She's a wonderful lady who wants to learn.'

'She mentioned this to me about a week ago. Thank you for taking care of my indifference. I'll speak with him now.'

James explained the situation to the principal who immediately understood, agreeing to change her tutor.

He turned to Hell. 'Clara will have a new tutor today. His name is Justin Black. He has a daughter with special educational needs, is English, and is held in high regard in the College. This should solve the problem.'

'Thanks, James. I hope you don't mind my interference, but I like Clara and will help her all I can.'

'Hell, I'm sorry you felt the need to get involved, but I appreciate what you are doing for her. It has not escaped me you're helping her to learn how to study. Thanks.'

Chapter 25

Clara quickly settled with her new tutor, with whom she had disclosed the true nature of her past and the challenges presented. He was full of empathy and suggested they double their tuition periods during which he would help her with her studies, but more importantly how to study effectively. Being a quick and enthusiastic student, she was soon coping well and enjoying the process. Hell could detect the rapid progress and enjoyed sharing the process as her fascination with the evolution of clothing increased.

The downside was her attention to chores in the apartment seriously diminished, albeit the lifestyle of James meant this delinquency was mostly unnoticed. She was grateful she didn't need to prepare dinners most evenings as his daily time at the office extended into evenings. If she spent time in the office with Hell after college, they would usually go home together, either dining at their now regular Italian, or collecting a takeout. Later, on reflection, this was the only time they had a proper conversation. However, she had to discipline herself to take care of household chores on Saturdays lest they have no food or clean clothing. As weekends blurred into working days for him, she was generally alone. She often reflected if the space she had was a blessing to allow her to pursue her own dreams. But the contra to this was the lack of the intimate fun had brought them together. She spent more waking hours with Hell than with James. *'Perhaps his dedication to his projects is what it takes to be successful. But at least he has others around him to share the load.'* She reflected on the loneliness for so long in her life.

Chapter 26

Her first semester was over, although she knew much additional work would be needed before returning to college in January. James had already declared they would go to his folks for Christmas but he could not afford any longer than a few days so they would leave for St Albans around lunchtime on Christmas Eve, and return to London Boxing Day afternoon. This was a relief to Clara, as she couldn't imagine spending any prolonged time with his mother.

Christmas passed without incident. Geoffrey significantly compensated for the attitude of his wife. Although always polite and friendly towards Clara it was still in her mind this was her son's mistress and housekeeper for a fixed term period after which he could find a more suitable woman as a wife.

Other than coaxing Hashem and Javid, and thus James, to spend New Year's Eve on the streets of Central London to participate in the festivities and the midnight fireworks display she hardly spent any waking hours with James in the weeks before she would return to college. Although she had much revision and preparation for her new term, the loneliness was taking its toll on her well-being.

Chapter 27

She couldn't wait to return to college, desperate for some social intercourse. Other than occasional telephone calls, she had no actual contact with Hell after Christmas. She visited with her material provider, and her local shops primarily to have contact with normal people. She was used to much interaction with people, feeling imprisoned in the apartment all day.

The spring term proved much easier to navigate as she became used to the routine and expectations. Hell was always prepared to help when needed, which was a welcome relief and time to chat with another human being. Time with James became even less frequent, so free to pursue her own dream, which was becoming less of a chore.

By the end of term for Easter break she was feeling relaxed about life in college, knowing she still had much to do to keep her place, but more in tune with how to achieve. Hell had been relentless in honing her learning skills and was most certainly her best friend.

Easter came and went with no regard by James. The weather was typical English Bank Holiday – awful and depressing. But her material provider, Rajeev, had looked at some of her creations with interest, introducing her to his extended family, all of which worked in the business. Specifically, Anisha, the oldest daughter, and the same age as Clara, had become very friendly. She showed Clara how to engage some of the more intricate sewing techniques for Indian-style clothes working with fine materials. She now had funds to purchase higher-quality materials and thankful to learn the skills to work with such materials from people who really understood the process. But Anisha was the primary designer for the family business and, as with many such Indian family businesses, she worked long hour leaving very little time to socialise.

The summer semester was very much about preparation for exams. Whereas she felt confident in the practical design and make process, nerves took hold about the academic requirements. Hell to the rescue, more to coach her in the techniques required to sit exams than subject knowledge. Nerves needed to be replaced by positive adrenaline. She trusted Hell so could feed off her confidence and obvious knowledge. After each exam, she would visit with Hell for a debrief and needed reassurance. Hell hid her frustration with James, taking no interest in her needs and support. Something she felt with her various boyfriends who generally showed little interest in her dreams and aspirations.

Chapter 28

She is sitting alone in the apartment. He didn't need her today for either chauffeur duties or to work in the office. The sun was shining – but outside. In her head and her heart there was only darkness and turbulence. Unsure about her performance in her exams was a metaphor for how she felt about her life. The latest EMULATE project due for delivery in a few weeks completely absorbed James meaning he only slept a few hours each day, spent most of every day working either in the office or alone in his computer suite into the night occasionally surfacing for a quick meal. The only time they spent together was in his bed, but even this was now periodic. No together showers in the morning. No fun at all, really. Even her birthday passed with no fun, not least because he'd never asked about her birth date.

She was evaluating her first year in London, feeling despondent. Yes – she was living in a nice apartment, had nice clothes, good food, and some money in the bank.

Yes – she had started to realise her dream as a fashion designer – if she passed her exams. But they never discussed the fashion engine James had agreed to build for her since leaving St Albans. He had achieved his part of their pact, and was moving on to greater things, but she was far from realising hers.

She felt trapped. If she left him, where would she go? Certainly not back to St Albans. Even if she passed her exams, she knew EMULATE was paying her college fees. Would her exam results warrant a bursary to continue – the premise of her entry to the college deprived student program?

Her love for this man plagued her *'or is he still a boy?'* who rarely noted she exists other than someone at his beck and call as mistress, housekeeper, chauffer, and occasional office dogsbody. *'Is this really what I signed up for?'*

'What to do? Back to a grotty life of shabby bedsits and long hours waiting tables. Depressing.'

The worst was feeling so alone, just as she felt when she lost her mother. She had no real friends she could talk to about how she felt. Her friendship with Hell stopped short of expressing her feeling lest this affected her attitude towards James. The lack of time to maintain relationships with her friends in St Albans since starting college was not a platform to share her depression, having lauded her new life when she moved to London.

She knew Hashem and Javid were there for her, but only to help her do things. They had excellent educations, were super bright, and from large, close families. What would they know about loneliness and the despair of having no family or close friends to confide in and hope for some shared joy? She knew of such loneliness and despair, having suffered four years as a lone carer, and a further three years trying to scrape a life from the bottom of the stack.

'*I have all of this, but I'm still alone and have no life to call my own.*' She burst into tears.

Chapter 29

Whilst awaiting her exam results, she needed to fill her lonely days after completing her daily chores. When not needed as a goffer for James, she took herself out during the day, determined to see the historic sites of London and scan the latest fashion in the best design houses. She even met with her student friends in the evenings but found five brief years' difference in their ages, and a whole world of difference in life experience limited compatibility. Most of her evenings out, she would walk the streets alone with the occasional movie or theatre show if the weather turned against her. Anything but sit in an empty apartment.

Finally, the day came. She could see from the envelope this must be her exam results. James, as usual, was not there to share this moment in their quest.

'*Come on, girl. You need to know where you are in your life.*'

She tore the letter open and extracted the contents. Scanning the results line by line. '*Not great, but not bad either.*'

The last line brought a smile to her face, "Congratulations. You may advance to your second year beginning 6th October."

She felt ecstatic for the brief moments it took her to realise she had no-one with whom to share her success. She reached for her phone and dialled James. It went to voicemail. She left a voicemail about her success.

About an hour later, she received a text message from James.

"*Great news. Knew you could do it. Hashem and Javid think we should take a break this evening for a celebration dinner. Come to the office around 6pm. Jx*"

She noted the idea came from his partners, not him. Knocked the joy out of the day. Now she knew she had to stay if she wanted to continue her studies, hoping things might get better for her.

Chapter 30

Laughter, lively chatter, and the clinking of glasses filled the warm summer evening as all the staff of EMULATE were celebrating the completion of their big animation engine project and the subsequent licence agreement, this time with an animated film company associated with award-winning blockbuster movies. Their table was outside and filled the space between the restaurant and the walkway.

Two dowdy-looking men came staggering along the walkway beside the restaurant, visibly the worst for drink. As they passed the table occupied by James and his staff, one man lost his footing and crashed into their table. James was nearest to him with Clara on his left. James was not happy with this disturbance, so let rip at the man now being helped to his feet by his friend. Once upright, the drunk looked at James with a fiery disdain. 'You fucking talking to me, mister. You fucking young spivs think you own the place. All your smart talk and money.'

Clara had moved next to James, hoping to diffuse this situation so the drunks could be on their way. This was more her domain than his. James countered, 'We're the people who work for a living and generate wealth for this country. Why can't we enjoy our efforts without being disturbed by people who expect everything for nothing?'

The drunk snarled his face while reaching under his jacket. A knife appeared in his hand. Before anyone could react, he lunged at James. Clara, realising James had frozen in fear, quickly pushed between them screaming 'No' hoping to push the lunging arm away. He was too strong for her. She took the full force of the knife into her upper thigh, stood motionless for a few seconds before collapsing to the floor. The drunk looked startled as she fell. His friend grabbed him to flee the scene as quickly as possible. Two men at another table quickly took chase.

James screamed, 'Clara. What has he done to you?' He dropped to his knees and turned her towards him. The handle of the knife protruded from her body. 'Oh, my God. Get me an ambulance quickly.' He supported her head in despair at what he saw as the blood started to stain her dress. 'Clara, please come back to me. Speak to me. Why did you do that? What have I done? Clara, Clara, please come back to me.'

Someone knelt beside her and checked her neck for a pulse and then put the back of his hand in front of her mouth. 'She's alive. Please don't touch the knife. I'm a paramedic. The ambulance will soon be here.'

They could hear the sirens as the ambulance approached. She was quickly stretchered to the ambulance. The paramedic spoke to James 'They will take her to The Royal London Hospital. Go, be with her.'

This ordeal confused James. He was kneeling on the bloodstained walkway repeatedly racking his brain '*What happened? Where's my Clara?*' His party could see his distress. Hashem grabbed his arm. 'Come with me. I'll get you to the hospital.'

Just then the police arrived. They had apprehended the two drunks. Now the police wanted statements. They were informed James needed to get to the hospital.

Understanding his distress, they took his address, after which Hashem led him to a taxi.

When they arrived at the hospital, they were told Clara was in theatre. She was alive, but critical as an artery had been severed. Hashem had the awareness to call their medical insurer to appraise them of the situation so she would get the best treatment possible. He went to advise the hospital Clara was a private patient and gave the insurance details.

James sat with his head in his hands, trying to come to terms with what she had done.

He took out his phone and dialled home. His mother answered. He broke down 'Mom, its James. Clara has been stabbed. It should have been me. She took the knife for me. What have I done? It wasn't her fight.'

Janice indicated to her husband he should listen as she selected speakerphone. 'James, where are you?'

'The Royal London hospital in London.'

'What's the situation with Clara?'

'She's in theatre, alive but critical.' He broke down again.

His father spoke 'Son, we're on our way. Phone us in the car if anything changes. We'll be there as quickly as we can.'

When they arrived at the hospital, they quickly found James and Hashem. His mother wrapped him in her arms whilst Geoffrey extracted a brief of what happened from Hashem. 'My God, Hashem, you're telling me Clara saw what was about to happen and deliberately put herself between the knife and James. What a lady. She said she would protect James, but this is above and beyond. Thank you for telling me.'

A man approached them in blue theatre fatigues. 'I'm looking for James Caldwell.'

'I'm Geoffrey Caldwell, father of James.' He pointed to his son, releasing his distress into his mother's shoulder. 'That's my son. What's the situation with Clara?'

'She's now in intensive care. She's weak, but we expect her to pull through. Thankfully, leaving the knife in place limited the loss of blood from her artery. The tissue damage will take some time to heal, but she's young and strong. We don't expect any lasting issues. But we'll know more in a few days. We hope to transfer her to one of our private rooms when she's breathing on her own and we've drained any excess fluids from her wound.'

'Thank you so much. Can anyone see her, so she knows we're here for her?'

'I think your son is probably too distraught to see her. Perhaps yourself, or your wife could usefully visit with her, but just for a few minutes.'

'Thank you for your help. Which way to intensive care?'

'I'll find a nurse to take you.'

'I think my wife would be better.'

'As you wish. I'll send a nurse.'

Geoffrey asked Hashem to take care of James whilst he appraised Janice of what he had learnt from both the surgeon and from Hashem. Tears were rolling down her cheeks; something he hadn't witnessed for years. 'We owe that woman. What courage and commitment to James. I'll go visit with her.'

She followed the nurse while Geoffrey sat with James and told him the situation. James wanted to see Clara, but his father told him his distressed state would not help her at this point. He could see her tomorrow.

When Janice entered the intensive care unit, the dull light revealed a row of occupied glass cubicles being watched by medics behind a line of computer monitors. The duty nurse took her to Clara. She saw her pale form; her face hidden by an oxygen mask. There was an array of wires and tubes from her body performing the necessary functions to keep her alive and to aid her recovery. Janice sat next to her and held her hand. Something erupted inside her. Maternal instincts, long buried, came rushing back to her. Her eyes welled. *'She could be my daughter.'*

Clara opened her eyes. 'Clara, my dear. It's Janice. We're all here for you. You are one magnificent woman, and we'll get you through this. Your surgery was successful, so you should be in a private room tomorrow. I'll bring James to see you then. They won't let him come to see you now because he's so distraught. Do you understand me?'

She nodded weakly, her oxygen mask not allowing her to speak.

'Would you like me to sit with you for a while?'

Another nod.

The duty nurse appeared. 'We'll put her back to sleep in a few minutes. She needs to conserve her strength.'

'Thank you, nurse. Can I sit with her until she sleeps? We owe so much to this wonderful lady.'

'I understand. I'll come back in a few minutes.'

Clara felt the warmth flow through her arm as she drifted back into the sanctity of sleep. Janice felt her hand go limp. '*Sleep peacefully, lovely lady. We'll get you through this.*'

When Janice returned to the reception area, she collapsed into the arms of Geoffrey in tears. He held her for a while to allow her distress to ease. James stood and moved to them. 'What's the matter with mom? Is Clara okay?'

She pulled herself together, realising her distress was not helping her son. 'James, I've spoken with Clara. She's alright but needs to sleep to conserve her strength. Why don't we go back to your apartment and get some sleep? There's nothing more we can do here this evening.'

Geoffrey thanked Hashem for his help and support before they retrieved their car and drove to the apartment.

James was still not focussed. His father decided it was time for some fatherly intervention. 'Son, can you tell me what happened this evening?'

'We were enjoying a celebration dinner. We signed a great licence agreement this week. Two guys the worse for drink came past our table. One fell onto our table, causing general mayhem. I was furious, so I let rip at him. When he got back to his feet, he had a go at me, so I responded. He pulled a knife. The next thing I know Clara's in front of me and then collapsed to the floor.' He descended into tears again. 'When I turned her over, the knife was buried in her.' Flood of tears now poured down his cheeks. 'Why did she do it? That knife was intended for me. What possessed her?'

His father put an arm around his shoulders to comfort him. His mother sat on the other side of him, holding his hand.

69

After some time, his father spoke again. 'James, listen to me. What Clara did tonight was truly courageous. You now need to be courageous for her. What has happened cannot be changed. But what you do next can make an enormous difference to her recovery.'

He looked pathetically into his father's eyes. 'What do I need to do?'

'You need to be strong for her. We all need to aid her recovery. Stop blaming yourself and start to think what you need to do to help her through this. You need to go to her as soon as possible and be strong for her. Let her know you care and you're there for her. Show her the love she clearly has for you. She'll probably needs a few months to recover. You must be there for her for as long as it takes. She put it out there for you. Now you must put it out for her. Do you understand?'

'But dad, I can't get it out of my head the knife was meant for me. Please help me.'

'First, you must sleep. Tomorrow morning, we'll phone the hospital to see when she'll be moved to a private room, or when you can see her.'

Janice piped in. 'From what I saw in intensive care, certainly not before lunchtime, maybe later. It would be normal for drainage purposes to keep her there for at least twenty-four hours, so it may even be Saturday morning before they move her.'

Geoffrey spoke again. 'Your mother and I will stay here with you until at least Sunday. If need be, one of us will stay longer. We'll be with you and Clara throughout this ordeal.'

'Thanks. I need help. Clara usually takes care of me. I must learn how to take care of her. She means so much to me.'

'Go sleep, son. Let's see what tomorrow brings.'

Janice and Geoffrey were in their bedroom. She sat on the bed and burst into tears. Geoffrey tried to comfort her. She looked at him. 'I'm so ashamed of myself. When I think of how I judged her in the past, I feel wretched. We must make amends. Irrespective of what happens between her and James, I want her to know she has a roof over her head, and love from our hearts for as long as we live. Can you forgive my abject prejudice?'

'My darling, I sense much soul searching from this, but not now. She certainly has a place in my heart, and I agree we should adopt her as family. But our role now is to help James come to terms with this. Tonight, we saw our boy, not yet man-enough to deal with such desperation. We have work to do as he must care for Clara for as long as it takes. We can help, but he must now learn human relationships are far more important than business, especially with such a heroic lady.'

He let this penetrate. 'Come. Let's try to sleep. We have some testing days ahead of us.'

Chapter 31

Geoffrey was preparing breakfast as Janice, and James emerged. He had already phoned his PA to alert her he would not be in the office today, and Janice had further advised her office she may not be there on Monday either. Her reborn maternal instincts instilled an overwhelming desire to care for Clara, and she was not about to leave until she knows she is safe and comfortable. Her son is clearly not capable of these tasks.

James looked drawn and sullen. Janice looked like she had spent the night in tears.

Geoffrey decided it was time to take charge of the situation. 'Come you two, time for some breakfast. Could be a long day.'

The first words from James were 'When can we go see Clara?'

His father responded, 'Son, I'll call the hospital after breakfast to assess the situation. Then we can make our plans, as I'm sure the police will want to speak with you. For Clara we will need bed clothes, toiletries, and her phone as a starting point.'

Janice joined the conversation 'I'll take care of the personal effects after I've spoken with her. I also need some fresh clothes for us.'

James was trying to remember 'I don't know what happened to her phone. I think it was on the restaurant table where she was sitting when the trouble started. She was using it to take pictures. I'll call Hashem to see if he knows anything.' He reached for his phone and dialled. Hashem quickly answered and asked him how he was. Wretched and desperate summarised his response. This conversation confirmed to his mother her son was not mature enough to deal with this crisis. He would need close supervision. However, Hashem confirmed Javid had retrieved her phone and would bring it to the apartment this morning.

Geoffrey rang the hospital. Clara had an uneventful night, but they would know more after her consultant examines her around 11 o'clock. No visitors until after consultant rounds, and then only one at a time for just a brief visit. Intensive care units are not geared for visitors, nor are they welcome in such controlled conditions.

Some ten minutes later, the door porter rang on the internal phone system. 'Two police officers here to speak with James Caldwell. Shall I send them up?'

They rang the doorbell and Geoffrey let them in. He invited them to sit at the table as he knew they were looking for a statement.

One of them started the process. 'We've contacted the hospital and therefore know the young lady, Clara Thompson, is in intensive care but out of danger and expected to recover over some months. We've recovered the weapon from the hospital. The assailant with the knife was apprehended and will face charges of aggravated assault, carrying a deadly weapon with intent, leaving the scene of a crime, and grievous bodily harm. He will appear before a Magistrate this morning for a preliminary hearing. We expect him to be held in custody pending further enquiries.' He paused.

'Can I confirm you are James Caldwell, and can you tell us your relationship with Clara Thompson?'

James, in a tone of exasperation 'Yes. I'm James Caldwell, and Clara is my long-term partner. She lives here with me.'

His father took exception to his tone. 'Excuse me, officer. James, these men are here to help you and Clara. You will please respect their task and co-operate fully in a civil tone. Do you understand me?'

'Sorry dad. I just can't deal with why she did this for me.' Tears were streaming down his face. His mother put a comforting hand on his shoulder.

The officer continued. 'Son, your father's right. We have a job to do, and this incident is serious, so we need your account of the events that took place immediately prior to the incursion of the two men, what you did, and your account of the attack. And could you speak slowly so we can record your statement.'

James related his account from the two drunken men approaching to the ambulance taking Clara to hospital. The police officer appeared satisfied with his account and did not feel the need for further questions.

'Thank you, Mr Caldwell. Your statement is consistent with the other statements we took last night. One observation you may need to consider with your solicitor should you be asked to give evidence in Court relates to your response when the drunken man fell against your table. We are not here to judge or advise, but it is likely your response to his fall, and your subsequent response just prior to the knife being produced could be argued as provocation and used in mitigation. His defence will argue, had you only helped him to his feet and sent him on his way, the stabbing of Miss Thompson would not have occurred. You should advise any counsel you seek of this likelihood.'

James was beside himself. 'Are you seriously telling me I provoked the attack which led to the stabbing of my lovely Clara. How was I supposed to react?' He was in tears at this revelation.

Geoffrey asked the officers if there was anything further. They had enough for now, so Geoffrey let them out. 'Thank you, officers. If you need anything else, we'll be here.'

'Dad, surely this can't be? Sure, I was angry because the guy was drunk, but I only used verbal, I didn't attempt any violence. Am I now partly responsible for what happened to her? I would never consider hurting her.'

'Leave it, son. They were merely making us aware of the legality of the circumstances. It's for lawyers to argue the merits of such defence. Come, we have work to do to ensure Clara has a caring and speedy recovery.'

The door porter rang again. It was Hashem and Javid. They entered the apartment and presented Clara's phone. Both expressed their remorse about what happened.

Geoffrey interjected. 'As all three of you are here, could I suggest you put your heads together and revise your plans for the next three months now James will need to spend all his time here caring for Clara. The technology is available for remote working, but the absolute priority of James must be the care of Clara. The only exception will be weekends when Janice and I will be here to give him some respite.'

'But dad, I can hire a nurse far more capable than me to care for her.'

He felt fury at his son's callous attitude. 'Absolutely not. I forbid it. You need to learn to care for those who love and care for you. This will be a valuable lesson for you.'

'But what about my business?'

'Son, what would happen to your business had the knife struck you, its intended target?'

James had not seen his father so assertive in years. He knew he would not win this argument. He took Hashem and Javid to his computer suite to discuss how they would manage their business over this three-month period.

Janice approached Geoffrey and gave him a big hug. 'My big angry bear. I'm so proud of you. He certainly got that message. Thank you.'

'Come, my dear. Let's use this time without James to work out what we need to put in place over the coming days, and then until Clara has fully recovered.'

'Are you serious about us spending every weekend here until she's well enough to cope for herself?'

'I think it's the least we can do. Is there a problem with this idea?'

'Not with me. I want to be here to care for her as much as possible. My concern is whether your golf handicap can withstand such a break.'

'We have been negligent with our son because we've been negligent with each other. We now need to put this right together and then provide guidance for our son. I'm so proud you want to care for Clara. We must educate our son. I would sooner lose my handicap than lose Clara. We'll stay together as family every weekend until Clara is fully recovered, and our son understands his priorities.'

'My wonderful husband. Does this mean you want to return to those days when we were first married?'

'I think it would be a good place to start. Let's relive the times we had before our careers dominated our lives.'

'You old romantic. I wish I could still have children. Maybe I would get the daughter I so craved.'

'My dear. Maybe you already have her.'

Chapter 32

It was over an hour before they emerged from the computer suite. James announced to his father they had a plan which would work, albeit likely to delay some new business.

'Gentlemen, this is excellent news. Other than two visits to the hospital each day by James, you have a week to embed your plan into your business practice. I estimate Clara will come home next weekend, after which James must assume his care duties. Thank you for your efforts and consideration.'

Hashem and Javid left to go back to the office.

'Dad, what type of care will I need to do?'

'Everything. I imagine Clara may not move around much until her wounds have healed. Say four to six weeks. Therefore, you will need to move her wherever she needs to be. You will help her to the toilet, have a shower, get up, got to bed, go for a walk. You'll need to feed her, ensure she has her medication, ensure she has clean clothes, take her for check-ups, talk to her, reassure her, and generally be there for her. She must always be in your peripheral vision, especially for the first few weeks, so no working in your computer suite. Use a laptop if you must, but don't let her out of your sight.'

'Dad, what do I know about such things?'

'Learn. We'll be here every weekend to help you and teach you. Caring for others makes us human. You've been cared for your entire life. Now it's time for you to reciprocate.'

He looked at his watch. 'It's past noon. Let me phone the hospital again.'

Janice, who had been busying herself with a list of tasks needing attention, albeit listening with one ear to the conversation with James, stopped to hear the news.

'She will not leave intensive care until early tomorrow morning. They will accept a visit as she is now breathing for herself, and she is generally more stable. She has taken her first food. But only one person at a time.'

Janice expanded 'These intensive care cubicles are small. They must put a chair in specially for visitors and then remove it because it takes up too much room.'

'I want to see her, mom.'

'Then we will have a quick lunch and visit with her. I want to speak with her about what she needs to add to her comfort, so you go first, and then I'll follow.'

They arrived at the ICU where they were greeted by the head nurse. Janice briefed the nurse about her son's instability in coping with this tragic event. With the nurse standing there, she briefed James. 'Listen to me, James. What you will see in there is not pleasant. If you so much as gasp when you see her, I've instructed the nurse to immediately walk you out of there. It's no shame if you cannot cope with this environment. What you must not do is distress Clara. And remember, she's heavily sedated. Are you ready?'

'Yes, mom.'

The nurse led him in. The first cubicle he passed looked like something out of a horror movie. As he arrived at the cubicle housing Clara, he could see her pale form through the glass window, apparently asleep. He saw the tubes coming from underneath her sheets into containers attached to the foot of her bed. Then he saw the IV drips, and the wires attached to monitors. It was all too much. He turned and left the unit into his mother's arms. 'She looks terrible, and it's my fault.'

'Stay with your father. I want to visit with her.'

Janice sat on the right-hand side of the bed. She reached for Carla's hand. The maternal sensation she felt last evening hit her again. She used her other hand to stroke her arm. Her eyes opened. She smiled. It took all her courage for Janice not to melt into tears. 'Hello my dear. You're looking so much better today, and no oxygen mask. We have progress. How do you feel?

Her words were slow and laboured. 'I'm okay. Can't feel much. But the nurse is lovely. She takes good care of me.'

'That's good to hear. You're being transferred to your private room in the morning, so I need to get you some things. Do you prefer pyjamas or nightdress?

'Pyjamas, please.'

'Full trouser length or shorts?'

'Shorts.'

I'll bring your telephone, charger, and ear buds. Do you need any other technology? Your room will have a TV and radio.'

'Nothing. Do you mean I will have my own private room?'

'Just like a hotel. Even your own private bathroom and dedicated nurse to look after your every need.'

'Wow. Sounds great.'

'You're now in the world of private healthcare; only the best for my lovely Clara. I'll also bring you toiletries. I've looked at what you use in your bathroom, so I'll get the same. What about books or magazines?'

'Fashion magazines would be nice.'

'At this moment they were interrupted. 'Ah. You must be Mrs Caldwell. I'm David Spencer. I'm the consultant assigned by BUPA to oversee the recovery of your daughter. When you've finished, could I have a word?'

'My husband and son are just outside. I'll join you in a few moments.'

Her attention returned to Clara. 'Anything else you need to while away the hours?'

'Will I be able to wear pyjama bottoms with these tubes? And what are they for?'

'One is a catheter into your bladder so you can urinate whenever you feel the need. They should encourage you to take in lots of fluids to keep you hydrated. The other is draining off any excess fluid from your wound. Neither should bother you, and they will remove both when you transfer to your room.' Using the knowledge of her profession. 'I'll get a couple of nightdresses for the first couple of days. Catheters tend to leave you with urges to urinate. Easier to get a bedpan into place under a nightdress.'

'They have only given me a brief visit so as not to tire you. Anything else you need?'

'Can't think of anything. How's James?'

'Still very distraught. He came to see you earlier, but you were sleeping. He sends his love and will see you tomorrow.'

'Thank you for being here. It helps to know you're around.'

Tears were welling 'My darling, Clara. I'll be around for as long as it takes for you to fully recover, and for as long as you want me around thereafter. You're family. What you did took great courage. You have my unconditional love for as long as I live.'

She gave Clara a kiss. I think I've overstayed my few minutes. As soon as I know you've moved to your private room, we'll all come to see you.'

'Is Geoffrey here as well?'

'Of course, he is. He's my rock, and yours as well. See you tomorrow, my darling.'

She joined Geoffrey and James, who were speaking with David Spencer. 'Ah. There you are, darling. Mr Spencer has been briefing us on Clara's condition and what the coming weeks will require. The biggest problem is the knife severed two major muscles in her pelvis. Until these muscles repair, she cannot walk on her left leg. Thus, a wheelchair will be provided. She cannot stress the wound for at least four weeks in any event. The good news is she should make a full recovery after extensive physio. A long process, but an excellent result.'

'Then my darling all weekend retreats are cancelled for the foreseeable future. We have a daughter to care for.' She turned to David Spencer. 'When will she be discharged from hospital?'

'Although this is not a private hospital as regards treatment, they have advised me moving her to a private hospital might complicate recovery. But I'm assured she will receive everything she needs here. I'll closely supervise her treatment during her stay here. I would think she will stay on the ward for five or six days if she has adequate care provisions at home.'

'I need to go back to my work and make provisions to enable me to care for her when she's discharged. Could we say Friday so I'm certain to be back in London for her?'

'I think we should take a cautious view considering the nature of her injuries. I'll delay discharge until Friday morning between 10am and 11am. She'll need help into a car.'

'Thank you, Mr Spencer. We will no doubt see you again in the coming weeks.'

'Come, boys. We have shopping to take care of.'

Chapter 33

Having finished breakfast, Geoffrey called the hospital. 'They moved her to her room at 9 o'clock having eaten breakfast with no problems.'

Janice felt her maternal instincts rising to the surface again. 'Listen up boys because this first visit together needs to be a *tour de force*. She must feel the love and commitment to her recovery. James, is there a decent florist nearby?'

'Yes, in the shopping parade.'

'Off you go. The most beautiful bouquet of flowers money can buy and make sure it's delivered to her before 11 o'clock with a very nice card from you.'

'When he had left, she sat with Geoffrey. 'Darling, I've been thinking about this next week. I think it's safe to leave here tomorrow evening. We will have the opportunity to observe at least two visits with James and make sure he stays strong for her.'

'I agree. I intend to give him another pep talk before we go to see her today.'

'Would you mind if I gave him this one? You have already imposed yourself twice. We need to let him know we stand shoulder-to-shoulder and I'm willing to impose myself as well.'

'No problem. One of us needs to; but doesn't matter which.'

'I certainly want to return on Thursday evening to manage preparations for her discharge. Are you able to take Friday off, or would you join us Friday evening? I'll need our estate car as it has the most room for her.'

'We all must be here for her, no question.' She touched his hand in appreciation.

'I'll stay here on the following Monday to ensure our son finds a weekday routine and understands his obligations. Again, you need to look at your work commitments.'

'I'll check when back in the office on Monday.'

'When we get to the hospital today, I want some time with her to get her cleaned up, into some nice fresh clothes, brush her hair and whatever else to make her feel presentable. I'll probably need around 30 minutes. Do you mind waiting with James?'

'Darling, I fully support what you're doing for Clara. You take as long as you need. We have no other engagements today. I'll take James for a coffee, and you text me when you're ready for us.'

'Thank you.'

James returned assignment complete. His mother indicated she wanted to talk to him.

'James, my darling, it's time for you to man up. You've now had two days of your righteous self-pity dwelling in a past you cannot change instead of dealing with the now, and the prospects for the future. When you asked Clara to engage in your journey, did you see yourself as her knight in shining armour rescuing a damsel from her miserable life and taking her into the land of happy ever after?'

'I guess so. I certainly wanted her to have a better life.'

'Can you remember from your school days if any of the knights were wimps?'

'Mom, this isn't fair. This is no fairy-tale.'

'What do you think these stories represent?'

'Good versus evil. Chivalry versus abuse.'

'Okay, let's take chivalry versus abuse. Which do you want for Clara?'

'Mom, what do you want me to do?'

Forget last Thursday. It's history. You have a wonderful lady who is somewhat battered; but will get better if her knight in shining armour stays true to his commitment to her. Stop thinking about yourself. Think about what she means to your life, and what you now need to do to restore what you so enjoy about her. Set this goal in your head and you'll quickly learn the means of achieving it.' She looked into his eyes to see if her words were penetrating. She put her hand on his shoulder. 'When we visit her today, reassure her, with conviction, that everything will get better, and you have set yourself the goal to make it better. Anything less will not be acceptable to myself or your father. We'll take her away from you and nurse her back ourselves. Your loss, our gain. Do you understand?'

'Boy. You two can be real hard asses when you get a cause. Why is Clara suddenly so dear to you? I remember what you said to me about her.'

'That was a terrible mistake for which I'm truly sorry and deeply ashamed. I saw the reputation. Your father quickly saw the qualities of the woman. As things stand today, she is far too good for you. But you can change this just as I recognised my shortcomings. Are you up for it?'

'Mom, I love Clara. I'll try to be equal to her, I promise. But I'll need a little guidance.'

'Good. Then let's get ready and go see her. Let her see us united in support of her recovery.'

Chapter 34

They reached the hospital just before 11am. Finding the private ward in this large NHS hospital took time as it was a recent addition with only six rooms geared for emergency cases who could afford the luxury of their own room. Janice had the items needed for Clara having washed and ironed the clothes she had bought, including a lovely new dressing gown. Now they knew the location, Geoffrey took James to find a cafeteria where they could have a coffee.

A nurse announced Janice to Carla. They hugged each other. 'How do you feel today, my darling?'

'Much better, thank you. You weren't kidding about the room. Lovely. Where's James and Geoffrey?'

'I thought we might clean you up and get you dressed before receiving visitors. I have all the clothes you need so how do you feel if I give you a bed bath, dress you, brush your hair and whatever else it takes to make you feel human again?'

'That would be lovely. Thank you so much.'

'My pleasure, my dear.' Looking around the room 'Do they have any packs of bed bath body wipes here?' She found them in the bathroom. 'Very nice bathroom. Have you seen it yet?'

'No. I'm confined to bed for now. Still hooked up to monitors.'

'Do you need the toilet before we start?'

'No. I did that just before you arrived.'

'Good. Let's start by getting rid of this hideous gown.'

She lovingly cleaned Clara from head to foot before dressing her in a nightdress for which the nurse needed to disconnect monitors to allow her arm to pass through the armhole, after which all were reconnected. Clara, her mind still blurred by medication, sat bemused by this attention. *This woman has been so cold to me in the past. Now it's like my mum used to treat me before she got sick.* She reflected upon the loss of her mother, imagining this was her mother caring for her.

Janice took her time brushing her hair. It was most certainly a bonding moment, and neither was in any hurry. She even found a dish for water so Clara could clean her teeth. She stood back to inspect her work. 'Now, my dear, you're ready to receive visitors. I'll alert the boys. I'll also put all the other items in my bag away for you. I've fully charged your phone, but I have a charger and ear buds for you. I'll put them on your side table.' The bouquet sent by James proudly adorned the side table. Excellent *choice, my son. At least you got this bit right.* 'I've brought you a selection of fashion magazines so they should keep you occupied for a while.'

It took about 10 minutes for the boys to arrive, during which they chatted as naturally as mother and daughter. The door opened. The nurse ushered in Geoffrey and James. Geoffrey allowed James to approach her first, as he wanted to observe his response to her. He stood back, thinking what a great idea to prepare her. She looked so lovely, and that big smile on her face certainly quickly put James at ease.

They stayed for about one hour, after which it was clear Clara needed to rest. The boys departed first. Janice stayed to make sure she was comfortable and to tell her they would be back this evening around 7pm. If she needed anything, pick up the phone anytime, 24/7. They hugged and kissed before Janice left.

On the way out of the hospital, Janice put an arm around her son's shoulder. 'You did well, James. Remember that smile on her face. She bears the scars, but she radiates warmth. Can you do that?'

'Yes, mom. She looked so lovely. All I could think about is how lucky I am to have her.'

'We have progress. Let's find somewhere to have some lunch. I'm famished.'

After lunch they shopped for food and other essentials before returning to the apartment, where they chilled for a while before returning to the hospital.

It was a little after 5 o'clock when they stirred to prepare to visit Clara. 'Mom, can I have a word.'

'Certainly, son. What's on your mind?'

'I've been thinking about what I can do to help her through this. For example, when you see newsreels about tragic situations, they always appoint psychological counsellors to help people deal with their trauma. Do I need to think about this for Clara?'

In her mind, she was angry. *'How ill-equipped he is to take care of her.'* She tried not to show her frustration. 'I think Clara is strong enough not to need such help. She doesn't need to continually relive that night; she needs to move on. Probably doesn't remember much in any event.

This is why I ask you not to speak to her about it; or ask her why she did it. If you don't already know the answer to that question, you do not understand that woman. If she speaks of that night, which I doubt, just listen to what she says and try to move the conversation into the now and the future. Concentrate on recovery and her future dreams. If either of you should experience nightmares, then let me know immediately as I know someone I trust to help. Does this answer your question?'

'Loud and clear. You did a fantastic job with her this morning. What can I do when you're not here?'

'Be there for her. You go to the hospital every morning around 9 o'clock to find out how she is, and if she needs anything. This is not a phone call. The knowledge you'll visit will incentivise her to wake up and prepare herself just like this morning. It starts her day in a good way. You select what you want to eat when you return for dinner, no later than 7pm. I'll show her how to organise her life in hospital. You need to realise this hospital environment is totally alien to her, especially as a private patient. Watch and learn how quickly she adapts and takes control. You need to learn this when you care for her. You stay with her for at least an hour in the evening unless she's tired, in which case let her sleep. Heeling is a process requiring sleep. Tell her about your day just as you would if at home. Try to emulate your normal life together. Even a brief call during the day, or just a text to show you're thinking about her, will work wonders for her recovery. Maybe on Wednesday take a bottle of wine with you as another step to normality.'

'Will they allow alcohol?'

'Of course. She'll only be two days from discharge so can return to normal life, even if only one glass. Make sure the caterer provides wine glasses. Attention to detail is essential.'

'Wow. No problem. Just one more question. Would you really take her away from me if I fail her?'

She looked him square in the eyes 'In a loving heartbeat'.

She let this sink in as she could see the shock on his face. 'Are you ready to go visit with her again?'

'Give me fifteen minutes. I want to clean-up for her.' He was off to his room.

Geoffrey had a wry smile on his face. 'I think our son is fast waking up to reality. No more time to think about last Thursday. Needs all his time to think how to prevent us taking her away from him. Clever lady.'

'My darling, I watch how you focus him, and follow your astute logic. He has a steep learning curve. Clara's recovery will not wait for him to figure things out for himself.' She paused. 'I need to freshen. These days have taken a toll, although I feel strangely invigorated by my awakened maternal instincts. I feel useful and wanted. It feels so good.'

Their visit to Clara was greeted with her lovely smile. She was more relaxed as she settled into this unfamiliar environment. Janice spent time with her explaining how things worked, what she could request to support her recovery, and how to order dinner for two every evening starting tomorrow. James looked on to this exchange, amazed how quickly Clara grasped this information and clearly relaxed with his mom. Geoffrey observed his son to determine if there were any further issues to address before they returned home tomorrow afternoon.

They agreed to visit again at 10am tomorrow.

Once back in the apartment, Janice found herself unusually tired. Adrenaline spent, she felt in need of her bed. As she rose to adjourn to her bedroom, she added one more advance to her son's education. 'James, why don't you help your father with breakfast tomorrow so you can see how easy it is.'

'No problem. Goodnight.'

Geoffrey was quick to follow his wife.

Chapter 35

Geoffrey and Janice were in bed, wrapped in each other's arms. Geoffrey wanted closure on the day. 'You did really great with Clara today. She looked radiant when we walked in this morning. And I really liked the valiant knight message to James.'

'He needed that, and it may have worked. As for Clara, much of her radiance is her infectious smile. When I was washing her that smile held even when the dressing on her wound was staring us both in the face and this area of her body was still stained in the antiseptic wash they use in theatre. When I brushed her hair, it felt so good I didn't want to stop. My love, it felt so good to care for her.'

'Do you think you may have found a daughter?'

'I would love to have her as a daughter. But would she forgive me for all the terrible thoughts and things I said about her, and she knows this?'

'You have one ace card in your favour. Words may not do it, but actions speak louder than words. We have the chance over the coming weeks to show her our change in family attitude, and I know in this time you will show your love for her in spades. Wait a few weeks until this terrible event has started to fade into the past. Find your moment and speak with her about your failings and your desires for a daughter. I sense that she also craves the mother misfortune took from her. The pair of you have a synergy that, at the right moment, could fuse into what you both desire.'

'And you will support me in this quest?'

'With love and open arms. I remember your cravings for a daughter after James was born. We foolishly missed that opportunity. Fate has dealt us a hand. This time we must grasp it.'

'You're a wise old owl. This weekend you've brought back so many of the memories of why I fell so madly in love with you. Quiet, unassuming, but a powerhouse of strength and wisdom when needed. I love you so much. Why don't we consummate our revitalised love in the way we used to?'

They embraced and made love together for the first time in months.

Chapter 36

Geoffrey was showing James how to prepare a basic English breakfast, not least calculating the timings so everything came together at the same time. They were chatting, but James had something on his mind.

'Dad, I've never seen you and Mom so committed to something outside of the family, or, can I say, to each other. What has happened to move both of you so much?'

He stopped what he was doing, putting both hands on the edge of the worktop in resignation. 'First and foremost, our son and the lovely Clara are in trouble. When we saw your reaction, we quickly realised our preoccupation with our careers over these past years meant we have not nurtured our son for such eventualities. Son, we failed you and has caused your mother and I to re-evaluate our lifestyle. Now we must rapidly help you understand and cope with this crisis. We are both changing our lifestyle to refocus on our family, including Clara. She, for all her misfortune, is a better human being than any of us and we have much to learn from her.'

He stood to face his son. 'Unfortunately for you, your learning curve will be very steep, but we're committed to be here for you every step of the way. Your mother will dramatically change her career workload in favour of being ready to come to your aid with Clara if need be. In short, we forgot our parenting duties, and we must make amends. We must make you understand the greatest ambition of any human way above business, sporting achievement or anything else, is to love, and be loved in return. You are blessed if you can achieve this. If we succeed in this, we will have restored our right to be called good parents.'

James was in tears as he listened to this confession of failure by his parents. He hugged his father. 'Dad, I feel so humbled. It's me who has taken Clara for granted. But with you and mom by my side, we'll put this right. I'll get Clara through this; I swear this to you. I owe it to her. I'll make you both proud of me.'

Janice had caught half of the confession and could see their son's response. '*I love that man so much*' she thought. '*How many fathers would confess to their son they had failed as a parent.*' But she also knew there was motive. This was intended to show James they must all play a part to ensure James does not attempt this rehab on his own just to show his parents he could stand on his own feet; but likely fail.

She let them bond for a while before announcing her presence. It was nearly 9 o'clock. She did not want to be late for Clara.

When they arrived at the hospital, Clara was ready for them. They had reduced her pain management; thus she was perkier. James selected his evening meal requirements from the menu so Clara could submit it to catering. She had mastered the conveniences of her room and had even ordered refreshments for them. She had never stayed in a hotel before. She was having fun.

'I have to go walkies today to see how much I can use my left leg.'

This hit James like a thunderbolt, but his father quickly saw the danger and gently nudged him to bring him back to the present.

Janice filled the role her son should have played. 'My dear, can you call me when you get back to let me know how it goes.' She knew a little pickup may be necessary if the outcome is not good.

After an hour, Clara needed to rest. They said their goodbyes and readied themselves to leave. Janice re-enforced that Clara could call her anytime, 24/7 and she would be back Friday to collect her.

When they were outside, James was down on himself. 'Dad, I screwed up again. I'm really sorry. The thought she cannot walk because of me took hold. I know I can't change the past, and I will try harder to stay positive.'

Janice responded somewhat annoyed with him. 'It should be you she calls with her news of progress. Please focus on her recovery. We already know she will have problems walking for maybe three months. Why was this such a surprise to you?'

He could see his mom was not happy. Geoffrey intervened. 'Okay, James. You're not there yet, but this is important. If you screw up with her during next week, you call us immediately so we can quickly rescue the situation.

And I don't mean when you return home. I mean within minutes of the event. Are we clear?'

'Yes, dad. I'm sorry.'

'When you return this evening, you want to know everything about her walk. If she's okay about it, be enthusiastic; a work in progress. If she's down, pick her up and don't leave until you succeed, or call us. A genuine cuddle could go a long way. And remember, when you hold her, she's not broken, so hold her as though you mean it.'

James was angry with himself all the way back to the apartment. His folks were totally alive to her situation. *'Why can't I tune into their thinking? I have much to learn about taking care of Clara.'* What hurt him most is he knew Clara would know how to take care of him if their roles were reversed.

When they arrived back at the apartment, they had a light lunch and then his parents prepared to make their way home. Much needed to change in their own life to facilitate their intentions toward Clara for the next three months.

After lunch Janice went to pack. Geoffrey sat with James.

'Dad, what am I doing wrong?'

'From observation I would say you still have the same mindset towards Clara you had when you brought her here. I really hoped when you stopped referring to her as your mistress your mindset had also changed. By definition, a partner is an equal, and you look out for each other. You may think you love her, but you have never entertained the idea of caring for her. You expect her to care for you, and your mindset tells you that you pay her for this service. Why should you have to concern yourself with her care?'

He let this sink in. 'Think about it for a moment. She is for all intents and purposes your wife. This is the role she plays for you. A mistress would not live with you, and a housekeeper would not share your bed. If she were your wife, she would be entitled to far more than you pay her, and divorce would be significantly expensive for you. If you decide you're bored with Clara, you can tell her to leave, and she has nothing. You treat her like a commodity, and this is both wrong and inhuman.'

'She does what she does for you out of love, and any doubts about her commitment to you were blown away last Thursday. You have always assumed people will care for you, but you now need to grow up and realise humans take care of those they love. If your mother were ill, I would care for her, and I've learnt the skills to enable me to fully achieve this. I would not dream of hiring help for someone so precious to me. We will take Clara away from you if your attitude does not change quickly. She has suffered enough in her short life. Abuse from my son is not acceptable to me or your mother. Change your mindset towards her and everything else will be instinctively obvious. Ask yourself what you have without her.'

'Thanks dad. Brutal, but I understand how much she means to me, so I must change towards her. I'm glad you and mom are here for her. Gives me a little space to learn from you all where my head needs to be. I don't see me getting everything right at first, but with you and mom on my case I have a chance to prove myself worthy of her.'

'That's a good start. We'll watch progress with interest.'

After his parents left for home, he sat contemplating events over the past few days. He could not remember a time when his parents were so together. And he could not fault their commitment to him, and especially Clara. He tried to think of a time he had so much conversation with them over such a short period of time. He replayed in his mind the confession of his father that morning, suggesting he had been a derelict parent. He would never describe his dad in such terms, but he knew his father as an intelligent and serious man, so this confession was no unguarded chat. He knew he must replay many conversations with both mom and dad. Much to digest to avoid them taking Clara away from him. Sitting alone in the apartment now was eerie without her there. She is the life and soul of their relationship. He needs her with him.

It was nearly time to leave to have dinner with her. How does he avoid making mistakes with her? What can he do to bury the guilt he feels about the pain he helped to inflict on her? His parents were not aware he cried himself to sleep these past three nights. Was this righteous self-pity as described by his dad, fear of what could have been, or genuine concern for what happen to her? He was so confused. *'Am I in any state to visit Clara on my own? Please God, no more pain for her.'* But he knew he had to go. He could not fail at the first hurdle. Both parents had made this clear.

As he was leaving, he had a thought. *'That's it. Take her iPad and pen. We can talk about her fashion project. Plenty of time for her to find data and for him to develop the computer graphic engine to bring her designs to life. Three months together at home should be enough. My folks want us to focus on the future. This project will certainly satisfy this requirement, and it will be worth a fortune to the fashion industry.'* He had a spring in his step as he made for his car.

He entered her room some fifteen minutes early for dinner. She was glowing as he approached to kiss her. 'Alone at last. I have so much I want to talk to you about. Can't wait to have you home again. How was your walkies session?'

'Not good, but not bad either. Early days yet, but the facilities are great. I'll need to come back once a week as there are no similar facilities anywhere near here.'

'Whatever you need, you'll get. And if there is any equipment we can usefully buy for the apartment, we'll get it.'

'Thanks. Your mum has been very kind to me these past days. She's so lovely when you get to know her.'

'My mom is on a mission to restore you to full health. Nothing can deflect her. Dad tells me she is going to reduce her commitments at work to spend as much time with you as possible. You have stirred maternal instincts in her.'

'I thought she didn't approve of me, or at least think me good enough for you.'

'She acknowledged to me she made a terrible mistake and is ashamed of her judgemental position. She's hell-bent on making amends. You're family now and my mom will make sure you know it.'

'Wow. That explains everything.'

Dinner arrived. James sat on her bed so he could share her over-bed table. The food was excellent. 'This restaurant's not bad. How's breakfast and lunch?'

'Great. So much selection; just like a restaurant.'

After dinner, he gave her the iPad. 'Thought you might like this. As I'll stay at home with you for the next three months, I think it's time to start our fashion project in earnest. It will be nice to work together, and I have some great ideas about the functionality of the graphics engine. But I need your input to make sure I get it right.'

'You don't have time to spend the next three months at home with me. What about your business?'

'All sorted. And the engine we'll build will be worth a fortune if we get it right, and we'll be 50:50 partners for this one. We build it together; we share the success together.'

'Are you sure my contribution is worth that much?'

'It won't work without your contribution, so yes.'

'Are you sure about this?'

'We started our journey with goals. I can now achieve mine. We should have started this before now. This next three months is the opportunity we need to concentrate and fulfil your goal, but together. I'm looking forward to our project. I've been thinking about it for over a year. Time to get on with it.'

'Great. What do you want me to do?'

He went through all the data he needed about sizes, yarn weights. Characteristics of different materials – everything a designer needed to design and make clothes. She knew much of this from designer college.'

He left her pleased she was in good spirits with some purpose. Likely a good report with his mother. He stayed within the realms of business, but this would give him time to learn the skills bombarded by his parents. But he was serious about building her fashion engine. It would be worth a fortune, and it answered one of his father's criticisms about her future if they parted. He had never considered such an event, but his father had made sure he understood Clara is no commodity he can cast aside.

'He sent a text to his mom informing his visit was a success. No errors to report.'

Chapter 37

The journey home for Geoffrey and Janice was subdued, neither wanting to say anything. Janice was thankful for some uninterrupted time to think through events of the past few days. Arriving home, they found the house empty. Sam must have gone to see her mother.

He knew they needed time to think through their future. Their lifestyle of recent years needed to change. 'Tea, or something stronger, my dear?'

'I think events call for a stiff G&T my darling. I need to tell you what I'm thinking, and how I feel about these past few days.'

'Two stiff G&T's coming up. Let's get comfortable. Much soul searching required this afternoon.'

She was sitting on the sofa, and him in his favourite armchair next to the fireplace. She was shaking her head. 'My darling Geoffrey, when did we stop nurturing our son, and why?'

'That we knew nothing of his activities for three years would suggest some time. As to why, I think we both know we became consumed by our careers. However, let's not follow the failings of James to reconcile himself to the present. We know where we are, so let's start to define our future. We have a wonderful lady in our family who committed herself to the safety of our son. We now need to care for her. She has no-one else, so we can nurture her as our own.'

'I'm so ashamed of myself. I failed as a mother. And my attitude to that lovely woman .... and the way I now feel towards her; what an explosion of emotions I've felt these past days. I need to rethink my priorities. I need to be a competent mother to our son, and care for Clara as though my daughter. She deserves our love and care, and we must help our son to care for her. My darling, my rock, I so need your wisdom and guidance to know what to do. Do I significantly reduce my workload, or even quit my job and concentrate on being a good mother? Or a sabbatical is another possibility. Help me here.'

'My first observation is I think you are about to become a fabulous mother to both James and Clara. But let's not get carried away. They are both adults on their own journey through life. We're needed to overcome an unfortunate but life-changing period for all of us. We have an opportunity to nurture a truly wonderful family, and we now know this is what we want for ourselves, and for them. But our concentrated effort is time limited to some three to four months, so let's remember we will still have our lives to fulfil our own desires. For both of us this is a project we'll relish, not least because it allows us to redefine our own lives together. But let's not make drastic changes to our lifestyle we'll regret once this project is over.'

'What changes do you think we need to undertake?'

'I'm not about to move to our London office, and you should not consider quitting your job. This is our home, and we have no reason to up-route ourselves. I think a three-month adjustment to our respective workloads on compassionate grounds is not unreasonable for the bank or your company after the years we have committed to them. We don't need to be with Clara in London during the week unless something goes wrong. She's very capable of taking care of herself and thus guiding James to satisfy her needs.'

She nodded her agreement. 'However, we need to be ready to take over should James fail or decides he can't cope. But we can bring her here to care for her. Sam is here during the day, and I'm sure we can find ways to ensure hospital visits, physio, and whatever else she needs can be accommodated between us. And we must be careful not to smother either of them. Our role is to nurture and mentor. Assuming responsibility for her care being the last resort. My suggestion is you reduce your workload for a few weeks so you can quickly respond with minimum disrupting to your work commitments. I can shuffle my workload as needed. How does that sound?'

'As always, darling, rational, and appropriate. I can take extended leave from the committees I Chair which will dramatically reduce my out-of-hours reading material. I can delegate my projects but retain oversight, which means if I'm needed when in London I can communicate by telephone as and when input is needed. Now we know the

94

horizon of three to four months I do not anticipate any management issues. Much of my Board duties tend to occur by phone in any event. I'll organise all this tomorrow. Thank you, my darling. I feel so much better.'

He leaned towards her. 'What about our lifestyle? I think we need to understand what we need to change in our personal lives to prevent us falling back into our old ways once this project is over.'

She didn't respond, so he decided to inject his own thoughts. 'My thoughts are we think back to when we had an active private life and start from there. For example, I think we need to revert to preparing our own supper together in the evening, and even occasionally go out to a restaurant. I don't think we need to lose Sam as this house is too large for us to manage whilst both working, but we should start to look after each other, leaving Sam to look after the house. Does this resonate with you?'

'Sounds lovely. To have the house to ourselves in the evenings allows a more romantic evening. Looking after each other used to be fun. I'm very happy to make this change. Any other ideas?'

'We must factor our son and Clara into our lifestyle as we will need to maintain a closer relationship with them, and I don't mean only by phone. And if you can develop a daughter relationship with Clara, how would this affect us?'

'My darling, if Clara would bless me with her consent to be our daughter, I have much catching up to do in the mother/daughter department. You would need to be understanding for at least some months as I would take every opportunity to foster such a relationship. I would try to make at least every other Saturday mother/daughter days. If in London, you could play golf in the morning and then join us in London for family evenings out to dinner or theatre. If they come here, you do boys' things with James while I'm out with Clara. This would give me so much joy and help to maintain a close family unit. Please God, let this be.'

'Such joy would indeed be a blessing. I'm starting to really see the woman I married. Let's drink to success in our new life.' They clinked their glasses.

'How would my darling husband respond to the idea of an early night? We have some catching up of our own desires for each other.'

'Why wait for this evening? We have time before supper to get some practice.'

She smiled her love to him as she grabbed his hand to lead the way.

Chapter 38

James awoke early on Monday morning. The silence was thunderous in his ears. He showered, dressed, and went to the kitchen. The coffee machine he could manage. But what about breakfast? He found eggs in the fridge, but where were the pans? He scouted around finally locating the pan his dad had used for eggs. Now, how to use the hob. How difficult could it be? *I'm a whizz at technology. Should be intuitive.* An array of touch sensitive controls confronted him. *To hell will this. I'll get something on the way to see Clara.*

The smile on her face lifted his mood. A big hug and kiss set him up for the day. He told her about his fiasco at breakfast. She laughed and suggested he come earlier to see her and have breakfast with her. He glanced at the breakfast menu and selected what he wanted. 'Same every morning, please. I'll be here by 8 o'clock.'

He remembered what his father had told him. Talk about normal daily activity. Where he was going. What he hoped to achieve and then ask if she had any special events during the day. Her visit with the physio department was to be daily to start mobility of her leg. The visit from her consultant meant more monitors disconnected as her recovery improved. He went to his office, relieved he was surviving any relapses to the guilt he still harboured.

Walking into the office quickly changed his mood. The atmosphere was sombre. Everyone wanted to express their concern and wanted to know the condition of Clara. He was close to breaking down. This was a test he could not fail. He must hold himself together. He stood in the middle of the office and called for the attention of everyone. 'Thank you all for your concerns for Clara. I can report she came though surgery without lasting damage. She will have a long rehab but will fully recover in the fullness of time. I have just visited with her. She bears her pain with the infectious smile we all know so well. She is the very example we all need. Let us take her lead and put this tragic incident behind us. Put the smile back into your work and show Clara we can move on and fulfil our goals. I'm happy to take any messages back to her this evening. Thank you.'

He quickly went to his office as he felt tears welling. Hashem and Javid followed him and closed the door. Hashem spoke first 'Brilliant news. And you did good out there. Javid and I have thought through our plan. No problems. We can do this, so you go take care of Clara for as long as it takes. We can always hook up on Saturday's if we need to.'

'Thanks, guys. She's my rock. I need to learn how to take care of her. If you know any good books about caring for such a lady, I'm interested.'

'Man, be there for her. The rest you pick up as you go along. I'm sure she'll be your best guide. She's the one who knows what she needs.'

'Hashem, you really are a genius. Besides telling me to be there for her, which is what my mom and dad rammed down my throat, you state the blindingly obvious. Brilliant. Clara can be my teacher. Thanks, Hashem. I can do this.'

'Your dad is some formidable dude. Wouldn't want to argue with him.'

'Hey, guys. I can't remember my dad so in my face. Boy, did he lay it out for me, as did my mom. They're certainly going to be on my case throughout Clara's recovery.'

Javid added to the conversation. 'James, they're right, man. Your priority is to care for her like she cares for you. That's what family is about. In my culture, the whole family would get involved. We all pull together. We take care of our own.'

'A new world for me. But I hear you.'

'We know what you must do, so we're here for you. Your dad's right. Had you took the hit, we would have to keep the show on the road. We have a plan. No problem. Go now if you want. We're cool.'

'Thanks, guy. I'm thinking of fulfilling a promise to Clara while she's in rehab. I want to build an engine specific to the fashion industry to support her fashion design ambitions. I'd like to spend some time this week with you guys looking at some very specific algorithms I'll need. My dad has banned me from my computer suite when I need to care for Clara. If we can get the basic engine together, I can refine it on a laptop. And by the way, they will discharge Clara on Friday morning, so I'll only be here for four days.'

'If you're ready, let's get on it.'

As he drove to the hospital, he recalled the conversation with Hashem and Javid. *'Am I the only one who doesn't know how to care for those we love? Where the hell have I been all my life? Hashem and Javid are bigger geeks than me, but caring is normal for them. I'm behind the curve. Time to change. Need Clara to help me.'*

Over dinner he told her about his day but excluding the detail of his conversation with Hashem and Javid. Her physio session went well. His mom had phoned twice for a chat. *'Failed again'* he thought, *'need to remember to call or text.'* He had already given her the bag containing Get-Well cards and flowers from his office.

'Clara, I need your help. I'm absolutely committed to care for you throughout your recovery, but you know more than anyone how useless I am at anything domestic, let alone caring. You, on the other hand, would be deemed expert, which you show to me every day. I originally considered using my mom to help me or find a good book. But then I realised the knowledge I need is with the person who needs my care, and she, being the receiver, knows better than anyone what she needs from me. I want you to teach me how to care for you.'

She smiled at him with love. *'He's still a boy, but he's starting to care. His heart is in the right place.* Are you sure you want to get your hands so dirty? Caring for an invalid can get very upfront and personal.'

Tears welled in his eyes 'This is something I must do to prove myself worthy of you. Will you help me?'

She could see the tears in his eyes. She put her hand on his cheek. 'I'll help you. But prepare yourself. It requires much love and commitment.'

'I can't fail you. If I fall short, you kick me back into shape. This is a goal I must achieve if I'm to be worthy of your love.'

She felt tearful. He had taken her for granted for so long. Could this be the turning point she had wished for since first taking him to her bed?

They hugged and kissed as he said goodnight. How would she report this conversation to his mum, who would most certainly call in the next thirty minutes?

Chapter 39

The week went smoothly until Wednesday evening when he realised the apartment looked unloved, with untouched dirty dishes and general take-away debris littering the place. He also realised the sheet and duvet cover in the spare room had not been laundered ready for his mom and dad on Thursday evening. '*And what to do about supper for them?*' Panic set in. What to do.

Washing up and clearing garbage was easy, except he did not know where to put the garbage. He knew she separated it into waste that could be recycled, and other, but where did she take it? He called Clara in the hope she wasn't sleeping. She was engaged, no doubt talking to his mom. '*There must be more bed linen*' he thought, '*but where?*' It took him a good ten minutes, rifling through cupboards to find the linen store. He found a fresh set of duvet cover, sheet and pillowcases and changed the bed. He stuffed the dirty linen in the linen basket in his bedroom. '*May as well change our bed as well, ready for Clara to come home. Maybe tomorrow night will be better.*' But left the linen out so he remembered to do it. He would speak with Clara in the morning about preparing the apartment and then get home early afternoon to execute before dinner with her, leaving him the option for clarification from Clara over dinner.

'Hi Clara. You look lovely, as ever.' He kissed her. 'This is the last time we breakfast here. Home tomorrow. Really looking forward to having you home.' He noticed a wheelchair in the corner.

'Good morning. I'm looking forward to coming home. Need to practice in my wheelchair today so I can manoeuvre properly.'

'Where are the motors? Thought mobile technology today had motors and joystick?'

'Don't be silly. This is just a temporary solution. I'm not a permanent invalid. I give this back to the hospital when I've finished with it.'

Breakfast arrived, which they enjoyed together.

He opened his notebook with his list of questions. 'Clara, I've hit some snags which I need to fix today before mom and dad arrive. Can't have the apartment looking like I've failed already. I found linen for their bed, and towels for the bathroom. What else do I need to do?'

'Did you clean their shower, check they have toilet rolls, and make sure there is bath gel and hair shampoo?'

'Didn't think of that. Do we have supplies?'

She laughed. 'How long have you lived there?'

'Okay. Have your fun. But help me here. At least I'm trying.'

'Let me see your list.'

She went through his notes, and he made copious notes of her answers, including where to find the garbage chutes. They decided the laundry could wait until the weekend.

'Thanks, Clara. I will learn how things work. But I need to get this done today or my mom will be on my case as soon as she arrives.'

She found this new James amusing. Janice had obviously let her thoughts be known about his lack of contribution to chores. Life was about to get interesting with him as her carer.

He left the office at lunchtime and was back at the apartment by 2pm. He finished his chores by 4pm and then went to their local store for the items they would need for supper tonight, and breakfast tomorrow. A quick shower, after which he noticed the bed linen he needed to change, and off to see her for dinner. He needed to get back for the arrival of his parents, so his visit was truncated. But Clara was looking forward to coming home, so no problem. She had mastered her wheelchair and crutches, so had no anxiety about leaving the security of her private room.

His parents arrived a little before 9pm, somewhat exhausted from navigating the rush hour traffic. Although they were driving against the evening traffic, the M25 orbital motorway was practically a car park early evenings. They were quickly impressed with his efforts to maintain the apartment. Janice had received a running account of his visits to see Clara, so she was satisfied she understood the progress of her son since their departure last Sunday. They enjoyed their cold supper washed down with a fine burgundy before Janice unpacked their clothes. When she returned, his parents were interested to know how his week had gone, and what he planned to do with Clara for the next three months.

He explained he knew she needed to make regular visits to the hospital for physio. He would also discuss with the hospital physio if it would be beneficial to have a physio come to the apartment on a more regular basis. As soon as the wound was healed enough, he would take her into the swimming pool downstairs as he knew swimming would be good for her, especially as she is already an excellent swimmer. But the news he wanted to impart was directed at his father.

'When I persuaded Clara to come with me to London, I agreed to help her achieve her goal of studying fashion design. As you know, she has finished her first year with good grades and will soon start her second year. I will visit with her college to make her classwork available online while she recovers, even if I must pay for this service.'

He took a sip of wine to allow this to sink in. 'More importantly, I agreed to design a graphics engine which will radically change the way the fashion world and online retailers can present their clothes to the public. I've been thinking about the structure of this engine since I first saw her sketches back in St Albans. It's time to build it as we could launch it at the next graduation fashion show where the graduate students will show their designs. We've agreed to focus on this engine for the next three months to see if we can get it to work. It requires much input from her. As dad has banned me from my computer suite, Hashem and Javid are building an outline engine on our office suite, which I can then refine on a laptop. This model will not be part of my business development. It will be a separate project where Clara and I will be equal partners. If we're successful, I see major interest in the fashion and online retail market with substantial licence revenues.'

His father listened with interest. 'Does Clara know about this plan?'

'Of course. She has been working on it in hospital for the past few days.'

'And this is just you and Clara. No payment to your company.'

'No. If I need specific expertise, I'll work it out with Hashem and Javid.'

'I'm impressed, son. Would you allow me to help you set it up because there are enterprise grants available for such projects? Will help with any specialist equipment you need to demonstrate the results.'

'Great idea, dad. I could use some of your expertise in my main company as well. We have some major opportunities knocking on our door. It's time to employ your skills to ensure we capitalise on these opportunities.'

'Let's get Clara settled and then talk about it over the next couple of weekends to see where I can apply any valuable input.'

'*Job done*' he thought, '*I'm taking care of Clara's future with or without me. Big tic.*'

His father quickly realised the intent of his son, but knew ambition is laudable, but delivery is the only measure of success. This project did not provide any security for Clara until it's realised and generating net income. He was happy his son would allow him to be involved in the structure of this venture, as it would allow him to secure Clara's interests. And to be welcomed in to look at the main business where he could determine the wealth creation since they moved to London was a bonus. He was determined his son recognise the contribution to his life provided by Clara. His marker: a settlement based on what would reasonably be awarded to Clara in the event of a divorce from his son based on wealth creation since they came to London. He was determined his son put an agreement in place for which he would be custodian to provide enough funds for Clara to start a new life should they separate. Clara would not abuse such a settlement agreement, but it would give her some leverage during the re-education of his son. He would agree such settlement agreement could be revoked once the revenues due to Clara under this proposed project exceeded the settlement amount. He also needed to investigate if it entitled Clara to a Personal Injury Award, not least because she could demonstrate little personal wealth but will be incapacitated for months from her injury. Something else his son would not know is available to her.

Chapter 40

They arrived at the hospital at 10am. Janice went in first as she had selected suitable clothes from Clara's wardrobe for her to leave hospital. Janice helped her to dress and recovered her hospital clothes and personal effects before allowing the boys in.

The pharmacist arrived with her take-home drugs. The physio had provided instruction for her at home, and an appointment card to continue her rehab. She was ready. She thanked the nurse for her kindness as James wheeled her out.

At lunchtime they celebrated her homecoming with champagne. She was clearly happy to be home amongst family. Janice was reading the notes provided by the physio. 'Listen up, boys. There are dietary considerations needed to aid recovery. We need to adjust our shopping list. James, you need to understand her dietary needs before we leave.'

Janice and James went to their regular supermarket to shop for the week. Geoffrey took advantage of this time alone with her.

'My dear, it's so nice to have you back. You gave us all a bit of a fright. But that's over, and our full attention is on your complete recovery. I know we haven't had the opportunity to chat, but I want you to know from me you can count on us for everything you need. We know James is not yet equipped to care for you, but I'm sure that between us you'll get all the care you need. We'll spend every weekend with you until you are fully recovered to not only give James some respite, but also to apply our parenting skills to improve his care skills. As you are aware, Janice has dedicated herself to your recovery, and I fully support her efforts. Should you ever feel the need for a little fatherly advice I'm here for you.'

'You're both very kind to me. And I know you're the rock in this family, so I know where to come. You should know James has changed this week. I agree he has much to learn, but I detect a willingness to change. He set a new goal this week to learn to care for me enough to earn my love. The one thing I'm sure about with James is he's very goal oriented. He doesn't set goals unless he intends to achieve them. The start will be rocky, but I think you'll be proud of him in time.'

'Your commitment to my son is breath-taking. He must learn how valuable you are to him. I've been delinquent as a father to him in recent years. This has now changed. We'll work together to allow him to achieve his goal with you. I can no longer imagine this family without you. Is there anything I can do for you?'

'Being here is enough. James needs your fatherly guidance and support. He told me about your little chats last week. He got the message. I think you scared the hell out of him, but he accepts you're right. Thank you.'

'My dear, I won't allow him to stray from this task. He has a steep learning curve resulting from my delinquency, so I must help him climb it.'

'By the way, you're probably due compensation under the Personal Injury Award scheme. Would you give me permission to pursue this on your behalf? From memory this could be as much as £12,000.'

'Wow. What do I have to do?'

'Nothing. I would make the application for you and include the police and hospital records. That's it. The conviction of your attacker will record you as victim of the assault.'

'That's very kind of you. Thank you.'

'My pleasure.'

'Could you help me out of this chair onto the couch? I feel the need for a nap.'

He carried her from her chair to the couch, retrieved a pillow and a wrap, and helped her to get comfortable. He agreed with his wife. She would be a wonderful daughter.

Janice and James returned with their shopping, awaking Clara in the process. She needed the toilet.

Janice was quick to respond. 'James. Let me show you how to get her to the toilet, help her, and then bring her back. Are you ready?'

'Yes, mom.'

'Lift her into her chair.'

'Now to the bathroom in your bedroom suite.'

'Park next to the toilet and put on the chair brake. Now lift her footrests so she can put her feet on the floor. Let her put her arms around your neck and then let her stand. Do not lift her off her feet as you may stretch her wound. Reach down to lower her pants and turn so she can sit lowering her gently.'

She looked at Clara. 'How are we doing my dear?'

She was smiling with amusement at the military-type precision rendered by his mother. She remembered getting her mother to the toilet in the early days of her illness before she became bed bound and thus used a bedpan. But her mother was somewhat heavier, especially for a fourteen-year-old. James's face was red with the exertion, but he was following instruction to the letter. *'He's doing good. Soon have him trained'* as she laughed at his serious red face. 'Why such a serious face, darling? You need to see the funny side of care activities if you're to survive.'

'I need to concentrate so I don't risk hurting you. I'll get used to it.'

She managed to wipe herself and readied herself to be lifted again.

Janice resumed control. 'This time James, lift her onto her right leg so she can stand. Then steady her to see if she can redress herself.'

She leaned against him while reaching down to redress herself. Her panties were fine, but her shorts had dropped too far down her legs.

'Okay, James. Sit her back on the toilet and then bring her shorts up to where she can reach them and help her stand again. Finally, she was dressed, and he reversed the process to get her back into her chair. Janice flushed the toilet and wheeled her out of the bathroom.

'Wait, darling. I need to wash my hands.'

He reversed and traversed to the basin, but she could not easily reach the taps.

Janice piped in. 'We need to buy a supply of bath wipes and put them within easy reach. This bathroom was not designed for people in wheelchairs.'

'I secreted a pack from the hospital. They're in my bag on the couch.'

Rather than retrieve them, he wheeled her to the couch where he opened her bag, found the pack, and extracted one wipe for her. Job done.

'Well done, James. First task as a carer completed without fault.'

'I need a drink. Anyone for a happy-hour refresher?'

Both women laughed, and Geoffrey was trying not to share their amusement at the expense of his son, but he was happy the funny side of caring is better than the alternative.

'I think a G&T would be welcome son, and then we must think about what to prepare for dinner.'

Clara wanted to sit on the balcony with her drink while the boys organised dinner. Janice sat with her soaking up the last of the afternoon sunshine.

My dear, do you have any thoughts on what you would like from us to make your recovery as comfortable as possible?'

'I've been thinking how to destress the coming weeks for all of us. I thought back to the start of caring for my mum. Those first few weeks were awful for me. No school, no socialising with my friends. When not actually caring for my mum, I had all the chores of running a home plus taking care of my brother. The strain on finances, trying to decide what I could and couldn't buy to put meals on the table.

The stresses on me were a heavy, depressing load.' She reflected on the emptiness and sense of injustice she felt. 'I reached a point of despair where I wanted to scream for help but knowing no-one was listening as I faced the inevitable death of my mother.' She was in tears.

Janice held her hand, feeling her pain. 'I can't imagine how awful it was for you. How did you cope with such despair?'

She continued to reflect on those terrible times. 'I was trying to move my mum and lost my footing. We both tumbled to the floor. When we looked at each other, we burst out laughing. We couldn't stop. Our uncontrollable laughter felt so good. We were laughing at our shared despair because I knew how guilty my mum felt about imposing this situation on me. That event changed everything. We would find any reason to have a good laugh together every day until her passing. Ironically, I felt worse after her passing because I was suddenly alone with no-one to laugh with. My brother had already started his cadet training in the Navy and only returned for the funeral. I was alone in the house, knowing I would have to leave and find somewhere else to live. All my friends had long deserted me. Where would I go? This started another depressing chapter in my life, very much until I bumped into James on the street. He instantly wanted to renew our friendship, and he was my platform for restoring my faith in humanity and making other friends.'

Janice was now in tears. 'My dear, I'm so grateful James has his own mind. I'm so angry with myself for not understanding your situation. I remember you being there when we needed a babysitter for James before your mother's illness. How insular we become when consumed in our own careers. We quickly forget we work to live; not live to work, even if we enjoy it. Only then can we spend time with the less fortunate. But this will change. We cannot change the past, but we sure as hell can learn from our mistakes to make the future more compassionate. Whatever you need during your recovery will be delivered. I commit this to you on behalf of all of us. But you must help me understand what you need because I'm prone to smother when unsure. You remind me you are the most experienced carer I know, so please help me.'

Clara squeezed her hand as she reflected upon the declared insecurity of this outwardly confident and assured woman. 'I think we need to concentrate on laughter. Worked for me and my mum.'

'Please help me here. I can't see the funny side of this situation. All I see is pain.'

'What was the expression used by Monty Python?' She started to sing, 'Always look on the bright side of life.' She paused. 'The distinct advantage this time is that I will survive and, will walk again. All we need to do is remember not to take things too seriously. We are where we are. Things will go wrong, but we'll get through it with a smile.'

Janice was now smiling. 'If your medication works this way, can I have some?' They both laughed.

'Seriously, Janice, I know what needs to be done. With you and Geoffrey around to share the load, the next few weeks will pass quickly, especially if we have some fun with it as a family. My biggest problem with my mum was being alone, carrying all the burdens. Here I'm surrounded by so much loving care. You have no idea how wonderful that feels.'

'Young lady, sometimes I just want to scoop you up and hug you. Geoffrey saw your qualities that first morning at breakfast. He's such a wise old owl. So how do we have fun with this?'

'I think the first consideration is James.'

She was shocked. 'Why James! He's not hurt.'

'I know how he reacts when stressed. I want to make this fun for us. I would like the more intimate needs to be just him and me. No pressure from anyone else. Allow us to find a way to laugh our way through getting up, shower, dressing, toilet – all those things that would be intimate between us. Our visit to the toilet earlier stressed him. I don't want to do that to him.'

'You are some lady. I'm so proud of you. Neither I nor Geoffrey will interfere unless needed.'

'Thank you. As for James growing up a little, we can all have some fun with this so long as we include him in the fun.'

'Okay. What do you have in mind?'

'Cooking, laundry and ironing could reveal some funny outcomes.'

With a wry smile. 'Do you seriously expect my son to take care of laundry and ironing? I expect this to be one of my weekend tasks. To get James to do it – my goodness. Could he survive such an ordeal?' They both had the giggles.

'If he gets cocky about caring for me, which he likely will at some point, it would be a fun way to ground him again.'

'I like it. I could teach him the basics of ironing, and then we could have a cocktail watching him try to apply that techy mind of his to more difficult clothing. I can see some fun in that. Let's have some fun with this idea.'

She recalled a distant memory. 'I remember Geoffrey telling me at university his mother's preparation for his university life was to iron a shirt, and to prepare basic meals. Sounds like an agenda to me.' They laughed again.

They continued to scheme, laughing at the potential fun involved. The boys could hear this laughter as they prepared dinner.

'They appear to be having fun out there. Can't imagine what's so funny.'

'Son, laughter's a good tonic. I'm happy they get along so well. I think we're nearly ready. Why don't you make a space at the table for Clara so she can stay in her wheelchair if she wishes and then go see if they're ready for dinner?'

'Ladies, dinner is served.'

'Darling, could you take me to the loo? That G&T has gone straight through me.'

He wheeled her to their bedroom, expecting his mother to follow; and was surprised to see she wasn't there giving her orders.

'Do you trust me to manage this on my own?'

With a wry smile, 'Not yet, but I think you care enough not to hurt me so we can manage on our own.'

His face visibly lit up. 'I'll take good care of you. You tell me what to do. I'll do whatever it takes to make you smile again.'

'A little playtime in bed tonight will certainly put a smile on my face.'

'That I can deliver – with a little guidance on what will please my lady.'

They smiled at each other as they finished their task and made their way to the dining table. Janice noticed their smiling faces. *'She knows my son well. I think my fears are unfounded. She knows what she needs, and she knows how to get it. That's my girl.'*

During dinner Geoffrey commented on the laughter they could hear on the balcony and if there was anything they could share. Janice looked at Clara. 'Do you think we should share our magic formula for the coming weeks?'

'Why not? Might be fun to see their reaction.'

Her tone was highbrow. 'Gentlemen, Clara and I have discussed the way forward for the coming weeks. She identified one specific ingredient that will certainly make our lives somewhat more pleasant. This ingredient is laughter. Last week was frightful. The coming weeks need to be frightfully funny.'

Both women were laughing as they looked at the expressions on the faces of the boys.

Geoffrey was first to speak, as James thought they were a little worse for their G&T.

'Ladies. I fully endorse this ingredient into our quest.' He raised his glass. 'To laughter, and may it fill our hearts in the coming weeks.'

They all followed suit with their glasses. The atmosphere was suddenly much lighter, conversation more buoyant, and everyone relaxed.

It was only 8pm, but Clara was feeling the need for sleep. James was determined they would not put her to bed alone, so they made their excuses and adjourned to their bedroom. Geoffrey and Janice sat on the balcony and relax for a while.

'Well, my dear, you two certainly appeared to have fun this afternoon.'

'Darling, it was lovely. We laughed. We cried, and then we laughed again. She was telling me what it was like for her caring for her mother and brother. So much darkness and despair until she accidentally fell with her mother, and they lay there laughing about it. It was the ingredient that saved her. But where were we? We knew this girl. She babysat with James. Why didn't we know or care what was happening to her?'

'People are too consumed with their own lives these days. No sense of community anymore. When I was a kid, the local community worked together to help with such tragedy. You rarely see it today.'

'Darling, before I forget, we've agreed not to engage in the more intimate aspects of her recover unless it's needed. She wants the two of them to work it out together. And who is she thinking about in this request? James, so he doesn't get stressed. Can you believe her devotion to him?'

'My dear, she has the experience and knowledge to know what works, and what doesn't work in such adversity. James has his insecurities and can lose it when stressed, as we've seen. She knows our boy, and what works for him. I would say she has the situation under control, and we should respect her knowledge and wishes. I'm sure our involvement comforts her she can manage the situation.'

'She told me how wonderful it is to have us around. She had no-one when she was a carer, or even after her mother died until James met her again.' Janice was crying. 'So much despair for someone so young. Never again will that woman want for love and care.'

He held her hand; but left her with her thoughts.

She looked up to him. 'I'm emotionally exhausted. I think it's time for bed. Much to do tomorrow.'

Chapter 41

Getting her up on Saturday morning was the first solo task for James. He couldn't think of a way to get her into the shower. She watched with amusement as he pondered how to rise to this challenge.

'Why don't you get the pack of wipes from my bag and give me a bed bath.'

He looked at her, thinking about this solution. 'Good idea. Will need to visit the chemist in the parade to get a stock of bed bath wipes', as he went to recover her bag.

She could almost hear his mind record this need.

Getting her dressed was the next chore, especially her bra. She decided to have some fun with this task, so did not intervene.

'Come on, James. You are very adept at taking it off. Surely your brilliant mind can work out how to put it back on' as she giggled.

'Is this what you mean about laughing our way through your care. I'm not seeing the funny side yet.'

'You will, and understanding a bra is an important part of our project. You need to get the hang of this task. I'm happy without a bra in the apartment but you need to be very proficient when we go out otherwise it will be very uncomfortable for me.'

'Now you are making fun of me. You can manage your own bra if you want to.'

'More fun if you do it. More intimate fun until we can resume normal activities.'

He understood. She wanted intimate contact as much as seeing him struggle with this task. He could see the funny side so relaxed. 'Okay. It might be more interesting for me to see your bra-less pert breasts poking through a T-shirt.'

In fun, 'Then let's do it. Pass me my T-shirt and forget the bra. But we will add putting on a bra to your list of tasks as you need this knowledge for our project.'

He smiled as he started to understand the need to have fun as a carer.

Geoffrey was busy preparing breakfast when they emerged from their bedroom. 'Good morning. How are you both this sunny morning?'

Over breakfast, Janice switched into military precision mode. 'What do we need to achieve today? Any further shopping to consider? There must be laundry. Can we re-arrange things here to make the place more wheelchair friendly?' Turning to Clara, 'Would you like me to take you to the park, my dear? Fresh air will be good for you after being cooped up in hospital.'

'Mom, I need to go to the chemist to get a supply of bed bath wipes until Clara can manage the shower.'

'You realise you can buy a special chair for the shower, but probably not from your local chemist.'

Clara realised this constant demonstration of how little James knows about caring was not good for him. 'It's okay, Janice. I'll look on the internet to see what's available. And I would love a trip to the park', hoping to diffuse her regimented approach. 'Such a lovely day.'

Geoffrey was quick to sense the problem. 'After breakfast can I suggest we all sit together and ask Clara for direction on her needs over the coming days. She is not only the person in need, but also by far the most experienced in knowing how to deliver it. I want us to calmly consider her needs and then plan how best to deliver. Darling, could you help me with clearing breakfast? James, can you take care of any needs for Clara? Then we sit together as family and plan our day.' He wanted a quiet chat with his wife before she applies any further regimented attitude.

'I must think how I get myself onto the couch, or onto a balcony recliner should I wish to nap on the balcony and, of course, getting into bed.'

Janice was quick to respond. 'You already have all of that, my dear. Goes by the name of James.'

'I think meals will be the hardest task initially. I can prepare cold dishes, but can't reach the hob, microwave, or the oven.'

Janice again quick to respond. 'You should not have to prepare any meals for yourself in the short-term. I will spend a couple of days with James showing him how to prepare basic meals that comply with your dietary requirements. You may get repeat meals initially, but I will expand his repertoire over the coming weeks. When you feel able, you can also supervise other meals to get some variety. Geoffrey and I will ensure your weekend meals supplement any shortfall during the week.'

Geoffrey frequently interceded, as Janice seemed unable to think of the impact of her tone on James. He reflected how smart is Clara in her approach to James. And to watch his wife's change from cold-hearted woman into a doting parent in just a few days bewildered him, although he was more than delighted with the outcome. '*A conversation when we're alone about the all-inclusive approach to this recovery exercise. She really must consider James in this process.*'

Clara soon needed a nap so was suitably settled on the couch whilst James and his mother departed to the local parade of shops to purchase a shopping bag full of suitable wipes, and then to W.H.Smiths to find basic cookbooks. They activated two loads of laundry in the communal laundry room in the basement.

After a quick lunch they all departed for a walk to the park to enjoy the lovely day and the radiance of colour now in bloom. They looked like a family enjoying some time together, and they felt the togetherness. Unfamiliar territory for both James and Clara, but comfortable albeit James spent much of the time in the park fiddling on his phone, apparently communicating with Hashem and Javid. Weekends are designated his respite days, so he thought nothing of it.

Chapter 42

Sunday was much calmer. Having identified as many concerns as possible on Saturday and finding solutions, there was less anxiety about the way forward. Now what they needed is to fine tune any issues and then settle down to the new normal for the coming weeks.

Geoffrey popped out to purchase a Sunday newspaper for himself and Clara, and magazines for her. James and his mother were in the kitchen teaching him how to prepare basic dishes that included the nutrients and vitamins specified in her dietary plan. He made copious notes, even though they had already purchased suitable cookbooks. Learning what pots and pans he needed and where they are stored, and how to use the hob, oven, microwave, and dishwasher was by far his biggest learning curve.

After a couple of hours, his mother could see he was at saturation. Heeding Geoffrey's warning about taxing their son too much she relented. 'Okay, James, enough for today.

We'll have a refresher tomorrow. But you can help me with dinner this evening to give you some practical experience.'

Clara found adjusting to this new environment somewhat overwhelming and certainly tiring. She parked herself on the couch taking frequent naps while the people around her busied themselves. Geoffrey, relieved of his duties towards her, parked himself on the balcony with his newspaper. He also needed some space to think through how to manage Monday morning, where the natural mindset would be early to rise and prepare for a day at the office. He needed to think of a trigger mechanism to emulate a bank holiday for himself and Janice, and a new routine for James.

After dinner, and Clara having called time on her day thus retiring with James, he sat with Janice on the balcony. Realising she was somewhat in hyper mode, he knew a soft touch was necessary. 'Janice, my dear, I think we need to agree a strategy we can put in place tomorrow where we take a different stance.'

'What do you mean?'

'When we leave here tomorrow, they will be on their own to fend for themselves. I think we can soften this situation by ensuring when we leave, we don't create a void that will most certainly stress James.'

'As usual, you make excellent sense. What do you propose?'

'I think James is feeling saturated with his new duties. I realise he has much to learn, but there is only so much he will learn at any one time. I'm comforted that in Clara we have an ace on our side. She knows better than any of us what she needs, and she knows our boy. I think tomorrow we need to step back and watch what happens – more an overseeing role, if necessary. Why don't we try to have a family day where we only make any minor adjustments necessary to engage Clara, but not overtly? It's our first opportunity to start our new family life. What do you think?'

She looked at him with love in her eyes. 'You're in your wise old owl mode. I have allowed myself to become overprotective of Clara, stressing James in the process. I can see it now. And, as usual, you have found a solution that will allow me to nurture Clara as family. What would I

115

do without you? Let tomorrow be the first day of our new life together as a family. If I stray, use one of your gentle jolts. I'll stay tuned.' She moved to him to kiss him. 'Thank you, my darling.'

'Tomorrow we need to remember neither of us are working. Think Bank Holiday. Nice lie-in. Casual dress. Leisurely breakfast. Both of us should avoid engaging with our work, as this will send the wrong message to James. If its nice outside, maybe a family walk. Then we watch to see if James is at peace with his role before we quietly leave them to it.'

'Sounds like a perfect family day.'

Janice was in perfect mother mode. After breakfast she sat on the balcony with Clara discussing her ambitions in fashion design, the project with James, and her hope for the future. When Clara needed to rest, she sat on the balcony studying Clara's collection of fashion magazines to familiarise herself to better engage with her desire for a mother/daughter relationship.

The more James realised his mother was not on his case, the more he relaxed into his new role. Neither Hashem nor Javid bothered him all day, so no reason to lapse. He was very happy to sit with dad to appraise him of where he was in his business ambitions, and why dad might add his vast corporate knowledge to help. He encouraged James to call anytime he might need advice. After lunch they went for a walk to get Clara out of the apartment, taking special note of any potential hazards in terrain for a wheelchair.

After a lovely family day, it was time for mum and dad to return home to prepare themselves for work the following day albeit not stated to keep James from contemplating work. They felt they had achieved enough to start Clara's recovery and rehab. More next weekend.

Chapter 43

Wednesday went well until Clara needed to move from the couch to her wheelchair. He was lifting her into her wheelchair. She hit the hard, wooden floor with a thud, screaming in pain. He panicked, realising he hadn't applied the brake to the wheelchair as it rolled away.

'Oh, my God. What have I done?' He was distraught. 'I'll get an ambulance' as he reached for his phone.

She could see his panic. She screamed at him, 'James, stop. Help me up and take me to our bed.'

This scream brought him back to the moment. Putting the phone down, he lifted her up in his arms, carrying her to the bedroom. 'I'm so sorry. I'm so sorry. Have I hurt you?'

After he carefully laid her on the bed, she lowered her shorts to see if the wound showed any signs of opening. No signs of any blood.

'Get me an oxynorm from the bathroom and a glass of water.'

He was on autopilot, his face sweating with fear and despair. He returned with the opiate tablet and water. She quickly swallowed her pain relief.

'Clara, what can I do to make this better? Do I need to get help?', still beside himself at his carelessness.

She was adjusting her body to find the most comfortable position. 'Come, lie with me, and talk to me. Distract me from the pain.'

He was quickly by her side, looking at her. 'How are you feeling? I'm so sorry.'

'Not good conversation. Try stroking my cheek and tell me about where we are, and how you see the future. Only positives, please. You're trying to make me feel good.'

He stroked her cheek with the back of his fingers, which calmed him as he gazed at the lovely women lying next to him. 'I've done some thinking these past days. I would like to share my thoughts with you.'

'Good start. Much better.'

'When I brought you to London, I eluded myself as a valiant knight on a white charger rescuing a lovely damsel in distress. Everything I did for you was with a puffed-out chest showing what life in my kingdom could do for you. I now realise how stupid I was. I didn't rescue you; you rescued me from my big-headed folly. I hit a problem, I throw money at it like confetti and hope it will go away. When you encounter a problem, you smother it in oodles of love and compassion. How do I aspire to your maturity and wisdom?'

'I like this story. What have you figured out?'

'The one thing I got right is my choice of woman. And, in my favour, I made that choice in the face of certain adversity.'

She smiled, knowing he was referring to his mother.

'I can't imagine life without you anymore. But I also know I have mountains to climb to remotely qualify to hold your hand on equal terms. But these mountains I will climb, probably with some help. I want you to look upon me as your equal so we can walk hand-in-hand, into the sunset together as true partners.'

She encouraged him to put his arm around her so that she could snuggle into his shoulder after planting a kiss on his cheek. 'You want to climb; I have the ropes.'

The opiate she had taken acted within minutes, but also made her drowsy. He could hear the breathing alerting him to her sleepy state. He lay back holding her close thinking *'I will climb those mountains and make you proud to have me as your partner. And I vow to get you through this, whatever it takes.'*

Chapter 44

The following weekend Janice and Clara decided it was time for James to undertake some of the more mundane chores of family life, so they tasked him with the ironing which included clothes added by his mom and dad.

At first, he found this demeaning and resented this chore, thinking *'this is not man's work'* but knew his father could iron clothes so not a good idea to vent any frustration.

He had just finished one of his own shirts, a classic fit business shirt, before picking out a shirt belonging to his mother. He became frustrated by the various shaping built into this shirt. The shaping around the breasts he could readily understand, but what was the shaping around the waist and hips – some being the cut of the fabric but others being pleated tucks? Picking a blouse belonging to Clara, a size 10, where his mother's shirt showed she was a size 12, he compared them. He noticed differences in the shaping curves. His mind quickly thought about the logic behind these curves and whether they followed a fixed profile which could translate into an algorithm, or a variety of shapes that would be independent of each other, but regular to a size. He found another shirt belonging to his mother, but this was a size 10. '*Why two different sizes for the same body shape?*'

His mind became immersed in trying to understand relative sizing, curvatures, cloth cutting against pleated tucks. He grabbed the pad and pen permanently located on the kitchen worktop and listed questions, drew shapes to remind him of the different curves he had found. Then he took his phone, put it into camera mode and took pictures of the shapes of interest. He would need to sit with Clara and explore these questions as they would be fundamental to his virtual model. Not much ironing was completed, but his mind was buzzing with the information he had assembled, and perplexed at how complicated it all seemed, especially that his mom could wear both a size 10 and a size 12 – '*what's that all about?*'

He found himself surrounded by his mum and Clara. 'I thought you were ironing these clothes, not merely looking at them.'

He looked at his mom. 'Why do you wear a size 10 from this manufacturer, and a size 12 from this one?'

'Because they are the sizes that fit me.'

'So how do you know which size to buy?'

'I try them on before I purchase.'

'But why is there no consistency in sizing that discourages you to buy until you have tried them for fit?'

It perplexed his mom. 'Different manufacturers have different cuts which change the way their clothes fit.'

'Mom, that's crazy. Why have a standard sizing which does not perform? There is no sense in what I've studied today. If I buy a 16" collar shirt with a classic fit, I know it will fit me just fine. Why is this not the same for women's clothes?'

They both could see he was totally engaged in this size issue. 'I don't know the answers, son. Perhaps the maker of the size 10 is trying to flatter me; remind me of my youthful, slim curves. James, you need to remember when you buy a shirt so long as the neck fits, the arm length is good, you can close the cuffs, and it tucks into your trousers – job done. This is not good enough for a woman. She needs to know that the curves in the shaping compliment her figure. May seem trivial, but it's the way it is.'

'Clara, starting Monday and for as long as it takes, I want to understand the construction of women's clothes. I want to know about every curve in cutting, every pleat tuck, why it's there, what are the differences in shape for different sized women, why does my mom have a size 10 from one manufacturer, and a size 12 from another. This is important in our quest. I must understand how pattern design works for women.'

Clara, completely taken by surprise, 'I know how the modelling works for different sizes, because body shape plays a significant part. But I sense this is important, so I'll find all the charts you need.'

'For our project to be successful, I must know everything about sizing for women. If there is no reliable standard sizing, I need to know the minimum measurements of a woman needed to determine her size, and what will fit her.'

This was a James his mother had not witnessed before; totally absorbed and focussed on an objective. The intensity of his desire for answers reminded her of herself when faced with a complex problem. All thoughts of his ironing delinquency dissolved as she realised this mattered. *'This is why he's successful.'* Okay, James, let's forget the ironing. You finish your notes and then join us on the balcony for a much-needed cocktail. We know what's needed, but let's enjoy the weekend before embarking on this quest.'

'And don't forget to turn off the iron.'

Dad was sitting on the balcony reading a newspaper, totally oblivious to what was happening inside but disturbed by the chatter upon their return. 'How's he getting on with the ironing?'

'He's not.'

Dad quickly put down his paper to go chastise his son. Mum put her hand on his arm to stop him. 'He's not being

120

delinquent. Totally absorbed by the cut of female shirts and is trying to make sense of it for his computer engine. Totally perplexed why I can be equally comfortable in a size 10 or size 12, albeit from different designers. He has made copious notes and drawings and is clearly focussed on understanding how women's clothes are designed and sized. Big project for Clara next week.'

Dad relaxed. 'I'd like to see how he works. Our delinquency for too long.' He headed to where James was still busy with his notes. Dad looked over his shoulder, amazed with the array of sketches, attempts to find mathematical solutions, and copious notes.

'Son, would you mind if I sit with you and watch how you work. It looks fascinating how you apply yourself to these problems.'

'Tearing my hair out at the inconsistencies I'm finding.' He spread the two shirts from his mum on the table. 'Look at this dad. Look at the seams and pleated tuck on the side of the shirts. They're slightly different in construction, but they create a similar overall shape. And look at these curves, they're not regular; more complex. How does a designer or cutter know the mathematics that goes into such curves? And then look at the sizes. One is a size 10 and the other a size 12. How can they be so similar in overall size?'

Then he pushed away the size 12 shirt and put Clara's size 10 next to his mother's. 'These two shirts show the same size. I think it reasonable to suggest Clara is a bust size larger than mom. Look at the difference in the cut. I can't work with these sizing conventions. I need to understand why one designer cuts one way, and another completely differently. How do they size?'

'Total mystery to me, son, but don't they use mannequins to make their designs into desired sizes?'

'Probably true, but how do they make the mannequins? What sizing conventions do they use?'

'Probably based on a model they know.'

'Good thinking. Not good for me in my quest, as such a process cannot easily be rationalised mathematically.'

'But son, aren't you overlooking a glaring reality, no two people are exactly the same size or shape? Perhaps the designer thinks about what body form will best suit the dress design and then produce patterns that will best fit a group of women within a base shape.'

'That's it. Brilliant. Not all clothes are intended for all body shapes. Must ask Clara about this. You should come work with me.'

'I don't have your skills, son, but I would like to follow this project as it develops. Truly fascinating. For instance, what will you do with the data you accumulated today?'

'If you don't mind me using my computer suite, I'll show you.'

'It's weekend so no problem.'

James fired up his system and loaded the wire-framed version of Clara. 'Dad, this is a mesh representation of Clara. Now watch what happens when she moves. Watch the mesh change shape.' She was walking, and they watched the mesh change as she moved.

'Now watch what happens if I increase the mesh size. Her walk is more stilted. And if I decrease the mesh size, her walk is more natural. The smaller the mesh size, the more fluid the walk. But the smaller the mesh size, the greater the processing power needed to have fluid movement. With the processing power available on laptops today, we need to balance mesh size against fluidity of movement. I need this much larger computer to achieve the movement you see when the mesh size is small.'

'One way to overcome the processing problem is to have different mesh sizes for different parts of the body. For example, there are several areas of the body that move as a mass where you have large muscles such as thighs, or bone structures such as the skull. A skill with my engines is knowing how to use different mesh sizes interactively to reduce the number of mesh squares but maintain fluidity.'

'Okay son, I think I've got that, but how do you get the movement because this wire mesh is surely a combination of mathematical formulae?'

'Think about celluloid movies. Your eye sees a fluid moving picture on the screen, but you know it comprises a series of stills being quickly passed through a projector lens. Someone calculated that if we passed these stills through a projector lens at 25fps your eyes would deceive you into believing you're watching a full motion picture.'

'We create several still frames which are a logical progression of the previous frame and do the same as a projector. Compared with the complete story of producing a graphic on the screen, this is the easy bit. Adding clothing that moves in harmony with the body is the next processing problem. If you look at most computer games, the clothing is tight fitting, so it moves in the same way as the body. The animation license we've recently sold changes this so clothes can overlay onto a wire mesh of a body having fluid movement, which combines the movement and momentum of the body with the type and weight of the clothing.'

'How did you manage this?'

'I spent about six months researching the way our brains process visual images. Do you know much deception and illusion by the brain forms much of what we think we see? Truly amazing ability by the brain to optimise its processing power. I thought about how to use these characteristics of vision to minimise the algorithms and thus the processing power. In its simplest terms we can take a logical expression such as IF A AND B THEN C. In conventional mathematics we need to solve for C. In our visual computation if I provide A and B, our brain will compute C. By understanding how our brain manipulates images I don't need to waste computer processing power when our brain will do it for me. Therefore, I can use the processing power for other more exciting tasks or be able to produce greater illusion of moving images on lesser computers.'

'Son. I'm embarrassed that all this incredible work took place under our noses, and we knew nothing of it. This is fascinating stuff. If not too much of a distraction, I'd like to follow this current project to understand the obstacles you face and how you conquer them. I'm so impressed.'

'Don't beat yourself up. When I was finding my way around these problems to produce the first engine, I had no logical pathway. I would have an idea and then pursue it until it either worked or failed. I could not sit and have this discussion with you then. It's only since I fully understood how to use the brain's use of visual data to create images, I understood how to optimise the use of graphics engines.'

'What challenges do you face with the engine for Clara's project?'

'Enormous. Mind blowing. Without Hashem and Javid, I would say impossible. They had some choice words when I first suggested what was needed – bonkers being a polite summary. Strictly between you and me the reason I kept putting off this project was delivery of the primary feature of this project is so far away from our current knowledge I hoped as we developed more and more sophisticated engines I could answer some seemingly daunting questions.'

'What types of problems?'

'We haven't discussed the most demanding of processing issues in graphics animation – rendering colour. If you look at a typical cartoon animation, it won't take you long to realise the colour palette is tiny compared with the ability of the eye to differentiate between millions of hues of colour. Early animations used just 256 colours. I can probably summarise with what one of the graphics people at the company who licenced our engine told me. Our engine allows them to expand their animation palette to one million plus colours. To generate the one thousand frames for just forty seconds of animated movie will take months. Before rendering, each frame will be multi-layered. These layers need to be flattened and harmonised for the final cut. This rendering for just forty seconds of action will take hours of processing power.'

'If it's as you say, why are you pursuing it?'

'Lots of reasons, not least a promise to a lovely lady. I will at least try. I now have the income streams to support such a quest. Javid, having studied my research on visual deception and illusion, has done a brilliant job rationalising and minimising the obstacles. And both are up for it even though it's not an EMULATE project.'

'Why would they agree to expend so much EMULATE resource without reward?'

'Hashem and Javid aren't driven by commercial interest. They see an exciting challenge. It consumes them. It becomes personal to them to apply their intellect to move the boundaries of knowledge. And they know if we succeed, we won't have merely raised the bar. We will have entered a new dimension. Javid has already purchased the special cameras that can see through clothing to capture the wire frame of a model as she walks onto the catwalk. First problem solved.'

'Are these special cameras? They sound intrusive. Are they allowed?'

'They use them in airports. Remember back some months when they were first installed. They capture somewhat more detail of the body than either necessary or respectful. I think Sony invented them. The airport versions have been amended to show less detail, but we have the full function versions. Yes, they are intrusive, but all we see on the screen is the wire mesh of the person so no embarrassment. And the people we use are professional models expecting to display whatever the designer requires. No problems to date. It will be interesting to see how models react when we undertake our study on breast movement. But at least the models don't need to be on the catwalk without tops. The cameras will capture what we need.'

Son, I'm in awe. Can't wait to see the outcome. We should get back to the ladies. They will think we've deserted them.'

As they were about to leave, dad saw Clara's sewing workstation. 'So, Clara works in here as well?'

'Yes. When she first bought her sewing machine, she quickly buried the dining table with cloth and patterns. We were eating off our knees on the sofa. Only way to get our dining table back was to buy her a good cutting table and suitable chair. And I used the wire mesh of her to have a mannequin made. You can see she was working on a project before that fateful night.'

'Doesn't her presence disturb you?'

'She usually works here during the day when I'm in the office. But even when in here together I get so absorbed in my work I don't really notice her, especially if I have headphones.'

'Has she shown any signs she wants to get back in here?'

'Too early, I think, both physically and mentally. But as she gets stronger, and tires of reading or staring at the life on the river, I think she will get itchy fingers to work again. When she does, is it okay for me to use my suite as my laptop cannot handle this sizing issue?'

Dad put his hand on his son's shoulder. 'The only requirement is you do not leave her alone until she can easily cope. If you are in here together, no problem.'

'Thanks, dad.'

They returned to the balcony. 'Boy's, what took you so long?'

'My dear, it's truly fascinating watching our son apply himself to this project. I've learnt so much today about motion graphics, and I'm eager to observe as this project develops. The technology requirements leave me speechless. But who needs a drink?'

Mum frowned. 'We're way past afternoon drinks as it must now be the cocktail hour.'

'Then cocktails it will be.'

During dinner Geoffrey remembered he had some news about the trial of Clara's assailant having followed the proceedings as part of his application for injury compensation. 'I have news of the trial of the two men who inflicted themselves upon you. The mitigation advised by the police officer was put forward by the defending Barrister but was dismissed by the Judge on a technicality because the victim, Clara, was innocent of any provocation. The man with the knife received a custodial sentence of six years for his various crimes, and the other man six months for aiding and abetting the attempted escape of the assailant. Leave was granted for injury compensation, which I am now pursuing on your behalf.'

'Thanks, Dad, that's a weight of my mind. What's the next step?'

'I've already made the application with some useful advice from the prosecution Barrister. I've added all the medical information so we can only hope for a speedy resolution. Put this sordid matter behind us.'

'Thank you, Geoffrey. Where would I be without you? You're so kind to me.'

'My dear, you are equally entitled to your common rights as anyone else in the country. Until the pair of you understand such processes, I will ensure they treat you with the same regard and respect as anyone else.'

James knew this was aimed at him. But not to be contested. He should know the ways of the world if he is to be a caring partner. *'Much to learn.'*

Janice, satisfied all relevant information, including the quiet chastisement of her son, had been aired, wanted to quickly move the conversation away from that awful night. 'Now that I can see Clara's project is most certainly in process, when do you expect having anything you can show to the fashion industry?'

Chapter 45

It was Monday afternoon. Clara had frantically searched the college digital library for the best data available to define the various female shapes used by designers. She was now sitting with James explaining what she had found. It immediately drew him to one diagrammatic representation.

'This is the data I need. Look at these shapes, each one has a geometric representation.' He was looking at a schematic of various body shapes overlaid with geometric shapes with specific characteristics listed underneath each. 'The Neat Hourglass shaped body has a truncated hourglass, the Full Hourglass is as it states, the Apple is ovular, the Pear is an isosceles triangle, with the Inverted Triangle shape being an inverted isosceles triangle, the Lean Column and the Rectangle being rectangular. These are all regular geometric shapes and thus easy to manipulate in algorithms. And the essential characteristics of each shape size in terms of shoulders, bust, waist, hips, and bottom allow me to configure three-dimensional algorithms. This is great. Now all we need is the dimensional information which dictates size. Great Job. We're moving forward.'

'So, what do you need from me next?'

'Any tables of data that translates these qualitative representations into quantitative data used by designers.'

'And just what does that mean?'

'Sorry. In laypersons speak what dictates the dimensions of each shape for any given size.' Pointing to the Pear shape, 'what is the width at the base of the triangle that goes with the vertical height to the apex or nape? Pointing to the Apple shape, 'this conic shape can be defined by a circle, a parabola and a hyperbola. What is the diameter of the circle and the conic length for a given clothing size? There must be tables of this data. Can you find them for me?'

'Got it. I'll get straight on to it.'

'And when you've done that, can you look at breast shapes and sizes, and whether we associate any breast shape with any specific body shape. Don't want to approach Rigby & Peller until I know a little about the subject.'

With that he was back to his laptop, ready to define the seven shapes geometrically before adding the three-dimensional attributes she had provided. He could then add the data tables to construct wireframe animations of each shape.

It was suppertime before they each emerged from their respective tasks. She quickly prepared a cold plate meal. They ate it only using this brief interlude to talk further before returning to their tasks until the body of Clara declared her day over. He put her to bed and then returned to his laptop for a further four hours before deciding he needed sleep before she would awake needing attention.

Chapter 46

It was now five weeks since the stabbing incident. Janice and Clara were sitting together on a park bench enjoying the afternoon sunshine. Clara had forsaken her wheelchair as part of savouring the atmosphere of the park.

'Clara, my dear. As we're away from the boys, could we have a conversation about a painful burden I carry to see if your compassion and wisdom can help me to heal this pain?

If you don't yet feel ready, I fully understand. It can wait for another day.'

'Janice, you've been so kind to me these past weeks. You treat me like family. If you have pain, of course I'm here for you.'

'It's important from the outset you understand your terrible trauma has nothing to do with my pain. It was only the catalyst that triggered a realisation for both Geoffrey and me, and we have vowed to make amends to our son and to you.' She paused.

'Something happened to me when I first visited you in intensive care. I held your hand. My ice-cool heart erupted. I wanted to scoop you up in my arms and tell you mum is here for you. In that instant I changed from Dr Janice Caldwell, biochemist, who just happens to be female, into a woman who first and foremost wanted to nurture her daughter. When I got back to Geoffrey, I cried in despair. Neither of us could remember the last time I was reduced to tears. I had to pull myself together because it was adding to the distress of James. But when we were safely back in our bedroom at the apartment, Geoffrey had to console my grief for some time. You should know we are both agreed that regardless of what happens between you and James, for as long as we live you will never be without a home and the love of a family.'

'Janice, I don't know what to say.' Tears welled in her eyes.

Janice held her hand. 'My lovely Clara, your love and compassion pales what we can offer, but we want to be better parents to both you and James. We have committed every weekend to spend with you until you are fully recovered. Much soul searching has occurred these past weeks with the realisation that the Caldwell members of our family comprises three largely independent people totally pre-occupied with personal desires. You are the only member with the wisdom and courage to care. Geoffrey and I have changed the way we live, and we hope these weekends together will help James realise he must also change to bring us back together as a family. Geoffrey is going to use his formidable skills as a corporate finance specialist to help James to optimise the structure of his companies. This will mean they will spend much time together both professionally and, more importantly, as father and son. Geoffrey will try to nurture James into a better outlook on life.'

Tears streamed from her eyes, 'My dearly beloved Geoffrey so openly accepted you that first morning at breakfast. He saw the lovely woman you are, not the misfortune. After your trauma he was quick to realise something had stirred in me, requiring both myself and James to change, and I bless him for his wisdom and love to put this family back together.' Tears were now in free flow as she reflected on the newfound love she shared with her husband.

Clara could feel her pain. 'Janice, I think this is wonderful. We have certainly noticed a difference over these past weeks. And the help you both give to us is overwhelming. I could not ask for better support. So why are you in pain?'

'I feel so wretched and empty. After James was born, I craved a little girl. I wanted a daughter I could nurture. But I put my career first. I was very successful in my work and could not find time for another child. So much regret, and now it's too late. Geoffrey now has James to nurture, and he's reborn in this endeavour. I can only watch, and it hurts. Where is the daughter I so craved I can nurture?' She was now openly crying.

Clara put her arm around her to provide comfort as she wept. 'Janice. How can I help you? I'll do whatever I can. You have been so kind to me.'

'You have no-one. I crave a daughter. I would be truly honoured if you would be the daughter I never had. I know you're too old to be adopted, but I don't care about the formalities. I so want to nurture you and care for you as my daughter. I want a special friend with whom to share joy exclusively ours. I want all those joys only mother and daughter share. You would make me so happy and proud.'

'But I'm already part of your family and I feel the love. What more is there?'

'As things stand, I see you as the partner of James. Therefore, every time I look at you, I can also see James. I so want to look at you and only see you, my lovely daughter who I can cherish, nurture, and be my friend.'

Clara reached around so they could hug each other. She whispered in Janice's ear. 'I would love you to be my mum, and I'll try to make you proud.' They were both shedding tears as they held each other tight.

Janice whispered back. 'I'm so proud of you already. Thank you. I'll try to be a good mother. You deserve to be loved.'

After a period of reflection for both, they unwrapped from each other but still held both hands. 'Do I still call you Janice, or can I call you mum?'

'Mum would fill my heart with joy.'

'And what about Geoffrey?'

'Watch his chest swell with pride the first time you call him dad or daddy. You can even change your surname to Caldwell if this will not cause you pain.'

'Let's see how things pan out with James. If we were to marry, then my name would change to Caldwell. If not, I would have no objection to Deed Poll, but what's in a name. The love of family is all that matters.'

'You see. Your wisdom makes my heart swell. I really hope James can see the love you have for him, and he for you. Be assured, we will not interfere in your relationship. We will, at last, try to be good parents to James and nurture him into a better place regarding human relationships and hope this will open his eyes. But we now have you within our family in any event, and that makes us both so happy.'

They continued to chat in their new roles as mother and daughter. It felt calm and reassuring to Clara she now had a proper family who wanted her. Her spirits were high. Life had taken another major leap forward in providing the security of family she had so missed.

They finally decided they should return to the apartment to tell the boys their news.

When they came through the door, they could hear activity. The internal vacuum system was working, so someone must be using the built-in vacuum cleaner. Janice pushed Clara into the living area to find both Geoffrey and James engaged in household chores. Janice looked at

Clara. 'You see, they really can do when properly trained.'
They both laughed.

'Hello boys. We're back. And we have some exciting news.'

They both stopped their chores in anticipation. 'Geoffrey, we have a new and wonderful daughter, and James, you have a new sister, but legally she can still be your partner.'

Clara watched Geoffrey's chest expand as he reached to kiss her. 'Clara, my dear, you have made us both very happy. Welcome to our family.'

'Thanks, dad.' She could see the tears well in his eyes.

'Thank you, my lovely daughter. We must celebrate. James, a bottle of your finest champagne is in order.'

'On its way, dad.'

After toasting this new relationship, James needed clarification. 'How can Clara be your daughter, and my partner?'

His mother responded. 'Very simple, my dear. In relation to your father and I Clara is our daughter. As for you, she is still first and foremost your partner, although if your partnership should end, she will still be our daughter. As there is no blood relationship between you and Clara, everything is perfectly legal. Are we clear?'

'So, I never refer to Clara as my sister.'

'My dear son, I was being euphemistic. But if your partnership ended in other than marriage, she would then be referred to as your sister as far as this family is concerned. Are we now clear?'

'I can't imagine a more lovely partner or sister, and I think this new relationship is great for all of us. Clara, my darling, welcome to our family.'

He reached down to kiss her. 'Help me stand.' He put down his glass and helped her out of her wheelchair. 'I would like a family hug to seal this deal.' They all hugged together. She had a proper family again.

That evening, when they were safely in bed, Clara felt concern how James might take this new relationship. 'Darling, how do you feel about your mum wanting to be my mum?'

'My mum always wanted a daughter. When she visited you for the first time in ICU, she fell into dad's arms in tears. You had aroused maternal instincts so long buried. I'm cool with the whole idea. Think where we started with mum, and where we are today.'

'Thanks. Didn't want to cause us any problems.'

'You'll have fun with my mum as she'll dote on you. Enjoy it. I failed you but will make good. Until then my mum will make good on my deficiencies, but I'll learn.'

Chapter 47

Mum and dad had left for home. James and Clara sat together on the balcony enjoying the afternoon sunshine.

'How does it feel to be my big sister?'

'*Is he teasing me?* You know what they say about big sisters and younger brothers. If the age gap is wide, the sister will probably "mother" the brother. But if the ages are close, a big sister can be very bossy and mean and even beat up on her brother. You're probably safer being my partner.'

'Ah, ah. But how do you feel about my mom being your mother now you've slept on it?'

'On one hand, it's crazy. Could you imagine your mother being even my bosom friend just 6-months ago? But these past few weeks she has been so kind to me. I've felt nothing but genuine warmth from her. On Saturday in the park when she explained why she so wanted a daughter, I felt her sorrow. And these past few weeks rekindled how I so miss my mother. And your dad is the rock which has held us all together these past weeks. I love being part of this family, and to have a mum and dad who genuinely love and care for me fills me with gratitude and joy. I was so alone when mum died. I had no one. Now I have the loving parents I've so craved for so many years. I feel blessed.'

'You're right. These past weeks have changed all our lives. Just think how bad things would have been if it were just me who had to cope, or not, with this.'

'I would have gotten you there even if I had to beat you to death.'

'Sure. What happy days they would be. But I'm closer to mom and dad than I think I've ever been. And it feels great. My dad has shown his true nature – strong, decisive, but compassionate. He's a rock and I'm proud to have him as my dad.'

'When your dad holds me in his arms, I feel so safe.'

'He's your dad now, so get used to it.'

Chapter 48

She spent much of her week thinking and fantasising about her feelings of having a mum and dad who really care for her. Her spirit rose, energising her determination to get out of her wheelchair, back onto her feet, and enjoy this much needed joy in her life. Any thoughts of her past loneliness were banished to the depths of her mind. Any thoughts of how she felt just a few weeks ago, mostly how their relationship had deteriorated to such a low level, were fading as she watched her boy slowly, but with commitment, learn to be more caring towards her. Her overwhelming gratitude was focussed towards her new dad who had used his strength of character and compassion to transform this family into a loving and caring unit. Just thinking about him gave her a warm glow. Her only regression occurred in the night when the pain in her pelvic region as she tried to turn in the night invoked flashes of that awful night. Rubbing the injury region to find some relief, invariable connected with her scar, reminding her of the horror she could not banish from her mind. She tried to believe that time heals but struggled to believe she would ever relieve herself of her nightmares. This secret pain she kept to herself.

Chapter 49

It was after 9pm when Geoffrey and Janice arrived at the apartment. Janice walked in carrying a lightweight wheelchair made of titanium; very compact, but clearly expensive. For effect, she was carrying it with one finger as she approached Clara. 'Hello my darling. This is your new F1 sports wheelchair for the remainder of your need. Can't have my daughter wheeling around in that awful hospital chair any longer.'

Clara examined it. 'But this must have cost a fortune, and I only need it for a few more weeks.'

'Fear not my dear. It's on loan from one of our suppliers who seeks favour from my company. We are 'testing' it. If you can record any pros or cons during testing, then I'm sure they will be grateful for the feedback.'

She tried it around the living space. 'Really nice to manoeuvre, and surprisingly comfortable. Thank you.'

After supper Janice turned to Clara. 'My darling husband tells me it would be very beneficial if he spent a few days here in his professional capacity to help James restructure his business. Apparently, this is quite urgent as James has a new contract to sign which would be more beneficial within a new structure. I'm minded the agreed rules are that James does not leave you alone during the week when we're not here. However, this restructuring requires James to visit with various institutions with your father. Therefore, it's time for a mother and daughter holiday. Any ideas where you would like to go?'

'I've no idea. I can't remember the last time I had a holiday.'

'I've noticed my son has been most derelict in his care for you. We are about to change this. What type of holiday would you like?'

'Sun, sea, fresh air, and nice surroundings. Flat would be better at present.'

'I'll go get my laptop and we'll see what we can find. We have a week to prepare.'

While she was away, James asked her if she had a passport. She had never needed one.

Janice arrived with her laptop. James spoke. 'Mom, Clara doesn't have a passport.'

'More dereliction. How do you expect to take her with you on trips if you haven't organised a passport for her?'

She turned to Clara. 'Do you have your birth certificate?'

'Yes.'

'Where is it?'

'In the side drawer in my bedroom.'

'James, please retrieve this for me.'

'First requirement is to find a local photographer open tomorrow morning for your passport photos. We can download an application form, and our company travel expert can do the rest. He has ways of securing a passport in a few days. Issue resolved.' She quickly found a local photographer.

'Now where to go. Sun and sea suggests Mediterranean. A hotel with lots of amenities and few gradients.'

James whispered to Clara, 'When Mom is in organisation mode, just go with the flow. It's a military exercise for her. Very organised.' Clara smiled.

'Something we should know, James?'

'Nothing, Mom. Just having a private joke with Clara.'

'I'm sure my dear. Anyway Clara, let me show you what I've found at such short notice.' They went through resorts in Spain, Greece, and Turkey. They selected one in Turkey and quickly booked. Flights from Gatwick next Saturday morning. Janice noted they would need visas, which they could purchase online once Clara has a passport.

'I'd like to try without my wheelchair. Just use my crutches.'

'My dear, your wheelchair will get us the best seats on the plane. If you want to use sticks at the resort, no problem. Swimming should really help your recovery.'

'Now my dear, as is traditional with us girls, we need to go shopping tomorrow. West End, I think as soon as we have your passport photos. The boys can take care of the chores.'

This all took less than thirty minutes. The boys just sat there, drinking wine as they watched Janice applying her corporate steamroller approach to organisation. Clara looked on in disbelief at the military precision being applied.

'Right, my dear, all done. I think it's time for bed. Early start tomorrow, and possibly long day as I don't think you have many holiday clothes in your wardrobe. Need to fix this.'

As she lay in bed with James, she was nervous about her shopping trip as she had no idea how much money she would need. 'James, how much is tomorrow likely to cost?'

'It doesn't matter. Mom will fund everything. She's having fun with her new daughter. Just go with it. She's right. I should have done this already. I'm sorry.' Then an afterthought. 'Darling, the domestic credit card you have is completely open to you. If you want to shop, no problem. If you need to use it on holiday, it will work. It's your card to do as you please. No restrictions. I'll increase the limit on Monday to be sure you never have problems.'

She turned to kiss him on the cheek. 'Thank you. I won't abuse it.'

'Clara, my lovely Clara, you would have to try very hard against your natural criteria to ever abuse it. It's time you had some fun. School when you get back, so make the most of your break. We must have a proper holiday next year. Must stop this dereliction of duty to my wonderful lady.'

They held each other close as they drifted into slumber.

Chapter 50

They were up, breakfasted, and out of the apartment in her new titanium wheelchair by 9am. They quickly found the photographer. Job done in 15 minutes, and he had a blank passport application form. Janice bagged these items, and they were on their way choosing a taxi over the underground.

Clara found navigating the large department stores on Oxford Street in a wheelchair daunting at first, having never had the funds to use them without James. But with her mum she soon relaxed and had fun. When trying clothes, Janice needed to help her, resulting in much ceremony and laughter. They even found bikinis that discretely covered her scar, which was still prominent. They bought so much she wondered how they would get it home until she remembered who she was with, and her organisational skills. 'Simple, my dear. We buy a suitcase with wheels, and we pack all our purchases. We don't need the bags.' They not only had to buy a suitcase which was packed full, they also needed a bag for the overflow. And, of course, they chose a suitable beach bag to fulfil this need.

They arrived back at the apartment after 5pm exhausted from their trip, but Janice was feeling very good about her day out with her new daughter. They had fun. It was lovely to have a daughter to shop with.

After quick refreshments they went to Clara's bedroom to unpack. They soon realised there were not enough hangers, so they removed labels and left the clothes folded as they would need packing next week.

Once all was packed away, they gather the debris ready for disposal. 'Thanks, mum. What a lovely day. And thank you for all the beautiful things you bought for me today. I'm so happy and grateful.'

'My darling daughter, it's been a wonderful day, and it's I who am grateful. I haven't had such a lovely shopping day in ages. We must do it more often. I'm sure there is much more space in your cupboards once we get some hangers.' They laughed as they hugged each other. 'Come. Let's see what the boys have organised for dinner.'

The boys did not even feign the traditional question of money spent. The smile and joy on Clara's face was enough to mitigate any cost. They could see the mother daughter relationship had cast away the dark clouds over the past weeks. Clara would soon be back to full health, and that's all that mattered.

Chapter 51

The following week was filled with excitement for Clara. There was a buzz in the air as she tried to imagine what she would need creating one list, then another, researching the holiday location, looking at tourist information and then changing her lists with this new information before exhaustion took over requiring a nap or even sleep to recharge her batteries before continuing her quest. At least one discussion each day with mum to relate progress and accumulate more information. She was in unknown territory, but like a valiant explorer, she wanted to be prepared for anything. James took full advantage of this distraction, allowing himself time to connect with Hashem and Javid. He only responded to her needs when asked.

Clara awoke buzzing. Tomorrow she will go on holiday for the first time in many years, and the first time in a foreign country. She had studied much about Turkey on the internet, especially the area around Antalya where they would stay. After much thought and debate with mum packing was now easy. Just keep packing until the case is full.

James looked on in amusement, but ready to help, if required. He had never seen her so excited.

'Sunscreen' she shrieked. 'I don't have any sunscreen.'

'Put it on your shopping list. We can get it when we go shopping after your physio session today.'

'What else do I need? I've never done this before.'

He handed her an envelope. She opened it to find a wad of currency. She took it out. The notes declared they were Turkish Lira. 'Thank you. How much is a Turkish Lira worth?'

'Think in terms of eight Turkish Lira equals one pound. You will also find some Euros at the back. In Turkey you can barter prices; and being able to pay in Euros for larger items gives you the edge. I've given you three thousand Turkish Lira and one thousand Euros. Should keep you happy for a while. And you also have your credit card. Tip people who do good things for you in Turkish Lira – easier for them to consume it.'

'Have you been to Turkey before?'

'Yes. We went there on holiday a few years back. Really interesting place, and the people are really friendly towards Brits who tend to treat service with respect unlike some of our European neighbours who treat them like servants. Treat them well and they will be very nice to you. On the other hand, when bartering with them the bigger their smile, the more you need to barter down the price. Only when they start to cry, do you know you are close to a good price. And if they offer you Turkish tea while you barter, they are taking you seriously so accept their hospitality with good grace.'

'Sounds like fun. I've always had to barter a better price to make my money stretch as far as possible. I know this game.'

'Then you can teach mom. She has the English attitude that the price tag is the price you pay. Come on, let's have some lunch and get you to the hospital. And don't forget to tell your physio you won't be here next week.'

A very excited mum arrived waving the passport for Clara and the visas they needed to get into Turkey, but no luggage.

'Your new passport, my darling. We're ready to go have fun in the sun.'

Clara examined it as though it was some ancient relic needing great care not to risk damage. 'My own passport. Wow. Never thought I would see this day. Thanks, mum. But where's your luggage?'

'I left it in the car. No point bringing it up to only to take it down again in the morning. Dad will take us to the airport. I've packed what I need for here in dad's case. Come, show me what you've packed. I've bought additional sunscreen just in case.'

The girls disappeared into Clara's bedroom. Dad turned to James. 'She's so excited she had a day off work today just to pack. Do we know this woman?'

They both smiled. 'Come, dad. You must need a drink.'

Chapter 52

Their plane departed Gatwick Airport at 10:40am so they needed to get to the airport before 9am. It was about a 40-minute drive so they were up and ready by 8am. Clara had chosen clothes to facilitate her using the toilet on the plane should this prove necessary. As she had never flown before she could only be guided by her mum but realised the space was tight so she would likely have to cope on her own.

They arrived at the airport in good time and Janice ensured Clara used her wheelchair for check-in knowing this would likely secure them good seats and priority boarding. Again, her infectious smile won the day with the check-in lady.

They said their goodbyes to the boys and made their way through security. As this was all new to Clara, they wondered through the duty-free shops and explored the departure area. They decided to have a toilet stop before boarding and hope this would suffice until they landed at Antalya.

The 4-hour flight was uneventful. Although Clara did need to visit a toilet about 30-minutes before landing, she held it until in the airport.

Whereas Gatwick Airport, being a hub airport, is convenient for wheelchair users, Antalya, being a provincial airport, required much navigation via lifts, including a much-needed toilet stop, to reach Passport Control. But this task was straightforward as their detour around the airport meant most of the queue had already been processed, and the officer handed her visa back without even looking at it, stamped her passport and waived her through. She waited for mum before making their way to the baggage hall to collect their cases. They both felt the dramatic increase in temperature since leaving Gatwick, as the evening temperature was still 24C.

The airport was buzzing with tourists and a multitude of holiday reps seeking their charges. They soon found their rep and were quickly directed to a waiting minibus, leaving their cases with a resort porter. There was only another couple so were quickly on their way for the 40-minute drive to their resort village.

As is normal in Mediterranean countries, the sun sets early and quickly. As it was after 8pm when they reached their destination, it was practically dark. All they could see whilst travelling the coast road was the near full moon shimmering on the sea.

The meet and greet was friendly, inviting them to sit at a low table to enjoy a cocktail and hot towel. Mum already knew this routine was an attempt to blur the onerous documentation process to check-in but knew there was no choice so get past it as soon as possible.

Their check-in lady, Angelina, had a name tag showing she could speak English, French, Italian and Spanish. She was introducing them to the resort. 'The resort has both a hotel and a village with individual villas. I see you have booked a villa in the Village', showing them on a map of the resort where they would stay. 'As your villa is some distance from the hotel, and it's not practical for you to eat at one of our village restaurants this evening, could I suggest you have something to eat at the snack bar here in the hotel which has a wide range of food, and then we'll transport you to your villa. We'll take your luggage now and have it delivered to your villa. Come to reception when you have eaten, and I'll organise a buggy to take you to your villa.'

Chapter 53

The sun was defeating the attempt of the curtains to block light entering the room. The air conditioning was in full voice, confirming the outside temperature was attempting to penetrate their controlled environment. Clara needed the toilet, but Janice was still sleeping. She reached for her chair but missed the arm, pushing it against the wall with a thud. Janice immediately awoke.

'My dear, what are you trying to do?'

'I need the toilet, but you were asleep.'

Janice jumped out of bed, helped her to the bathroom and planted her on the toilet. 'Now you listen to me, young lady. If you need help with anything, I'm not asleep; I'm not too busy. Do you hear me? Even in the middle of the night. We're here to have fun, so no stress. You're my lovely daughter. Get used to having a caring mum around. I've waited years to have a daughter. Indulge me.'

Clara sat on the toilet, smiling. 'Yes, mum.'

'Now we're up how about we shower and go see what this place has to offer for breakfast?'

The breakfast area comprised a central, partially covered assortment of self-service servers backed by a series of covered booths where hot food is prepared to order. To the front there were several covered eating areas. As they approached, they noted two people greeting guests – a short stocky man probably in his 30s with a boyish face and short-cropped black hair. A younger and pretty blonde female flanked him. Once at the entrance, the man came to greet them.

'Good morning and welcome. My name is Birkan, and I'm the restaurant manager.' Looking at Clara, 'As I would remember your lovely smile anywhere, this must be your first visit.'

'Yes, it is,' acknowledging his cheeky charm. 'My name is Clara, and this is my mum, Janice.'

'Dear Clara, may I show you and your lovely mum around our humble restaurant to show you where you can find what you want?'

'That would be very kind of you. Thank you.'

She started to rotate the wheels of her wheelchair. 'Excuse me, dear Clara. We have taxi service here to ensure your safety. We will first have guided tour of the restaurant, find you nice table, and then will collect what you wish to eat.'

Birkan took the chair handles and started their tour, making beep-beep noises when he needed people to make room for them. After showing her the total fare on offer, he wheeled her into the adults only section and parked her at a table for four. A waiter came to join them.

'Clara, this is Omer, our most prized waiter who will take care of you throughout your stay with us when you use this restaurant. He will now come with us to collect what you wish to eat and then take care of you.'

Janice, realising her daughter's infectious smile was yet again attracting the required attention, went to secure poached eggs on toast. Soon they were both sitting together enjoying breakfast. 'This is so lovely, mum. These people are so nice, I'm having fun already. Thank you for bringing me here.'

'My darling, you deserve oodles of fun. Let's go with the flow and enjoy ourselves. What would you like to do after breakfast?'

'Maybe we should explore our options and then plan accordingly. Now I can see this place in daylight, it's so beautiful. Magnificent gardens, and so much beach front.

Why don't we go change for the beach and then go exploring?'

They soon discovered the site comprised two parts, the hotel complex, and the Village complex, each having their own pool, bar, and restaurant area. They passed through the Village complex to find an Adults Only area with infinity pool, bar, and sunbed area. Back towards the Village complex they walked through a parade of small shops, past the open-air theatre, arriving at the rear of the spa complex where they found a 20m long aqua pool. 'Mum, this is what I need. Can we try it?'

The aqua pool was empty. The aqua jets were at peace. Janice helped her to sit on the poolside at one end with her feet dangling in the water. She got in to help her daughter into the pool. There were rails on each side just below the water level, which they noted was 1.4m. She held onto the handrail with her left hand. Mum was on her righthand side, holding her other hand. She stood for a moment to get her balance. Her instinct was to put her weight on her right leg, but knew she had to let the left leg know it needed to share the load. Gingerly, she moved some of her weight to the left leg until she thought she had equilibrium. 'Okay, mum, let's try this.'

'One step at a time, my dear. We have plenty of time.'

She sent a silent message to her left leg to instruct it to lift and move forward. Her leg started to rise, using her foot as a lever. She was now on her toes. Another instruction to lift her toes. The pain shot through her abdomen. Mum felt the jolt and the tension but said nothing. She tried again but this time with the expectation of pain which made it more tolerable. Her foot was floating above the bottom of the pool. Her next silent instruction was to move her left hip forward. The hip responded, but the resistance of the water on her leg caused further pain. She gritted her teeth and moved her leg forward before planting her foot back on the bottom of the pool. She then moved her right leg to the same place, momentarily putting all load on her left leg. Mum looked at her. The pain had brought tears to her eyes.

'One small step, my dear. Do you want to try another?'

'I want to get to the end of the pool if you can bear with me.'

'My dear, you set the goal and we'll do it together.'

It took over 20 minutes to cover the 20m length of the pool. The left side of her abdomen was racked with pain. She turned to mum, tears rolling down her cheeks; half from the pain, and half from the joy of completing her goal. Mum wrapped her in her arms '*What a gutsy lady*' as tears welled in her eyes. Clara held onto her mum until the pain had dulled and she could stand again with minimal support.

'You did really well, but that's enough for now. Let's go relax a little.'

'Mum, I want to come back later and do this again. I could move my leg. I want it to understand it must do better.'

'With you as it's mistress, it will most surely comply but be a little patient. Listen to your body. Come, let me help you out, and I'll fetch your chair.'

Once back in her chair wrapped in a towel, mum noticed they were outside the spa building. 'Let's go see what they have to offer. You might need a massage after your aqua therapy.'

They approach the reception desk to be greeted by an infectious smile, almost as beguiling as Clara at her best.

'Welcome to our spa. Can I show you what we have on offer?'

At that moment a woman, tall, slim but strong, probably early 30s came towards them.

Speaking to Clara, 'Hi, my name is Tanya, the physio specialist here. I just watched you in the aqua pool. You are some gutsy lady. Can you tell me about your injury, and can I help you with your recovery?'

'My name is Clara, and this is my mum, Janice. Someone stabbed me nearly eight weeks ago here,' pointing to her wound. 'I want to use your facilities to try to walk again.'

'My God. Who would stab such a beautiful woman?' She turned to the receptionist, 'Book Clara in for a free assessment with me now.' Turning to Clara, 'What's your room number?'

'103A in the Village.'

'Come with me. Let's see what we can do for such a brave lady.'

They entered a treatment room. 'Can I help you onto the treatment couch?'

'But I'm still wet from the aqua pool.'

Tanya put a towel on the couch. 'Don't worry about that. I need to get you where I can examine you', as she helped her onto the couch.

'Now tell me as much as you can about your injury.'

Clara related the incident and the hospitalisation with mum filling any gaps. Clara showed her the scar.

Tanya, pointing to her scar, 'So the knife entered here puncturing your femoral artery. Thus, the likely muscular damage is Rectus Femoris, Tensor Fasciae Latae, and the Sartorius. Would you mind if I had a feel to check this, as the artery puncture will have healed by now. This might feel uncomfortable. If you can avoid tensing the area, it would help me.'

Tanya probed deep into her pelvis around the scar. 'And you only have physio once each week. Does your physio probe you like I just did?'

'No. She concentrates on mobility.'

'Clara, let me tell you what I can feel, and what I think. If you then want me to help you, we need some concentrated effort, as once each week, and no attention to the extensive amount of scarring tissue I feel, will not get you back to normal walking.'

At this point mum interjected. 'Could you explain to me what you have diagnosed and your proposed treatment? I'm a biochemist so you can be technical.'

'Great. We define neuromuscular control as the unconscious trained response of a muscle to a signal regarding dynamic joint stability. The movements of the lower extremity, including the knee joint, are controlled through this system, which needs to provide the correct messaging for purposeful movement. Neuromuscular training programs should address several aspects of sensorimotor function and functional stabilisation to improve objective function and alleviate symptoms. Based on biomechanical and neuromuscular principles, the aims are to improve sensorimotor control and achieve compensatory functional stability. Unlike conventional strength training, neuromuscular exercise addresses the quality of movement and emphasises joint control in all three biomechanical/movement planes.'

'Interesting prognosis. What would you suggest is needed?'

'Neuromuscular exercise has effects on functional performance, biomechanics, and muscle activation patterns of the surrounding joint musculature. Simply restoring mechanical restraints is not enough for the functional recovery of a joint because of the coordinated neuromuscular controlling mechanism. A lag in the neuromuscular reaction time can result in dynamic joint instability. The hip, in this incidence, will without doubt be compromised. Therefore, both mechanical stability and neuromuscular control are probably important for long-term functional outcome, and we must consider both aspects in the design of a neuromuscular rehabilitation program.'

'Impressive. What do you see as the issues that have not been addressed, or need address?'

'Impairments are present at different levels of the sensorimotor system, from sensory input through integration and processing of information in the central nervous system to motor output to perform voluntary movements and maintain postural control. Some suggest that sensorimotor dysfunction also may play a role in the development and progression of degenerative joint disease. Neural inhibition caused by factors such as pain, swelling, inflammation, scarring, joint laxity, and damage to sensory receptors in the joint prevents the muscle to be fully activated, likely through altered excitability of spinal and supraspinal pathways.'

'Sensorimotor deficiencies will also be found in the non-injured leg compared with controls possibly because of factors such as physical inactivity after the injury, inherently poor function, and/or disturbed sensory feedback from the injured joint with an inhibitory effect of muscle activation also on the non-injured side. We have repeatedly shown that training the non-injured side has beneficial effects to the injured side, prompting strength and proprioceptive gains.'

'I see what you're saying. She needs to consider mobility issues for both legs after this 7-week period of inactivity. What do you propose?'

Clara is listening to this conversation, thinking it sounded like the geeks having a discussion. She could only lie back and marvel at such a technical discussion with her mum. *'Good job she's here with me.'*

'In normal circumstances I would suggest that we consider blood restriction training but as we have an arterial involvement, I think this contraindicated.'

Thinking for a moment, 'The involvement of electro-stimulation would without doubt be beneficial in this case as this modality is ideal for including through active movement rather than in static isolation. Placing this equipment on a patient whilst cycling or performing lower limb exercises increases muscular recruitment to 100% muscle fibre engagement compared to an active cognitive contraction of around 40%. If we build a program for Clara, I'll take you to Christina, or Chrissie to her friends, our performance coach, who has the skills and equipment to radically improve recovery and mobility.'

Janice was in awe. 'I'm impressed with your knowledge. What is someone so well versed in rehabilitation doing here?'

Chrissie and I are physio and rehab specialists for elite winter athletes, so we spend our summers here. After 6-months in winter training camps with an injury rate that would test most medical facilities, we come here to relax and study as a sprained ankle per day is about as testing as it gets here. We occasionally get excited when someone has a tumble playing tennis or soccer.' They all laughed. 'But Clara needs help, and I would like to help her after what I witnessed this morning. And I'm sure Chrissie will be happy to help. Getting people back on their feet is our speciality.'

'What type of program do you propose?'

'I'll need at least two half-hour sessions with Clara each day, and a good massage towards the end of the day will help. I could do this, or one of the other masseurs can do it. We'll have to talk to Chrissie about her involvement. We will have to charge you for the formal sessions, but we can add a few informal sessions as well. Each time Clara goes into the aqua pool I want to spend a few moments preparing the nodes of her muscles as her chair will likely relax them again until we can convince them to fully awaken and stay awake.'

'Don't concern yourself about cost. If you can get my daughter back onto her feet, it will be worth every penny. What do you think, my darling?'

'Sounds great to me. I'll do whatever it takes. I have my sticks with me if this will help.'

'That's useful to know, but not today. Let's put a plan together after we've spoken with Chrissie.'

Janice was now truly connected using her technical skills. 'What do you think you can achieve in the six days available?'

If Clara is willing to put in the effort, which will involve some pain, we could probably have her walking a few steps on her own, but further with aid. I can certainly deal with the scaring and reactivate the muscles. She will need some strong anti-inflammatories, but I have suitable ones if you will allow me. She will need much more effort when she gets home. I have a colleague who takes care of the UK Winter Sports Team. I could contact her to see if she can help if you wish. She's not in London, but not far away. I'll email her with your consent to see if she can help, and where.'

Clara piped in. 'Please do whatever you think will help me. You'll have no complaints from me. Just tell me what to do.'

'Okay. We'll go see Chrissie when we've finished here, as I would like to start on this scarring. This should have occurred in the early rehab phase – but has not been done. It's sad when physios don't address this. I appreciate there is an arterial issue, but with the deftest of touch, if they do not compromise the wound, it can work well respecting any tissue layer issues. Scars stick down and trauma causes soft tissue to stick together like tar on a blanket, so early scar management and hydrotherapy movement patterns will be our initial way forward. I want to start to break this scarring so that the lymph system will take the

149

inflammation away. Then we get you back in the aqua pool later today. Can I start? It won't be pleasant, but in a few days, you will reap the benefit.'

'Go for it.'

Tanya wove her magic around the scar, slowly penetrating deeper and deeper into her pelvic region. Janice could see the tears of pain welling in her daughter's eyes, but not so much as a whimper. *I've been blessed with a truly magnificent daughter. I will get her through this whatever it takes.'*

After some minutes Tanya stopped her treatment. 'That's enough for now. We'll try again after your aqua pool session, which I suggest between 4 and 5 o'clock. I'll reset your muscle nodes before you enter the water. You should notice a significant difference to your efforts this morning. Are you on any medication?'

'No. I have pain killers when I need them.'

Tanya reached into her bag and produced a blister pack of pills. 'Stop any other medication and use these only when you need them. No more than 3 per day and keep one for about an hour after your last treatment each day to help ease the pain and flush out any inflammation overnight. I think you need one now. I'll get you some water.'

Whilst I think of it, we'll need to look at your diet. Are you eating well such as essential fatty acids, vitamin C, digestive enzymes, and magnesium?'

Janice was quick to respond. 'I've ensured her diet complies with the requirements for a fast rehab. I've also increased her intake of zinc, selenium, magnesium, and iron in readily absorbed forms.'

'Sorry, I forgot your biochemist background. Sounds good. Lots of good fresh fruit and honey here, so take advantage of it.'

Chrissie was a tall, blue eyes, and long blonde hair, classic stereotypical skier. The gym was large, well-equipped, but devoid of people. Chrissie explained people use the gym at the beginning of the day and late afternoon, preferring the beach during the day. Tanya quickly appraised Chrissie of the problem, and the need for a rehab program. Chrissie examined Clara's legs, asking her to try to lift them, first her good leg, and then her injured leg. More talk between Tanya and Chrissie.

Chrissie squatted in front of Clara. 'Okay Clara, you have one good leg that has been asleep for 7-weeks and one not so good leg that needs to start working again. What I want to do is to wake up your good leg to let it know it needs to work again and use this to get your other leg functioning again. We want your not so good leg to learn from your good leg. This makes for a faster, more balanced recovery. We good so far?'

'What do you want me to do?'

'We start this afternoon at 3 o'clock here. Bring your sticks so we can see how well you manage. No accidents in this program. I will bring my electro-stimulator so we can announce to your quads in both legs that they need to wake up. I will also assess what exercises will best help you. Then you go see Tanya, who will reset the sleepy nodes in your pelvic region after which you go into the aqua pool with your sticks, so you are uniformly balanced. But only use the sticks for balance. The less support by the sticks, the more your legs will need to work. Your mum can be there to encourage, but you need to be balanced when you walk. After that you go back to Tanya for an assessment, massage, and possible ice bath. That will be more than enough today for your pain thresholds.'

'Your daily program from tomorrow will be here at 10 o'clock, then quickly to Tanya for node reset, into the aqua pool, and then take it easy until 3 o'clock, back here, over to Tanya, into the pool, and back to Tanya for assessment and treatment. We'll get you onto sticks as fast as we can. If you feel like a swim during your rest period, it would be useful. But only crawl, not breaststroke. You can also hold on to the poolside and kick your feet. Sound good?'

'Sounds great. Thank you so much for helping me.'

'We enjoy helping people who realise we are not a golden bullet. You have shown your grit to Tanya so let's make this happen.'

Both Janice and Clara left the gym feeling buoyed by the commitment of these lovely ladies to help with her rehab. Time to explore more of the site, have some lunch, and then chill before showtime at 3 o'clock.

They sat relaxing in the open-air restaurant after dinner, reflecting on the day. The afternoon session with Chrissie was more about what she could do in the way of exercise. And the electro-stimulator attached to her quads was a source of great amusement as her muscles appeared to dance as the stimulator forced the muscles to contract.

Tanya had come to the poolside to activate her nodes before she and mum lowered her into the pool. Mum had stood facing her, walking backwards as she progressed, ready to catch her if she stumbled. The difference from the morning yielded tears of joy rather than pain as she completed the walk in just 8 minutes.

Tanya was pleased with progress, giving her more scar treatment and a massage before 5-minutes in an ice bath, and then relaxing with some herbal tea. She had taken her second pill of the day just prior to leaving their room for dinner. No pain, only a funny sensation in her quads and knees from the stimulator session. 'Mum, I think my legs have got the message they need to wake up.' They both laughed.

Although they knew there would be a show at 9 o'clock, they both felt an early night was in order after such a gruelling day with more tomorrow.

Janice went to sleep reflecting on the day feeling good about her new role with her daughter. *'What a great idea to come on holiday together. Now I feel like her real mum.'*

Chapter 54

Back in London, James and his father were meeting with EMULATE's corporate auditors, who were also assuming the financial accounting role until such time as the company undertakes this task. Although one of the larger accountancy companies, it impressed his father that EMULATE commanded oversight by a partner, and this partner, Alan Bishop, was conducting the disclosure to his father as corporate banker.

They spent over four hours, including a working lunch, plotting growth since incorporation, projecting revenues for the reasonable duration of existing licence agreements, projecting revenues for agreements under negotiation, and how to structure the company to take advantage of enterprise grants from both the UK and the EU. Geoffrey was stunned with the quality of the information provided, having to check himself as he was there as a corporate banker, not as the father wishing to congratulate his son on the incredible performance of his enterprise. However, Geoffrey was able to suggest valuable considerations regarding the nature of a corporate restructure, and it was agreed the partner would participate in a meeting with the corporate lawyer tomorrow to define the earn-in for Hashem and Javid, and to modify the licence agreements not least to allow for transfer of ownership without disturbing the integrity of the licence.

Once out of the building, Geoffrey could not contain his pride in his son's achievements. 'Son, I'm truly impressed with what you've achieved. When I proposed to my bank that a less than 3-year-old corporate warranted corporate banking oversight, there was clearly some scepticism, especially as the owner is my son. When they see these numbers, they will certainly want you as a client and offer you preferential treatment. This will be a fee-based relationship as you don't need any financing, although I will suggest you consider using leases for your technology acquisitions, not least because the way you use technology renders it obsolete quickly. We can provide lease finance cheaper than you could arrange an overdraft. Although you will tell me you can pay for technology out of cash flow, leasing will be more tax beneficial. Now I have some ideas of your projected technology spend I'll put an example together to illustrate the benefits of leasing.'

They saw a Costa coffee shop, so stopped for coffee. 'What we must do son is to find a valuable use of your spare cash flow. This evening it would be useful if I outline some ideas I have as I'm sure you will not have considered the idea of targeted acquisition, for example, where we, the bank, identify a corporate target that needs development finance in exchange for a valuable interest. As a bank, we cannot engage in such financing, but we can offer it to our preferred clients as a private placement secure in the knowledge we will have used our expertise to fully evaluate the prospects of such business, so you don't need to seek these opportunities, or to conduct expensive due diligence. Likewise, you may identify a target during your activities you may want to quietly build an interest. We could do this on your behalf thus not alerting the target to your interest.'

'Is this what you do as a bank? Seek out targets and then place them with your clients. Will a bank like yours be looking at EMULATE as a target?'

'If not now, certainly within the near future. Your revenue streams will attract much attention. But this is another of our roles. We will seek out anyone taking an interest in one of our clients. We will alert you to such interest and evaluate whether this attention should be pursued, but on our terms, or to protect you from any hostile approach. This is all part of our corporate banking product, and why we charge for these valuable services. You will get most, if not all, of my time this week as an introduction to my bank. I will make you a formal proposal to act as your corporate banker. If you accept, we will agree a fee retainer, and then our fees for various activities we can offer. That's how it works.'

'Wow. I have much to learn about the corporate jungle. Glad I have you on my side.'

'If my bank knew I am actively restructuring EMULATE this week without charge, they would not be happy.'

'But dad. I don't want to cause you trouble with the bank.'

'Fear not, son. I'm merely endorsing what has already been proposed to you by your auditors and conducting the due diligence with your lawyers to ensure the level of corporate integrity required by the bank. When they see you have oversight from a partner at your auditors, and your lawyer is a partner of a reputable law firm, any thoughts of impropriety on my part will evaporate. I know my bank and how they think.'

'As long as you're sure. I can happily pay you for this week.'

'I know son, but what I do this week I should have offered long ago as a father. Come, let's away. I have much to consider for our meeting with your lawyer tomorrow.'

Chapter 55

When they arrived at the corporate law firm, Alan Bishop was already there. They were quickly shown to a meeting room where Simon was already present.

They went through the proposed changes to the companies' Articles of Association, the earn-in proposal for Hashem and Javid, which had been prepared in draft form after a conversation with Geoffrey during their meeting yesterday. Geoffrey further explained the transfer of banking arrangements, the agreement to recognise the interest of Clara in the fashion project, and other thoughts he had for consideration. After some two hours, all agreed on the way forward. The draft agreements for Hashem and Javid would be available for collection in the morning.

Having finished their meeting, they went back to the apartment.

'Son, can I talk to you about something that has been bothering me, and for which I have a proposal for remedy?'

'Sure. What is it?'

'You remember we had a chat about using Clara as a commodity.'

'I don't use her as a commodity, but I understand what you mean.'

'Tell me son, what happens to her if, God forbid, something happens to you? What does she have? Where does she go?'

'To you and mom by all accounts.'

'But what assets will she have to rebuild her life? Have you made a Will, for instance?'

'No. Haven't thought about it.'

'I would like you to put this right both in terms of a Will, and a Settlement Agreement if you part company for any reason.'

'The Will is easy. Everything goes to Clara. What do you mean by a Settlement Agreement?'

155

'I've drawn up an agreement between you and Clara, and for which I will be custodian, that makes provision for Clara as would be appropriate if you got divorced. I would like you to do this for Clara and let her know why you want such an agreement to protect her interests.'

'Dad, I have already made her an equal partner in our fashion project. I expect the result to be worth millions. Isn't this provision enough?'

'That's in the future, thus still speculative. I want you to provision for her now, so she has certainty. I think you owe her certainty, even though I don't believe she will ever use it on her account. It will be you who terminates your relationship or causes termination, not her.'

'Dad, I love Clara. There is no way I want to end our relationship. She's my rock and my very reason for being. Why would I even consider termination?'

'Then you should have no objection to such an arrangement unless you marry her.'

'That makes more sense to me. I think I've known from the beginning she's the one for me.'

'Then why haven't you asked her to marry you?'

'Sure, Dad. I come to you and mom in those early days and tell you I want to marry a girl with her background. Mom would go ballistic. Today it's possible, but will Clara accept my proposal? I haven't exactly shown myself worthy of her.'

'Son, the one thing I'm sure of is you and Clara are made for each other. This has been clear to me from the day you both had breakfast with us. I agree your mother would not have seen what I saw in her back then, but everything has changed. Your mother would certainly give her blessing, but I sense Clara still needs you to show her you really care for her. Until then I think you need to provision for her to at least let her know you want to care for her.'

'What is this agreement you want me to sign?'

'It provisions a little over £500,000 for her in the event you separate. I calculated this amount from your books, considering the likely award in the event of divorce.'

'Wow. Some settlement.'

'She's worth more for what she's done for you.'

'Sorry dad. Didn't mean it that way. The Will is fine. This should be easy. If we have time, we could go back to my lawyer and do this tomorrow. As for the settlement, I would like to try proposing to her first to see if she will marry me.'

'Okay son, but I suspect you need to be ready for her refusal. Don't go for the traditional on your knee proposal – could be embarrassing for both of you. Just talk about it in conversation. Don't take refusal badly. Use the refusal to extract what you need to do to win her hand. Remember, faint heart never won fair maiden. She's not about to leave you so no burnt pride. You'll learn much about where you are in her eyes. Valuable information for your cause.'

'Do you really think she'll refuse my proposal?'

'I suspect she might think you are asking out of guilt for what happened. Or she still does not yet see you as the man to take care of her. Who knows, but my instinct is she's not ready to say *yes* to such a proposal.'

'Wow. But at least let me try. If you're right, I'll look at your agreement as, in principle, you're right that I need to do something for her after everything that has happened. I'll try to find the right moment during this next week.'

'Good enough, but prepare for the worst, and accept a rebuttal as a first step to achieving your goal.'

'I hear you.'

'By the way, I forgot to tell you I now have an injury settlement agreed for Clara. They have awarded her £12,000 which will be in her account when she returns. I can invest this for her if she wishes, as her account is very liquid. She could benefit from investing in an ISA with us. I must admit I have some reservations about speaking to her about the outcome of the trial as I don't want to revisit that awful night with her just yet, but she will see the funds in her account.'

'Are you telling me my wise owl of a dad can't find an answer to this conundrum? Only joking. I agree we should not revisit that night any time soon. What about if I casually tell her after you and mom have left, probably Monday, that she should receive a settlement into her account feigning I don't know the details, but you could invest it for her if she wishes? She should speak to you when she next sees you and hope she forgets all about it. If she wants you to invest it, either of us can give you a heads up and you can bring any paperwork you need next weekend.'

'Okay, son, I'll go with that. Don't want to distress her after so much excellent progress.'

'By the way, what was the outcome of the trial? I wasn't asked to attend Court.'

'Apparently the observation by the police when they visited for your statement regarding mitigation was presented to the Court but rejected on a technicality that Clara was the victim of the stabbing, but she did not provoke her assailant. The assailant, a repeat offender, was jailed for 6 years. The Injuries Compensation Committee did not challenge me regarding the claim I made for her.'

'Thanks, dad. I wouldn't have thought about compensation. Much to learn. Let's have dinner.'

Chapter 56

First thing Wednesday morning James phoned Simon to alert him he needed a Will and life assurance in favour of Clara. Simon confirmed the draft agreements for Hashem and Javid are ready for collection, as is a copy of the amendments to the Articles of Association.

After collecting these documents, they visited the office to sit with Hashem and Javid to explain their agreements. Geoffrey offered the services of the bank as trustee to their agreements if they so required. They appeared happy and would seek execution when they had studied them. They then had a meeting, including Hell, where Geoffrey explained the new corporate structure and banking arrangements. Hell was the interface with the accountants, so needed this information. Geoffrey noted her capable attention to detail having ignored her unconventional dress albeit not out of place in this environment.

It was lunchtime so James, Hashem, Javid and Geoffrey adjourned to Fredericks for lunch where discussion showed to Geoffrey the enthusiasm for the fashion project, albeit they aired complications that would take some effort to overcome.

After lunch Geoffrey left James at the office as he wanted to visit another client whilst in London. They agreed to meet back at the apartment.

Chapter 57

They were sitting having breakfast. 'Son, we have successfully completed our restructuring, and I hope you're happy with the outcome.'

'Sure, dad. I've learnt so much this week. Thanks for spending so much time with me.'

'It was a genuine pleasure and eye-opener to see just how well my extraordinary son is doing. I'm happy I could add something to such a wonderful enterprise. But we have a couple of days before the girls' return. I'm not inclined to return to my office as it gives us the opportunity to spend some time together. Any thoughts on what we could do?'

'I've taken the opportunity of this break to meet with Simon Attwood, the Principal of Clara's college at 11 o'clock, and then to lunch. I need to sweeten him to ensure Clara can get her college lectures online as she's due to start again in a couple of weeks, but she's not ready to attend.'

'Would it be appropriate to join you as I would like to see where she studies.'

'No problem, as he will surely ask where we are with the fashion engine project. Your being there will alleviate any thoughts he might have I'm overselling the story. After all, you're not only my dad, your also my corporate banker. Would I exaggerate in front of such integrity?'

They laughed. 'Do we need to be dressed?'

'This is an art college. What do they know about suits and ties?'

They arrived at the Principal's office to be greeted by his PA, Jan. 'Hello, James. How's Clara? We all heard about that nasty attack. When will she be back with us?'

'*Do I need reminding of this?* She's doing fine. Not ready to come back yet, but hopefully only a few weeks away.'

'That's great news. Please give her our best wishes.'

159

'Thank you. I will.'

'Simon's ready for you, so please go in.'

As they entered, Simon rose from his desk to greet them. 'Hi Simon. This is Geoffrey, my father, and EMULATE's corporate banker. He wanted to see where Clara studies.'

'Very pleased to meet you. Nothing like keeping it in the family. And how is darling Clara?'

'She's getting back on her feet, and the reason I wanted to visit with you. As things stand, she's unlikely to be ready to start college for a few weeks yet, but I don't want her to play catch-up. With your permission I'd like to deploy some of our technology so we can stream lectures to her at home, and email notes to her.'

'You're willing to deploy your own resources to facilitate this?'

'Of course, so long as it's not intrusive. We have the technology to do this.'

'Is this the technology for our fashion project? And how is your project progressing?'

'The technology we need for streaming lectures is trivial compared with the technology for our fashion project. We've invested around £500,000 on this project to date, over half of which is in technology, and I've budgeted this to more than double over the coming months. Computer engines of such sophistication do not come cheap. Our target is to be ready for your end-of-year graduation show, but we're really having a problem understanding how designers pattern their clothes. It's a real headache trying to find the detail we need.'

'Our librarian informs me Clara has been keeping her busy for a few weeks now. But I sense the detail you need is still beyond her knowledge. I think you should have a meeting with our most senior design lecturer who understands this mysterious subject to find what you need. Your impressive investment to date certainly warrants our assistance.'

'That would be incredible. When can we do this?'

He reached for his phone and selected the speed dial for Professor Cynthia Crawford, Senior Lecturer in Design Techniques. 'Cynthia, my darling, we are part of a project to develop a computerised fashion simulator. The very bright designer is sitting with me in need of some sophisticated aspects of clothing design. It would be helpful and appreciated if you could spend some time understanding his obvious frustration and relieving him of his pain.'

'Thank you, my darling. When would suit you? His availability will concur with yours.' He looked at James. '3 o'clock tomorrow?'

James indicated this was okay. 'Great Cynthia. I'll make sure he finds you. Thank you so much. Bye.'

'That's wonderful. Thank you.'

'Do you need any other assistance as I'm intrigued to know what you intend to deliver?'

'This project is a real learning curve, so one step at a time. Rigby & Peller have provided fantastic data about different bust types and bra design. And they'll help us to dress models as we run simulations on our catwalk.'

'You have your own catwalk? My goodness. And support from such an elite establishment. Now I really am intrigued.'

The credibility job done, he wanted to get Simon back onto the subject of streaming lectures. 'Our intention is to revolutionise the way the fashion industry relates to its customer base. But we still have the issue of ensuring Clara does not fall behind with her studies.'

'This is no problem. Why do you think we're all here in our so-called summer recess? This college runs summer school programs, which are also streamed all over the world, and we contribute to the Open University, so we have all the technology to ensure the heroic Clara misses nothing. I will ensure they activate this until she returns.'

The relief on James's face did not go unnoticed by his father. '*Well done, son. You are one hell of a charmer. You'll go far.*'

'Thank you so much, Simon. I came here with two weights on my shoulders, and you've lifted both. I owe you an excellent lunch. Shall we?'

Chapter 58

'Good morning, my darling. It's our last day here. What would you like to do?'

'After breakfast, and my morning walk in the pool, I think a little shopping, especially for the boys, might be in order. A last walk this afternoon and visit with Tanya and Christina, not least to thank them for their kindness this week. I have some local currency. A good tip for both is in order. And we must not forget the kindness of Omer. What a lovely man.'

'Sounds like a busy day. We better get ourselves up and out of here.'

As James and his father were enjoying breakfast together, it became apparent to both that their endeavours during the week left the apartment looking neglected. This would not be the appropriate welcome home for the girls tomorrow.

'Okay, son, you have your meeting with Cynthia Crawford this afternoon. Any idea how long you're likely to be with her?'

'I think as long as it takes whilst I have the opportunity.'

'Can I suggest we stock the larder this morning and start to repair our neglect of the apartment before lunch? Then you go to your meeting while I finish here. We can reconvene for dinner this evening. Does this sound like a plan?'

'Sounds good to me. Why don't we have a quick pub lunch and go to Arabella, our local Italian restaurant this evening? Give us a chance to recap on the week.'

'Good idea. Let's get started. Better make a list for shopping so we don't forget anything.'

After lunch James needed a little time to reflect on what he wanted out of the meeting this afternoon, as this meeting is an unplanned opportunity he did not want to waste. He retreated to his computer suite whilst his father continued to restore the apartment to the anticipated expectations of the girls.

He left at 2:30 with a list of questions he wanted to ask, and unusually nervous. He felt decidedly lacking in knowledge to be facing a professor.

The PA to Simon led James to the office of Cynthia and made the introductions. Cynthia was probably in her early 40s, of slim build with an attractive face with a chiselled jaw which gave her a serious, but not forbidding look.

'Simon has briefed me on your project, and your association with the lovely Clara. Please give her my best wishes, and we look forward to her return as soon as she feels able. How can I help you?'

It was past 5:30 when James left, knowing he must immediately visit with Hashem and Javid. He called his father to alert him the meeting went so well he now needs to speak with his partners and would call again when leaving the office.

His excitement during the meeting with Hashem, and particularly Javid, enthused them to the opportunity on offer by Cynthia. It was an offer they could not refuse, not least because this project would now be a mainstream project of EMULATE where James would surrender his 50% share into EMULATE Corporation. They all agreed, without reservation, Clara must retain her 50% share, but the project now needed to move up a gear and would need the resources of EMULATE to make it work. Having agreed strategy with his partners, it was now time to alert his father to his alternative plan as some restructuring would be necessary at a corporate level. He phoned his father to say he was on his way, and then Arabella to inform them he and his father would be there within the hour.

It was 8:30 by the time they were seated for dinner. His father detected a level of excitement in his son as he quickly ordered and ready to speak.

'Dad, we need to change some work we did this week. Cynthia was great. She so loves this project she wants to contribute, and all she wants out of it is the exclusive right to publish papers about the project when completed. She will contribute her own time and thus we can keep all our work secret from the college until we're ready to launch. I sense Simon is a self-promotion junky, stealing all the limelight from his staff. She suggested I keep the detail of our work secret from him before we unveil it. He has the air of a latent rockstar.'

'Slow down, son. I can see you're excited, but remember I was not a fly on the wall this afternoon so can you explain what happened.'

'Sorry, Dad. This project has just taken a step-change in sophistication which even has Hashem and Javid buzzing. We need to embrace this opportunity, but we also need to adapt the way we develop this engine. The resource commitment requires this to be an EMULATE project, and I agreed this with both Hashem and particularly Javid who will work directly with Cynthia as there is no way Clara can deliver so we need to be sensitive to how Clara will react.'

'Stop, son. Tell me how this will affect Clara as this is supposed to be her project.'

'It's okay, dad. I will stay true to my commitment to her, but she needs help, which is not part of her curriculum until her third year. Cynthia is prepared to change the curriculum for year two to incorporate some of the detailed knowledge required to keep Clara relevant. But I need this data now. There is no intent to usurp Clara. It's just a case of timing as Clara will eventually have all the required knowledge but not in the required timeframe.'

'Son, you must learn to take people with you. I understand the issue, but you cannot discard her. She will never forgive you, and neither will I. You better tell me what you're proposing as we may have a delicate period on our hands.'

'Clara will not be aware of Cynthia's input, as Javid will keep this relationship away from the visibility of the project. To Clara, it will appear that Javid is applying his incredible mind to this project. She already knows I rely heavily on both Hashem and Javid for complex algorithms, so this will not arouse any suspicion. I will explain to Clara that I need their input, and significantly more investment, thus have surrendered my 50% to EMULATE. However, she keeps her 50% with our blessing, and you need to restructure at a corporate level to protect her interest. Dad, I can now deliver for her, and I'm very alive to our conversation to keep Clara relevant. This is her project and I'm committed to deliver for her. But I must compensate for her lack of detailed knowledge until she has advanced her studies.'

'Okay, I hear the commitment to Clara and respect your intent. What I want us to agree is the process as I suggest we keep the detail to ourselves. Not even your mother should know the detail, as she will most certainly discuss it with Clara.'

'Let me tell you how I see it. You look for defects. We need far more sophisticated technology than we currently have. We also need to create a virtual walkway in the office with a multitude of measuring technology to capture and accurately emulate how clothes respond to different shaped bodies. The information to be provided by Cynthia is complex but has defined parameters, which means we can develop accurate simulation algorithms. This will all take place out of sight of anyone other than me, Hashem and Javid, so even if Clara talks to people in the office, she will not detect these details. Dad, if we get this right, the whole of the animation world will bang on our door. No longer will characters in animated movies look animated; they'll look real. Think clothes on people equals fur on animals. When I'm working with Clara, the input she provides will be relevant, and needed. Remember, it's Javid working with Cynthia, not me. I will only see the impact on my screen of her input, albeit created by Javid. I promise to continue to work with Clara as we work today. The only difference to Clara is the inclusion of Hashem and Javid to get the desired result.'

'Can you really afford to resource this alternative version of your project?'

'No choice if we want to be successful. You remember I told Simon I thought another £500k would be invested? I've now doubled that expectation. Any development funding you can get your hands on will be most welcome. But we can afford it. And the potential revenues when we get it right will be enormous. I should add that Clara's 50% will relate exclusively to the fashion world. Using the engine in the animation industry will be EMULATE, as we will have to further adapt this engine to that industry. Clara's interests will relate to the application, not the engine. But I see a massive ongoing application of this technology in the fashion world so she will be very rich.'

'I'm amazed at the revenues you generate. I told my office a small porky when I suggested I needed an additional two days to get this right. I wanted to save my annual leave in case I need it for family. What you've just told me eliminates any such notion. I probably need more days to ensure your corporate structure takes full advantage of anticipated business. I can only sit in awe of your achievements, and your commitment. I've noted the modification to Clara's interest and will need to think this through, but I'm at peace with it. I will be proposing in my formal report to you that you are now in need of a competent Financial Director, and we can find one for you if you prefer. Such a person will be best placed to secure whatever Government grants and development funding are available.'

'If you tell me we need one, I must listen. So long as such a person does not attempt to dampen our enthusiasm, and commitment to push the boundaries, so be it.'

'Don't worry, son. You don't need an FD to manage your financing because you don't need any. However, leaving large cash balances in your bank account is great for the bank, but could be better utilised by a skilful FD. And should you engage in acquisitions, a competent FD will protect your interests.'

'Okay, dad. I'm listening.'

'What we need to do is agree what we tell the girls about our week together, and especially the outcome of your meetings today.'

'I think we adopt a keep it simple approach. After considering all the information available, and the resources needed for all projects, including Clara's fashion project, we now have a corporate structure which will maximise our resource management and allowing investment requirement where needed. This required me to integrate my 50% of Clara's project into EMULATE to facilitate the anticipated investment requirement, and the need for Hashem and Javid to contribute to the specialist algorithms required. However, you have secured Clara's interests, or will complete this task in the coming days. Do we need more?'

'No. I like it. What about your visit to the college?'

'I went to the college to secure online access to lectures for Clara until she can return. I had the opportunity to investigate some questions I had on sizing, which I've passed on to Javid. Cynthia certainly won't mention our meeting. Not even Simon will be briefed.'

'Good enough. I'll email my proposal regarding Clara's interests early next week. I think we're ready for the return of the girls.'

Chapter 59

They were standing at the exit to the Customs Hall. James saw them first. He couldn't believe his eyes. 'Dad, look. Clara's walking.'

The vision they could see was Clara pushing her wheelchair with her suitcase lodged where she would have been sitting. Janice was by her side, wheeling her case. James couldn't help but wave at them in total excitement. He couldn't wait for them to leave the Customs Hall. He went to meet them, wrapping his arms around Clara who was sporting her usual smile. 'You're walking. It's fantastic. Hi, mom. What happened out there?'

He took her suitcase out of the wheelchair and wheeled it himself. Geoffrey greeted his wife before turning to Clara. She could see the tears in his eyes as he wrapped her in his arms. She so loved her new dad, always feeling comfortable in his arms. It was like a sanctuary where she felt safe.

He held her at arms-length. 'Look at you. You're walking again. How fantastic. You must tell all.'

'I'm not fully walking yet. I can walk short distances on my own, but I still need support to walk any distance. But it feels great to be mobile again.'

Clara took her dad's right arm as slowly they made their way to the car.

James put her case back into the chair, but quickly realised it was easier to fold the chair and roll the case. He caught up with his mom. 'How was it? You really got some colour.'

'It was great. We had a wonderful time. And to see her walking again brings tears to my eyes. She's so strong. I'm so proud of her. How did you get on with your father?'

'We did good. My corporate restructuring is done, and dad has given me some excellent advice to go forward. I'm moving our accounts to his bank, which means he can provide general oversight without charges. And he's there when we need to package our deals.'

'Can you now refocus on your project with Clara? She needs private rehab three times per week, and to be in the swimming pool for her walking exercises every day when not in rehab. She was so brave out there to get where she is. Now it needs daily maintenance. The professional rehab lady is in Hatfield, so I will take her on Saturdays, but you must take her Tuesday and Thursday.'

'No problem, mom. Her walking again takes a load off me. I'll do whatever it takes to get her walking properly again.'

She put her spare arm around his shoulders. 'It's all going to be good again. She's one determined lady. I'm so proud of her. Come, let's get home. Much to tell.'

By the time they got back to the apartment, it was after 4pm. Both girls wanted to freshen after their long flight. For once Clara felt the freedom of showering on her own, albeit not an experience she wanted to repeat very often. The difference was she didn't need help anymore, which was liberating. She could now return to enjoying their showers together without feeling an invalid.

Dinner was set for 6pm. James had helped his father to prepare a welcome home dinner, putting the dining room chair back at the table where for weeks the space was reserved for Clara's wheelchair. They all felt good about her progress.

Over dinner Clara, but mostly Janice, relayed events of the week with much laughter as they recalled funny incidents throughout the week. The resort was very much a sports venue with much support facilities such as a spa, a gym, and an aqua exercise pool some ten metres long. This pool had both static and resistance capability where jets of water would resist progress. Clara related, with the help of her mum, how she used this pool twice every day, under the guidance of the lovely Tanya and Chrissie. The first two days were very difficult for her needing much support from her mum. Her mum recounted the pain she endured in those first days, but with gritted teeth she persevered. But the rehab program under Tanya and Chrissie yielded the results they witnessed at the airport, and this rehab must continue privately as the hospital physio cannot yield the desired result.

They invited Tanya and Chrissie to join them for dinner on their last evening to find they were partners in actual life, and Tanya is a trained medical doctor and osteopath after realising that much surgery could be avoided with a little manipulation. They spent their winters at the training camps with elite winter athletes, and summer in the Turkey resort chilling other than treating the occasional sprained ankle, using the couple of months between the end of the winter season and the summer season to travel.

They related how they did everything together, never leaving each other's side. It was obvious they had fun. Janice was clearly a reborn mum, enjoying life with her beautiful daughter. James, particularly, could see his mother really has the daughter she so craves and could easily take Clara away from him, if necessary. But that threat had receded. He had succeeded in his task to care for her and was happy to have her back. Although the week with his father was interesting, especially the corporate work, he so missed her lovely smiley face in the morning on his pillow. He didn't need the actual sun, the beaming face next to him provided all the sunshine he needed at the start of each day.

An early night was in order after the long day for the girls. Both couples made tender love to rekindle their need for each other before gently descending into a peaceful slumber in each other's arms.

Chapter 60

At breakfast Geoffrey announced they would make an early start for home, as they had their own chores to take care of after a week away. They were packed and ready to leave by 10am.

The farewell hug between mother and daughter seemed endless. 'Thank you, mum for such a lovely holiday. I'll never forget it.'

'Neither will I my lovely daughter. I think we should have a girlie holiday every year. The boys can go fishing, or whatever boys do.'

'That would be lovely. Something to look forward to.'

'And next weekend, after rehab, we go shopping now we know what's missing in your wardrobe. Another fun day, I think.'

'That would be great. I'll talk to you in the week to keep you up to date with progress.'

'At least once every day my darling. You brighten my day when we talk.'

After they had left, James wanted to hear about how the holiday went from her point of view, his mom having dominated much of the discussion over dinner.

'Mum was really great. She spoiled me rotten. And we had everyone at the resort looking after us. It was incredible. We could not have asked for more. And such a lovely place. We should go back there. Everyone was so warm and friendly.'

'Mom tells me we need to go to rehab three times a week in Hatfield. How did that happen?'

'As mum said last night Tanya and Chrissie are professional physio and rehab specialist for elite winter sports. They know the head of physio and rehab for the British winter sports team, Jules, who has a clinic in Hatfield. She has agreed to finish my rehab program.'

'Wow. You really did find the right people. Mum also tells me you need to walk in the swimming pool every day. Do you feel up to it now?'

'For sure. It's much easier now, so let's change and go down to the pool. I also want to use the gym afterwards as the lovely Chrissie showed me some exercises that really worked for me. You need to help me with one of them.'

'Let's go. Show me what you need.'

Over dinner Clara wanted to know about his week with Dad.
'Fantastic. My corporate structure is now as it needs to be for our future activities. I have embedded my interest in our project within the company, but Dad has secured your position. We need the cash flow of the company to fund this project. Hashem and Javid are happy with their deal and love their involvement in our fashion project. There are some personal details raised by Dad you and I need to discuss, but not tonight. It was a good week. I learnt a lot, but I missed you.'
'Then we have some catching up to do, especially with my new mobility. Won't be long before I'm fully mobile. What do you think about needing to take me to Hatfield twice each week?'
'Clara, the vision of you walking at the airport yesterday is all I need to know this is a must do. Am I thankful mum took you where you could get the very best of treatment, and can continue now you're home. My folks are continually showing me my delinquencies towards both of us, especially you. I need to learn how to take care of us. What will you do about your Friday sessions at the hospital?'
'If it's okay with you, I'd like to end them. When you see the difference at the elite end, there is no benefit to continuing. Mum has agreed to pay for Jules, so not constricted by private medical rules.'
'That's my responsibility, not my mom's.'
'You take it up with her, but I think you'll find she's adamant about this. She told Tanya to convey to Jules that whatever I need will be covered. She told me she doesn't want any restriction by your corporate medical plan, as you would likely ask your medical insurer to cover the cost of treatment.'
'This is not fair, but I'll talk to mom. You are my responsibility, and I must learn to take care of my own. You will get whatever you need from me, no question.'
'Wait. What's with this responsibility crap? I'm not your possession, your servant, or your child. What mum

and dad do for me is not out of responsibility, it's out of love we share. If mum or dad became ill, I would happily care for them out of love, not responsibility.'

'But I got you into this mess, so I feel responsible to get you out of it.'

'Which mess are we talking about? The despair I felt before my injury, or the injury. If you mean the injury, it was my decision to try to protect you. I'm not your paid bodyguard. I felt no responsibility to protect you. I did what I did out of my love for you.'

She could see he was rattled. 'Mum is enjoying her new maternal life. I think it's as much therapy for her as it is for me, and it's great to feel the love of a mum again. Don't let this bother you. All will settle once I'm back on my feet.'

He was angry with himself. 'This will only settle when my parents don't feel the need to think for me. If you feel there is no value in your Friday sessions, close them out. I'll strive to do better.'

'And I'll be still by your side when you get there. But where are we with our project? Can't imagine much got done with Dad around.'

'Not true. We advanced our needs, Hashem is meeting with Rigby & Peller this week, Javid is spending money on equipment as if we have infinite resources, and I met with Simon Atwood, who sends you his best wishes, and has agreed all your lectures will be streamed here until you feel able to return to college. I'm in a better place, which means we're in a better place.'

'Sounds great. Early night tonight, I think. Let's go remember why we work so well together.'

Chapter 61

Monday started well with a together shower and breakfast, after which the reality of back to work struck her.

On Tuesday morning, it took a little over an hour to find the clinic belonging to Jules. Fortunately, it had its own car park close to the entrance. Once inside, they were confronted with a reception area with two receptionists dressed in identical sports gear. The walls were plastered with framed pictures of sports people, some of which they recognised, most sporting medals or trophies and, without exception, expressing thanks to Jules in hand-written notes.

One of the receptionists greeted them. 'You must be Clara here to see Jules. Could I ask you to complete this form with some contact details for our files? Dr Caldwell has already contacted us with payment details, so ignore that part of the form. And before you leave, can we agree dates and times for appointments for the next month?'

James chose to not show his feeling about the reference to his mother. Clara dutifully completed the form thinking, *'what am I doing here amongst such stars of sport?'* She handed back the form. James was already working on his laptop, so didn't notice her anxiety.

'Let me take you through to Jules' as a receptionist wheeled her through a sizeable gym into a treatment room.

A slight lady confronted her, probably mid-40s, with jet black hair, looking very fit in her British Sports tracksuit.

'Hello Clara. Nice to meet you. Heard some good things about you from Sonya who sends her regards. There are some formalities we need to complete before I can treat you. Tanya has sent me a full brief of what she found, with the treatment and rehab program conducted by her and Chrissie. As I have a very high regard for both if I could ask you to read what they have sent and accept it, I can use it as the required assessment I need to work with you.' She handed Clara a lengthy email.

After reading the whole email, 'other than the technical bits I agree with what it says.'

'Excellent. Now I need to examine you. If I hold your chair, could you stand for me? Use the treatment bed for support if you need it.'

Clara slowly raised herself to her feet. Once upright, she let go of the arms of the wheelchair but not reaching for the couch.

'Are you okay if I move the chair away so I can see you standing?'

Clara acknowledged she is okay. Jules walked around her, observing her stance.

'Let me help you to the treatment table where I would like you to remove your slacks and then lie on your back.'

Once she had complied, Jules conducted a detailed examination, occasionally referring to the email from Sonya.

'Okay, Clara. Everything is as described by Sonya. Today I'll do some soft tissue work and passive mobility with electro-stimulus to keep your muscles awake after your journey home. On Thursday I would like you to bring shorts and a top so we can work in the gym. We don't have an aqua pool at this facility, so we will need to use resistive bands. Oh, if you have sticks, could you bring them? The sooner we get you out of that wheelchair the better.'

'I have sticks. And I have a pool where I live and have been walking in it twice since I got back.'

'Excellent. Sonya informed me of your commitment.'

'Could I ask you why you're helping me? It looks like you only work with top sports people.'

'This clinic deals with anyone who needs help, but you are right in that I tend only to work with elite sports, usually at our Loughborough facility. But I have a lot of respect for Tanya and Chrissie, and work with them during the winter season. I wish they would come work with me here. But they like the sun. Tanya told me about your dogged attitude. Looking at this email, it wasn't a very relaxing week for you in Turkey. I wish some of my elite athletes had your grit, determination, and commitment to recovery. You did well in Turkey but need to continue for a few more weeks to complete your recovery. I'm happy to help you. Might even introduce you to some of my more derelict patients so they can see what it takes to fully recover from traumatic injury.'

With that Jules started her therapy, which took some 40-minutes. 'Enough for today. Get dressed and I'll see you Thursday.'

Clara retreated to her wheelchair. 'Thank you so much for helping me. I feel privileged to have met Sonya and Chrissie, and now you. I will do whatever I need to do to walk again. I'll be in the pool this afternoon and tomorrow.'

'My dear, your commitment is clear and why you deserve the effort. See you Thursday.'

On the way out she agreed her schedule of appointment for the next 4-weeks, all at 10am. James logged them into his digital calendar before driving home.

Chapter 62

Wednesday had gone well. He could see Clara was in good spirit. Her leg was getting stronger every day, and her trip to Jules confirmed she was close to full walking capability.

They were having dinner together. It was time to talk with her about the future.

'When dad was helping me to reshape my corporate existence last week, he raised some issues that someone my age would not necessarily consider but would now appear important. I had no life assurance, and there was a need for key man insurance to protect the business, all of which are now in place.'

'One of the important issues he raised is how I provision for you in the event something happens to me. He came up with two scenarios. The first is in the event of my demise. This one was easy. I have put a Will in place where you inherit everything, including my business interests. The second is what happens should we part for any reason as we are not married and thus you would not legally be entitled to a divorce settlement. My dad gave me two options; marry you, which is my preferred option, or a Settlement Agreement where dad acts as custodian of your interests as he is doing with your interests in our fashion project.'

'Today we live as man and wife in all but legal standing, and I certainly could not imagine life without you. Would you consider making our relationship legally recognised and marry me?'

'She looked at him. She could see his unease with this conversation. What hit her most was it was dad who had provoked this conversation. The boy was not yet man-enough to think this through for himself. Whereas she was grateful that provisions were to be put in place for her, they had little to do with the loving relationship she needed.

175

'James, we made a pact in which part of my role is to protect you from marriage until we achieve our goals. I have diligently helped you avoid marriage, and you agreed to help me fulfil my dream of trying my hand as a fashion designer. To date, we are on track to complete our commitments to each other. We are together living our respective dreams as per our pact. Why would I allow an event that could distract us from our goals? Talk to me about the future when we have both achieved our respective goals and our pact is complete.'

'Nice speech, Clara. But we both know we belong together. This has been the case from the start of our relationship. What do I need to do to convince you of my commitment to you; to us as man and wife?'

'Deliver for me.'

'And what do I need to do to deliver for you?'

'When you know the answer, ask me again.'

He was getting frustrated. 'Clara, please tell me what you need from me. I will deliver for you.'

'I know you will. But let us first finish what we started. This is very important to me. I don't want dependency on you. I want to be on equal terms. You offered to give me a life. I now ask you to deliver for me. On Sunday you spoke of responsibility. This is your only responsibility towards me.'

He sensed this conversation was over, short of an unnecessary argument – to be avoided. His father had predicted the likely outcome, so no point in pursuing marriage at this time. He needed to deliver for her.

Chapter 63

Thursdays visit to Jules cemented their relationship. Clara thought it time to end her physio sessions at the hospital as they could not usefully add anything to her therapy with Jules.

On Friday she attended her usual hospital appointment, but with some anxiety. It wasn't she didn't like her physio, but her treatment with Tanya and Chrissie, and now Jules opened her eyes to the difference between conventional physio and what could be achieved by elite physio. But how to express this to her hospital physio.

At the end of the session, she declared she has been lucky in finding Jules who has put a rehab program together to complete her recovery. Fortunately, the physio knew of the reputation of Jules and thus understanding. But Clara would need an examination as part of a sign-off. They would organise this for the following Friday. In any event, in her anxiety, she had forgotten she would have to surrender her hospital wheelchair. The long corridors, various doors, and failure to bring her titanium wheelchair made it impractical to leave behind the hospital wheelchair. It would need one more visit. She alerted James to help her remember to bring both chairs next week.

Shopping done, and session in the pool completed, it was time to prepare for the weekend. She helped James to prepare a hot supper for mum and dad.

Chapter 64

Janice and Clara rose early and, after a quick breakfast, were excitedly on their way to rehab followed by shopping at Brent Cross on the way back, leaving the boys to their chores.

'How did it go with Clara?'

'She turned me down flat. And she won't consider our future relationship until we have completed the original goals we agreed in St Albans.'

'How do you feel about her response?'

'Gutted. I love this woman, but she doesn't think me good enough for her.'

'In terms of your relationship, she's right. But it doesn't mean it can't be fixed. If you truly love her, as we think you do, then you need to apply that ingenious mind of yours to win her over. You must have encountered obstacles developing your computer models, but you overcame them. Now you need to apply your mind to overcome the hurdle with Clara. Our dereliction as parents means you don't yet have the knowledge for this hurdle, so I now offer to work with you to win this wonderful lady.'

'Dad, will you please stop giving me this parental dereliction crap! You gave me the space to develop what I have. For that, I'm truly grateful. Sure, I came up short when Clara was stabbed, but you and mom helped me to overcome these shortcomings. Ironically, Clara's care for her mother made her my best teacher as she knows her needs better than anyone and what I needed to learn to deliver for her. She helped me to help her, and mostly it was fun once I got my head into the groove of caring for her. You've said it many times. Her infectious smile makes obstacles evaporate. She made it easy for me. But she wants more.'

'What she wants from you is to know you're as capable of looking out for her as she is for you – a true partnership. In its most basic form, she wants to see the boy she agreed to help is now a man capable of helping her. What about you and I have a goal of winning this lady over?'

'Dad, you're nuts. My dad is going to help me win the woman of my dreams. How weird is that?'

'I'm only offering the guidance any father would give to his son, so not weird at all. Just a little late. But never too late, especially as the prize is worth the effort. Her criteria is for you to delivery for her. You can do this, so what's the problem? A genuine effort, combined with a little patience, and you'll win. She's not going anywhere, so relax. Be positive. Deliver her dream as you promised her. Treat her as your equal. You will win your prize; and what a prize.'

'Okay. These past weeks have been an education for me, so what do you have in mind?'

'I first met your mother at university. She was hell-bent on a first-class honours' degree with the singular expectation to advance directly to a PhD. She was totally focussed on this objective to the exclusion of everything else. I was more laid back. A good degree was the extent of my student ambitions. If I were to move onto an MBA programme, I wanted to participate as a working banker sponsored by the bank. No more living on a State grant.'

'What I noticed about your mother was the more obsessed with her goal, the more insecure she became. She expected perfection in an imperfect world. I found myself constantly having to reassure her and pick her up when she failed any unrealistic goal. She became more and more dependent on me to be there for her as she intensified her efforts. She was already good enough to reach her goal, but she wasn't secure enough in herself to know it. The weeks before her finals, she drove me nuts. But she never forgot I was there for her; calm; reassuring; never judgemental or angry with her. Although you see your mother as strong and organised, she still relies on my calm in times of trouble when her insecurity kicks in.'

'I've seen this, especially over the past weeks. I remember when she broke down after the first visit to Clara in the intensive care unit. You were there for her, and she recovered quickly; I guess not to upset me further. Now you mention it, her military precision is a mask for her insecurity. She functions better when she thinks she's in control.'

'Well observed. How about if I suggest to you, as you progress your project closer to your goal, Clara will become more and more insecure. Remember, she didn't finish school. You are taking her where knowledge is more important than streetwise. The complexity of this project will make her feel more and more irrelevant. You said Cynthia Crawford expressed Clara does not yet have the knowledge you need. You need to identify this insecurity and keep her relevant. Coach her and teach her what she needs to know to feel relevant. And when she feels overwhelmed by the whole project, stop, pick her up, and reassure her. The prize will be one very grateful lady, and one wonderful wife.'

James put his hand on top of his father's hand. 'Dad, you are most certainly the wise old owl in this family. I get it, and I've already noticed pangs of insecurity. I can do this; and will happily keep her relevant. This is her project. I'm just the techy. Thanks dad.'

'As nothing material will progress in your relationship until you complete this project, why don't you execute the Settlement Agreement I gave to you? Present it to her in good faith. Your first step in demonstrating your concern for her well-being and security. I'll hold it in safekeeping for her so it won't be abused; not that I would ever consider her capable of such abuse. She loves you dearly. She just wants you to step up to the plate for her. Then try to coax out of her where she feels fragile in your project and reassure her and impart the knowledge she needs. Can I suggest that every Friday afternoon you sit with her and recap the week so you can quickly resolve any issues before she feels you've left her behind?'

'Okay, dad. Good advice, as always. I'll do it tomorrow so you can take it away with you.'

'How about lunch in the local hostelry? Lubricate the wheels before our chores this afternoon.'

'Good idea. Let's go.'

The girls burst through the apartment door a little after 4:30 laughing and joking as they manoeuvred her wheelchair and a myriad of shopping bags into the apartment. The boys were on the balcony as they became aware of the cacophony of sounds invading their peaceful calm.

'Hello boys. We're back, but not finished. We wish to dress and be escorted to dinner this evening. So, gentlemen, as we extend the honour to you to escort us this evening, could you please organise a restaurant suitable for two finely dressed ladies, and let us know what time our carriage will be available.' It was obvious they had also visited with a hairdresser.

Clara was in fits of giggles as she watched the stunned faces of the boys as they were appraised of their instructions, so elegantly delivered.

'Come, my dear. Let us go unpack our purchases and decide on our dress this evening before refreshing ourselves.'

Janice wheeled her to her bedroom where giggle and laughter continued.

Geoffrey turned to James. 'Where on earth will we find a good restaurant at 5 o'clock on a Saturday evening?'

'Dad, there's only one I know will try hard to accommodate us. Let me call them.'

He scanned his telephone directory looking for Fredericks in Camden Passage; his regular choice when working. He hit the dial button.

'Hello. Restaurant Fredericks. Stefano speaking. Can I help you?'

'Hi, Stefano. It's James Caldwell.'

'James! How are you? And how is the lovely Clara?'

'She's much better, thank you. Still in a wheelchair but, hopefully will be walking again in the coming weeks.'

'This is good news. We have missed her. What can Stefano do for you, my friend?'

'Clara has just returned from a shopping trip with my mom and informs me, for the first time since that horrible night, she wants to get dressed and go out for dinner. Can you help me?'

'For such a hero Stefano will make this possible. How many?'

'My mom and dad will be with us, so four.'

'Let me look as we must find the right table, so the beautiful Clara has no problems. We must avoid the theatre crowd as we are so full. If you can arrive at 8 o'clock, it will honour us to receive such a hero. Stefano will put a bottle of our best Champagne on ice, compliments of the house, to welcome back our dear friends.'

'Thank you so much, Stefano. You will certainly put a big smile on her face.'

'Such a beautiful smile will make Stefano happy. See you at 8.'

Geoffrey put a warm hand on his son's shoulder. 'Well played, son. Better go tell the ladies their carriage will arrive at 7:45.'

He informed the ladies of his success and when they must leave. He retreated to yet more laughter.

'What did they say to cause yet more laughter?'

'Mom informed me, with continued theatre, they will expect us to dress as is proper for escorting beautiful ladies. Ties are optional, but jacket is a must. Smart casual is our instruction. Furthermore, I'm told I should retrieve what I want to wear no later than 7 o'clock and get ready in your room. Mom and Clara will get ready in my bedroom.' He was carrying a bag.

'My goodness. I came here from the office yesterday, so I only have the jacket I was wearing. Better see what shirts I can wear with it.'

'I think mom has thought of that', as he pulled two shirts out of the bag. Looking at the sizes, 'This must be yours.'

'Thank goodness. Better see if it needs ironing.'

'This isn't fair, dad. If this situation were reversed, all hell would let loose about not giving enough time; nothing to wear, no time for hairdresser, etc. Whatever happened to equality?'

'Equality in a relationship? Son, you have much to learn, especially about marriage. The fairer sex feel it's they who have to go to great lengths to adorn themselves for our benefit. It's a natural expectation we will honour such effort with no consideration how this might be achieved at short notice. We are expected to comply without complaint. How is irrelevant. How abouts a G&T to ease the process?'

'Love to, but I'll be driving.'

'Why don't we order a cab? Much easier for Clara in her chair.'

'Good idea. Stefano will make sure we get a cab home. Let's have that drink.'

It was 7:30. Both boys were dressed and ready, both having used the option not to wear a tie but otherwise compliant with their dress code.

The bedroom door opened. Janice, beautifully dressed in a chiffon cocktail dress, wheeled out the wheelchair but only adorned with two shoulder wraps. She moved the wheelchair to the side and then stood beside the door.

'Gentlemen. May I present Princess Clara, the belle of the ball.'

Clara moved into view and walked through the door. The jaws on both men dropped to the floor. She looked radiant in a silver-grey lace and linen cocktail dress, and of course sporting her intoxicating smile.

'Wow, Clara. You look stunning. Princess doesn't do justice to the vision before me.' He moved towards her, held her hands, and kissed her on both cheeks. He moved to one side to escort her, but dad wanted his turn.

'My darling daughter, you look spectacular. It will be an honour to escort you to dinner.'

'Thanks, dad, You're all so lovely with me. It's great to feel human again.'

The internal intercom rang. James went to answer it.

My darling wife, you too look absolutely stunning. You two certainly had a good shopping day.'

'Thank you, my darling.' Pointing to Clara, 'When I saw this stunning dress, I knew it was perfect for my darling daughter. She tried it. The vision stands before you. But where could she wear such a beautiful dress? The rest is where we are. Nice shirt, by the way.'

'Thank you for thinking of the need.'

'Clara bought a shirt for James, but I note he isn't wearing it.'

'Needed ironing but he has plenty of choice of his own.'

'But my darling, it looks like you ironed yours.'

'Yes, dear. My need was greater.'

She turned to Clara, 'still a work in progress with James.' They both giggled.

James returned. 'Our carriage is waiting.'

The cab dropped them at the door of Fredericks. The doorman opened the door as James wheeled her into the cloakroom area. Stefano was quickly notified of their arrival.

'My goodness, we're blessed with an angel. Clara, my darling, it is so good to see you, and what a picture of beauty you paint. You lift the darkness of your absence with the brightness of your light. Let me take you to your table.'

'Thank you so much, Stefano. It's so nice to be back.'

He wheeled her to their reserved table, but with only three chairs and a space for her wheelchair.

'Stefano, would it be possible to have a chair, preferably with arms. I want to feel as normal as possible.'

'Of course, you can.' He shouted across to another waiter asking him to bring an armchair for her. When it arrived, he placed it slightly turned towards her. 'Can I help you, my dear?'

'Thank you, dear Stefano. Just give me your arm.'

'Madam, just tell Stefano what you need, and it will be.'

She was comfortably seated; the wheelchair folded and returned to the cloakroom area, and parents introduced. The champagne was already in a bucket on the table with five glasses. Stefano opened the champagne, poured all five glasses, and handed them around keeping one for himself.

'I wish to toast the return of a good friend and incredible hero to Fredericks. Clara is a true and beautiful princess, and we wish her a speedy recovery so her light shines in our humble restaurant again. Clara, our heartfelt thanks for returning to us. To Clara.'

They all toasted her.

'Stefano, you're spoiling me. But thank you so much. I feel better already.'

'Whatever you need, Stefano is your servant. Enjoy your evening. This table is yours for as long as you want it.'

'Dinner was delicious.

'Mum, this is a lovely idea. Thank you.'

'My darling, you do not go shopping to buy beautiful clothes to hang them in a wardrobe. And you look so beautiful in that dress. As soon as I saw it, I knew only you could compliment such a dress. And I am right. We need to do this more often.'

'Mum, I need to go to the toilet.'

'Do you need your chair, or can we manage together?'

'I think the alcohol tonight will numb any pain, but it may also numb my balance.'

They both laughed. 'Which side would you like me – left or right?'

'I think left would be best.'

Mum helped her up and waited until Clara felt ready to move. Stefano noticed what was happening as she took her first steps. He quickly moved into position in front of them to make sure none of the other diners inadvertently blocked their way.

'You can walk. Fantastico.'

'Only a little yet, but I'm getting stronger.'

'This is so wonderful. When Hashem tell me you couldn't walk, my heart cried for you. But you are strong woman. I pray for the day you walk through our door on your own.' He opened the door to the ladies' cloakroom and waived them in and then kept his eyes peeled for their return. '*Nothing horrible must happen to this lovely lady in Fredericks.*'

It was after 10pm. The post-theatre crowd would soon be here. Clara was showing signs of tiredness. Time to leave. James paid the bill, including a good tip. Stefano brought the wheelchair to the table. 'Madam, your carriage.'

She smiled at him as she transferred to her wheelchair. Once comfortable, Stefano wheeled her to the cloakroom area. Dad was quick to follow.

Stefano moved in front of her as dad took up the rear. 'My darling princess Clara, any time you need to eat lunch or dinner you call Stefano. We will always have table for you.'

She turned to dad. 'Can you hold the chair for me?' He immediately responded.

'Stefano, will you give me your hands to help me up?'

He instantly offered his hands, which she took and pulled up to a standing position, and then put one arm around his neck and kissed him on the cheek. 'Thank you so much for a lovely evening. I so needed to have such lovely company.'

She held both his hands again for support so she could see his face. There were tears in his eyes. 'I will pray for the day you can walk through our door again. It has been so lovely to see you.'

James and mum arrived as she sat back in her chair. Stefano turned to James. 'James, please take good care of my princess. She is welcome anytime. We always have table for our special friends.'

'Have no fear, Stefano. Only the best care for my lovely Clara. And thank you for a lovely evening.'

'It is my pleasure.' Stefano turned to mum and dad. 'So lovely to see you both again, and what a lovely family you make. Hope to see you all again very soon.'

With that, he wheeled Clara out to the waiting cab and helped her to get comfortable. They were soon on their way home.

Once through the apartment door into the living room, she locked the brakes on the chair. 'James, would you help me up, I need a family hug.'

He smiled as he helped her to stand. They all hugged. 'Thank you all so much for a lovely evening, and mum for such a lovely day. I'm so happy in this wonderful family.'

They all hugged and kissed with no urgency to part.

Clara was first to speak. 'Could we get a selfie to remember this lovely evening?'

Mum was first to respond, 'how silly of me. Should have thought of this earlier.' She reached into her bag to find her phone.

'Mum, my phone is on the table. I would like a picture.'

Mum handed the phones to James as they huddled to get into the picture. Both pictures taken, mum wanted a full-length shot of Clara in her beautiful dress. James stood with her for support as several photos were taken on both phones. As always, her beaming smile filled the pictures.

It was time for bed. 'Clara, my darling, do you need any help to get to bed?'

'It's okay, mum, James is very proficient at putting me to bed, so we'll manage. But thank you.'

As James and Clara curled up in bed, she held his face. 'After such a lovely day I would encourage some playtime, but I think it must wait until the morning.'

He smiled as he thought how lucky he is to have such a lady as she drifted into a deep sleep. In the other room, mum and dad decided that playtime was the best way to end such a lovely day.

Chapter 65

Back to work on Monday. James had set her tasks that required apps she was unfamiliar with and needed help.

'Would it be possible for Hashem to come to help me understand these new aps? I'm struggling.'

'I'll call him now to see if he's free.' He called Hashem.

'He'll be here around noon tomorrow. He wants to sit with me later, so he'll probably spend the afternoon here. I'll organise lunch.'

Hashem arrived a little after noon displaying his normal geeky boyishness. He quickly spotted the F1 wheelchair. 'Wow, this looks fantastic. Can I try it?'

Without waiting for a reply, he was in the wheelchair manoeuvring it around the living room, increasing speed as he became familiar with its capabilities. 'This is great. Handles cornering really well.' He stopped and raised it onto the main wheels as though climbing a kerb. 'Rear wheel axle is set back behind the centre of gravity so more stable against falling backwards.'

Clara could only watch in both amazement and amusement as she observed this kid with a new toy testing what he could do with it.

'Do you still have the hospital wheelchair?'

'Yes. It's in the computer suite.'

He quickly retrieved it and put the two chairs side-by-side studying every detail and difference. He then sat in her hospital wheelchair and repeated his manoeuvring.

He turned to Clara. 'Do you have your phone handy?'

'Yes, I have it here with me.'

'Good. Find the stopwatch app. Let's put these chairs up against each other. Three laps of the room.'

He started in her titanium wheelchair, tearing around the room as fast as he could for three laps. He then switched to her hospital wheelchair. As he came around the last bend of the third lap, he lost it, turning the wheelchair over, throwing him out onto the floor. Clara could only lie on the sofa laughing, 'Are you okay?'

Hashem got to his feet. 'You see, rubbish design. Your new one is far superior. Designer really thought about the dynamics involved.'

'Hashem, I don't think they built the hospital wheelchair for racing. It's only for normal mobility.'

'Just because you're confined to a wheelchair doesn't mean you can't have fun.'

She could only laugh at his boyish sense of fun. Then she remembered what Janice had said about any observations relating to her titanium wheelchair. 'The manufacturer who lent me this chair wants to know if I detect any problems, or any improvements that would make the chair easier or more comfortable. Do you have any input I could feed back?'

He looked closely at the chair again and then sat in it. 'Did it come with a seat cushion?'

'No. Why?'

'I find the side rests about 2 – 3cm too high for comfort. These side arms should be at waist height, as would be the case with a normal armchair other than for leisurely comfort. This implies there should be a cushion that will compress so your elbows can rest comfortably on the arms without you having to scrunch up your shoulders.'

'Bring the chair here so I can sit in it. And please apply the brake,' remembering her fall.

He helped her into the chair. 'You're right. These armrests are a little too high for comfort. Anything else?'

'How do you find having to reach backwards to apply the brake?'

She reached backwards to reach the brakes. 'You're right. Not great.'

'They designed this brake for someone pushing you. Responsibility for the brake should be the occupant. It needs to be ratchet on/off but cannot be under the front of the armrest as you need that area for support to get in and out. But perhaps on the front of the armrest upright would be good, so you have control without inconvenience.'

'Brilliant idea. Thanks, Hashem. I can see why you're such a genius. So much attention to detail.'

The door intercom sounded. James, who had been working on the dining room table until the spectacle before him attracted his attention, knew lunch had arrived. His culinary skills were still not advanced enough to engage with proper lunches, so take-away pizza would have to do. Normal intake for Hashem in any event.

After lunch it was time for work. 'James tells me you have some issues with your iPad that you need some help.'

Sheepishly, 'I've got a list.'

'No problem. Where will you be most comfortable?'

'As you like my wheelchair so much, how about I lie on the sofa, and you sit next to me in my wheelchair?'

He helped her to the sofa and perused her list. 'Okay. I can see the knowledge gaps which will deal with most of these issues in one go.' They started to work.

James had resumed his work on the dining room table. He looked up to see the strange picture of these two working, deciding he must capture this moment. He grabbed his phone, set it on camera, and stealthily moved around the room away from the front windows to steal his shot. They were so engrossed they didn't hear the click of the camera. His stealthy zeal was unnecessary as he sauntered back to his work.

After some two hours she was tiring but had grasped the valuable input from her patient teacher. Hashem needed a drink, so moved to get one.

'If you two have finished, I would like to go through some ideas whilst you're here.'

'Let's do it.'

'Darling, I know I should not use my computer suite, but it would really help if I could whilst Hashem is here.'

'Why don't you take me to the loo, and then I can enjoy a nap whilst you and Hashem do what you need to do, leaving doors open where necessary so at least one of you will hear me if I need help. I think this solution technically complies with dad's instructions.'

He smiled as he reached to kiss her. She reached for her chair. He stopped her, lifting her into his arms. 'We haven't had a cuddle since breakfast, so I'll carry you.'

After she was comfortably back on the sofa James and Hashem retreated to the computer suite remembering to leave the door wide open. She tried out her newfound knowledge whilst Hashem was still there. But soon the weight of her eyelids took control as she drifted into a peaceful slumber.

When she awoke, Hashem and James were sitting on the balcony having a drink. She alerted them to her awakening, indicating she would like to join them. She sat in her wheelchair for convenience reasons.

Hashem spoke. 'When you're feeling better, I would like you to bring this chair to the office so that I can do some runs on our new walkway with it.'

James, somewhat surprised, 'You have the walkway up and running?'

'Yes. We could only get about 20m of useful walkway, but that's about 40 steps by an average person each way so should be enough to get our data. But I still have a problem that's bugging me. I had Hell and Jenny walk for me. When I looked at the data, it looked like they were slightly lobsided as they walked. Thinking this may be the way the lighting was set I asked a couple of guys to do the same walk. No problem. Perfectly balanced walking. So, I've put a couple of cameras outside the office window to capture people walking along the pathway to see if I get the same data as on the walkway.'

James laughed. 'Are you sure you can record people on the pathway without consent?'

'Don't know. But I only need a few days, preferably under different weather conditions.'

Clara realised she had read something about this at college. 'I remember reading a paper at college that refers to women putting more weight on one step than the other. Something to do with carrying a baby which is usually in their non-principal hand and the side on which they apply more load when they're walking, even without a baby. I think this is one of the reasons models are taught to walk with one foot in front of the other to counter this tendency. I don't think you're going mad. Just more of that incredible observation skill you have.'

'Thank goodness for your knowledge. Made this visit valuable. I thought I was going bonkers. I checked the floor was level, looked along the walkway to see if we had anything which made the horizon slightly skew and even the lighting to see if they were casting shadows which would affect the visual. Now I find its probably normal. Females on the walkway need to walk like models to get the data we need. Thanks, Clara. I can sleep at nights again.'

Chapter 66

It was time for her Friday physio session at the hospital. But on this visit her hospital wheelchair would be taken, but not return. A symbolic gesture that a page has turned and recovery imminent.

That evening, when mum and dad arrived, Clara was standing to greet them without support, albeit close enough to the table should she feel the need for support.

Mum reached for her. 'My darling, you're standing! Can you walk?'

'I'm walking around the apartment, but not confident enough to walk outside. But we're getting close. I can now swim, which helps to strengthen my legs.'

Mum had tears in her eyes. 'I'm so proud of my beautiful daughter. We must celebrate.'

Dad was carrying a good bottle of burgundy but realised that it may, or may not, be opened for dinner as James retrieved a bottle of champagne.

During dinner Clara told her mum about the antics of Hashem in her wheelchair and explained his thoughts on design faults.

'Thank you, my dear. I'm certainly pleased we can provide such valuable feedback to the supplier.' She paused. 'I constantly hear about the incredible work of Hashem and Javid but, although they visited to return your phone, I've never properly met either of them. I feel a void in my knowledge as even Geoffrey speaks of them in high regard. When can I meet them? My curiosity is overwhelming.'

Clara smiled at her mum's expression of exclusion. 'Why don't I invite them here for dinner tomorrow. You'll have time to get to know them. There're really lovely people.'

James joined the conversation. 'I'm up for that. I'll call them now.'

Clara put her hand on his, 'Please darling, allow me.'

He conceded that they certainly would not refuse her, no matter what else they had planned.

'Hashem, it's Clara. My mum feels deprived of the pleasure of knowing my favourite friends. Could you both come to dinner tomorrow, say 6 o'clock here?'

'That's great. Don't need to dress. Just your usual casual selves. Don't need to bring anything. Your boyish charm is more than enough to win my heart.' She giggled with him. 'See you tomorrow. Give my regards to Javid. Bye.'

She returned her phone to the table. 'We need a menu away from their staple diet of pizza, pasta, and burgers. I think wholesome English cuisine. Neither has probably had a cooked vegetable for a while. What do you think, mum?'

'I think a meal complicit with your nutritious dietary requirements is in order.' They both laughed. 'Time for a list, I think.'

Much laughter ensued as they composed what they termed a geek menu. As usual, Geoffrey and James observed this drama relaxing whilst sipping excellent wine. No input required.

Chapter 67

The rain was lashing against the apartment windows, and the surface of the river Thames looked like a boiling cauldron. Not much river traffic this morning even though breakfast was later than usual because Clara wanted to prepare it herself, albeit mum was close at hand in case of mishap.

Once all seated, mum voiced her plan for the day. 'As we have significant progress on the walking front, and James probably needs a little respite from the apartment, I think Clara and I should spend some time today in the pool and gym after our visit with Jules to see if we can progress further. We have decided a menu for this evening and made a list of the items we need. I think you boys should go shopping, and if desired, visit a suitable hostelry for lunch. The preparation to receive our guests this evening won't take long if we all pull our weight. Any comments?'

James spoke first. 'Good with me. I have some other shopping I want to do.' Looking at his father, 'We can go to the main shopping centre to escape the rain. I also need to pass by my wine merchant as stocks of both wine and fizz are running low. And I must remember to get Indian beer. Javid only drinks beer, and he's very particular which brands he drinks.'

'Okay, son. Let's get our shopping list and be on our way.'

After nearly one hour in the pool, Clara was feeling the strain. Mum, a driven person herself, was far more encouraging than James to go that extra mile in both swimming and their aqua walking exercises. She eventually realised her lovely daughter was feeling distressed, if not in pain, knowing she would keep pushing until she dropped. Mum held her in her arms to take the weight off her thigh. 'Enough for today, my darling. You have worked so hard, but now you need to rest. Your determination overwhelms me. There is no question you will walk again within the next few weeks. We will certainly celebrate that day. Shopping, lunch, more shopping, skip through the park, and whatever else takes our fancy. Let's go get changed ready for the gym, but only the exercise you learnt in Turkey. We need you rested and perky for our guests this evening.'

They changed into gym gear and entered the gym. Being a Saturday and raining, the gym was very much in use. However, the exercise equipment needed for Clara was soon available, and they only needed it for ten minutes before retreating to the apartment.

'Do you need any help in the shower, my darling, or can you manage?'

'I can manage, thanks mum. See you in ten minutes for a nice cup of tea.'

Once secure in her bedroom, the first act was 500mg Paracetamol. Then a warm shower before donning her house clothes and retreating to the sofa. Within a few minutes mum emerged heading for the kitchen to make tea.

Mum delivered tea to the sofa and sat beside her. 'Are you okay, my darling? Did I push you too hard? You look in pain.'

Clara stroked her cheek with a loving smile. 'We're both strong women. If the pain is too much, I'll stop. I really appreciate you pushing me. When James detects the slightest expression of pain, he gets all protective and wants me out of there. But you and I know no pain, no gain. If you have time before you leave tomorrow, I would like to try again.'

'My darling if you feel up for it in the morning then it shall be. Now what would you like for lunch?'

Javid and Hashem arrived punctually and welcomed by James. A little nervously but without hesitation they introduced themselves to Janice, acknowledged Geoffrey and then straight to Clara who was sitting in her wheelchair.

'Hi, guys. Will you help me stand?'

They both extended a hand which she used to lift herself up to standing, steadied herself and then put an arm around the shoulders of both pulling them towards her.

'It's so lovely to see you both,' as she kissed their cheeks.

Javid leaned backwards, 'You can stand. Fantastic.'

'I can walk a little as well. If you two gentlemen will give me your arms, we can take a stroll around the apartment.'

They stood each side of her so she could take their arms and then led them around the room. As she sat back in her chair, there were tears in Hashem's eyes.

'Clara, this is so wonderful. So lovely to see you back on your feet. Must have a pic,' as he reached for his mobile, encouraging her to stand with Javid.

Janice watched this spectacle with great interest. *'These two are not just partners, they are family to my daughter. Therefore, they are family.* James, I think champagne to greet our guests.'

'No problem, but Javid and Hashem only drink beer.'

Hashem quickly responded. 'To celebrate the lovely Clara back on her feet, we will have just one glass of champagne. Beer doesn't do justice to the joy I feel.'

Celebrations over Hashem, Javid, Janice and Clara elected to sit on the balcony while Geoffrey and James prepared dinner. Janice decided this was really her evening to get to know Hashem and Javid.

'I'm so glad to meet you both at long last. I've heard so many wonderful things about you both. And now I see how kind you are to my lovely daughter I can only assume you are family. My two boys in the kitchen both know you well, as does my daughter, so I have another two boys in the family I need to know. Can you help me by telling me a little about your backgrounds, and how you met James?' She thought for a second, *'sounds like the inquisition.* Sorry if that sounded a bit inquisition. Please, I have a genuine interest to know you both as you are such an important part of this family.'

Hashem looked to Javid to respond. 'We're from India and have known each other since we were kids. We're both considered geeks and share the same interests in mathematics and computer sciences so naturally drawn together. We went through the University of Mumbai together, both graduating with Ph.D.'s. Our families know each other well. My father is an industrialist and Hashem's father is into Hitech. They are of a generation where class and status are important so agreed to send us to England to translate our Ph.D.'s into Cambridge Ph.D.'s which is a one-year process. We arrived early last year to allow us time to get to know the UK and travel Europe. We arranged to start at Cambridge in October last year, but then we responded to a question James posted on the internet. We arranged to meet with him. After listening to what he had already achieved and where he wanted to go with his engine, we agreed to spend the time until starting Cambridge working with him.'

'But you didn't start Cambridge.'

Hashem picked up the story. 'Once James had secured his first major licence, and we saw the revenue streams, we knew he was serious and had the funds to follow his dream. He asked us to join his company on an earn-in basis and have never looked back.'

'What did your families think about your change of direction?'

'We kept it quiet until just before we were due to move to Cambridge.'

Reaching out to hold Clara's hand, 'Sounds familiar. Parents always the last to know.'

'At first our parents were not amused. We're both the oldest siblings, so expected to return and support the family business. After signing the animated movie license, we knew we were where we wanted to be. My father has a joint-venture relationship with a major technology company in the UK. Unbeknown to us he had their auditors take a close look at what we're doing. When they reported back that James, just 19 years old, without a university degree, was a multi-millionaire with projected income streams expanding rapidly, he was only interested in our earn-in agreements. Thankfully, Geoffrey has satisfied that request. Now both families want to invest, but we don't need any investment.'

'Geoffrey told me you are both well on your way to becoming millionaires yourselves. Your families must be proud of you.'

Javid picked up the interrogation. 'They want to come to see what we're doing, but now is not the right time. Clara's project is so interesting we want to spend our time getting this engine right. If we can conquer this requirement, we will change the landscape of amination in every commercial sector. Realtime rendering of complex computer-generated images changes the game.'

She turned to Clara. 'My dear, you're challenging some superior brain power. Can't wait to see the outcome.'

'We've asked our folks not to come until we have it working. When they descend, it will be the entire family, probably at least twelve people who won't come all this way just for a few days. Don't have time to entertain family until this project is working.'

'Big families. Are there any other members I need to be aware of?'

Javid laughed. 'I have two younger sisters who can be very pushy, especially in pack mode, but they're no match for Clara. Hashem has a younger sister and brother both still at university.'

'So, you think my daughter can hold her own?'

'Clara is our stability. When any of us, including James, has conflict with the outside world, who do we call? Clara. When we get agitated, spiralling out of control, who calms us? Clara. If any of us steps out of line, who steps in? Clara. And we know if it gets physical, there is only one street fighter. We do not argue with Clara. She's our sister. In our culture family take care of each other.'

'Wow. Such affection. You're most certainly welcome members of this family, and I'm so grateful to meet you both. What an aura of positive energy I feel. Exciting times ahead, I think.'

Hashem reached into his pocket, extracting a memory stick. 'Nearly forgot. Hell gave me this for you. Says you'll know what it is.'

'Thanks. She's a real sweetheart.'

Janice was looking confused. 'Who has a name Hell?'

Hashem spoke. 'She's our super-duper office manager. Her proper name is Helen, but she's goth so wants to be called Hell. She keeps the business running while Clara is recovering. Keeps us all in line and shields us from all the outside World garbage we want to avoid. And who found her? Clara. What a find. And she found Jenny, our receptionist and admin lady.'

Janice turned to Clara. 'You hired a goth to run the office? What must she look like?'

Wanting to gently remind her mum about forming opinion based of perception, 'Mum, you would certainly like her. Strong, capable, knows what she's about, and a great stabiliser for these guys. She's not the black clothes and makeup type of goth. If you watch NCIS on TV, think Abbi.'

'I see. Your dad watches NCIS, so I think I know who you mean – the lab woman. Has dad met her?'

'Yes. he speaks with her regularly, and she has assembled data he need to help James with our project.'

'What does she do if you also have Jenny?'

Hashem was quickly on to this question. 'She makes sure everything runs properly. And boy, do we need her to keep models in line. Some of them can be real divas.'

Geoffrey arrived to announce dinner.

'Darling, have you met this woman they call Hell?'

'Oh, yes. What an asset she is. Very capable.'

'What about her appearance?'

'She looks great, and certainly not out of place in that office. I sense it's not just a job for her. She's found her resting place where she's accepted for who she is and what she can offer.'

'Well, Clara. Sounds like I need to visit the office to meet her. I'm behind the curve, as usual, in this wonderful venture of yours. Interesting people to meet. As soon as you're back on your feet, I'll stay an extra day so you can take me to meet all the people involved in this remarkable adventure.'

Geoffrey thought for a moment. 'If you want to visit the office, I need to spend some time with the accountant and Hell to specify the quarterly report the bank would like to support the £half million+ leasing requirement for their next equipment purchase. We could stay an extra day next weekend, and all go together. I'm sure Clara would like to see the changes since she was last there. And I'm sure James would like to get back there if only for a day.'

She turned to Clara, 'what do you think, my darling? Are you ready for a day at the office?'

Hashem reached for her hand, 'please Clara. We've all missed you so much, and we have new people who constantly hear your name as an important person in the business but need to meet the person.' As an afterthought, 'And bring your chair. I want to try it along our catwalk.'

'Let's do it. Can't wait.'

Chapter 68

It was now approaching the end of September. The atmosphere was more buoyant. Clara was slowly but surely adjusting the mindset of James to accept she is no longer a fragile invalid so they can return to normality. Whilst working, his mind was fully engaged with the project, but when relaxing she knew he still felt guilt for what happened, and his inability to care for her. He was trying to prove himself by delivering the fashion engine, but she so wanted him to concentrate on proving himself man enough to love and care for her. He had not faltered in his commitment to learn to care for her, but he saw it more as a required function than a natural response. She needed his love with no guilty sense of obligation.

She was constantly bemused by how quickly the coldness of Janice had transformed to unconditional love and genuine friendship. And the comfort Geoffrey brought to the relationship; the dad she always wanted. Neither had anything to prove regarding their love and commitment for her. How to change James. This must be her primary quest. Having faced so early in her life that one must adapt to what life throws at you, deal with it and move on, she understood that wallowing in resignation or self-pity was a waste of valuable life.

She was happy they were all going to the office next Monday, as this would certainly connect James back to his business. Removing this shackle had to be a good first step in her quest, and she knew she had to convince mum and dad she is now strong enough and mobile enough to allow James to return to the office when he felt the need. The sooner any sense of guilt is in the distant past, the better.

Chapter 69

Clara had committed much effort to walking again, swimming as often as possible, and using resistance bands throughout the day. She kept James away from her efforts as he was still not happy to see the pain she endured during this process. Only when mum is with her is she prepared to share her pain.

Friday evening. Mum and dad would arrive soon. James had been in his computer suite since they returned from shopping, albeit with the door open. She was no longer in her chair within the apartment, having ensured her routes to any part had adequate means of support for her if needed. She did have a walking stick if needed. Her only remaining difficulties were sitting on a hard seat for any length of time and walking up and down steps without support. This weekend she is determined to be fully on her feet when mum arrives as part of her quest.

'Darling, mum and dad are on their way up.'

He quickly shut down his computers, and out of the room before they arrived. The doorbell rang. He advanced towards the door to let them in. But she indicated she wanted to go. She opened the door. The shock on mum's face to see her standing there caused her to drop her bags on the floor and wrap her arms around Clara. Tears filled her eyes.

'My darling, you're walking again. What a lovely surprise.' She moved to her side with one arm around her waist. 'Come, you must tell me everything that has happened this week. So wonderful.' Her bags were forgotten. As soon as they were in the room, James went to help his father retrieve the bags on the floor.

'My darling, are you ready for shopping tomorrow?'

'Probably not tomorrow, but we can try next weekend.'

'We have a date. Boys, Clara, and I will go shopping next weekend after physio, and I think out for dinner in the evening. Could you please set your diaries.'

James looked at his father in resignation. 'At least we get a week's notice this time.'

Chapter 70

Geoffrey and Janice were dressing for their day at the EMULATE offices. He chose casual slacks and a shirt with a sports jacket. She dressed as though going to her office.

'My dear, could I suggest your dress code is somewhat too formal for a group of geeks and a goth. I think more casual attire will make you feel more comfortable in their office environment. When I first went there in my suit and tie, I felt overtly conspicuous and thus uncomfortable.'

'Sorry, my darling. Dressing in autopilot, not thinking where we're going. Will slacks and a shirt be better?'

'Perfect.'

They were soon on their way to the office, Clara using her F1 wheelchair but also taking her stick as she imagined with some amusement Hashem turning the office into a racing track as he tests her chair to destruction inflicting general mayhem. She was looking forward to returning to see Hell and meet the new staff recruited since that fateful day. Far too long away from her friends.

James held open the main door, allowing Clara to wheel herself inside. Everyone was in the reception area, including Sonya from the recruitment agency. There was bunting everywhere, Hashem had printed a full-size poster of her standing with Javid with "Welcome back our Hero" printed across it. The screens in reception had "Clara the

Invincible" beaming out of them, and everyone clapped in delight at seeing her.

She wanted to stand. Geoffrey steadied her chair as she rose to her feet. First to greet her was Hell, who wrapped her in her arms. 'Welcome back, Clara. We've so missed you.' Sonya joined them in a triple wrap. Tears were in abundance.

'Come, let's introduce you to everyone.' Hell helped her to move to Jenny, a wispy 20something with long blonde hair simply tied back in a ponytail revealing her freckled face. 'This is Jenny, our receptionist, diary keeper, and general admin. Sonya found her for us, and she has settled well in this crazy but lovely environment.'

'Lovely to meet you. You're quite a hero around here.'

The geeks lined up, now six of them from a variety of races. 'This is Phil, our one and only truly home-grown member of the geek pool.' He was stocky, good looking, ear to ear smile with a thick crop of black wavy hair and charming manner.

'*Wow*', she thought, '*a sporty good-looking geek. He certainly keeps himself in good shape.*'

'Lovely to meet you, Phil.'

'Delighted to meet you, Clara. We've all heard so much about you. So happy to see you mobile again.'

'Nearly mobile but thank you.'

She moved on to Danny and Sammy, most certainly Chinese, looking like they should still be in school, both sporting thick-rimmed glasses. They informed her they were from Hongkong, albeit they both graduated from Cambridge University.

Janice watched this welcome in awe. So much genuine outpouring of love for her daughter having never met her before. '*These geeks are all super-intelligent, but they treat my daughter as their hero.*' She made a mental note to herself '*Never again will you ever judge someone until you really know them. I must eradicate prejudice from my thoughts.*'

'Mum, come and meet Hell.'

The sound of that word "Mum" here, in public, brought tears to her eyes. She had watched proceedings under the close supervision of Geoffrey but was now quickly next to her daughter, wanting to be a part of this moment.

James had long since escaped to his office with Hashem and Javid to appraise himself of current work, and keen to see the walkway and their research using various models and was soon absorbed.

Geoffrey was still by the door, observing this lovely welcome. *'This was a great idea. She needs this connectivity.'* The door opened behind him. He turned to be confronted by no less than the partner from the auditors. 'Hello Alan, so nice to see you. Didn't expect someone of your stature for this meeting.'

'When I heard you called this meeting, I assumed it important. We need to take care of this client. Could be one of our biggest in the future. Did I miss a party?'

'No. It's a welcome back for my new daughter, Clara, my son's partner. Before you ask, we've adopted her. Such a wonderful lady.'

'This is the hero Clara who took a stabbing for James?'

'Same lady.'

'Can I meet her? Much love here for her.'

'Clara, my dear, could I introduce Alan Bishop. He's the auditor who takes care of the company finances.'

Once things had settled, Sonya, having said her farewells, retreated to her own office. Clara and Janice settled with Hell to get a quick update on events before her meeting with Geoffrey and Alan. 'It's ok if mum listens in?'

'Sure. Might be boring for her.'

Feigning whispering but clearly audible, 'My mum is a director of a big pharmaceutical company,' having forgotten the name of the company. 'She's Dr Janice Caldwell, biochemist extraordinaire.'

'Okaaay.'

At that moment, Hashem appeared. 'Can I borrow your wheelchair?'

'Sure. Try not to break it and remember the speed limit around the office.'

'I will need you to do some runs for me when I've calibrated our cameras.'

'Why me? What are you looking for?'

'I need a wireframe of you wheeling your chair. As the only qualified wheelchair driver around here, you are the natural choice.'

'But why do you need this?'

'Not everyone who buys clothes walks. Many need wheelchairs. We're not building an engine that discriminates against people who cannot walk.'

Tears welled in her eyes as she stood. 'Come here, you lovely man. You deserve a big hug. What a lovely thought.'

Janice could not let such a moment pass as she also stood. 'Hashem, you truly are an inspiration. Your compassion is overwhelming. I can only aspire to your thoughtfulness. I'm so happy to know you. You truly have a heart of gold. Thank you for being part of this venture.'

Once Hashem was on his way with the wheelchair, in it; not pushing it, Hell continued. 'The only news since we last spoke is Hashem and Javid have hired a female geek, Estelle is her name. I've met her briefly. I don't see her fitting in here. Obviously very intelligent, but a tad too full of herself. Looks down on mere mortals. Starts in a couple of weeks so you might see a few sparks until I get her trained in our ways.' They both laughed.

Clara and Hell had agreed on Friday the idea of a corporate lunch. Hell had briefed the geeks unit to clear their laptops from the Starship Enterprise cluster by midday so caterers could deliver a plethora of sandwiches, dips, and drinks for everyone. Meeting over with Alan, they all gathered around the cluster, relaxing together as a single unit. They overwhelmed Janice with the positive energy she could feel in this energetic arena of intellect and humanity. She had never experienced such a gathering.

Around 3pm, all runs completed by Clara and feeling the overwhelming impact of such a day, it was time for her to retreat. Mum was first to spot this need and alerted Geoffrey. James wanted to stay longer, so they left without him. Once back at the apartment, Clara made herself comfortable on the couch.

'Whilst James is not here, can I express my views on the way forward now I'm practically mobile?'

'Of course, my dear. What's on your mind?'

'James still feels beholden to stay here every day when we all know he now needs to be back in play. This is stressing him. I'm now able to fend for myself. I would like your agreement that when he feels the need to go to the office, he has our blessing. Obviously, he still needs to be here when I need to go to physio and any other appointments, but otherwise he should be free to attend to his business. As you saw today, much of my project is playing out in the office. This is where he needs to be. And I'm happy to go with him if needed. I've missed what you experienced today. Both of us need to retreat from isolation and slowly return to normality.'

Janice sat next to her and scooped her into her arms. 'As always, my darling, you know what's best for our boy. If you're ready to let him return to his business duties, you have our full support. And can I say what I experienced today is truly remarkable. I want to do this more often. When you're ready, Geoffrey and I would like to host a party here for all the wonderful people involved in your project. I could feel the energy. I want to stay close to this wonderful group of people. I have much to learn from their approach.'

'Thanks, mum. I know this will be best for all of us. I'll speak with James about a party. Probably Christmastime will be best as they'll need a break by then.'

'I sincerely hope you and James will join us for Christmas. It's time we had a proper family Christmas.'

'I think you and dad need to speak with James about Christmas. Could we invite Hashem and Javid if they have nowhere else on Christmas Day?'

'My darling, they are very welcome. They could join us on Christmas Eve and stay over to Boxing Day. Such delightful boys. Let's discuss Christmas as family next weekend. I accept James is focussed on this project, but he must consider others, and a few days break to recharge could well be what they all need. Leave this to me and dad.'

'Thanks. *Good luck with that idea.*'

'If you're sure you can manage without James, dad and I should be on our way home. Truly wonderful day.'

'I'm fine, mum. Probably take a nap. But I'm mobile around the apartment, so no problem. Need to spend the rest of the week shaping up for our shopping trip next weekend.'

'Of course, but no overdoing it. I know your grit and determination, young lady, but I know when to put the brakes on you. No sliding backward, you hear.'

'No mum. I'll be careful.'

Geoffrey decided he needed to move things on. 'Come dear, let's get ourselves organised and leave Clara to nap. She's already had a busy day.'

It was after 7pm when James returned. She was still napping on the couch.

'Sorry I'm so late, but much has accumulated on my desk that needs attention. I know I've broken the rules but boy, did your return lift the place today. You created a real buzz. Do you think we could do it more often?'

'Come, sit with me. I have the agreement of mum and dad that so long as you are not derelict in your duties towards me, you can go to your office when you need to be there. Which means that if I don't need you to help me, you can go as often as you like. Does this solve your problem?'

'Will you come as well?'

'College starts for me in two weeks. But until then, I would like to come for a couple of days. Maybe we could go on the way home from physio. It felt good to be amongst those people today.'

'Fantastic. I don't know how you convinced mum and dad, but thanks. What are we doing about dinner? Shall we go out?'

'I've had enough excitement for one day. How about you order our favourite take-away?'

'Consider it done', as he reached for his phone.

After ordering, 'Will be here in 30 minutes.' Looking at her reluctance to move, 'Are you okay? You look wiped out.'

'It's been a big day today. Needed to get us some slack to return to normality. I'll be okay after a good night's sleep.'

'I sensed you pushed yourself last week. Now I understand why. I love you so much for the way you manage our lives, but a few more weeks is okay if you need it. We've come so far. Please don't do anything to spoil the journey. I know I'm champing at the bit to get back to our project, but not at your expense. I committed to look after you as you would look after me, and that commitment still stands.'

'Come, hold me. We need to move towards normality again, but in a fresh way. I will work hard this week to shop with mum next weekend without a chair. I want next weekend to be the last they feel committed to come here. I'll need weekend space for my college work, and we need some time together on our own. I want you to commit weekends for us. I'll try to wind down mum and dad to every other weekend and then phase out their commitment to a normal family engagement. You will have to help me achieve this to convince them you are now mindful of your responsibilities. I want us to control our lives again. Do you understand?'

'My darling Clara, you tell me what you want me to do. I commit to you I will deliver.'

'That's all we need.'

The building intercom sounded. 'Dinner's here.'

Chapter 71

The week went well. James went to the office Monday, Wednesday, and a half-day Friday so they could shop in the afternoon. When she wasn't engaged with her streamed classes, she worked hard in the pool and the gym, ensuring she had an afternoon nap so as not to cause any disquiet with James in the evening. They both went to the office after physio on Tuesday and Thursday but left early so she could use the pool, and she could watch her recorded classes.

Once back at the apartment on Friday afternoon, they sat together discussing how to ensure her plan would work.

'By the way, mum and dad want to discuss Christmas. They want us to go to St Albans for a family Christmas. We can also take Hashem and Javid if they have nowhere to go.'

'Is this already arranged between you and mum, or do I have a say?'

'I'm only telling you what they have expressed to me. This is a family discussion, so we all can agree. And mum wants to host a party here for all the office staff. She wants to stay connected with them.'

'That won't work. I know my mother's idea of a cocktail party. Too stuffy for our staff. What we could do is to hire a private room at a restaurant or hotel and do something themed to make it different. Need a variety of food types as well. Maybe some music or some theatrics after dinner. I'll give it some thought. I like the idea, but not my mother's way.'

His mind was working. 'I've seen billboards for themed places in London. I've seen one themed on The Great Gatsby. Just across the river, I think. Even if our staff brought other halves, we probably don't have the numbers for such a place. Could invite some key collaborators to let them know they're valued team players. Could you scan the web to see what you can find, including minimum numbers and costs?'

'Sure. I'll do it next week after mum and dad have left.'

'Okay, my beauty, what do we need to do to get you bright and perky for our plan?'

She was smiling inside to see him relaxed and ready to have his shackles removed. 'I want to go for a short swim to loosen up. Then a nice shower would certainly help.'

'Go for your swim while I get dinner organised. Then, we should have time to play before our shower. We have a couple of hours before they arrive.'

Just before mum and dad arrived, she took a painkiller as insurance. Her left hip was still causing her problems, but Jules assured her this would subside as she strengthened her muscles to full fitness. For her plan to work she must not show any sign of pain to mum, and she wants to drive for their trip to see Jules to further endorse her return to full mobility. As their car was an automatic, this should not pose any objections from her mum.

Chapter 72

'Back to college today. Are you up for it?'

'I'm looking forward to it. See my friends and get back to my studies. I've learnt a lot working with you, but it won't pass my exams. Can you drop me off on the way to the office?'

'No problem. Are you ready? And when you finish at college come to the office, by taxi if necessary, so I can bring you home.'

'Good exercise, that will be. If I'm okay, I'll take the underground. Need to keep up the exercise.'

'Please, no heroics. If you need a ride home, you come to the office, especially if the weather's not great. I want you to stay in touch with the project. Need your experienced eye on what we're doing so you need to come to the office at least once every week. You can always have a swim in the evening if you need exercise.'

She liked this caring James. 'Why don't we agree if you need me specifically to come to the office, send me a text. I'll come at least once every week to keep in touch with Hell. I also want to stay in touch with Jules but can only see her after college so I can stop by the office on the way back. Are we good?'

'Great. This project is now too big for my system at home. Need to be at the office most days. I want this system ready to demonstrate in June for the end-of-year fashion show.'

Clara's return to college was greeted with much interest. Everyone knew of her heroics, changing their minds about this unusual woman. There was also a noticeable change in the maturity of the students as those who failed to adjust to life after secondary school had fallen by the wayside, as is the case after the first year in higher education establishments. Those who survived had adapted to the more mature attitude of college education, and Clara was no longer the oldest student as two students somewhat older than her had transferred from other colleges. Clara, herself, had now adjusted to the demands of education, and enjoyed the warm, comforting feeling of family. She was no longer an outsider; she was no longer alone in the world.

The first semester went well. Demands of project work learning about working with different fabrics to explore the nature and characteristics of the multitude of man-made fibre versus more natural fibre meant many hours in the evening at her machine in the computer suite. Although there was little interaction whilst both engaged in their respective quests, she felt a togetherness so missing during her first year in London. The demands for information by James put additional demands on her studies, which she took in her stride as she now really felt she had the opportunity to fulfil her dream, embracing these demands with vigour and purpose.

Christmas was a lively family affair where she felt the love and joy of family so missing in her life for so long. Even the pain in her abdomen had gone; a distant memory as full mobility had returned. They spent a week in St Albans where her newfound mum spoilt her rotten including two days shopping in the Christmas sales. Laughter was her tonic, and love was in her heart.

Hashem and Javid were with them from Christmas Eve until Boxing Day, both lavishing technology presents on Clara, spending time to teach her how to use them. It was their way of engrossing her into the technology surrounding her at home and in the office. They genuinely care she feels part of the team.

Sam could not believe how this girl of misfortune had transformed this household from three disconnected souls into a loving family of four people totally connected with each other. This house now felt like a home, and she savoured the joy it gave her as her only other life was caring for her old and fragile mother, now immersed in heart-breaking dementia. It overjoyed her when Clara went with her to see her mother, having heard much about this unfortunate young woman but unable to fully engage as they had never met. Her mother could now put a picture to this woman connecting all the pieces accumulated but fractured in her depleting mind.

James decided they should spend an evening at the restaurant where Clara was so abused encouraging her to host their table, noting the discomfort of the proprietor who dealt with wine orders as he took their order from her. He was clearly uncomfortable as Clara relished the idea of turning the tables, especially her new apparent prosperity.

She also sought some of her past friends. Some were pleased to see her; others had moved on, no longer recognising the person they knew. In all cases, she decided not to spoil such a joyous Christmas recounting the events of that terrible night in August. It was in the past. She was grateful for the resulting transformation in her life but recounting her horror as she felt the knife enter her body, with the heat of the ensuing pain, was lodged deep in her mind, as far away from her conscious memory as she could bury it. Not a word to James about the flashes in her mind of that event as she knew she would arouse guilt which would stress him, spoiling the joy she now felt in her new life. She had worked hard to reduce the scar on her abdomen to remove this constant reminder. Complete removal of this scar is something she has studied and is on her agenda.

New Year's Eve was spent at Fredericks with Javid, Hashem and his new lady friend, Amanda, who was also geeky. She had a doctorate in Social Evolution and lectured at the London School of Economics on subjects such as evolving social effects on economic growth, and the role of women in the workplace and politics. Clara could not relate to Estelle, a female geek in the office who was apparently very capable but liked people to be aware of her superior intellect. Okay in the office, but not for socialising. In contrast, Amanda was down to earth friendly. Clara thought the gulf between their intellectual capabilities could probably be bridged by their understanding of loneliness. Although a beautiful woman, it was evident her intellect frightened most men away. It was also obvious in Hashem she had found a soulmate and they were very relaxed and happy together. Clara could not wish happiness on a nicer person. She regarded Hashem as a brother and a lovely person deserving of a good mate. His boyish charm hid his caring nature. He had quickly spotted her distress in those early days and was always there for her.

During conversation Hashem let it slip that he and Amanda were looking for a place to live, and which was clearly news to Javid. Although Amanda lived in Greater London, owning her own apartment, it broke his 10 – 15-minute walk to the office rule, the primary reason they settled on the office in Camden as commuting on public transport to Hashem is an alien pastime to be avoided. He could now afford London prices so a serious venture for the start of the new year.

The customers in the restaurant this evening were all regulars who knew each other, if only by sight. They even included some recognisable celebrities. As midnight approached, the atmosphere coalesced into a party with much mingling and champagne. As the party erupted on the sounds of Big Ben chiming in the New Year, Clara could not help but reflect on the difference a year makes. This time last year James had taken a brief time-out to have dinner together but back in his computer suite early the following morning.

Chapter 73

From the middle of January until the end of February the weather was dreary with long, hard frosts and much snow, even in London. Moving around London was slow, and the general mood reflected the dark grey skies that forever loomed in the sky. The eerie mist rolling along the river Thames much of the time blanked the view across the river, creating a sense of isolation. Clara spent most of her waking hours either engaged in her own college studies or seeking data for James. Although still spending much time on her own when not at college, she could always stop and speak with her new mum, who was never too busy to take calls from her newfound daughter, and to Hell who had become a good friend and soulmate.

On one of these particularly dreary days, Hashem and Amanda were visiting because Hashem wanted wireframe scans of Amanda. The scanning pod was still in the computer suite. As it was a Sunday, they made it a lunch, and part social as everyone needed a break. Clara helped Amanda to use the pod, having now been inside several times, while Hashem captured the images he wanted. Amanda was clearly happier using this pod in private, realising the intrusive nature. She could not imagine using it in the office, even in the evenings, knowing how much office surveillance was present.

Clara prepared lunch catering for any taste, having forgotten to ask Hashem about any dietary preferences of

Amanda. So pre-prepared cream of pumpkin soup followed by a table grill of various meats, vegetables, eggs, cheese, and pasta with salad on the side so they could eat at leisure. A tiramisu purchased from their favourite Italian would round off the meal for anyone still seeking additional delights after the table grill. James had remembered to stock up on Hashem's favourite and preferred beer, with a medium burgundy wine for anyone else.

Once the grill was fully loaded with each person's preferences, Clara used the occasion to find out where Hashem and Amanda are with their search for somewhere to live. Amanda explained that the pressure of his work and the gloomy weather meant they spent whatever time available at weekends together at her apartment. Although she did recount an interesting Saturday visit to Rigby & Peller being measured for the seamless bra she needed for the wireframe scan.

Clara looked at Hashem, 'how are you getting on with Rigby & Peller? Do you now understand the confounding variety of shapes and sizes of busts?'

'Every time I think I understand different types of bra they throw another set of variables at me. Sometimes I think they enjoy watching me try to make sense mathematically trying to emulate bra shapes and effects. So complicated. They try to make the whole concept of bras a mystery to see if a mere man can understand the magical transformation a bra provides.'

Clara is amused by his discord. 'You need to remember underwear for women is recent in terms of evolution. We're talking late 19th century for the first modern bra and still not generally adopted by some cultures. The history of bras is inextricably intertwined with the social history of the status of women, including the evolution of fashion and changing views of the female body. Although there is evidence dating back to the Egyptians relating to some form of female underwear, even female panties as we know them today only started in the 1940s. Until then most females went completely commando.'

'You should consider modern bras functioning as a tool of deception more than a means of support. The idea is to make the upper body more appealing. If a woman wears a bikini top, it tends to be minimal, showing no visible signs of support. Many bikini tops provide no support, only the barest of modesty. But would you expect to see a woman wearing only a bra as an upper body covering? A bra is intended to provide a more favourable profile for her outer clothing, thus only serves as a utility, not a fashion statement.'

Hashem slaps the table. 'That's it. Clara, you've done it again. All my discussions with Rigby & Peller are about separation, support, and cleavage, but not once have they used the word utility. Of course, women do not display their bra because it only provides utility. Now I know how to use this data. A bra only defines a shape to the upper body. Once selected, it only modifies the wireframe. Brilliant. I don't need to consider a bra as a piece of clothing requiring any rendering, just a modification to upper body shape. I'll finish these algorithms in a few days.'

Hashem remembered an observation he made. 'Explain this for me. When we had the camera hanging out of our office window, I made several observations, some of which I could rationalise, but other still evade my understanding. As you're studying evolution of fashion, maybe you can answer these anomalies.'

'Okay. What puzzles you?'

'Why do females wearing shorts, jeans or trousers walk with a more confident gait than when they wear a skirt or dress? For the same shoes even their length of stride can be different.'

'Wow. Your observational skills are incredible. You miss nothing. I think this is all about consciousness of revealing underwear or even more. In trouser-type clothing a woman feels completely covered and more carefree in her movement.'

Hashem: 'That makes little sense. Some wear leggings that reveal far more than a skirt.'

'Ha, but they feel in control of this exposure. Think on this one. A female will lie on the beach or around a pool in the skimpiest of bikini bottoms but as soon as she moves somewhere else, she will tie a wrap around their middle or don a pair of shorts or even some type of dress to cover their crotch area, but a man won't bother. There are many such contradictions you will observe with females as they both instinctively want to control their apparent availability but want to show what is on offer should they select you. Do you know the human female is the only female in the animal kingdom with pubic hair?'

Hashem, in disbelief, 'No. Why is that?'

'From my studies it appears we are the only animal that understands life, death, and procreation. Back to the Adam and Eve story – conscious realisation. Pubic hair provided a natural cover post-puberty before clothes.'

Amanda was laughing at Hashem's naivety. 'I think Hashem needs to come to your classes.'

Clara, still giggling, 'It gets even more bizarre. Females consider their public hair as a psychological cover but what do they do to stop this hair either bulging their skimpy bikini bottoms or escaping through the sides, they have it removed whether a bikini wax or a full Brazilian. We must take all these seemingly irrational activities into account in our design work. It would surprise you how much design calculation goes into the design of a bikini bottom to minimise coverage without exposure. And then we must choose materials that will not disturb this fine balance when wet.'

Amanda and Clara were still laughing at this craziness. Amanda turned to Hashem. 'And you think you can conquer all these quirky female traits. When did men ever really understand women and their ways?'

Hashem, feeling he was the butt of a joke, 'then why is it most of the major fashion designers are men?'

Clara: 'Good question. Historically, women have not been encouraged to be senior to men in design, but this is changing rapidly. Historically, a woman adorns her body to attract a man – again the opposite to the animal kingdom. So, it has always been assumed a man will know better than a woman what will attract a man to her.'

Amanda decided she could contribute to this discussion. 'There is evidence to suggest our species is some 150,000 years old. But it is only in the last 10,000-years that the coming together of people in ever-increasing numbers that technological revolutions radically affected the relationship between men and women. Yet we are still programmed to be tribal hunter-gatherers. The substantial creation of wealth and resulting social upheaval upon the rise of agriculture, then industrialisation, and most recently technology have obscured this important fact in the relationship between men and women.'

'The most critical legacy of bygone times was a sharp division of labour between men and women – a necessary condition for the survival of the species. Many of the sexist biases and social institutions that persist in the world came into being as a result, the two most pervasive of which are misogyny and patriarchy where I define misogyny as a disdain for women and general denigration of feminine values, and Patriarchy as a set of institutionalised social rules put in place by men to control the sexual and reproductive rights of women.'

'My primary interest of study at present is how the inherent differences between man and woman play out in the business arena. Very topical as we see more women climbing the executive ladder.'

Clara had been studying the importance of the 1960s to the evolution of fashion. 'Surely 1960s women changed the game in the free world when they finally found their freedom of choice with control of their reproductive systems with the introduction of contraception. Women have subsequently fought for their rights to equality ever since. In the fashion world, there was even a period of women going topless. Then it went too far when the feminist movement, wanting to emulate man, burnt their bras.'

Amanda jumped back in. 'You're right. The contraceptive pill changed everything. Women are no longer shackled to the patriarchal view and can express their desirability as they wish. Women can now choose if, and when they have children and with whom. Although men are physically stronger than us women, we have control over their desire for both pleasure and heirs in such a way we can achieve equality within a relationship. A woman's ability to refuse a man's advances is the source of their power. Men have needed to up their game in how they present themselves to women to find a mate. Although an expression of wealth is still an aphrodisiac by far the most compelling is the attractiveness in presentation and behaviour towards women.'

Clara: 'Fashion plays its part in the visual presentation. Even in religions and conservative cultures where women are still suppressed, if you look beneath their outer clothing, you are likely to find modern fashion.'

James: 'When I think of glamorous fashion, I think of the spectacular Hollywood movies of the golden era. Not a bra in sight, just beautiful dress design that made even the less glamorous of women look good.'

Clara: 'Anyone in particular?'

James: 'Cyd Charisse, Rita Hayworth, Leslie Caron, and of course the iconic Audrey Hepburn. She could make any clothing look good, and she would always radiate through with her smile. What I see today is a race by women to get noticed by revealing as much as possible, leaving little to the imagination.'

Clara: Leaning towards him with a glint in her eyes, 'This is a new James to me. So what makes a woman attractive to you?'

James: 'A woman feeling comfortable being feminine. I hear Amanda's view on the fight of women through the ages, but since Adam & Eve when has man won an argument with a woman? I'm all for equality but not for woman trying to emulate man. It's the difference between man and woman that makes relationships attractive and interesting.'

Clara: 'What do you see in me?'

James: 'Besides the obvious fact you're a beautiful woman, you don't try to compete as a man, and your infectious smile is my most calming influence. Wasn't it Marilyn Monroe who said her most important make-up is her smile? I remember the first time I visited you in hospital. I was totally stressed about what to expect. I walked into your infectious smile. Made me relax. Everything would be fine.'

Clara: Reaching over to kiss him. 'Thank you. Means much to me. *Playtime later, I think.*'

James: 'I like what we have together. I don't want you to compete with me as a man. I like that we're different.'

Amanda to Hashem: 'Why are you attracted to me? When was the last time you had a social conversation with me or even Javid? Do you realise I have little idea of your taste in women, music, or even your politics?'

Hashem: 'I can relate to what James has stated. Besides being a very beautiful woman, you are interesting and extraordinarily intelligent, active in essentially a man's world, but you know who you are. I feel very comfortable with you in my life.'

Amanda: 'Very much appreciated. Thank you. We should talk more often.'

Hashem: 'My politics are simple. Mostly mediocre people seeking celebrity with populist views, making mediocre decisions in the name of progress. Very rare to encounter someone with a meaningful ideology that captures the imagination.'

'As for music, I'm not into genres which appear to expand regularly for no logical reason other than people cannot think in expanse. For me there is wonderful music, and noise. Of the wonderful music, I have my preferences but not dictated by genre. I enjoy being called a geek because it allows me to explore anywhere my mind wants to go without needing to justify myself.'

Amanda: 'And how do you see the future for us?'

Hashem to Amanda: 'In the short-term you can educate me about women and relationships to help me understand all these female contradictions. I accept this project places much demand on my time, but I hope you understand the cause is worthy, and the likely outcome exciting.'

Amanda: 'I wouldn't be sitting here if I didn't understand your commitment to this project. I like what you're doing and want to be a part in any way I can.'

Hashem: 'Let's see how many pairs of shoes you wear out walking the catwalk for me in various attire so I can compute the likely outcome given any set of parameters.'

Amanda: 'You expect me to model for you? What about Hell, or one of your professional models?'

Hashem: 'You're prettier, nicer, and available during the evenings. I will want to start you fully clothed, then remove a layer, and another layer until there is nothing but

217

a bikini so I can see the changes in how you walk. Then we try a diverse range of clothing for me to understand what works for you and why. Can't expect Hell or a model to do this in the office during office hours. Also, I now have your wireframes and I can put you through the tunnel in the office with and without clothing to accurately motion capture your natural movements. With you as a control model, I can learn so much.'

She looked at him, 'you seriously expect me to spend all my evenings modelling for you?'

'Not just modelling but helping me to think this through. When I can show you what you do, you are bright, so can help me to understand why. I need your intellect and your body.'

She gave him a long stare to see if he looked serious. 'So, this is our evenings for the foreseeable future. If you're serious about working together, I think it might be interesting, and fun. If we find anything really interesting, can I write it up as principal author?'

Hashem: 'So long as we retain commercially sensitive information, I see no problem in this. What do you think, James?'

James: 'You've aired the commercially sensitive piece, so leave me out of your domestic affairs. I think it's a great way of a controlled experiment so long as you survive without killing each other.'

Clara: 'I'd like to be there when you're trying something new. Might have another word or two to help you.'

Hashem: 'Not only would your presence be useful, I think you should be there because you're the one with the knowledge we need.'

Clara: 'Just let me know when my presence will be useful to you. What's Javid up to?'

Hashem: 'He's trying to make sense of how different shaped bodies expand through sizes. He now has all the algorithms for the standard shapes used in the fashion world. Working out how each changes shape for sizing is challenging, but there must be set parameters because brands can put the same clothes out there in different sizes and they will fit the intended body shape. I sometimes think

218

we're trying to be too perfect when the underlying situation is far from perfect.'

Conversation continued around the sizing of people and how clothes helped people to look good or hide bodies that are not well maintained. This conversation continued late into the afternoon with no one interested in leaving the table.

Amanda: 'We should do this more often if only to have a break from the continual subject of algorithms.'

James: 'But we have a project we must deliver with a fixed deadline. We don't have time for socialising, maybe afterwards.'

Amanda turns to Hashem: 'How much time do you think you've saved after one simple word from Clara?'

Hashem: 'She has refocused my task, so I accept your argument.'

Amanda: 'You may not have noticed, but Clara and I are young women, the primary focus of the fashion world. In addition, I lecture on social trends and Clara studies fashion. I think we should consider regular lunches. Certainly, Javid should join us, and maybe we should include Hell as she has an interesting perspective. She was telling me about her previous experiences in the workplace regarding her choice of clothing. What's interesting about her experiences was she was working in the media sector amongst celebrities considered fashion icons.'

James to Hashem: 'What do you think?'

Amanda (before Hashem could answer): 'As I am asked to sacrifice much of my free time to this project, or become a project widow, I propose we have regular Sunday lunches to express views and we should include Javid and Hell. If you and James see this as a loss of project development time look upon it as a valuable working lunch. Clara, do you agree?'

Clara: 'Absolutely. Look at us today. We've sat at this table for nearly four hours. It must have been interesting to share ideas and knowledge. And what a great way to spend time together. You have my vote. What about you, Hashem?'

Hashem: 'I agree today has been valuable to me, and worth the discussion. What about you, James?'

James: Thinking he is being usurped but then tempering his disapproval after remembering his dad's valuable advice, 'Okay, we do this again next week including Javid, and Hell if she wants to come as today has been interesting.'

Clara: 'Hell will jump at the opportunity to join us. She has been trying to get closer to this project for ages. At some point soon we will have media attention. As she has a background in media, we should foster her skills.'

After Hashem and Amanda had left, having helped with the kitchen, Clara pressed her need for intimacy before he considered returning to the computer suite. 'You were very nice to me today. Deserves some special playtime. Are we good?'

As they lay replete of any need for any more immediate intimacy, she turned to him, 'Great afternoon. What do you think?'

'It concerned me that such a discussion might make you feel out of it. But you not only held your own; you were right in it. It was me who was out of it. You and Amanda seem to get on well. She's an interesting lady when you take the trouble to speak with her. I can't argue we advanced our cause today, so let's see how these lunches progress. If, as you say, Hell has a keen interest to contribute, let's see what she has to offer. I completely agree we should foster her media skills because we will need them. Better in-house than some agency.'

Chapter 74

Monday at college finished for the day, Clara visits the office, not least to chat with Hell. After some chitchat about the taming of Estelle as they made her face the reality she may consider herself an intellectual, but some other geeks, especially Hashem and Javid could easily outgun her. Hell enjoyed putting Estelle into situations where her weaknesses were exposed. Whereas no one overtly said anything to her, Hell made sure she understood her attitude was not conducive to the office environment hoping she would leave. She chose to modify her behaviour.

'Hell, I need to ask you something. Hashem was at our apartment yesterday with Amanda so Hashem could get a wireframe scan of her in the pod, which is still in our computer suite. We had lunch and a great chat for four hours. Along the way, we found answers for some issues we face. It was so good we made these lunches regular and wondered if you would like to join them as you have some interesting angles and ideas. I think you can add to the mix. What do you think?'

When and where will these lunches be?

'At our apartment on Sundays.'

'Who will be there?'

'Amanda, Hashem, Javid and you.'

'Count me in.'

'Great. If you arrive between 11 and 12 o'clock and be prepared for a long lunch.'

'Thanks for thinking of me. You know I love what's happening here and I want to contribute. Any dress code needed?'

'Think Hashem and Javid and be as casual as you like. Any dietary concerns I need to know about?'

'Nothing to be concerned about. How did you get on with a table full of nerds?'

'I have an ace; I know the fashion world. You have at least two aces. It will be interesting to see them in action.'

'And what aces are you thinking about?'

'You have media skills and experience, and you know who you are. Both valuable.' As an afterthought, 'And I think a first from Oxford is one hell of a qualification – excuse the pun.'

They both laughed as Amanda came through the door. Hell was first to speak. 'Hi Amanda. Early today.'

'After the discussion yesterday, Hashem wants to reset some parameters for upper body sizing. Are you joining us next Sunday?'

'Wouldn't miss it.'

'Great. With three of us there we can teach these geeks a thing or two about women.'

They all laughed as Amanda made her way to where Hashem was sitting. Clara made her way to spend some time with Javid to see if she could help him with sizing. She quickly realised how much she enjoyed being with these lovely geeks, and how much she learned observing them ply their skills. She spent as much time with them as she could afford thereafter.

Chapter 75

The week flew by as they realised it was Saturday morning and they needed to plan and shop for their expanded working lunch tomorrow. Over breakfast James remembers next Sunday is Easter Sunday. 'It's Easter next week. Mum and dad will be here for their last weekend before the show. We'll have to cancel lunch next week.'

Clara, quickly realising the opportunity presented for mum, and the likelihood if they were to cancel lunch, it would likely set a president, 'Think about it for a moment. Mum is desperate to stay in touch with our wonderful team. Remember, she wanted to have a party before Christmas. If we have our lunch as usual, it will keep her sweet as we won't see them again for some weeks. I think they both would love being at such a lunch, and we have the situation under our control.'

He looked at her somewhat bemused. 'Do I know this beautiful, but scheming woman? Boy, has your education developed one formidable woman. On balance, I like your thinking. I agree mom and dad will enjoy the company, but how many of our group will have other plans for Easter?'

'We'll find out tomorrow.'

The dilemma she faced was what to provide in the way of food. She wanted to be at the table, not in the kitchen. *'Think, girl. Think working lunch. Cold buffet, or caterers, or home delivery.* James, I don't want to disjoint our lunch with working in the kitchen. I can only think of hot/cold buffet, or home delivery. Any ideas?'

'I liked your idea last week with the table grill. Allowed everyone to feast as they liked. The weather forecast tomorrow suggests a warmer day than last week, so we

222

could do a mix of hot and cold buffet. Let's go see what we can find. Must get more beer for Hashem and Javid.'

Sunday morning started with playtime followed by a leisurely shower together. After a quick breakfast, it surprised her that James was prepared to help her prepare for lunch. *'He's serious about partnership. I like this version.'*
They selected so much choice she envisaged dining on leftovers for most of the week. All hot food could either be quickly microwaved or left in the oven until needed. They would leave all veg raw, prepared to be accompanied with a variety of dips, including some Indian dips they found in a deli. Various pies and cold meats were divided on to two serving plates, one for each end of the table. James popped out to the local bakery who provided a range of fresh breads, the aromas of which filled the room.
Javid arrived first, soon followed by Hell, and then Hashem and Amanda. As soon as Amanda saw Hell, 'Wow. You look great. Now we see the real Hell in all her glory.'
Under her leather jacket Hell wore a leather bikini top, choker with silver studs, a leather miniskirt and knee-length platform boots – all in black. Black shoulder-length shiny hair with a fringe and black leather studded watch strap completed this stunning picture.
Amanda's comment triggered a missing component in Hashem's work. *'Must get a study of her in platform boots. Hadn't thought of this. Another benefit of these lunches. We need these women to help us.'*
James: 'What's everyone drinking? I have beer for Javid and Hashem, and red and white wine and a variety of soft drinks. For you, Hell, I bought a token black beer not knowing if Goths have a preferred drink.'
'Fresh bull's blood, but if you don't have it red wine will do nicely.'
The amusement in this exchange created the relaxed environment needed to start their lunch.
Clara to Javid: 'As you were not here last week the benefit of these lunches, besides ensuring you have some nutritious food at least once per week, is to air any challenging issues in the hope we can help think it through,

away from your computers. Do you have something you can share with us?'

Javid: 'One problem I have relates to online selling. I can assemble a wireframe from the dimensions keyed by the buyer to show the clothes. But what about the head? Not sure it's a good idea to have people use their webcam for us to create and render a head.'

Hell saw her chance to contribute her knowledge from her media activities. 'Why not use the methods out there today? Fashion catalogues use models, but you're back to a one size picture. The best form of promotion by brands is to find popular celebrities to wear their clothes at functions or on the street where media photographers will take pictures that will appear in the media. This is by far the most effective way of selling. If it's good enough for her to wear, its good enough for me. If the brand has a stable of celebrities in different body sizes, your system can use the closest celebrity to the size of the buyer and achieve a double psychological connection with the celebrity and the clothes. If she looks good in it, and she's my size, I'll look that good as well. Great selling platform.'

James: 'Hell, I owe you an apology. Knowing of your background, I should have realised months ago you probably have much experience to contribute. Welcome to this forum as a valued member. Anything you ever want to throw into the mix please do not hesitate.'

Hell: 'This company has a great bunch of special people, and this project is mind-blowing. I want to be as big a part as I can contribute. So, thanks. I'm on it.' Hell and Clara smiled at each other.

Hashem: 'I would like you to walk our catwalk in those boots. It only occurred to me today when I saw you, we haven't profiled someone who walks in platform boots. Don't want to get caught out if any of the students are punk or Goth. But I will also need a wireframe of you for simulation purposes.'

Hell: How do you get the wireframe?

Clara: We have a scanning pod here in our computer suite. Less intrusive than the office.

Hell: What do I do?

Hashem: 'First we need to find you a bra which optimises your upper body shape. Do you have a bra you think is a perfect fit for you we could lend to Rigby & Peller to make you a seamless skin-coloured bra for scanning? You will also need skin-coloured underwear, seamless and with no elasticated edges.'

Hell: 'Goths don't wear conventional bras. I only wear a black bra in the office as a compromise just for the office. As you can see, I'm not wearing one today. They're always tops in one form or another. I have a seamless bra-like top they could use. Traditional Goth clothing is mostly leather.'

Clara, wanting to diffuse any insecurity towards Hashem, 'Along with fur, the most enduring of clothing materials. As people migrated to colder climates over the millennia, the demand for warmer clothing increased. The only option was leather and fur. Man had to face the dangers of pursuing ever larger animals to provide more coverage. Fur has an evolution unmatched in the clothing business with leather as a derivative. Even though fur and leather are frowned upon by animal rights activists, it is still the covering of choice in the colder climates. In the UK there are difficulties because of our generally mild winters, but not so in Central Europe where temperatures can dip to levels where only fur will suffice. Even in the UK, fur is returning as a fashion accessory. Leather is the obvious alternative in our milder climate.'

Turning to Hell, 'I'll come into the office on Monday and explain what Hashem needs and how we achieve it. This is not a problem as Diane from Rigby & Peller will be in the office on Tuesday.'

Amanda detected Clara's defence of Hell. 'You look stunning without a bra. But I've been through this process. Diane's a very interesting lady. You'll be amazed what she can teach you about breast shape and support. It was worth the scan just to speak with her.'

Hell wanted to move the conversation away from her breasts. 'Thanks, Amanda. Not a problem. Are you studying anything interesting?'

Amanda, noting the deflection. 'As it happens, I have two areas of current interest. In society we have evolution of society, and we have short-term fads. I include equality campaigns between man and woman but not by wrote. Patriarchal man still has difficulties understanding that contribution needs to be based on merit, not gender or indeed statute.'

'My serious research has much to do with the elevation of women to lead corporations and, indeed, countries. If we look at the evolution of humankind, we notice that the rules for women have not changed over time because they bear children. It is man who has adjusted to changing rules from hunter to gatherer to provider and now to colleague. If you look at typical TV product ads in the 1950s and 1960s, you will immediately see the massive change in attitude men have been forced to adopt over a single generation. Women proved their capabilities in the workplace during the war, but then told to keep house and bear children during what they called the baby boom. Men quickly and convenient feigned memory loss to secure control again. But now the men in our lives are asked to make radical shifts in attitude and behaviour fuelled by our recently found independence and control over our own procreation lives. The only real issue for women is leaving the decision to have children too long in preference for a career. It's an interesting balance that women need to face in their desire for equality in the executive workplace.'

Hell: 'But surely this is a problem that you, Clara, and me are facing in our careers, but with no obvious solution.'

Amanda: 'True. But women are relying on men to find a solution. My current paper suggests that women need to find a solution that works for all.'

Hell: 'Interesting. Must read this paper when finished.'

Clara: 'But what about your current fad? We base fashion on fad, so I'm interested to know your current thinking.'

Amanda: 'My current fad of interest is veganism, heavily supported by lobby groups who suggest we stop eating meat to reduce the need for farm animals blamed for significant methane emissions resulting from their grazing diet, and all in the name of climate change. My concern is man, or to be precise women, are carnivores for a specific reason – their need for large supplies of iron, animal fats, and amino acids throughout menstruation, pregnancy, and suckling. A woman needs to provide large quantities of these supplemental ingredients in her breast milk during the first year to facilitate the doubling of the size of her infant's brain and create healthy babies to protect the expansion of the species.'

'I certainly cannot rationalise how to secure the large quantities of natural elemental iron with a plant diet. Her stomach would probably need to enlarge to process the extra intake she would need plus quality supplements. This will do nothing for the ideal visual of the ideal feminine child-bearing form throughout the evolution of humankind as depicted by the ancient Greeks in Venus de Milo through the Renaissance by Venus de' Medici and The Birth of Venus. Today think somewhere between a size 10 and size 12. This expanded plant processing process will certainly result in the same methane production we see in grazing animals. Therefore, I think vegans merely move the methane production to man rather than eliminate it.'

Clara: 'So why is veganism so popular?'

Amanda: 'This is what I'm trying to reconcile because if a woman does not supplement her iron requirements normally found in meat, future generations are likely to suffer growth issues on a progressive basis.'

Clara: 'So when we feel low during a period, it's our iron levels that have dropped. Is this why doctors prescribe iron supplements?'

Amanda: 'Yes when medical science finally understood menstruation. Before then, men were afraid of menstrual bleeding. They thought it a source of power because women were invigorated again afterwards. Many cultures adopted bleeding a sick person. George Washington died because his misguided physician bled him excessively after a non-life-threatening injury.'

Clara: 'James, don't get any ideas of becoming a vegan. My periods are bad enough already. More juicy steaks, I think.' Much laughter.

This discussion totally perplexed James. Totally out of his comfort zone. 'Reminds me of the Puritan's creed of celibacy. No Puritans anymore.'

Javid: 'The logical progression at the top of the curve of the vegan population, having maximised the reduction in farm animals; cull the vegans. We will have less methane producing farm animals and vegans, culminating in a reduced global population. A win-win for mother earth.'

Everyone realised that, although interesting, this conversation was not progressing their cause. James brought the discussion back to the project. 'Hashem, where are we now with upper body profiles?'

Hashem: 'After the brilliance of Clara last week, all upper body algorithms are working. As already mentioned, Diane from Rigby & Peller will be in on Tuesday to try out our emulations of different bust sizes for otherwise same build women. My first attempt did not consider the impact of gravity versus skin elasticity. If I can get this right in the coming week, and incorporate Hell's solution for heads, if I can find which heads are currently in use, we're in good shape.'

Javid: 'I think I can get the head data from Cynthia, and consent to use them. She will know the right people.' Turning to James, 'Where are you on the rendering issues?'

James: 'Still expanding the use of the human brain to overcome the vast processing requirement to render full-size people in real-time. Our brain is very clever at illusion. I want to understand and capture as much of the illusion powers as I can. Means we can do more with our computing power. A new portable but powerful computer arrives this week. Can't wait to render moving wireframes to see what's possible.'

Clara: 'Where do you guys expect to be this time next week?'

James: 'I think next week we try to consolidate some of our activities to ensure they work together. I certainly want to integrate Hell into the project group, so she is part of the team and participates in all discussions. Hell, if you have any input, no matter how vague, please air it as many times it takes a small piece of information to trigger a great solution.'

Hell: 'Thanks. Much appreciated.'

After much general conversation, James thought the lunch had run its course. 'Next week is Easter Sunday. My folks will be here, but Clara and myself would like to continue our lunches for those who have no other plans.

228

My mom wants to stay close to her new "family" so no problem. What about you, Hell? Do you have other family commitments?'

Hell: 'You've just got me out of them. I have a brother and a sister, both married with young kids who will assemble at my parents for Easter lunch. I don't mind spending time with my nephews and nieces, but I do object to being hounded about when I will settle down and revert to being a normal woman. So thanks. Will be here.'

James: 'Great. We'll get your wireframe done as well. What about you, Amanda?'

Amanda: 'Similar issue, and going without Hashem will also raise unreasonable questions, so count me in.'

James: 'Full house. Proper festive lunch with all the trimmings, I think. I'm really enjoying our working lunches, both informative and fun.'

Chapter 75

College was closed for Easter, not that it changed anything regarding study whether towards her exams or providing more input to the project. She spent Monday, Tuesday and Wednesday in the office observing progress, sitting with either Javid or Hashem when needed, taking a keen interest in progress with Rigby & Peller on Tuesday helping Hell to understand the bra requirement for the pod. She needed Thursday and Friday to prepare for the arrival of mum and dad for Easter.

She had informed mum about Easter Sunday and briefed her about Amanda. She was excited about meeting these people again insisting she and dad will host the lunch including preparation.

Mum and dad arrived early Friday afternoon for their long, but last weekend before the Graduation Show at college. A final girl's day out in the West End on Saturday was certainly on the agenda, although no specific needs other than a day together. Dad had become absorbed with the project, so he and James spent Saturday morning shopping for groceries, lunch at the pub, and then to the office for dad to be updated on progress. Dinner at Fredericks rounded the day nicely.

Chapter 76

Sunday morning, after breakfast, mum went down to their car, returning with a sizeable box sporting a large Easter bow. She presented it to Clara, who found an enormous Easter chocolate bunny rabbit within. They all looked at mum rather bemused.

'I've never had the opportunity to buy an Easter egg for my lovely daughter before, and I couldn't resist this lovely rabbit. Happy Easter, my darling.'

After breakfast, mum and dad busied themselves preparing a traditional Easter lunch with all the requisite trimmings. James and Clara busied themselves ensuring the table, which was large enough for eight people, was suitably set and decorated. James also ensured all likely drinks were close at hand.

Hashem and Amanda arrived dressed for the occasion, Amanda in a lovely spring dress, Hashem in traditional Indian dress. Javid came as Javid, although his T-shirt looked new as it only had packaging fold marks. Hell came full Goth dress code, but with a sheer blouse over her leather bra top.

Clara took Hell to the bathroom in the computer suite to prepare her for her scan whilst Hashem booted the scanning computer. It surprised Hell how well the seamless bra fitted and the upper body shape it gave her. 'Diane offered to make me Goth tops if I like the shape. Must talk to her on Tuesday. Feels good.'

Clara ensured Hell was settled in the pod, allowing Hashem to secure the wireframe he needed.

Janice greeted all with a tray of prosecco and Indian beer, truly excited to be amongst these extraordinary people. 'Can I say how lovely it is to see you all again. We wish you all welcome and thank you for coming to join us today. Geoffrey and I can't wait to hear news of your wonderful projects. Cheers to you all.' She made an additional effort to foster a relationship with Amanda as the new person in the group.

As they sat at the table, Janice looked around at their guests. 'I don't think I have ever been so excited to meet such a diverse range of people and who exude so much positive energy. Hashem, my dear, you clean up well, and thank you for your lovely dress code. Hell, do I owe you an apology. You look great. Amanda, so pleased to meet you. Heard good things about you. And Javid, I love you any way you choose.' They all laughed.

Geoffrey thought he should contribute, having been on kitchen duty since everyone arrived. 'Dear friends, it is our pleasure to host you today. I'm ready to serve lunch. Tradition has it there is no starter, but the generous nature of this festive meal is more than enough for anyone concerned about being able to walk from the table.' They laughed as they understood his joke.

Amanda: Janice, as a woman who has made a successful career for yourself as well as being a wife and a mother, what challenges did you face?

Janice: We're all family at this table so we can speak freely together. I'm so happy to have the privilege to be part of this incredible group of people, so would like to be an insider. If I can bring anything of value to this wonderful project, I'm available.'

'As for your question, I'm happy to declare my success is due primarily to the love and support of my darling Geoffrey. He has put up with all my doubts and insecurities as I grew into my career, giving me the confidence and courage to fight my corner. Challenges: the same as every woman wanting to fulfil her desire to have children.'

Geoffrey: 'My dear, you give me too much credit. You are successful because you have the credentials and experience. We are a team.'

Janice: 'Thank you, my darling. Understated, strong, and adorable.'

Geoffrey to table: 'James told me you started these lunches a few weeks back. Are they truly a working lunch?'

Amanda: 'To date, the benefit of these lunches is adding a female perspective to this project. Our previous lunches have revealed the wonderful geeks on this project

231

are certainly impressive in their digital world, but we have revealed flaws in their understanding of the analogue world of females. They are finding complex 3-dimensional algorithms trivial compared with the contradictory nature of female behaviour.' Much laughter, including dad. 'As mere men they are too young and inexperienced to understand women, not that they ever will.' Laughter all round. 'But I hope we can seriously contribute to their endeavours as their cause is worthy of success.'

Janice: 'Bravo. Well-articulated, Amanda. What can I contribute to the success of this venture?'

Amanda: 'You must be of an age where you have seen and witnesses much change in the corporate environment. What was it like when you started your rise, especially dress code and dealing with men in the workplace?'

Janice decided to have some fun with this question. 'In my youthful days – yes, I was once a desirable woman,' much comment from the assembled, 'there was much of what today would be considered undesirable attention. However, in those early days the labs had female researchers and we wore lab coats all day and with little makeup which calmed predator instincts. As I elevated to executive status, dress code became important. If you went to the office looking like prey to your male colleagues, expect problems. I learnt quickly to dress as a corporate executive, not as a woman seeking male attention. A woman who overtly flaunts her sexuality is at risk of her career, and likely the love of her life.'

Hell: 'What would you define as executive dress code. Surely you're free to express your own identity?'

Janice: 'Hell, my dear, my prejudicial thoughts when I first heard of your dress code in the workplace were borne from what I've learnt during my career. I acknowledge my prejudice was inappropriate, but you would not be accepted in a corporate Boardroom dressed as you are.'

Hell: 'What difference does my dress code make? I can still perform the same task thus deliver.'

Janice: 'You've found a natural resting place in this company because it's very genius is derived from its lack of respect for convention. In a typical corporate environment, the executive must resemble and think like a team. If you think of sport, teams wear the same or similar strip which psychologically binds them together in a common cause. Individuality is what you bring to the table, not your dress code. When I dress as an executive, I think team strip which has the added advantage my male colleagues see a capable colleague even though a woman. And before you say this suppresses my identity as a woman, this is not the case. I'm a member of a team and must show my commitment to the team.'

Hashem to Javid: 'We need to think this through. There's an angle to this if we can design for the corporate environment. We must look at teams that have both male and female members to see how the strip differs whilst still smacking of team.' Turning to Hell, 'Next week we want you to help us understand how we can design acceptable clothing for the executive workplace without losing too much of your Goth identity. You said last week you already compromise by wearing a black bra in the workplace. Let's explore how far we can be creative with materials and looks. If we can solve this for the extremes of Goth, we will have a real feature to explore.'

Hell: 'Great. I'll give it some thought.'

Janice: 'Designers need to understand that career women need to fit into the corporate environment, but not lose their identity.'

James was listening to this exchange thinking, '*How short-sighted have I been? Even my mom has sparked value into this project. This forum idea is valuable. Must continue.*'

Clara: 'Mum. what was the impact of contraception in the workplace?'

Janice: 'My darling, I'm not that old! Contraception came into play in the 1960s. I started my career in the 1980s. But even then, contraception was a two-edged sword. It gave women control over when they had children. It also gave philanderers the freedom to avoid paying the price of their conquests.'

Amanda wanted to further explore the experience that Janice brings to her current studies. 'What about career versus children?'

Janice: 'Difficult. Very difficult. I felt my choice was children or career. Horrible choice. Today it's changing, but still not there. I wanted so much to have a daughter after James was born, but I risked losing my career. I'm now blessed to have Clara as a daughter. I've learnt I should never put career before family. So many regrets, but fate gave me a second chance and I would sacrifice my career tomorrow if my lovely Clara needed me. All I can say to you lovely women is follow your natural instincts, especially now the corporate world is starting to understand. Never put yourself into a position of regret.'

Amanda: 'Wow. What a powerful statement. Could I interview you for my paper on women in the corporate executive workplace?'

Janice: 'Certainly my dear. Would love to share my experience with such a gifted woman. Let's exchange contact details before you leave.'

James: 'Dad, how does the bank view us? As mom said, our strength is our lack of respect for convention. I think it's more we let our minds go where others fear to tread, without the constraints of conventional shackles.'

Geoffrey: 'Banks, on the outside, need to project crusty and dependable to invoke trust. However, they know success when they see it, and want to engage. They have difficulty understanding the way you operate, but they can't argue your income streams, and your professional support. Hell provides a good interface, albeit I have to agree with your mother that to present Hell in person to the bank would disturb the more crusty members. Better leave that to your auditors until we find you a FD.' Turning to Hell, 'I like you, Hell, and you're very capable, so I'm delighted to see you at this table, as I can see you have much more to offer. But you have experienced dress code problems in the past. One day the world may catch up with your request for identity. For now, I'll come to the office when I need something, not least because I enjoy your dress code. Always intrigues me to see how you express your identity.'

'As for what you do, I'm truly amazed and proud to know you all. To be part of so much creativity must be so exciting. My trips to London would not be complete without a visit to the office to watch this business grow.'

Hell: 'Would it embarrass you to be seen out with me?'

Geoffrey: 'Goodness no. I know the person. The next time I come to the office, I'll happily take you to lunch. And I hope you will join our dinners at Fredericks, where you will fit in better than me. Please don't take our comments personally. We're merely expressing experience and observation.'

Hell: 'It's okay. No offence taken. I know the person.' They warmly smiled at each other.

Janice: 'Now that our interrogation is over, I think it only fair if each of you lovely people explain your fashion project to us and where you are with it. I understand it needs to be ready by the end of June, so you must be well advanced by now. Geoffrey tells me you will spend more than £1million on development. I can't wait to see the outcome. So, who will start?'

Discussion went on for some time, only interrupted by the need to clear away before dessert. Much joy and laughter throughout, especially while Hashem is animating his description of trying to get his head around busts and bras. After dessert, Clara put her enormous Easter bunny on the table. 'No-one can leave the table until we have consumed Bunny. For Hashem and Javid, this was the equivalent of a yummy picnic.

Janice to Clara: 'Well, my darling, it sounds like you have a fabulous project supported by these fantastic people. Can't wait to see the result.'

Clara: 'Hopefully soon.' Addressing the entire table, 'Before we leave this table can I say, in front of my trustee dad, that all my wonderful friends and colleagues at this table will share in my good fortune should this system prove valuable. To have you all in my corner is a privilege. I could not have hoped to fulfil my dream without you.'

Chapter 77

It was Easter Monday. Mum and dad enjoyed their family break, but sad that it was their last weekend in London until the night of the Graduation Show. Although tickets were strictly limited to two per graduate, James had secured two tickets in a prime location on the front row from

Simon. The remainder of the tickets were reserved for trade professionals and media.

Parents already on their way home, James tells Clara he has a message from Javid stating that the fashion engine has new sizing algorithms.

They sat in his computer suite playing with the new engine. He thought to himself, *'these are way past anything Clara could specify. I don't like deception, but I must say something to her about Javid and Cynthia before she doubts her contribution. Here goes, and please God, don't let me get this wrong.* What do you think of the way the models work with the clothes?'

'Wow, these sizing images are brilliant. So lifelike. How did he achieve this?'

'I guess it's Javid and his liaison with Cynthia Crawford. Hashem tells me he has frequent meets with her. Would love to be a fly on the wall.'

'What are you saying? Do you think Javid has a relationship with Cynthia, Professor Crawford from college? She must be nearly twice his age.'

'You're older than me, but does it matter? You used to be my babysitter.'

She poked him in the ribs, 'I'm only 4-years older than you in age, although I'm much older in worldly wisdom. And pretty enough to look younger than you. Javid is 24 or 25 years old, looks boyish, and Cynthia certainly looks in her 40s. Hardly a fair comparison.'

'Hey. Who are we to say who Javid can date? If he likes older women, so be it. All I can see is the fantastic info he's obviously extracting from her. These algorithms are spectacular. Long live their relationship if this is the result.'

'How long has it been going on?'

'You remember I went to see Simon to organise streaming your lectures until you could return. During that conversation, I mentioned the sizing problem I had with yours and mum's blouses. He introduced me to Cynthia, but her answers were all gobbledygook's to me. I asked if she would meet with Javid to see if he could get his head around it. They've been liaising ever since, mostly in the evenings. And the last time I spoke with Simon, he mentioned nothing about it. He's such a gossip, so he doesn't know of her involvement.'

'Are you suggesting they're having a relationship?'

'All we know is he keeps these meets secret. Not in the office, and not at college. Correction, I think she has been to the office once or twice to see what Javid is creating. But out of hours when no one else is there. Hashem noticed activity on the office computers from his computer suite at home. When he checked to see who it was, he detected Javid using the system and then he tapped into the office security system to see Cynthia with him.'

'Javid and Professor Crawford. I would never put them together in a relationship.'

'We don't know what's happening between them. It may just be a platonic interest in what we're doing, but Javid knows our work is secret, so they must be closer for him to expose our project to her. To date, the results are impressive. And that Simon knows nothing of this relationship gives me confidence Javid is staying within the bounds of our confidentiality rules.'

An internal sigh of relief that she showed no concern, 'I've got your wire frame image on my system here. Why don't we try it in Javid's new engine?'

He loaded her wireframe into their latest animation engine. 'See how you move. This is our animation engine, which now is very fluent with movement. Whether you walk, turn, bend down it all flows as in real life. This engine handles the movements of your body. Now let's put some clothes on you and add Javid's engine to control the interaction between you and your clothes.'

He started her walking on the screen. Her clothes moved smoothly as she walked.

She moved closer to the screen, aghast at the reality of the movements. 'James, it's incredible. You've done it. I can't believe it.'

'Let's see if I can increase you by one dress size and see what happens.'

'She watched herself increase in size and start to walk again. Again, the clothes responded, but differently.'

'Wow.'

'Javid built this so please remember we've done it with the brilliant collaboration of Javid and Hashem.'

'You were right to involve them. Truly lovely and brilliant people. And whatever is happening between Javid and Professor Crawford, he's doing a magnificent job translating her knowledge. This is going to work. Thank you so much.'

He started to make notes. 'I can see some problems Javid needs to address. They don't show other than with a trained eye on this size screen, but full size they would show as imperfections. Did you notice he did not change the shoes for the size 14 image? I don't think a size 14 can easily manage 6in heels. We need to understand how to manage shoes for different body sizes. Something we've not encountered in animation engines, but certainly relevant here. He's getting close, but more work to do.'

'Can you come to the office after college tomorrow? We'll go buy you shoes with different heal sizes. You can walk the catwalk to see how the legs change, and how it affects your walk.'

'I'm not a good example. I don't wear heels other than a couple of inches occasionally. Never had the need nor the clothes.'

'And what do you intend to wear with your dress on the catwalk?'

'Haven't really thought about it yet. Need a good dress design first and then worry about shoes. But certainly not high heels. Need some practice before considering anything other than a few inches.'

'Then you need some practice. We must buy a variety of heel heights to see what works for you. You can bring them home after we've captured them on camera so you can practice here. Think about what would match your dress design so we can get suitable colours. Let's see what else needs to be considered.'

After watching the computer model move some more, 'It's usually these small refinements that require the most time to fix, and we only have a few weeks before we need to have this working. I see some long days ahead. Thankfully, this time you have preparations for your exams, so both busy.'

Clara quickly understood that playtime was about to be limited. 'Then before we become strangers for a while, why don't we celebrate with a little fun.'

'Can't wait to see what my nymph of mischief has in mind.' As he joined her in the bedroom, *'Okay, so far. Don't like it but needs must.'*

Chapter 78

She was just one week away from exams, and they were three weeks away from the graduation show as final year students were in the process of completing their exams to give them time to complete their designer creations they want to showcase at the graduation show.

This year revision was not such a chore for her, not least because she now knew the process and the demands placed on her for information by James meant she studied beyond the expectation of her year. All playtime other than Saturday evening into Sunday morning, culminating in a swim as the only exercise he took, had been suspended until after the show to maximise the time to prepare. However, the pressure to produce a dress worthy of showcasing on the catwalk was certainly taking its toll. She was well used to making alterations and repairs to clothes as this was her way of life during her teenage years. She also enjoyed making clothes for herself out of necessity, or just for fun. But this was different. Now she needed to design and make a dress which would define her capabilities, and paraded along a catwalk in front of people in the fashion world. Sketches on paper are one thing, converting to the standard expected, quite another.'

They were both working on their respective projects in the computer suite. She was audibly struggling with her dress design constantly disturbing his concentration refining the engine processing dynamics to optimise the speed of presentation.

He swivelled to look at her. 'What's the problem? All I can hear is stress.'

'Sorry. I can't get the side panels to sit properly.'

'What type of dress are you trying to make?'

She handed him her iPad, showing her sketch.

'This looks like a slappers dress from the roaring twenties. Mom had one of these with a headpiece with a broach and a feather. She wore it at some Great Gatsby gig with dad in his black and white brogues. So, your shoes will be heels with a band across, so you don't lose them when you Charleston. What's with the elongated diamond side pieces?'

'A slapper dress does not touch the waist or the hips. But today dresses tend to accentuate the shape of the waist and hips. My idea is to add this diamond shape in a silver shimmer material from the armpit to the hem to give the illusion of a waistline. But it's not working.'

'As you will wear this dress for the show, why don't we key all the material parameters into the system and see what our algorithms produce. We need to test this to ensure we can render the wispier and larger sizes on screen. Ready with the data?'

After watching how her design transformed into a perfect pattern, uncertainty, buried for some weeks, came to the surface. 'James, this is not my work. I could not begin to solve some of these problems, let alone participate in the development. What of me is in what we have just seen?'

He could sense her insecurity. It prompted a reality check that he had let the system build without taking her with him, thinking she would be too absorbed in her studies to notice. The cautionary words of his father came crashing back to his mind.

He turned to her and held both of her hands. 'Clara, my beautiful Clara. I've made another of my foolish mistakes, for which I apologise. And you are allowing the stress of your upcoming exams to get to you. Where is the unflappable lady I know?'

'Don't know what you're talking about.'

'Okay, first let's deal with your exams. Last year you were rightly concerned about your exams because it was the first time for many years you had sat a formal test, let alone an exam. What did you do? You called upon a resource, Hell, because you know she is well versed in exams, and would help you. You used your initiative, found the right source of help, and you got through your exams. Are we good so far?'

'Where's this going?'

'This year I've not detected too much stress regarding your exams, but I know you had the misfortune of starting your year late. Plus, how much of your valuable study time have I called upon to help me with this system. And you now have the added burden of designing a creation that would normally occur at the end of your final year, and I know you feel the stress of competing with the final year students. But you can do this. Remember what started this entire process, your wonderful drawings that morning at your bedsit in St Albans. You can do whatever you set your mind to do, albeit sometimes with the help of a collaborator or two. Because of your help with this system, you now have the resource to help you finish your dress creation, ensuring that it perfectly fits you. All you need to do is apply the magic in your fingers to sew it together like the professional you are.'

'But I recognise little of my work in your system.'

'This is your idea, our system. How many times have I torn out my hair looking for answers which you provided? My mistake in recent weeks is not keeping you informed of progress. But, more importantly, I have never explained to you how I finished my first engine, the foundation of where we are.'

'When I first thought of attempting to build a graphics engine, it was just a dream. I convinced myself I had the mathematical skills and the design ideas to make it happen. After some 18-months, I knew my ambition was beyond me. I put a call out for help on an online chat forum. Hashem and Javid were two of the respondents. Can you imagine what it was like meeting these super-educated geeks? But they had the knowledge I needed. I finished my engine and sold my first licence. This convinced Hashem and Javid to help me develop a more advanced version. I had the vision. They could fill the gaps in my mathematical knowledge. Great teamwork.'

'And that's how you met them? Trying to solve a problem?'

'Yes. I used to secretly spend 3-days each week with them in London to develop engine no.2.'

'So that's why you came to London every week.'

'Yes. I needed collaborators who could fill my skill gaps.'

'Do you remember when we came upon sizing issues. We worked out the basics of sizing, but it wasn't until I met Cynthia, I realised it was beyond us. I couldn't develop these wonderful algorithms. And neither did I have enough funds of my own to develop the system requirements. It is our project, but we needed help. Step in Javid with his brilliant mind working with Cynthia, and the resources of EMULATE.'

He encouraged her onto his lap. 'Success is not about doing something on your own. It's being smart enough to know you need collaborators and knowing how to find them. This fashion project is your idea, my knowledge in converting your idea into a system, and the wonderful collaborators we have in Hashem and Javid to fulfil your dream. Your current role is to pass your exams and show what you can produce in your dress design. My role is to check the work by Hashem and Javid delivers on our dream. If you have time each week, I want to sit with you and show you where we are as you might spot something we've missed. So, stop beating up on yourself and let's get this dream out there.'

She wrapped her arms around his neck. 'I'm thinking you really love me. And I know you will deliver for me. I just didn't realise how important our collaborators. Lovely guys. I think of them as family. Do you really think we can finish the system in time for the end-of-year show?'

'We have no choice if we want a great launch. So why don't we break for something to eat and then get this show back on the road. Much to do.'

She gave him a loving kiss before bouncing off his lap and taking him by the hand to the kitchen.

Chapter 79

The following morning, he was at his computer early and would soon be on his way to the office for yet another long day. As soon as he left, she focussed back on her dress design, re-cutting material to match the pattern generated by the system. But her efforts did not produce the desired result. After an hour of trying to perfect her stitching of the critical diamond shape, she sat back in despair. Then a thought occurred to her *'time to find a collaborator, I think.'*

The materials were all from her favourite supplier in Whitechapel, and all originated from India. She bundled the dress parts into a bag along with the design and pattern pieces and made her way to the shop.

'Hi Rajeev. How are you?'

My dear Clara, so nice to see you. What brings you to my humble shop today?'

'I'm trying to make one of my dress designs from the lovely materials you suggested, but I can't get the stitching right. Can you help me?'

'Let me see what you have.'

She emptied her bag on his cutting board, the only empty surface in the shop. He examined her design, the pattern pieces, and the unfinished dress. He could see the materials were purchased from him. 'What are you trying to achieve?'

She explained the basic design for a cocktail dress is based on a 1920s slapper dress but using a contrasting precisely designed diamond shape on each side to give a more feminine shape to the bodice and torso.

'So, this diamond piece is critical to your design?'

'Yes. But I can't get the stitching to sit properly.'

'Take your dress up to Anisha. She is best designer with these materials.'

She climbed the narrow bare wooden stairs now familiar to her leading to the sewing shop. As she reached the top Anisha spotted her. 'Clara, how nice to see you. What a surprise. I thought you would be studying hard for your exams.'

After a hug and kiss 'I'm having a problem with a dress I must make. I need help.'

'Come. Let me see what you have.'

243

They went through the design, and she explained the distinct purpose of the elongated diamond shape.

Anisha pondered the design. 'I love the idea, but these materials are not really suitable for such a challenge. Can I suggest two others, but far more expensive materials, which would probably work very well, and we need a weight closer to chiffon for the lining. Come with me. I'll show you what I mean.'

'Cost is no problem. I must get this right.'

Anisha opened a cupboard where they kept the very finest of materials usually reserved for the well-heeled wanting a special dress for their daughter's wedding – no expense spared. She quickly identified a fine blue-turquoise material with streaks of silver thread through it followed by a similar silver material which shimmered in the light, and a soft silky material for the lining.

'Is your pattern correctly dimensioned?'

'Yes. Exactly sized for me.'

'Let's go to the cutting table and prepare the pieces we need. I assume you will not wear a bra with this dress so will need a little support under the cleavage. This is where the lining will help.'

Some 2-hours later her dress was ready for pressing. 'Come. I'll show you how to press this material. You need to be very careful not to damage the silver threading.'

This was a steam press. Mental note to get one.

'Why don't you try it to see how it looks. Dressing room is over there.'

She knew as soon as she adjusted her bust into the dress everything was perfect. She walked out into the sewing room to gasps of delight from Anisha and the other girls, who stopped their machines to examine this creation. Mahima, the mother, walked in with lunch for the girls.

'Clara, my dear. You look lovely. Is this one of your designs?'

'Yes, Mahima, but it was Anisha who made my design work for me. She is so clever with your lovely Indian materials. I need to come here for lessons.'

They all laughed as Rajeev came up the stairs to see what was happening. 'Clara. Now I see what you intended. So beautiful, my dear. Can we have an Indian version, as this idea will sell well among the younger adults?'

Anisha wanted something similar herself, as the shape would fit well on her. 'I could help Clara convert this idea into an Indian version, as I would like one. Is this possible?'

Clara looked at Anisha, 'For you it is possible but not for another 3-weeks. When I show this dress at the end-of-year fashion show 3-weeks on Friday it must be original, and my design, to qualify for the show.'

'Don't worry. We don't have a dummy close enough to my size to quickly make this dress. The diamond width at the waist is the key to your design. Just a small amount too little or too much in width and it won't work. I see your patterns are printed. How did you size your dress?'

'On a computer that has a wireframe of my body around which I fit my design and then it prints the patterns.'

'You have this technology?'

'Yes, and more. I'll show it to you after the show where it will be launched for the first time.'

'Tell me, tell me. I want to know more.'

'It's complicated, but I'll try if you have the time.'

Mahima, still holding the lunch tray, 'Clara my dear, go change so you do not spoil your dress. You join us for lunch, and you tell us what you will launch.'

When she returned, they had made a space for her and invited her to help herself. Rajeev invited her to explain what she was using for her designs. Some quick thought on her part as if she spoke about the scope and expense of the fashion system having pleaded poverty in securing materials this might not go down well. She decided to give a little of her background regarding her mum and lack of schooling and being rescued by James who helped her into college and saw an opportunity to apply his existing animation technology to use her ideas to change the way design, presentation, and delivery of fashion to the consumer market. If it all works, she will profit from this technology. Just enough of the story to indicate James had money, but not her until the system is successful. They were already aware of her stabbing incident, so no need to rekindle that horror.

Mahina reached over and put her hand over Clara's hand 'so sorry to hear of your mother. It must have been a lonely time for you. We are blessed with family around us. You need us, we here for you.'

'Thank you, Mahina. It means a lot to me to have such kind support.'

Rajeev was keen to progress, 'what does this system of yours do?'

'*Where to start*', she thought. Turning to Anisha. 'Let me take your desire to have a similar dress to mine as an example, but you know the precision necessary to get the diamond pattern right is fundamental to the dress. Let me tell you how we approach this problem, and I will offer this to you after the launch. The first step is to solve the problem of an exact dummy of your body. For this we will scan your body using 3-D laser technology, so your digital wireframe is a perfect replica of you.

Rajeev was quick to react. 'Aren't lasers dangerous, and what is wireframe?'

Anisha, being more tech-savvy. 'Peti, it's okay. I know what she is saying.' Pointing to a workshop dummy, 'she is talking about a digital version of a dummy, but far more accurate. We need this. And the lasers are no more harmful than our photocopier. Sorry Clara, Peti has not joined the computer revolution, but we will get him there one day when he sees how valuable it can be. Please continue.'

Mahima wanted to know more. 'How do you do this laser scan?'

'There are two types of scanner. One is a static scanner, which is essentially a large tube. It has a door for you to stand inside. The door closes. You stand perfectly still as the lasers scan you. We have one of these pods at our apartment. It takes a couple of minutes so long as you don't move while it's scanning. This provides a green wireframe computer model like a dummy but full body length.'

'What do you wear in this tube?'

'For very accurate wireframe only what you would wear under the dress you want to model. No jewellery. For more general use, Rigby & Peller have made us a range of wireless and seamless bras to emulate upper body as best we can.'

'Ah, quality,' as Mahima animates with her hands. 'Rigby & Peller are famous name. They associated with your system means it must be very good.'

'Once we have your wireframe, we then need to add your design. The system will fit your design to the wireframe as best it can, and then you can modify the design until you are happy with how it looks. Then you print the patterns.'

'Wow. And you say I can use this system for my clothes.'

'Anisha, I'm very grateful for your skills today. You help me turn my ideas into lovely clothes and I'll gladly help you do the same.'

Mahima, being a stereotypical very attentive mother, 'you say you have two such scanners. What is the other one for?'

'At our studio in Camden, we have a tunnel scanner. This one records how you move when walking. In this part of the system, you not only input the design but all the information about the materials you want to use. Once you are happy with your static design, the system will then show you how the clothes react to movement when walking, sitting, or bending. For example, will the materials gather. If so, you can modify the design or the material to prevent this happening.'

Anisha is radiating excitement. 'Incredible. We must have one. How much does it cost?'

'I don't know. What I do know is it has cost over £1million to date to develop. To use the animated engine developed by James for computer games, I think the licence cost is about £100,000 per month.'

'Not for small businesses like ours. But it would be so nice when we have an order for a very expensive dress. Far too much measure, cut, measure again, refine cut sometimes over weeks. Your system can do this in a few hours.'

'Anisha, I commit to you when you next have such a complex requirement, you can use our system to help you. I would very much appreciate your eye for detail as you are far more experienced than me.' She had an idea, 'once I've finished my exams, after next week, we will have some dummy runs at the studio ready for the show. These runs will be evenings. If you're prepared to not say a word to anyone about what you see, I will take you with me so you can see it for yourself. You cannot interfere in the demo but if you see anything you think is wrong, or could be better, you can tell me. Interested?'

'Of course. Peti, you hear. I cannot speak of what I see until after the show, so please don't ask.'

Rajeev turned to Clara. 'And who are these people in this studio in Camden? Can I trust my beautiful daughter in such a place?'

She smiled. 'Besides James, the two most incredible people working on this system are lovely and Indian. Both from good families in Mumbai and both have PhD's.'

'Ha. I should have known the exceptional computer skills found in India are involved is such a project. Are they married?'

Everyone laughed.

'They're geeks. Don't have time for marriage.'

'Ah, but if they are from good families, we expect them to breed the next generation. Their father's will ensure this happens. They cannot be secret so, my daughter, you can tell me about these nice Indian boys when you return. And now we must back to our work. Very interesting project. We only charge you today for materials and we test your system.'

On her way home, she had a real spring in her step. She had her dress, a beautiful dress which both complimented her design, and fitted perfectly. The big surprise was she could describe at least parts of the system to people who understand designing and making clothes. A real boost to her confidence. *'Collaboration is good. Time to do justice to my exams and look forward to the show.'*

Chapter 80

Beautiful dress hanging in her wardrobe, and much happier she was part of her dream project, exams went well. Hell gave her a pep-talk before exams started and then a debrief after each exam. The practical exams did not challenge her beyond comfort level. The week went well. She couldn't remember seeing much of James, but they relaxed for an entire morning on the following Sunday before their now regular Sunday working lunch.

'Clara, we want to start our dummy runs on Tuesday evening. We need as many females we can trust to act as models. With you, we have four. Could use one more.'

'No problem. I'll bring Anisha with me.'

'Who's Anisha?'

'She's one of the daughters from the shop I get my lovely Indian materials.'

'Are you sure she will not put what she sees all over social media. We must have certainty with confidentiality, and will she make an excellent model?'

'Wait, a moment. I want to show you something.' She went to the bedroom and changed into her dress. He hadn't noticed or enquired about progress on her dress – too pre-occupied.

She walked back into the computer suite.

'Wow. You finished it. You look fantastic. Have you changed the materials? My memory suggests you were working with a more mauve-like colour.'

'This is the brilliance of Anisha. I took your advice and sought out a collaborator. Rather than show me how to make it myself, we sat in their workshop and made the whole dress. You like it?'

'Beautiful. You'll certainly wow the audience dressed like that.'

'Anisha has been my friend now for nearly two years. We are like sisters. She knows how secret our project and has the experience to spot detail we may have missed. She is the chief designer for some very expensive weddings.'

'Okay, if you're sure, we could use her. Could you both wear a skirt or dress so we can see the impact of movement? And bring the shoes you want to use with your dress.'

'What time do you want us there?'

'I think we will be setup by 5:30. We want staff not connected to leave for the day before we start so we can focus.'

'We'll be there.' Afterthought 'Anisha is Indian. She could come in typical Indian dress to see if this presents any challenges.'

'Interesting. But can she bring some Western clothes as well? Too late to adapt for Eastern dress if it doesn't work. We can add this later if needed.'

Clara couldn't wait to tell Anisha but warned her it could be a very long evening. 'These geeks do not relate to clocks, just hunger and the need to sleep.' She was invited to go to the shop early for late lunch so it would fuel them for as long as it takes.

She took the car to collect Anisha, knowing she could park on the side street by the shop, and no problems getting home no matter how late.

Rajeev invited her to go straight upstairs, where she was greeted by Mahima. 'Come, my dear. Anisha is so excited. Let us lunch and you can tell us more.'

They were soon on their way to the office where they were greeted by Hell who quickly took to Anisha. Amanda was also there, as was Angelina, or Angie to her friends, a professional model friend of Hell, and who had been hired to bring her experience to the show. All were asked to stay in the waiting area to receive instruction from Angie on how to conduct themselves on a catwalk. Much laughter as they tried to master the way models walk on a catwalk – particularly challenging for Clara in 4in heel shoes so alien to her. But she would be on the catwalk during the show so needed to master the walk and the shoes.

After about an hour of walking torture, the office door opened to reveal Cynthia, taking Clara quite by surprise.

'Hello Clara, lovely to see you. How were your exams last week?'

'Did my best. Hope my best is enough.'

Reassuringly 'I'm sure you'll be okay. And what a fantastic project you have here. I'm overwhelmed with the detail being built into this system. I feel so privileged to be part of it. You deserve to do well.'

She noticed Anisha. 'Who's your friend?'

She turned to Anisha and beckoned her closer. 'Anisha, this is Professor Cynthia Crawford from my college. She is head of design and working closely with Javid.' Turning to Cynthia, 'this is my good friend Anisha. Brilliant designer and seamstress of exotic materials.'

'Pleased to meet you, Anisha. I would love to see how you work such materials as I know it's a skilful task handed down through generations. Perhaps I can visit you with Clara when we've finished this project.'

'Lovely to meet you. I would be delighted to invite you to our workshop. Clara knows where we are in Whitechapel.'

'I will most certainly do that. But for now, the pressure is on to get this wonderful project finished. See you both later.'

As they walked back to their walking lessons, 'you have some incredible people working with you.'

'James drummed it into me that to be successful you need the right collaborators, and they are all around you in this room. You feel their energy.'

This evening was focussed on lighting that would provide a uniform white backdrop to the models. The computers they could reasonably transport to the college were not powerful enough to render images at the required speed unless the background was totally uniform and thus eliminated from the rendering process. The models were continually walked along the catwalk to identify anything that would create problems to the emulation generator such as shiny jewellery which they found should be avoided.

The next task was to optimise the walk-rate of the models to avoid image lagging. And then the reset time as the models twirled at the end of the catwalk to start their walk back. Angie was very tuned to these requirements so took the lead and then showed the drafted-in models how to comply; a very important task for Clara as there would be no rehearsal for her on the night; only the graduate students modelling their own creations.

At one point they stood the models down whilst the techies examined the replays to see where they were. Anisha could see them huddled around a matrix of screens and wanted to take a peek. 'Clara, can we go see what they're looking at?'

'We can, but you must remember what we agreed. Nothing you see must leave this room and don't speak while we're close so as not to distract them. They are in geek mode – do not disturb.'

She whispered, 'no problem.'

They quietly wandered along the room to a spot a couple of metres behind the geeks. Anisha's eyes saw the images on the screens. She quickly put her hand to her mouth to hide the gasp she wanted to let out as she stood frozen to the spot, watching the image transformations on the screens. After a couple of minutes, they retreated to the others. Once out of hearing range of the geeks 'that's incredible. Now I understand the secrecy. Amazing how you change the sizing. One model, five sizes. Are they standard sizes?'

'For the show, we're using standard sizes provided by Cynthia. But we can change it to whatever you want. In its simplest form you could test a top by having the same model emulated with different bust sizes to see how to optimise the design to sit well on as many upper body shapes as possible.'

'Incredible. I love it, but beyond our budget.'

'I heard James discussing this with a major online seller, I think Amazon. They would buy a licence and make it available to small manufacturers like yourselves as part of their small business community. Which means if you have an Amazon shop you get to use the system for your customers.'

'That would be great. Getting Peti online might be a challenge, but me and my sisters are all familiar with online shopping, so no problem.'

Eventually it was agreed that enough progress had been made today, and it was late. Everyone was asked to return tomorrow at 5pm after identified corrections have been applied to finish the setup.

It was after midnight when they dropped Anisha back at the shop. 'Thank you so much for letting me see into your incredible world. Your secret is safe with me. I'll see you tomorrow. Goodnight.'

She let herself into the side entrance leading to the apartment behind the shop where she found Peti and Mama waiting for her.

'How was it my dear?'

'Incredible, amazing, exciting. I must have walked that catwalk fifty times, but if they wanted fifty more, no

252

complaints from me. Fantastic project and most certainly Clara's vision. Those fantastic people work so hard to deliver her dream and give her the night of her life. I have never seen so much technology in one place. Peti they want me to go back tomorrow as there is still much to do to get their lighting, cameras and projectors perfectly set for the most amazing show. I will work Sunday to catch up on my work, but I must go. I feel so excited with my small roll in this spectacular project.'

Mama spoke, 'my dear, you do not need to tell us about your excitement. I'm surprised your feet stay on the ground. You shall go. We will make good your work. Rajeev, you see this is important for our daughter' which was her way of telling her husband she was using her prerogative as a good wife and mother to make this important decision.

'As you wish, Mama. But Anisha, what about the Indian boys?'

'Ha, Hashem and Javid. Truly lovely and brilliant. They treat Clara like a sister. Javid certainly has my heart, but he is far too consumed with this project to even notice me. He is most certainly the lead in making this show work. Hashem already has the lovely Amanda.'

'Then my daughter, you can stay with these people to see if Javid will notice how lovely you are.'

'Peti, so keen to get me married. I tell you one thing. We can use this system, or part of it, as it will probably be available through the likes of Amazon. And I will know how to use it properly so we can develop a bespoke online business, allowing us to reach customers all over the world. Such a fantastic idea. Clara has wonderful vision.'

Rajeev, with puffed chest, 'And she is family so we will have advantage. I knew the day Clara walk into our shop that this girl will go far. You must sleep. Busy day for you tomorrow.'

Chapter 81

When she awoke the following morning, James had already left for the office. *'How can they survive on so little sleep?'* went through her mind. Her feet were telling her they required TLC after walking so much in her heels on the catwalk. *'Thank goodness I only need to walk the catwalk twice on show night. A swim might be a good start to the day.'*

Her carefree, leisurely swim and breakfast suddenly hit the wall. *'Damn, I have to be in Harley Street at noon.'*

Her dark secret relationship with her stabbing scar had moved her to research her options to remove, or at least minimise the scar that always reminded her of that awful night. She found a cosmetic surgeon in Harley Street who claimed to 'remove' scars. She had plucked up the courage to make an appointment.

Reading the literature in his waiting room, she gathered his speciality was removing stretch marks, and the scar left after a caesarean section. *'Close enough'* she thought.

The consultation went well, but the verdict was not to her liking. He thought it a little too early after the event and would like her to wait a few more months, after which he could likely help her. She wanted to rid herself of this scar before talk of a holiday. But he told her even if he could treat it now, it would not heal in time for a holiday, so take the holiday and then come back. She resigned herself to finding more bikinis that hid this dreadful mark on an otherwise flawless abdomen.

They arrived at the offices for their evening workload to be informed that part of last night would need to be repeated to check they had now removed the flaws before moving on to the next stage. Then it was beat fixing the walk pace such that the model does not get ahead of the emulations. One of the other geeks familiar with music would pick catwalk music with the appropriate beat for each model.

The final task this evening was to determine the optimal distance apart when all models return to the catwalk for the finale. Also needed simple choreography so that the first person wasn't left standing idle for too long.

Angie supervised this activity with great professionalism, endorsing Hell's suggestion to James he should hire her to choreograph the show.

All exhausted, it was again after midnight when they started the drive back to Whitechapel, Clara driving, Anisha in the passenger seat, and James sleeping in the back.

'Clara, I'm so excited for you. I so wish I could be there on the night. I offered Javid my body for a ticket but to no avail.'

'You did what?'

'No, just joking, but it would be worth it. I asked him if I could be a roady on the night, but I don't have the skills. He is, however, streaming the show live to his folks so will add me into the stream. I can watch the show at home. I'm so excited. Can't wait. He'll give you the logon information I need. Mama and Peti will be over the moon. I will tell Peti you organised this for us as he is trying to marry me off to Javid, which is okay with me, but I don't want to encourage Peti.'

They both laughed at this marriage-maker tradition. 'I'm glad you'll see the show, and you will have access to this system once things settle afterwards. I think it might help you achieve your dreams.'

Chapter 82

Javid was very alive to the fact they could not take their main computers to the college and could not rely on broadband speeds to use them remotely. Thus, compromises are needed to maximise presentation. He had to remove as many unnecessary variables out of the rendering function as possible to achieve a realistic response time.

They arranged a dress rehearsal at the studio on the day before the show to both define the catwalk protocols and to familiarise these non-professional models with the disciplines they need to keep models and portable systems in synchronisation. They mandated Angie to drill the models in catwalk protocol and then work with each student to establish their individual walk. This took some hours to achieve displaying none of the emulations to the students. Clara was there to observe the entire process, learning much from Angie.

Finally, all 23 students were fully drilled in their personal walk, and the finale walk where they would walk in procession along the catwalk, keeping a one metre distance apart. When the first student reached the end of the catwalk, they would stop for a count of two, rotate 45degrees left to face the press and invited guests posing for a count of five, and then rotating 45degrees to their right and pose for pictures from their family guests. Each would wait for the person in front to complete this task before starting themselves ensuring that the first person did not stand idle for too long. Cynthia was there to help each student to present their creation in its best light and to collect the description she would use in her commentary on each design.

Chapter 83

The room was set. The catwalk extended out into the room with fifteen metre Cinemascope screens curving around on both sides. Sound, imaging cameras, processing computers, and projectors were all set, aligned and ready. There were just three hours to showtime. It was time to clear the room and test that everything works.

James stood on the catwalk. 'Can we please clear the room of everyone except my technical team? Clara, could you please get changed ready to walk the catwalk.'

Simon, the college Principal, approached him. 'Would you mind if I stay as I'm responsible for the success of this evening?'

'Sorry, Simon, of course you can. But please do not disclose what you are about to witness to anyone. We want it to be a total surprise.'

Cynthia Crawford came through the door. She quickly located Javid. 'Hi Javid. We ready to rock 'n roll with the show?'

'Sure. But we keep everything secret until this evening.'

'I'm not about to spoil this show. I want to see people's faces.'

Room vacated, doors closed, and lights dimmed they applied spotlights to the catwalk. Projectors lit the two screens. 'Hashem, queue music. Okay Clara, start your walk.'

The imaging cameras locked on to her as soon as she appeared onto the main catwalk, projecting her image onto the screens. As she walked a further two metres a second image of her appeared but one clothing size larger. Another two metres and a third image appeared behind the first two images, but again a further clothing size larger. Simon noticed these images were not just increased body size, but the dress materials reacted differently in each body size, reflecting what would be the case in actual life. 'James, this is spectacular. Your emulations are incredible. Wow. You allow the catwalk to relate to people of all sizes. Amazing. Would you mind if I make some calls to the fashion industry and press to tell them of this spectacle without disclosing what they will witness. This will be fantastic publicity for the College.'

'No problem, as long as you do not disclose what they will see.'

'Don't worry. I want a camera on the audience to capture their reaction. What a scoop. Thank you, James. This is wonderful.'

'Don't forget this is Clara's creation, and she has contributed much to this achievement. This creation will be in her name. Without her, I could not have delivered this technology. I want her to lead the show tonight, even though she has not graduated. I want her to show the graduates how to conduct their walk and what to expect. If I do this before the show, it will be all over social media within fifteen minutes.'

Simon looked towards Clara, who was still standing at the end of the catwalk, but now looking at the screens.

'Clara, my dear, this is wonderful. What a scoop for the college. Thank you so much. Beautiful dress, congratulations.' He turned to James. 'Your request is unusual, but I completely understand. I also want this scoop.' He thought for a moment, *'If this incredible technology is in Clara's name, another famous name associated with this college, Perfect. If Clara designed her dress, she is a worthy participant.'*

'It's her design, and we used her design to test the design aids on this system to ensure it exactly fitted her and reacts as expected to her movements.'

He held James by the shoulders, 'Please James, no more information. You will put us out of business. The people I'm about to call will probably think we've nurtured another great designer, as is the legacy of this college. But what they will see is a major change for the whole industry. I'm so excited. I must go to make my calls. See you later.' He skipped out of the room, rubbing his hands in glee as he prepared himself to make his calls. He knew if significant people from the fashion industry agreed to attend, so would significant media. *'What a scoop for the college. Must organise a proper reception party afterwards. My goodness, so much to do.'*

Clara turned to James. 'It's fantastic. Unbelievable how lifelike the larger sized models appear. We did it. I can't believe how realistic it is. I'm so happy.'

Javid cut the projectors and restored normal lighting. People needed to finalise preparations, and he needed to confirm the stream to the Savoy Hotel where both his and Hashem's family will host a private screening of the show. There was no possibility of securing seats for fourteen family members from India, no matter what they were prepared to pay.

Cynthia turned to Javid and hugged him. 'Fantastic, Javid. Truly fantastic. You're one brilliant dude. Will you help me write this up?'

'No problem. I could not have done this without your input.'

'I need to make some calls as well. This night will be a major event for this college. We must go celebrate after the show.'

'By the time we've moved all our equipment back to our studio, it will be late. But tomorrow night we celebrate. Our families are here. My father has booked a private dining room at the Savoy for all of us, and you are most certainly welcome to join us.'

'Thank you. I would be honoured to join you. Give me the details later. Must go.'

James and Clara hugged their success. 'My darling James. Our goals and dreams are fulfilled. You delivered for me. Thank you.'

'My darling Clara, you are as much part of this as me. I could not have done this without you. And I don't mean just this spectacle. I mean everything I've achieved with you in my life. What a wonderful outcome, despite the problems along the way. Tonight, the world will know our names and what we've achieved together.'

For a few moments they were locked together, oblivious to what was happening around them. They were quietly celebrating their success.

Javid broke the moment. 'We still have much to do to make this spectacle a success. Angie, will you ensure you brief the other models that when you all come out together at the end of the show, they must stay in the same order as their walk and at least one metre apart. They must not bunch.' He turned to Clara, 'beautiful dress. It looks great on you. I have a little surprise for you during the finale even James doesn't know about.'

James looked at him perplexed 'What surprise?'

'It won't be a surprise if I tell you. But you won't be disappointed. We developed it in honour of Clara. It's her night and we're going to make it real special for her.'

Chapter 84

All student models were preparing for makeup and dressing. Angie took each to finalise their walk with Hashem setting the length of each piece of music. The catwalk at college was much longer than in the studio, so the music must give each model time to get back and beat-match the music for the following model. Then she collected all of them together to rehearse the finale walk. Hashem, responsible for all sound, was happy, allowing the models to return to getting ready, not really questioning why Clara was also getting ready. They had seen her at the studio, so knew she must be part of the show.

Once ready, Angie gathered all graduate models to her. 'There is one last thing you need to know about this evening. You are the first people in the world to showcase your work using an incredible new technology. This show will undoubtedly go global, so do as I tell you and you will shine. Do not fail me or you will fail yourself.' She paused to let this sink in. 'Jennie, you are the designated lead, but it's not fair to put you out there before you know the spectacle you will create. You will probably freeze, which is not good for you or the show. It's better you know what to expect so you stay focussed and deliver a fabulous walk.'

Again, she let the expectation build. 'This show is Clara's creation. She will lead off so you all can see what happens as she progresses along the catwalk. Watch it on the screen so you can see how the spectacle unfolds and how important you play your part. I will marshal you onto the catwalk. I will trigger each walk with Ready-and-Go. When I say **Ready,** I want to see posture and attitude. When I say **And,** you prepare to move. When I say **Go,** you step out without hesitation remembering your step beat. Three steps to the centre of the walk. Wait one beat. Turn to the catwalk. Wait two beats to get your balance, then start your walk. Do not lose your concentration. I will give each of you a copy of the show to take home and view at your leisure. What a way to showcase your work. Any questions?'

Little did they know both stops were needed to capture their rendered wireframe. They had five systems driving the images. The first captured the real model data, and the other four each provided a different emulation. These systems were not powerful enough to undertake high frame rates but Hashem and Javid had calculated they could use the visual features of the eye and brain to create the impression of a smooth image at just 4-frames per second so long as the images are not synchronised with each other. So much information for the eye to absorb over five images, the brain will smooth the picture.

One of the male models spoke. 'Why didn't we do this in dress rehearsal?'

'Part of the expectation of the show. No-one has seen it. At the rehearsal in Camden yesterday it was playing out before your eyes, but only on hidden screens. Look at your screens. There are important people out there from this industry and the press. They must be first to see it. And you must play your part. As a professional model, I would give my back teeth to be out there tonight. Your potential sponsors are out there, so shine. Are we good?'

A resounding 'yes'.

'Then go get ready. The show is about to start. Jennie, you watch on my screen, so you are ready to go as soon as Clara returns.'

Chapter 85

It was now 7:30. Showtime. The room was heaving with people. Far more than expected, including recognisable faces from the fashion industry, and a jostling throng of press photographers and media. James looked on as all seats filled leaving standing room only. '*Whoever Simon and Cynthia called this afternoon, it worked. What a launch for our technology.*'

All the graduating models plus Clara had spent much of the past hour in hair and makeup, all looking their best to showcase their creations. There was a buzz in the air as they realised how many people were crammed into every available space and the number of media people jostling for position.

Amanda and Hell rushed through the doors to find Hashem having bolted from their offices to witness the culmination of so much hard effort to which they had also contributed. Panting for breath, they took to the side of Hashem. They were not about to miss this show.

Simon was clearly excited as he walked along the catwalk to start proceedings. He was at his most flamboyant and clearly dressed for the occasion. 'Good evening and welcome to the Central Saint Martins' graduate passing out show. We are privileged to have the exciting launch of a

261

fresh way to present our work to our audience and customers.' He elevated his voice to stimulate anticipation. 'This has never been seen before. You are the privileged few to witness a revolutionary way to present the world of fashion. Let the show begin.'

The other models, having heard Simon, stood around screens in expectation of Clara showing how to present themselves with this technology; must duplicate her movements. The music started. Cue to start the show. Angie queued her. She stepped onto the catwalk wearing her beautiful creation and her infectious smile. Her image was immediately captured by the motion cameras and projected onto the screens. After two metres along the catwalk the second image appeared one size larger. Then another two metres and the third image appeared yet another size larger. There were gasps from the audience as they realised what they were seeing, especially how the fabrics changed dynamic as the sizes got larger. As she reached the end of the catwalk, she twirled. The models on the screen rotated in synch with her. She stopped to pose for the audience as Cynthia performed her low-key commentary. Cameras flashed as the audience stood to clap their appreciation. She turned and made her way back with the simulated models on the screen following her.

Backstage the graduate models were awestruck. As Clara returned backstage, Jennie was ready to go. 'That was amazing.'

'Go do as I did. You'll see your other images as you walk back.'

'All twenty-three models did their individual walks before Jennie led all of them out for the encore to rapturous applause, each one remembering to leave at least a one metre gap. The room was filled with Javid's surprise – 3D emulations of each model scattered around the room, posing, and then rotating before moving on. Simon returned to the end of the catwalk with a mic.

After wallowing in the applause, he indicated he would like the noise to subside so he could speak. 'Good evening, ladies and gentlemen, friends, and honoured guests. Was that a spectacle worth attending?' The cheers and clapping resumed. He allowed the noise to subside. 'I would like to applaud the final year graduates who designed the creations paraded here tonight with this wonderful new technology. Let us congratulate them on their fine work. We hope they will always remember this momentous event and look forward to their progress in this wonderful industry.' Further applause. He knew it was his duty to praise his fresh graduates; but knew the media would only print one aspect of this evening and he wanted to be full on and centre in the story. The models dispersed from the catwalk to their respective supporters. Clara waited with Angie in the wings.

'To those who came at very short notice, thank you. I hope you feel your efforts rewarded. Although I've been aware of the development of this technology for some time, I did not know just how spectacular the result you have witnessed tonight until mid-afternoon when it was demonstrated to me for the very first time. I couldn't believe my eyes. I could not help but alert my friends and sponsors in this industry of this spectacle, and so proud to have it launched at our esteemed college.' More applause.

'I'm so proud that the origin of this fantastic technology is a collaboration between one of our second-year undergraduates and her technology partner. Clara, could you please return to the stage.'

Angie, with tears in her eyes, 'Ready girl, GO LIVE YOUR DREAM'. This time Javid did not use size emulations as she walked the catwalk. He staggered full life images up the screens and then floated them over the audience in 3-D images. The applause in the audience, Whitechapel and the Savoy were rapturous as she smiled her way to Simon.

'James, would you like to join us.' The entire audience rose to their feet in applause. The press were in a frenzy – exactly what Simon wanted – his picture with this incredible pair and association with this new technology. He wanted decoration unabashed by the irrelevance of being an imposter.

The 3D images of Clara in her lovely creation were still floating around the room and the various size images were beaming out of the screens. Javid was having fun with this technology, even though it was not part of the show plan. But this was family, important family. The press loved it. So would the families from India with their private showing at the Savoy Hotel.

Someone in the audience shouted, 'How does it work?'

James indicated to Simon he needed the mic. Simon handed it to him but was not going to fade from the picture. During the noise, Clara looked around the audience. Just to her right on the front row she spotted mum and dad; waved and smiled at them. She could see the tears of joy streaming down mum's cheeks. She turned to James and whispered in his ear, 'Mum and dad are here.'

'You didn't really think they would miss your day in the spotlight. They're staying with us this weekend to celebrate.'

James waited for the noise to subside. This was his moment to announce himself, Clara, and his company to the media. It was time to have their work recognised. He held Clara's hand. He wanted her to project her infectious smile. 'Ladies and gentlemen. We're overwhelmed with the reaction to our new fashion platform technology. Thank you.' Much applause.

'The origin of this technology occurred over two years ago in a bedsit in St Albans where I was looking at some incredible design sketches produced by Clara.' He wanted the people who had abused Clara in her past life in St Albans to know, yes, this is that same Clara. Now look at her.

'I had already produced an animation graphics engine for the computer games industry. We thought about how her designs could be presented in 3-D, which led to the idea of graphically producing a lifelike catwalk show to parade her designs. Then it occurred to us that catwalks are generally limited to a specific model size, which limits the connectivity to only people of the same size as the model. What about if we could emulate all sizes accurately, including the dynamics of how the materials would react to different body sizes and weight? We could then connect design to all standard body sizes. What you have witnessed this evening is phase I of our development.' Tumultuous applause.

He returned the mic to his mouth to indicate he was not finished. The noise subsided as they were gripped with this story and wanted more. 'This technology allows us to transform the online experience as a customer can key their own body sizes for clothing. This will generate accurate 3-D images of how the selected clothing will look on them. When Clara designed her dress for this evening, we scanned a wireframe of her body, entered her design, enabling her to fit it to her wireframe until she achieved the desired result, including motion, and then we printed the patterns.' There were gasps from the audience, followed by much whispering between professionals. This is big, and they knew it. 'As you can see around you, a feature still under development will allow a shop to model a variety of clothes for a buyer in their size. Using 3-D emulations, we can create a virtual model of any size to provide a private fashion parade for a buyer.' More gasps. 'This is the first phase of an exciting novel way for the fashion industry to relate to their customers. We now need the fashion industry to help us understand their views on the future for this technology.'

A shout from the audience, 'When will this technology be available to the industry?'

'You've seen the catwalk technology. It's available. We will quickly add the 3D capability you see around you. The online capability is ready for shipping.'

Another question. 'How difficult is it to use? The fashion industry is not known for being techy savvy.' Much laughter from the audience.

'This morning this room was empty. I have three technical staff with me. This is the first time we have used this equipment outside of our studio.'

A woman in the second row stood and revealed herself. There was a gasp from the audience. Clara whispered in his ear. 'This is amazing. That's Este Vanne, one of the top fashion designers.'

Once the audience was silent again, Este spoke. 'James and Clara. Congratulations on a wonderful show. And Clara, my darling, wonderful dress. You must tell me where you get your fabrics. You look stunning.' She paused 'James, I find it difficult to understand how two such young people not yet embedded in this industry can develop such a creation. Your model emulations are fantastic. I noted how the fabrics flowed differently on the different sizes. Tell me how you approached this as it is important in fabric choice.'

In Whitechapel, where Rajeev and Mama had invited family, friends, and selected clients to watch the show, there was much joy as Rajeev repeatedly told anyone who would listen that Anisha had helped with this dress recognised by one of the top fashion designers, and how proud he is to have Clara as part of the family. His pride in what he was viewing was clear to all. 'My Clara has changed the world of fashion.'

James thought to himself this was a discussion for the office, not in open forum. But he also knew this exchange would be on YouTube within twenty-four hours. It was a chance to shine and tell the world about their new creation. He had already noted that several photographers were using their cameras in video mode. Other members of the audience were using their phones to either take pictures or record video. And he knew Javid is recording the entire event using a gamut of cameras. His mind was racing to ensure he got real value from this exchange.

'I'm just a techy nerd, so please forgive my ignorance, but Clara informs me you're Este Vanne, the famous fashion designer. We're truly honoured that you attend our humble show.'

She responded. 'The honour is mine, I assure you.'

'When we started this project, I knew the model emulations needed to be as true to life as possible, just as is required in the computer gaming industry today where our emulation engine is still the market leader.' He most certainly wanted this promotion out there. 'If I can contain my illustration to women, I noticed how clothes worked on different sized women. We used models of different sizes in our simulation studio to parade the same clothes to capture the differing movement of the materials. The larger the model size, the more momentum in the material's movement. We would like to express our deep gratitude to Professor Cynthia Crawford, who provided much data in our understanding of designing clothes for different body shapes.' More applause as Javid turned a spotlight on her. They all knew who she was.

'We then developed algorithms to emulate these different dynamics. Using Clara's knowledge of fabrics, we also played with the idea of different yarn densities for the same fabric. The lighter density we used for smaller sized models to get a wispier look, whereas for the larger sized model we would use a heavier yarn density to provide less chance of gathering whilst providing a more elegant or even sassy sway. We developed algorithms to calculate the different yarn densities for the same material to suit different sizes and preferences for the same dress.'

Este interrupted him. 'Wait. You're telling me you calculate how to take the same dress material and make it perform differently on different sized women.'

'Yes. This is really Clara's domain, but we found that more curvaceous women swayed their clothes more, whereas smaller sizes liked a wispier look. Thus, we needed to understand how to calculate the different weight of material to achieve these looks, considering the additional material for the larger sizes.'

'Amazing. Please continue.'

'Our most difficult task was to emulate the vast array of bust shapes and sizes so we could achieve lifelike upper body emulations. We are very grateful to Rigby & Peller, who I see represented here this evening, and who shared a tremendous amount of data with us, as well as making a multitude of different seamless bras for us to scan on real models to ensure we could accurately create virtual models of any size. This we use in our virtual models to show the best contours possible for any given top and inform the customer about the optimum bra type and size to wear with the top.'

Este interrupted again. 'This is truly remarkable. Most women tend to wear the wrong bra size. But you're telling me this system will educate them as part of the buying experience. Incredible.'

James added, 'And it provides an addition sales opportunity to supply the bra with the top or dress.' He wanted to let the audience know he had commercial skills as well.

There was much discussion in the audience, so he took a moment to let this information sink in. 'Another real benefit of this system is to optimise the purchase experience. Once a customer has keyed her sizes, the system will optimise the selection for her. For instance, if the customer has a size 14 upper body, and a size 12 lower body, the virtual model will select these sizes to provide the visual and inform the customer of the choices made. It's an anomaly in the current fashion industry that there is inconsistency in sizing. A woman can buy a size 10 from one label but needs a size 12 from another. And this is not just a female issue. Am I a size L or a size XL? I've found it very much depends on the label. The system will know the actual finished sizes of the clothes in detail, so will make the optimal choice for the customer. This should substantially reduce the need for returns.'

Again, he gave the audience a moment to absorb this information.

'The obvious next step is to move to bespoke. Let us consider a dress for our size 14 upper body, but size 12 lower body. If the patterns for this dress resides on the system, it can seamlessly blend the patterns to cater for this sizing and either print a bespoke pattern for make-up or pass cutting instructions to a computerised cutting machine. It will be possible to offer a bespoke service to the mass market.'

Anisha was excited already knowing the possibilities, 'You see Peti, we can use this online to expand our business all over the world.'

What type of models do you use for the online?

'Our best solution to date is to use the current promotion platform of celebrities apparently captured by media photographers at functions or just on the street. If a brand has a stable of celebrities of different sizes compatible with a targeted general population audience, the system will select the nearest to the sizes input, tweaking a little if necessary, showing the buyer her clothing selection modelled by a popular celebrity of the same or similar size. Use the psychology hook of if it looks good on her then it will look good on me.'

Este, still standing, started to clap her hands. 'Truly remarkable.' The audience joined her in applause.

He waited for the applause to subside. 'There is another feature of this system which may interest you. During our research about the way different sized people wear their clothes, we hung a camera out of our office window to observe the considerable footfall along the street. We were struck by the number of people who did not have two good legs to propel them. We have emulated the needs of clothes for these people, whether partially mobile or confined to a chair of whatever description. We realised they have their needs in design to give them the looks they want but with the freedom of movement to propel themselves. Our system can show your world how to design for this sizeable market.'

Este stood for a moment, not sure how to respond. 'I am truly humbled that two new entrants to this business have identified and solved the needs of a market generally ignored for so long. I can't wait to see how your system solves this requirement, as I would love to include this important audience into my work. You should be very proud of yourselves for showing us the way.' She clapped again quickly followed by Simon moving to the side just in-front of James and Clara leading enthusiastic applause as he realised the college could take the lead in this new opportunity – another first for the college. He was visibly overwhelmed by the revelations of this evening.

The applause subsided with Este still on her feet. 'When can I see the full capability of this system?'

'You are welcome to visit our studio here in London and we'll demonstrate all the capabilities that exist at present. We would most certainly be grateful for any feedback that would help us better serve you.'

She smiled 'You have already given me much to think about. I see this changing the relationship with our customers and extending our reach to important new customers. Let us agree on a date.' She sat down, clearly satisfied.

He was exhausted, and seriously in need of a drink but was happy with his delivery – acknowledged by an icon of the industry. He could visualise the income streams.

A shout from the back of the audience. 'How much of this show was pre-recorded. It's not possible to emulate one fully rendered figure in real-time, let alone four.'

James felt offended. *'Always someone wants to spoil our night of celebration.'* But he knew this time he must keep his cool. 'Everything you have witnessed was in real-time.'

'Not possible' came the response.

He looked to the professional audience, looking for a suitable candidate to demonstrate the truth. 'Is there anyone around a size 10 prepared to walk this catwalk to satisfy our doubter?'

Este could sense the alienation felt by James at this intrusion. She stood. 'I'll do it. It will an honour to be one of the first to use this technology.' She dropped her cloak onto her chair, revealing one of her magical creations, and made her way to James at the end of the catwalk. 'James, what would you like me to do?'

'If you could go to the entrance of the catwalk, you'll find Angie, a professional. She'll instruct and queue you. I'll have a one second step beat rhythm ready which we'll play before you start so you have a feel for it. Then just follow Angie's queue. You don't have to do the return leg.'

'But I must if I want to see my multiple images on the screens. Are you recording this evening?'

'Yes.'

'Then you will please let me have a copy to show my friends.' With that, she made her way to Angie.

James guided Simon and Clara off the catwalk out of the way of the system cameras thinking *'Jesus, I hope this works or we're in real trouble.'* Later he would reflect that fortune was shining on his courage as his volunteer was well versed in catwalk discipline. Luckily Javid was unaware of the potency of this situation – it was just another walk – reset systems and cameras, synch to music.

Simon was beside himself. 'Este Vanne on my catwalk on this momentous evening. I think I will faint.'

James turned to Hashem. 'A one second beat and play it when ready. Enough for a full walk.' These are simple 12-bar riffs so easy for anyone to follow. They could not expect the graduate models to perform to complex arrangements.

Hashem quickly played the music so Angie could queue Este. She poked her head around to Hashem to indicate Este was ready. Audience lights dimmed.

Music starts, Angie queues the walk. A very elegant Este followed instructions perfectly appearing to enjoy every step. She was used to the spotlight and bathed in it. The audience were in raptures. The photographers hustled each other to get the best angles. Simon had his hand over his mouth, *'These are the pictures that will adorn the media tomorrow. Este Vanne with this wonderful technology at my esteemed college. My goodness, must prepare for interviews.'*

When she returned to the start, she turned to face the audience, curtsied, and strolled back to James, her smile beaming at the audience as they continued to show their appreciation. She took the mic from James and looked towards the doubter. 'Are we now satisfied?'

'Miss Vanne, and James, I humbly apologise. As a graphics animator, I would never have believed my eyes. Your technology is extraordinary. I'm so sorry to have doubted you.'

Este returned the mic to James, turned to Clara 'That was fun. We must talk after the show. Your dress construction is so clever.' And returned to her seat.

Another audience member spoke. 'Where can we get it?'

'I will provide a business card to those interested at the end of this evening.'

'Is there a press release?'

'Leave your details and I will email it on Monday.' Thankfully, Hell had quietly worked on a draft for some days in preparation.

'When will Clara's dress be available for the shops?'

He handed the mic to her with a loving smile. She responded. 'When I can find someone to produce it. I can provide the source of these special materials.'

Someone else stood 'I'm the buyer for Selfridges. We have our own preferred make-up companies. All we need are the patterns, source of materials, and a licence agreement. As no doubt this beautiful dress will adorn the media in the coming days, the sooner the better.'

271

She looked to James for guidance. He took the mic. 'Let's talk afterwards.'

Rajeev was in raptures as he pumped his chest. 'She remembers her family. We will supply fabrics to Selfridges. Wow.'

Hashem and Javid, still engineering the production and now flanked by Amanda, Hell, Angie, and Cynthia, simultaneously received a text message from the father of Hashem. '*Congratulations. Wonderful show. Fantastic work. We must take this back to India. We take the license for India. Worth a fortune.*' They both looked at each other and smiled.

Another voice from the audience, 'What's the next step?'

James saw his opportunity. 'Good question. If you would indulge me for a few moments, I need to discuss this with my partner.'

He turned to Clara, but still using the mic. 'Clara, my lovely Clara. We have achieved the goals we set for ourselves a little over two years ago; and fulfilled the commitments we made to each other. We endured a serious setback when you were brutally stabbed, protecting me from a drunk. I had to grow-up and learn how to care for you, but we used your recovery time to focus on this challenge. We're at a crossroads. Where do we go from here? We're back to a blank sheet of paper. Is our future together developing more ideas, or do we go our separate ways?' Everyone was spellbound. Talking to the audience, 'I need to say a little pray here'. There was laughter from some of the audience as he lowered himself onto his knees, still holding her hand.

'Clara, I know I've proven unworthy of your love in the past, but I've tried so hard to be guided by your love, compassion, and worldly wisdom. I pray I've now done enough for you to consider me worthy of your hand in marriage. Please, will you be by wife, my partner, and lifetime companion?'

The audience were so quiet in anticipation you could hear a pin drop. The audience in Whitechapel froze as the tension grew. She looked at the boy turned man with tears in her eyes. 'Yes, James. I would love to be your wife.'

The entire audience rose to their feet, erupting with good wishes. He encouraged her to her knees. The press were in yet another frenzy with their cameras. He did not want Simon in this picture. They embraced as lovers as journalists thrust audio capture devices forward, seeking comment from these new important faces in the business.

The audience in Whitechapel had a similar response, with Anisha and her sisters jumping with joy. Anisha turned towards her father. 'Peti, we must make her wedding dress, a beautiful wedding dress.'

'She is family. We take care of our own.'

She hugged him, 'Thank you Peti' as tears streamed down her cheeks.

He held her at arms-length so he could see her. 'My daughter, she has no family of her own. We take good care of her.' She hugged her father tightly.

Mum and dad, in tears, pushed their way through the chaotic throng of photographers and journalists. They knew their son intended to propose this evening, but not the spectacular nature of his proposal. They are satisfied that their son is now worthy of the love of Clara, and they have fulfilled their nurturing as parents. A family hug is in order.

End of rebirth

Ingram Content Group UK Ltd.
Milton Keynes UK
UKHW022320160623
423544UK00014B/283